Nancy Peach is a writer of romantic comedy, a mother of three, an owner of various ridiculous-looking pets, and a practicing GP working for the NHS and a national cancer charity.

She has been longlisted for the Comedy Women in Print Prize 2020 and shortlisted for the HarperCollins / Gransnet competition 2019. Nancy is a member of the Romantic Novelists' Association and is represented by Tanera Simons at Darley Anderson.

nancy-peach.com

 twitter.com/mumhasdementia
facebook.com/NancyPeach.Writer
instagram.com/nancy.peach

D1461428

LOVE LIFE

NANCY PEACH

One More Chapter
a division of HarperCollins*Publishers*
1 London Bridge Street
London SE1 9GF
www.harpercollins.co.uk

HarperCollins*Publishers*
1st Floor, Watermarque Building, Ringsend Road
Dublin 4, Ireland

This paperback edition 2021
1
First published in Great Britain in ebook format
by HarperCollins*Publishers* 2021
Copyright © Nancy Peach 2021
Nancy Peach asserts the moral right to be identified
as the author of this work

A catalogue record of this book is available from the British Library

ISBN: 978-0-00-849626-5

Printed and bound in the UK using 100% Renewable Electricity
by CPI Group (UK) Ltd

MIX
Paper from
responsible sources
FSC™ C007454

FSC
www.fsc.org

This book is produced from independently certified FSC™ paper to ensure responsible forest management.

For more information visit: www.harpercollins.co.uk/green

To Mr Peach and the three little Peaches

Chapter One

"*I*t is a truth seldom acknowledged but nonetheless unassailable, that there are few moments more pivotal in the life of a young woman than finding her boyfriend in bed with someone else. Particularly when that someone happens to be another man.*"

Occasionally, the voice narrating segments of Tess's life had a pleasing Regency tone, a genteel feminine inflection evoking Royal Baths, Pump Rooms, and leafy Georgian squares. Having Jane Austen describe her past and plot her future course would have been Tess's preference, she thought as she wandered the supermarket aisle and chose a large tub of ice cream from the freezer cabinet. It would have been reassuring to know that whatever other calamities may befall her, they would be dealt with in a sturdy, prosaic fashion, perhaps accompanied by an avuncular vicar or an elegant great-aunt swathed in crinoline.

Unfortunately, her usual commentator was the oily

daytime television host, he of the orange tan and the crocodile smile of preposterous whiteness, he of the paternity test results revealed in front of a live studio audience. It was this man whose blokey, jocular, mansplaining voice was most often in her ear. And rightly so, Tess told herself as she pulled a multipack of biscuits and two large slabs of chocolate into her basket and made her way to the checkout; rightly so. Because his was the most appropriate voice to document her *coup de grâce*. It was after all a storyline worthy of a bad soap opera or a tabloid front page, and he was an experienced commentator in this field, far more so than dear Miss Austen, who might have balked at the finer details.

Driving home, the bag of food sat like a smug toad on the passenger seat and she thought of the *"Day her life was turned upside down"* as her television host called it – each word delivered with emphasis and captioned at the bottom of the screen. The host was able to articulate the things she could not – indeed, this was his very reason for being – but recently he seemed to have taken on a life of his own. Constructing an alternative character to channel her positive energy had also proven challenging, but for different reasons. Whereas the television host had outgrown his role, in her ear on an almost daily basis, her Jane Austen creation was struggling to muster even the most basic of witty asides and could certainly not be relied upon to put in an appearance when needed. Frankly it had all been very disappointing.

As she might have predicted, it was the television host's voice she heard as she sat in the kitchen with her bag of confectionary goods, and he'd brought his imaginary studio audience with him.

———————

Looking back, Tess realised she had known as soon as she entered the flat that something was wrong. She had replayed it countless times, dissecting those moments between blissful ignorance and betrayal. It almost always left her with a feeling of utter bewilderment, the type of incredulous reaction she had learnt to quash when hearing about some of her more interesting patients' outlandish life-stories. She thought it through as she sat at the kitchen table in the semi-darkness, the food assembled in front of her like the Last Supper (just with no disciples or wine – or Jesus, come to that). Had there been clues? *The Golden Hind* of hindsight had proven to be an elusive beast, galloping off into the sunset without so much as a backward glance, let alone an explanation. And how could she trust her own judgement when it had previously led her so wildly astray?

She knew the punchline. She felt it with the force of a custard pie to the face – a pie thrown by a particularly resentful clown who had anger management issues. But when had she first realised the joke was on her? The television host led her through the reconstruction like a crime scene as she shovelled in biscuit after sorry biscuit:

"So, Tess," he said. *"You arrived home at the end of a long shift on the labour ward?"*

She nodded miserably as he addressed the audience.

"*That's right folks; she'd been up all night, bringing new life into the world. Ahhhh!*"

The audience responded with sympathetic clucks and mutterings of consternation.

"*And it seems you'd been working in obstetrics and gynaecology for a few months, concentrating on women's problems whilst your boyfriend was concentrating on… Never mind, we'll get to that.*"

They processed his clue, his little joke. A snigger rippled around the studio.

"*And you didn't notice the unfamiliar coat on the chair, the additional wallet and keys on the hall table, the two empty wine glasses in the sink? Is that right?*"

She nodded again, keeping her eyes fixed on the food.

"*Of course, that's understandable. You were tired, weren't you? Exhausted. And coming home earlier than planned to surprise him? Well, you certainly did that!*"

Another giggle, this time louder, the audience growing in confidence as they neared the main event. He continued:

"*But you did notice a few things in your sleep-deprived state, didn't you, Tess? The new smell? A different aftershave? The fact that Scott wasn't up and about, in the shower, getting ready for work as he would usually have been?*"

The host's attention was diverted by a scuffling noise in the audience. The sound of a tissue being pulled from a handbag and a muffled sob of feminine distress. Some of this was clearly close to home.

"*And so now you're starting to realise something is not right?*"

Tess unwrapped another bar of chocolate.

"And you're making your way down the corridor to your bedroom. The room you share with Scott, yes? And you push the door open... and what do you see?"

There was a dramatic pause. She wondered if a drum roll would be dubbed over the soundtrack.

"I see Scott." Her voice was muffled; she was halfway through a mouthful of chocolate and her tongue stuck to her teeth. *"He sees me. He sits up. Puts his hand out to sort of... fend me off. He's anxious, confused. It's like there's guilt radiating off him. I see the other pair of trousers on the floor, the shape in the bed next to him, moving..."*

"And that shape, Tess? What is it? Who is that shape?"

There was a delay while she up-ended the ice cream tub, letting the molten remains trickle down her throat, and when she spoke her voice was quiet. A tiny mouse of a voice drowning in chocolate. *"I see him."*

She imagined the rows of people, on the edge of their seats, craning forward to hear her.

"Sorry, Tess? You'll have to speak up. You see who?"

"I see a stranger. A man. On my side of the bed."

The host gave his usual sharp intake of breath to indicate astonishment, which was followed by the predictable gasp from the audience, the voyeurs expressing their pleasure, imaginary rubberneckers in what felt like Tess's car-crash of a life. It sounded as though they'd got what they came for.

Tess started to cry; ragged, untidy sobs, knowing it was better to let it all out in the privacy of her own home. She regretted not having been able to offload her distress at the time of the discovery, but she had been numb, struck dumb

5

by the surreal nature of events. By the time the anger had caught up with her, Scott was long gone, liberated, forging ahead with a new life, a new relationship, an entirely new sexual orientation, and all she was left with was the riddle of how a supposedly intelligent woman could have been duped in such a spectacular fashion.

In the early months, after they had separated and she was on her own, she had revisited the scenario every night in her dreams, waking anxious and confused, hating herself. She had fought for a return to sleep, hoping her neural pathways would reconfigure and provide her with a different waking image, but usually it was futile and the familiar lurching sadness would stay with her for the remainder of the day, an unwanted companion glued to her side for lack of other friends.

A year later, the dream was now infrequent, the pain and humiliation less invasive, but the memories could trigger off at any time of day, in any scenario. Tess had given up trying to make sense of it. Instead she managed her self-loathing in the only way she knew how: by stuffing her face. Desperate to fill that aching void with something, anything, she filled it with food.

Chapter Two

The following morning Tess woke early, her tomcat Morris kneading the soft crease of her neck with painful enthusiasm and fishy breath. She poked a toe out from under her duvet to confirm that the room was bloody freezing, the type of cold that left a trace of frost inside the window pane where her breath had condensed overnight. Later it would thaw into small pools on the sill as the glass warmed in the weak February sun, and Morris would dab his paws in it as he patrolled the house like an overzealous security guard checking for hazardous substances. She rolled to the edge of the bed and shoved his warm gingery weight onto the floor, swinging her feet down to find her slippers. The clock showed six-thirty and the radio alarm came on, filling her room with the chatter of an aggressively cheerful DJ. The noise was harsh above the peaceful drone of city traffic and the hum of their dodgy extractor fan left on in the mildewed bathroom.

"Tess?" came a loud stage-whisper as Kath, her housemate, nudged the door open and peered through.

Tess blinked as her eyes adjusted to focus on Kath's skinny silhouette in the chink of light. "You all right?"

"Yeah, fine." Kath hoisted her bag onto her shoulder. "Just heading off. I wondered if you'd be up for a drink later? A few of us from the department are going…"

Tess's heart sank. "Oh, I don't know. It'll be busy today. We've got a couple of new patients coming in. Thought I might stay late…" She registered the look on her housemate's face and turned her palms up. "Sorry."

"You're going to stay late again? Is there not somebody covering the evening shift?"

"Well, yeah but…"

Kath sighed. "Don't worry. Give me a shout if you change your mind though?"

"Thanks, will do."

They both knew she wouldn't.

She found her dressing gown as she heard the front door slam and made her way downstairs. In the kitchen she saw that Kath had left the usual trail of breakfast devastation in her wake. It appeared Morris had already sampled the milky dregs of the half-empty cereal bowl before heading upstairs to nudge his owner into action.

The weatherman on the radio confirmed what she had already established from the rain hammering against the window pane. He reported that here in the south it was cold and wet with torrential rain, a deluge expected, and back home in the north where there were blizzards and sleet, driving conditions were described as treacherous, as if roads were something humans could usually put their faith in. Accordingly, she dressed for warmth rather than glamour as she pulled on a fleece-lined cagoule. It looked more like something a sensible middle-aged woman called Barbara would wear for a brisk walk in the Peak District, armed only with a thermos of tea and her friendly Labradors. She briefly envied this imaginary woman striding across the moors and almost checked the cagoule pockets for crumbled remnants of Bonio biscuits before remembering that she didn't actually own a dog. Morris eyed her sternly from the stairs. Idle thoughts of dog ownership were not to be tolerated in this house, thank you very much.

Before leaving for work she caught sight of herself in the hall mirror and paused, trying to be objective. She saw dark, wavy hair that many would envy, but to her appeared unkempt and messy – and not in an attractive, recently-shagged way, more as if she'd been recently electrocuted. Deep-brown eyes went with the dark-brown hair, but they were puffy after last night's tearful overeating, and her brows, despite relentless plucking and shaping, still had the potential to straggle outside their boundaries and pop up where she least expected. She was bound to end up like one of those whiskery, old ladies she sometimes saw on the ward, hair sprouting from their faces with the reckless abandon of weeds in a carpark. The curse of the dark hair, the Latin colouring, was perhaps the only trait inherited from her wayward Italian father; indeed, it was her solitary reminder of him. Her olive skin was clear apart from those tiny pale acne scars at her hairline, marks that told of teenage low self-esteem, feelings she thought she'd outgrown, or at least dealt with, until last year.

"You can't run away from it, Tess." the television host's voice whispered in her ear. *"Although, with a face like that I can see why you'd want to."*

She sighed once, the exhaled breath fogging up the mirrored image, and drew a smile through the condensation in an attempt to force a reciprocal one onto her actual face, before she headed out of the door into the drizzle, leaving Morris grooming himself enthusiastically in the hall.

———

Tess drove with caution along the reportedly treacherous roads, occasionally aquaplaning through a vast expanse of surface water. Her car wasn't the most robust of vehicles and would likely collapse if she so much as slid into the soft verge, so she clung onto the steering wheel like a drowning man as she navigated the city traffic. She had to be at work by eight for the handover from the night staff and was eager to return to a place where she was useful. At least this was something she *knew* she was good at, and the security of her career had in many ways been her salvation over the past year whilst everything else fell apart. The tranquillity of the hospice provided a respite, not only for patients and their families, but for the staff too, and as she walked into the coffee room the tangled knots of tension in her shoulders began to loosen, and the gentle voice of Miss Jane Austen echoed in her head.

"What pleasure is there to compare with the companionship of

*friends, the meeting of like minds and the attainment of gainful
employment in a situation worthy of one's talents?"* Jane gave a
contented sigh, evidently pleased with her observation.

Tess's senior colleague Farida was sitting in one of the
tattered armchairs, a mug of tea balanced on the edge of one
arm. She waved over at Tess and mouthed, "Good
weekend?"

Tess shrugged, thinking of the empty ice cream carton
and biscuit wrappers in the bin. "Just the usual," she said
and then realised that Farida was genuinely interested.

"It was a bit of a quiet one, to be honest." She slipped
into the neighbouring chair. "Some friends have recently
got engaged so they had a dinner party on Friday but it was
pretty sedate, you know, one of the girls was pregnant and
not drinking, others had work the next day…"

She trailed off but Farida was still listening, her head
tilted to the side, eyebrows raised in eager expectation.
Having only known her for a few weeks, she was already
aware that Farida was happily married and therefore
desperate to hear details about a single life to which she no
longer had access. Tess tried her best to oblige, despite the
fact that her single life was currently as exciting as a trip to
the dental hygienist. She assumed that Farida was after
comedy stories, ones that she could repeat to her husband
later that evening as they sat down to supper and thanked
their lucky stars that they were out of the dating meat-
market. She hadn't yet shared with any of her colleagues
the details of her last relationship. It wasn't really
something one bragged about, the fact that your previous
boyfriend had run off with a bloke, and although she liked

Farida she wasn't ready to hang out that particular piece of dirty laundry just yet. She decided to aim for 'mildly amusing' rather than 'tabloid shocker'.

"So, they'd invited another friend, Ryan, to even the numbers up…"

Farida nodded.

"And as soon as he finds out I'm a doctor he asks me about his intractable verruca problem."

"No! At a dinner party?"

"Yep. The classic conversational opener, made marginally worse by him asking whether I thought these verrucas were exacerbating his athlete's foot. 'It's funny because I'm not much of an athlete,' he said. Which, to be honest, was fairly obvious from his general demeanour. Anyway, verruca-laden Ryan works in a council office by day but by night… he's a gamer. And I'm not talking about the odd bit of *Grand Theft Auto* or whatever it is people usually play. I mean he is a serious gamer, goes to conventions, you know."

"Oh."

"Well, yes, that was sort of my response. I mean, I've got nothing against guys who spend their time on computers, but it just feels a bit like you're having a chat with a little boy. He's talking about which level he's completed like he expects me to be impressed, and I'm just nodding and trying not to think about his foot problem."

Tess settled back further into the armchair, keeping an eye on the door for the night team.

"He told me this story and it was like his only anecdote the entire night, about how he had played a trick on a colleague by making some minor change to his screen saver so he couldn't access his documents."

"God, how annoying."

"I know, right? He must be a dream to work with."

Farida sipped her tea. "So, basically, he's a socially awkward gamer who plays hilarious tricks on his colleagues and has a chronic verruca problem." She paused. "He's certainly ticking a lot of boxes, what are you waiting for? Did you get his number?"

Tess grinned. "Well, look, at least it's not as bad as the guy I was attempting to flirt with at a party who got a Tinder alert and left halfway through our conversation, or the one who had that weird thing for Mary Berry. But yeah, not the best."

Farida giggled and moved her attention to the patient list in front of her as the night team filed in. Tess felt a twinge of guilt for mocking Ryan's social inadequacies, but then the chance of him meeting Farida was slim, and so what if she'd made him into a bit of a caricature? She had been responding to the pressure of delivering an anecdote, after all. Farida would have been an attentive audience regardless, but Tess suspected that her ideal scenario would have been to hear her colleague unveil a story of blossoming romance, or failing that, a steamy account of a night's passion and intrigue. There was bugger all to report along either of these lines, and an itemised list of the number of bars of Dairy Milk she'd consumed last night would probably not meet the criteria either.

She turned her attention to Rob, who'd been on call. His face had a grey shadow of stubble and his scrubs were crumpled. He thumped into the chair beside her, brushing against her arm.

"Rough night?" she asked.

He jolted at the contact and, seeming embarrassed, rubbed a hand over his eyes.

"Do I look that bad?"

"No, not at all! That's not what I meant."

But he had already pulled away shyly, as if fearing he might accidentally touch her again.

Rob fished a scrunched-up piece of paper out of his pocket and smoothed it out on his lap, his voice husky with lack of sleep as he recounted the details of various inpatients and their individual management plans. Reaching the end of his list, he looked over at Tess and his cheeks flushed.

"There's a new lady coming in… Mrs Russell. Sixty-four. Ovarian cancer with bone mets. Transferring from the General. Ambulance is on its way so she'll be here"—Rob looked at his watch—"pretty soon. Are you happy to clerk her in?"

Once the handover meeting had finished, Tess made her way to the nurses' station set back from the main reception area. She scrolled through the pathology lab results that had come through from the hospital since Friday, and was halfway through the patient list when the sliding doors from the lobby opened and a burly paramedic arrived at the desk with a large file of notes, dropping them onto the counter with a thud.

"Mrs Russell," he announced. "Where d'you want her?"

He bent closer to Tess and said in an undertone, "She's a

lovely ol' gal. Proper lady. Son's a right pain in the arse though." He straightened up quickly as the doors slid open again and Tess could see a wheelchair edging through the gap.

The occupant of the wheelchair was a smartly dressed woman in her sixties who wore a weary expression as she turned her head up towards the tall man walking beside her chair. They paused in the doorway. The man, who still had his back to Tess, seemed to be immersed in a conversation that he didn't want interrupted.

"If you'd just let us contact Dr Hamilton-Jones again? Hmm? Mother? I've got his secretary's number. I know he'd be happy to see you, talk through the options…?"

His voice sounded vaguely familiar to Tess as he turned with an exasperated huff, but her attention was focussed on the wheelchair now approaching the nurses' station. She leant over the lower part of the desk, extending her arm out to shake hands with the lady sitting in it, who on closer inspection was looking exhausted.

"Hi," she said as the woman clasped her warm hand. "Mrs Russell? I'm Tess. I'm one of the doctors who'll be looking after you while you're here at St Martin's."

Mrs Russell gave a weak smile. "Thank you. Everyone's been very kind."

Tess returned to her chair and glanced through the summary notes.

"Good," she said. "Now Mrs Russell, if you just give me a moment I can let you know where—"

She was interrupted by another irritated snort of disbelief from the man standing next to the wheelchair and she looked up in surprise, her gaze travelling over a well-tailored suit into a pair of deep-blue eyes.

She felt a thud in her chest. Those eyes, that face… She knew there had been something about his voice. It took her back to that night, years ago now, before Scott, before the humiliation, before any of this. Her mouth started to form the shape of his name but she realised, in the few fractured moments before blurting it out, that the recognition was not mutual. Or at least, if it was, the warm feelings associated with the memory were certainly not reciprocated. He was glaring at her, the animosity radiating off him.

"Nearly embarrassed yourself there, Tess!" the television host hollered in her ear and she winced, her cheeks flushing crimson, but she continued to stare up at him, willing him to show some sign, a flicker of response. However, the owner of the blue eyes had no time for fond memories. He had other things on his mind and was evidently struggling to contain his frustration. His mouth was set into a thin line and he raked a hand through his hair as he looked from Tess to the paramedics and back.

"My mother shouldn't *be* here," he said. "She's not *terminal* or whatever it is that you people call it. She shouldn't be in a *hospice*." He hissed the word with obvious distaste and turned to face the wheelchair. *"Mother!* Won't you let me speak to the oncologist? Please?"

Mrs Russell moved her head a fraction, her face set in a determined expression despite her obvious exhaustion.

"Edward. Leave it. Please. Just for now." She looked up at her son. "I would like a bit of rest, darling. Let them do what they need to do." She took a long breath in and her eyes fluttered shut for a few seconds.

Tess was still trying to gather herself. The blood continued to pound in her cheeks and time seemed to have slowed to treacle. A barrage of images and fragments of memory were clattering around in her head, vying for attention with the television host and Miss Austen, both of whom appeared to be as bemused as the other by this inner turmoil.

Tess motioned to the paramedics. "Bill, can you take her to room two?" she asked. And then, regulating her breathing, she turned her attention back to her patient. "Mrs Russell, I can see you're in some discomfort. We'll get your pain relief sorted out first of all and I'll be in to see you once you're settled, okay?"

She scanned the bundle of notes, keeping her attention on the desk while Bill pushed the wheelchair away. The son remained, leaning his elbow on the raised counter of the nurses' station, cracking the knuckles of his left hand and radiating a tense energy. Tess risked another surreptitious look. Yes, it was definitely him. Edward. Eddie he'd been then. A younger, more carefree version of this angry, awkward man she saw now. She was on the verge of trying again – perhaps if she called him Eddie he'd respond… But no. That was ridiculous. One didn't go around using diminutive names for patients or their relatives, even if you knew them really well. It wasn't appropriate.

But how about if she said, *It's Edward isn't it? You look familiar. I think we've met*, or something like that? Something casual and low-key. It might put him at ease, even if he didn't remember her. It might establish a connection? She rolled the sentence around her mouth, wanting it to emerge naturally, but as she processed the words she knew they would be as weighty as a boot to the head, and that he would pick up on it immediately, and it would be awkward – hideously so. And, God, why didn't he just go? Follow his mother into her room and leave Tess to her thoughts?

But then what if he did leave, and this was the last chance she ever got to see him? The prospect caused her to glance up again, commit the lines of his face to memory once more. Add them to that warm, little bundle she had buried deep. Surely, he couldn't have forgotten her?

"I think he ha-as," the television host sang softly in her ear.

Edward's expression was inscrutable as he stared at the door behind which his mother had disappeared. He was tense from his neck through his shoulder and forearm to the fingers now drumming upon the raised countertop. Tess's eyes were drawn from his face towards the tips of his fingers and their restless rhythm, close enough to see the whorls and grooves that would make up his own individual prints. She had held that hand, once, a long time ago it seemed now. She was struck by an urge to place her own hand across his once more and cease the movement altogether, to trap those agitated digits and feel them straining against her palm. To say, *It's me. Remember? That night? Remember?*

But she didn't do this. She wasn't a complete idiot. Instead, she shook herself out of her ridiculous daydream, focussed on the job at hand and pulled out Mrs Russell's drug chart with a professional flourish that was slightly spoiled by her dropping it on the floor.

"Aha! She's due some Oramorph," she said as she bent to retrieve it. "That'll make her feel a bit better."

Edward scowled down at her, his eyes sharp. There was nothing there. Not even the hint of an expression that Tess would later be able to cling to and analyse, to turn over in her mind for hidden significance. He was looking straight through her. She could have been anyone; merely a worker in an institution that he wanted no part of.

"The morphine might make her feel better," he said, "for a few hours. It might drug her up. Won't bloody cure her though, will it."

And he turned on his heel, disappearing out into the lobby, leaving only the faintest waft of clean linen and a memory of tense, static charge in his wake.

Chapter Three

It was early afternoon by the time Tess managed to get in to see Mary Russell, who'd been dozing in her room since the morphine took effect. Over lunch of half an egg sandwich and a packet of stale crisps, she'd had a stern word with herself and with the television host and even Jane Austen, whose advice regarding matters of the heart and unrequited passions was beginning to grate on her nerves. *It's nothing*, she told herself. It never was anything. Just a transient meeting between two people, just a 'ships that pass in the night' thing; they were ports in the storm, feathers in the wind (was that even a phrase?)... She ran out of rubbish allegorical references, finished her lunch, and with a decisive scrunch of her sandwich wrapper she'd banished both her narrators (although to be fair, the television host had already informed her that he had more important things to be getting on with, including a date with a C-list actress who'd fallen upon hard times).

Tess took a deep breath before going into Mrs Russell's

room and repeated the words *I am a confident professional* to herself a couple of times as she straightened her skirt and knocked on the door. She found her patient propped up in bed, peering at a tray of hospital food. Tess wrinkled up her nose.

"What's today's lunchtime delight then?" she asked, pointing to the gelatinous mass in Mrs Russell's bowl. "Looks suspiciously like frogspawn."

Mrs Russell smiled, "Tapioca, I think?" She looked doubtful, "Maybe not? Maybe rice pudding?" She poked at it with her spoon. "It's not bad actually, I've just got no appetite. All these years I've been watching what I eat and now I can have whatever I like, I just don't fancy it. It's not fair, is it?"

Tess was struck by how attractive her face was, in spite of what she'd been through. There were strong sculptured cheekbones underneath the steroidal puffiness, and the tired lines crinkling at the corners didn't diminish the dazzling blue of her eyes.

"No, Mrs Russell. You're right. It's not fair." She pulled up a chair beside the bed and opened the notes out on her lap.

"It makes for pretty grim reading, doesn't it?" Mrs Russell said, inclining her head towards the heavy manila file. "I wouldn't want to have to wade through all the gruesome details. It can't be easy for you, having to deal with people like me all the time."

Tess was surprised by this. It was unusual for someone in Mrs Russell's position to be concerned for the feelings of their attendant healthcare professional. Most of the time –

not unreasonably – patients with significant medical conditions were absorbed by their own diagnoses and didn't necessarily consider the lives of those working around them. She tried to reassure her.

"Actually, I love it," she said. "It's really rewarding, and I like getting to know my patients properly. We don't get the chance to do that anymore in most medical specialties – it's all such a rush."

She flicked through Mrs Russell's notes, scanning for information. "I've only been working at the hospice for a few weeks so it's all still quite new…" She glanced back up, noting her patient's look of alarm.

"Oh, gosh, no, please don't worry," she said. "I'm not like a total novice. I do know what I'm doing. It's just that General Practice training is all a bit chaotic. There's so much to learn and you basically lurch from one specialty to another overnight. I was doing paediatrics before this, over Christmas actually, which was fun but also a bit, you know, frantic."

Mrs Russell now looked more amused than alarmed. "I can imagine," she said.

"It's a slower pace here. We have more time to chat, which I like, obviously, and it means we get to find out what our patients want and how they feel about everything, not just the medical stuff. Speaking of which, I'm rattling away about how lovely it is to listen to people whilst not letting you get a word in edgeways. We need to talk a bit more about you. I can get most of the clinical details from your notes, but I think it's maybe better to hear your take on things, if you're feeling up to it?"

Mrs Russell nodded, sank a little further into her pillows, and began to tell Tess about the events that had led her to this point: the grumbling lower abdominal pain that she had attributed to irritable bowel syndrome for too long, the look on her doctor's face when she mentioned that she'd lost a stone in weight, the scan results showing something suspicious on her right ovary, the further scans that revealed the extent of the spread. "And now here we are. I'm riddled with cancer and all my son wants is for me to go through more tests and treatments. And there's no point to any of it. I'm tired." She looked across the room to the window and her voice quietened. "I'm *dying*, for goodness' sake. The only thing I have any power over is how I choose to do that, and Edward just wants me to give it up, hand control over to the medics like everything else. Sorry..."

"It's okay. You take your time." Tess handed Mrs Russell a tissue.

"It's my fault... That's the thing. I'm so cross with myself because I could have made it easier if I'd let them know a little sooner, but I didn't, and as a result they're panicking. I didn't want to worry either of them. It's only a couple of years since their dad died. Maddie's over in the States – has been for years – so it's difficult for her. Edward is so busy with work – he's a lawyer. He's very successful, very focussed, you know. I didn't want to trouble him..." She poked her spoon back into the bowl of pudding.

"So in the end I didn't let either of them know about the tests. I had plenty of friends nearby who took me to appointments and waited to drive me back from my scans, and all the time they were asking me, 'What does Edward make of it? When is Madeleine coming back?' not knowing that I just wasn't brave enough to tell my own children what was going on. Until it was too late. And I had to tell them. There was nothing they could do, and they were devastated. And furious. As you'd expect. I'm so sorry, do you have another…?"

Tess pulled another tissue out of the box and handed it to Mrs Russell. She dabbed her eyes delicately.

"Madeleine has just been on the phone non-stop, to me, to Edward, to the doctors… And I think she has led Edward to believe that he should have somehow taken better care of me, that he shouldn't have allowed this to happen in her absence. Completely unreasonable, but you know, they're siblings. What can you do? It's always a bit of a power struggle."

Tess considered her own brother, Jake, and their wrangling over much more trivial matters than these. "It's not that unusual, you know. There's always a lot of guilt around when someone has a difficult diagnosis, and families react in different ways. Sometimes it really brings people closer together."

"Well, we'll see."

"We do have family counselling sessions here at the hospice if you think it might help, with Ed… with your son? No? Well, have a think about it. He might surprise you. I'll leave you be for now, but if there's anything you need, let me know. All your medication's written up."

She reached over to place the box of tissues onto Mrs Russell's table and, seeing that her eyelids were starting to droop, she patted her hand and left the room.

Tess didn't speak to Mrs Russell again that day. She and Farida were kept occupied by a dramatic showdown in the family visiting room where Mr Johnson's mistress, Ms Frost, had arrived just as his wife and family were leaving. The ensuing slanging match had resulted in security being called and many of the staff were pulled in to administer cups of tea and sympathetic ears to both sides of the party (Mr Johnson being fast asleep and blissfully unaware of the unfolding drama). Much as the staff were familiar with extremes of emotion at the end of life, they were less used to dealing with displays of open aggression, and some of the language hurled from wife to mistress and back again was enough to make your eyes water. Eventually, the betrayed Mrs Johnson settled the matter by slapping the enigmatic Ms Frost across the face with a copy of *Reader's Digest* magazine. Ms Frost dropped the potted plant she had been carrying and fled the building to the refrain of Mrs Johnson wailing, "He doesn't even like begonias, you silly bitch!" and calm was restored.

By the time Tess left, the supper trolley was meandering through the hospice distributing cod mornay and Mrs Russell's door was shut; the nurse in charge said she was sleeping. There had been no further sightings of Edward, angry or otherwise, although Tess understood that he was likely to be visiting later that evening. She was keen to get home for once. There was too much going on in her head and she needed to sit down with Morris on her lap, put something mindless on the telly, and open a bottle of wine.

She knew of colleagues who dealt with far more complicated conflicts of interest during their careers than simply treating the mother of a man you'd once misguidedly thought might be "the one". This scenario didn't really constitute a professional crisis but she couldn't deny it had been a shock to see him again. It was almost as if she'd persuaded herself over the years that he had been a figment of her imagination. And in a way, she supposed he had. Or at least her notion of him was fabricated; the connection they'd shared had been entirely in her own head.

The rain was lashing down as she made her way across the car park, pulling her coat tight across her body and trying, but failing, to position her umbrella in such a way as to make it remotely effective against the gusting downpour. She was just crossing the ambulance bay when a large BMW thundered around the corner, headlights on full beam and splashing through the pot-holes. Tess stepped back, dazzled by the lights as the car thumped to a halt beside her, soaking her feet. The passenger window glided down and she felt the thump in her stomach again as she saw the tense, handsome face of Edward Russell staring back at her through the gloom.

"There's nowhere to bloody park."

"Well you can't park here. It's the ambulance bay," she replied in as dignified a way as she could whilst grappling with her brolly like a deranged Mary Poppins. "Look," she softened a little, seeing his plaintive expression, "you should really park in the visitors' section but I'm just heading home now. You could have my spot?"

"Excellent." There was a pause. "Well. You'd better hop in then. I can't very well follow you in my nice dry car and leave you battling the elements." He leaned over to release the passenger door and nodded quickly. "In you get."

His movements and tone were so decisive that Tess didn't really feel in a position to refuse, despite her car being only a short distance away. She put her umbrella down before getting in, all the while questioning just exactly what she was hoping to achieve by spending more time in close proximity to this man. The rain drove sideways through the open door and made small puddles on the leather upholstery. Edward gathered a collection of papers into a document folder and moved it from the front to the back seat to make space for her, the fabric of his shirt stretched taut across his upper arm and shoulder as he did so. Tess clambered in with minimal elegance, the electric window gliding noiselessly back into place and steaming up as her breath hit its cold pane. She settled into the leather seat and balanced her sodden umbrella across her knees, watching it drip into the footwell. She was aware that every inch of her seemed to be emanating a damp heat into the arid BMW interior, her hair was plastered to her forehead, and little rivulets of water were trickling down the back of her neck.

There was an impatient drumming of those restless fingers on the steering wheel and she looked across to where Edward sat, dry and composed. His blue eyes were fixed on her face as he enquired as to her car's whereabouts. With a nervous laugh she pointed to a red Fiat parked only ten metres away. "It's just over there. The little Punto? The red one?"

"The little Punto. Indeed." The BMW purred across the tarmac, rolling towards the space. "Well, thank heavens we saved you such an extensive journey. God knows how you'd have made it otherwise."

"Absolutely. Quite the hero." She smiled. "At least you get a parking space for your trouble. I'm so sorry, I appear to have introduced a monsoon into your car. I hope I haven't wrecked your interior."

She reached for the door handle but then paused; maybe she should say something now? Could she make her voice casual enough when her throat felt this tight? But it would be weird anyway, wouldn't it? To suddenly start talking about a party she'd attended five years ago when he was clearly in a hurry and, you know, waiting to see his dying mother and therefore perhaps not in the most receptive mood? Maybe better to talk about the obvious thing. "She's nice and settled," she said. "Your mum. She's a lot more comfortable now."

It was the wrong thing to say and the mood in the car shifted noticeably. Tess felt the recently broken tension return with a vengeance and almost wished she *had* talked about the bloody party instead.

"I'm sure she's more comfortable, thank you." He turned towards Tess and again appeared to look through her rather than at her. "But she's not going to give up. I've been in touch with her oncologist this afternoon. He thinks she has other options to consider and I value *his* opinion regarding my mother's care. We're obviously extremely grateful for all you do here," he waved a dismissive hand in the general direction of the hospice building, "but I doubt she will be staying with you for long. Little point in her getting *settled*, as you put it."

Tess felt suitably told-off. Her cheeks flushed, but she responded in a measured tone, "Of course." She gathered her things and glanced across to Edward, now staring resolutely forward, deep in thought and chewing on his lip. "Well, thank you for the lift."

There was a long and uncomfortable silence while Tess awaited a response. Seeing that none was forthcoming, she opened the door and stepped back out into the rain, wrestling her bag behind her. Reversing out of her space with a little more pressure on the accelerator than was strictly necessary, she made her way out of the car park, still clenching her teeth with frustration.

"Truly, the gentleman is insufferably rude." Jane Austen's voice was just loud enough in Tess's ear to compete with the windscreen wipers frantically bobbing up and down through the torrents. *"It is not to be borne."* She sighed. *"Certainly, he is blessed with a noble countenance and perhaps one can make small allowances… But are you quite sure that this is the same gentleman to whom you once felt an attachment? Can it be that he is so altered?"*

Tess shook her head. "Tell me about it, Jane," she muttered under her breath. "Tell me about it."

Chapter Four

"**D**o you remember that party when we were, like, third or fourth years?" Tess was trying to jog Kath's memory, but seeing as Kath had consumed the best part of a bottle of Bacardi whilst out with the A&E lot, she was not having much luck. Kath wrinkled up her nose, "Mebbee?"

"Maybe you weren't there. I can't remember which firm we were attached to, but it was the F2 doctor, Dan. He had a flat in Clifton, a really lush one. It was a duplex; he had the basement and the garden and—"

"Not ringing any bells yet, my love." Kath slumped down onto the sofa and gathered Morris up into her arms, burying her face in his fur. "You're a fine cat, so you are Mr Morris. A handsome devil. Aren't you? Aren't you?" Morris gave her a disdainful look and padded back to Tess.

"He can tell when you're hammered, you know." Tess smoothed her hand down Morris's back and he settled into her lap. "Anyway, this party. I went… we'd been invited – I guess it must have been me and Donna. It was when we were doing the ENT block…"

"Wasn't me then," Kath said. "I did ENT in Gloucester, remember? Got off with that tasty registrar, the one that was doing the research project about tonsils. Or maybe it was just my tonsils…"

Tess ignored her. "Well, this party. We didn't know anyone else there – it was mainly proper doctors – and I think the only reason we'd been asked was that Dan had wanted to get into Donna's knickers. But there was this bloke there. Do you remember me talking about him?"

Kath pulled a face. "Well, you're going to have to be a *bit* more specific… I mean, a bloke at a party, five or six years ago. A party I didn't even go to…"

"Yeah, yeah, okay. It's just that I'm sure I told you about him. Maybe not if you were in Gloucester. I certainly wouldn't have told Donna… Anyway. I was still going out with Pete so nothing happened, but it was one of those nights when it felt like everything happened. Do you know what I mean?"

Kath looked confused and Tess sighed. "I know I'm not explaining this well."

"You're not wrong."

"But I met this guy, Eddie. He was a friend of this doctor, the one who owned the flat…"

"Yes, yes."

"A friend of his from school, or they'd grown up together or something. But anyway, he was from Bristol, this Eddie, but he'd moved to London and he was starting out as a lawyer. Bit flash, you know the type."

"Player."

"Yeah, a bit, I guess. But we just hit it off, immediately. We just, you know, clicked. It was like, I don't know. It was like it was meant to be. Don't give me that look."

"Sorry, something stuck in my teeth, that's all."

"I know it sounds ridiculous. I do realise that. Especially when you hear the latest, but at the time it felt really special. He didn't know anyone else there and neither did I, Donna spent most of the night tangled up with Dan, and I was really just hanging around out of a sense of duty, wanting to make sure I didn't leave her in some bloke's flat on her own. Anyway, I bumped into him, Eddie, in the kitchen, where he was getting a bottle of beer, and he said something funny and I smiled and it was one of those shared moments, you know. He asked me what I did and I asked him, and we just chatted about working versus being a student, about Bristol, about him being in London. About the fact that he wasn't sure he really wanted to be doing law, that he'd wanted to be a vet. And how I'd always wanted to be a doctor. And we talked about friends and holidays and books we'd read, and loads of other stuff; art we liked and history and things I wouldn't normally talk to a bloke about; things I wouldn't talk to most people about…"

"Okay, getting the picture."

"Yeah, well." Tess poured herself another glass of wine. "D'you want one?" she called to Kath, getting another glass from the kitchen in anticipation of an affirmative response.

"And a plate. Please." Kath unwrapped the pack of chips she'd come home with and popped one into her mouth. Morris circled her feet expectantly. "Oh, so you're interested now, sunshine," she said to him sternly. "Hmmm, chips and wine. Food of the very angels, so it is." She stretched her feet out in front of her, luxuriating in the ludicrously fluffy socks she'd pulled on as soon as she got in the door. "So, you really hit it off then, you and this random guy from five years ago at some bloke's flat in Clifton?"

Tess laughed. "I know. It's a shit story."

"Ah, well, no. It's got potential. Does it improve? Pick up the pace a bit? Is there some actual riding goes on, or is it just, you know, chatting like?"

"No actual sex. Sorry to disappoint. We did spend the night together, as in, we were in the same room all night, but he was the perfect gentleman, insisted I got the sofa, he was on the floor on some cushions. It seemed sensible really, for me to stay. There was plenty of room. Donna was upstairs with Dan. It was really late by the time I even looked at my watch, like maybe three in the morning. So, we just carried on talking, and talking. And it was as if neither of us wanted the night to end. There was that feeling of pretending that the outside world didn't exist for those few hours. When we were on our own and everyone else had gone home. It was just the two of us, with the occasional thump from the bedroom upstairs, but even that wasn't awkward, the fact that both our friends were actually having noisy sex in the room above us. It was just…"

"The perfect soundtrack?"

"Hmm."

Kath continued with the steady procession of chips. "So, did you end up going out with him or what? I honestly can't remember ever hearing about an Eddie."

"No. I was still with Pete, I told you. And I told him, Eddie, about Pete, I mean. He knew I had a boyfriend. I think he might have had a girlfriend too, back in London. But he asked if… well…" She cast her eyes down to the sofa.

"What?"

"He asked if he could see me again. He asked if I wanted to spend the day with him, before he went back to London. And I said no. Because of Pete. And, you know—"

"Because he was a bit of a player and you thought he'd mess you around and you didn't want to risk it?"

Tess nodded sadly. "And I never saw him again. I tried casually mentioning him to Dan when we were at the hospital the following week and he just sort of said, 'Oh yeah, Eddie took a bit of a shine to you, didn't he?' but then we were on a ward round, you know, and I couldn't really go on and on about him. And we finished the ENT block that week so I didn't see Dan again, and he was the only connection I had. I tried googling him but I didn't know his surname, so I was just putting in things like 'Eddie, lawyer, London', which didn't exactly narrow it down. And I don't know what I'd have done if I *had* been able to contact him anyhow. He still seemed like this unattainable dream, like, who was I kidding, thinking that he was really interested? Anyway. As it happens, it's a bloody good thing I didn't track him down. I keep imagining what might have happened, me phoning him or turning up at his London flat declaring undying love, now I know he doesn't even remember me…" She cringed, hunching her shoulders up. "God, how *mortifying*."

Kath had paused in her chip consumption. "Wait, so how do you know…?"

"I saw him. Today. That's the reason I'm telling this over-complicated rambling story."

"Ahhh." Kath nodded wisely. "Sure, I knew there had to *be* a reason."

"Yeah. His mum was admitted."

"To the hospice?"

"To the hospice. He was there. It was a massive shock."

"I'll bet. And did you fall into each other's arms and it was all, 'Oh my God, where have you been all my life, you beautiful woman…'?" Kath was acting out the dramatic moment.

"No! You're not listening. He didn't remember me. He didn't remember any of it."

"Oh." Kath looked contrite, "Sure, sorry. That's pretty shite."

"It meant absolutely nothing to him." Tess's face was downcast. "That night, all the things we talked about, him asking me out, it all meant nothing. I was probably just one of a long string of girls he routinely chatted up, and he forgot all about me as soon as he hit the M4."

Kath passed her the plate with a few fragments of chip remaining on the greasy paper. "Go on," she said. "You have 'em. No?" Tess shook her head. "Well, look, I can see it's not, like, a nice thing to have happened but, in the grand scheme of things…"

Tess stood and pushed Morris off her lap. "I know. It's no big deal really. It was a shock like I said, but…"

"Wait, though." Kath licked her fingers in contemplation. "ENT… Was that not your peroxide pixie-cut phase?"

Tess frowned. "Yeah, I think it might've been." She paused. "Yes, you're right, it was. It was in the last few months of going out with Pete, wasn't it? I wanted to do something radical."

"That haircut was pretty bloody radical all right."

"And Pete hated it, d'you remember? Kept going on about my 'raven locks' and why had I got rid of my 'crowning glory'?"

"Which was of course subconsciously why you did it. Looking for an excuse to push him away."

"All right, Freud. What's your point?"

"Well, your man here, this Eddie, he sees you today with your 'raven locks', like, sure, it's not beyond the realms of possibility that he simply didn't recognise you? Seeing as last time you'd gone full Britney Spears?"

"I hadn't shaved it all off."

"No, but it was, what, an inch long? If that. You said it was really liberating, d'you remember? And it was like platinum blonde?"

Tess smiled, reminiscing. "It *was* pretty fierce, wasn't it. Roots were a bitch though."

"Anyways." Kath leaned over to tickle Morris behind his ears. "All I'm saying is that you looked quite different to how you do now. And men aren't great with faces."

"Men aren't great with faces? You crack me up." Tess

laughed. "But seriously. We talked for hours. We talked *all night*. He'd have recognised my face, my voice, surely? I mean, if I'd meant anything to him."

"Ah, you'd be surprised..." Kath stretched her arms above her head in an expansive yawn. "Look," she said. "It's a one-night stand, that actually wasn't even a one-night stand as such, and you've turned it into a grand love story in your head when maybe it wasn't, and that's a bit tough, but we've all been there, imagining Prince Charming in every frog we meet."

Tess snorted. "You don't do that."

"No, sure. Too bloody right I don't. But I'm not especially representative of my gender. I was meaning more that we've all misjudged things in the past. It's easily done. And sounds as though this fella was quite a charmer. Knew how to make you feel special. And then you find you weren't quite as special as you'd thought. That's what they do, these types of blokes; it's like their own unique skill-set."

Tess shrugged. "I guess. Yeah, you're probably right." She gathered up their plates. "He's not so bloody charming now, though. Gave me a right earful at work. Wanted to make it *absolutely* clear that he didn't want his mum in a hospice and that he had no faith whatsoever in our clinical judgement."

"Well, you've seen plenty of that kind of attitude before," said Kath, following her out to the kitchen. "Hospices, palliative care. It does that to some people. They think it's not like real medicine. And, you know, he's cross, he's upset, he's hurt your feelings by not remembering your momentous night of romance…"

Tess flicked Kath on the shoulder. "Oi! Don't take the piss," she said. But she was smiling again. "Thanks Kath," she said over her shoulder as she went upstairs, trailed closely by Morris. "You've put it in perspective. Like you always do."

Kath held her half-empty glass aloft in a toasting gesture. "My pleasure," she said. "And if it's any consolation, he must be a bit of an arse not to remember a cracking babe like you."

Chapter Five

The following morning after handover Tess was asked to the nurses' station to answer a call from consultant oncologist Dr Hamilton-Jones. He informed her that he would be visiting Mrs Russell later that day at the family's request and could she, Tess, please ensure that the patient's paperwork was up to date before his arrival. He had the tone of a man who was used to being obeyed and his request was delivered as a command that he clearly assumed would be acted upon as a priority. Tess bristled at the other end of the phone and assured Dr Hamilton-Jones that they went to great lengths to make sure every patient's records were updated in as timely a fashion as possible, but by this point the oncologist had hung up, evidently happy that his instructions would be carried out to the letter without any further need to engage with a mere minion from the hospice. Tess replaced the phone in its cradle with a look of incredulity. What was it with this family and their attendant male authoritarians? She felt a twinge of anxiety for Mrs Russell, who, it seemed, was in for a barrage of high-handed bullying dressed up as a consultation. She remembered the woman's words from yesterday when she had first arrived at the hospice. It seemed she felt that some decisions were being taken out of her hands. Tess was resolute that Mrs Russell must be allowed to choose for herself, and it was her job to enable that process. She was not going to be intimidated by the domineering Dr Hamilton-Jones or allow herself to be distracted by an angry Edward Russell.

"You, dear girl, shall be a shelter in the storm. A warrior for those who cannot defend themselves. A knight in shining—"

"Yes, all right, Jane," said Tess. "I get the picture."

In the event, she did not have to chain herself to her patient's bed or barricade the hospice doors. The reality was much more civilised – on the surface anyway. The consultant arrived in a whirl of tailoring and self-importance. He whisked the notes into Mrs Russell's room and raised his eyebrows a fraction as Tess followed him in, but did not openly question her presence. A few moments later Edward Russell entered the room, a similarly surprised expression on his face as he observed Tess, who was trying to look authoritative despite a slight trembling as the consultant deigned to shake her hand. Her position was further undermined by a brisk, "It seems your senior colleagues are not currently available?"

The question was delivered with a surprised smile as if Dr Hamilton-Jones was unaware that medical staff may be occupied elsewhere and were not necessarily beholden to his own timetable.

"*He's asking where all the proper doctors are,*" the television host whispered in her ear. "*To be fair, we're all thinking the same.*"

Dr Hamilton-Jones launched into an emotive lecture on the importance of "availing ourselves of every opportunity", "staying strong", and "fighting the cancer", directing his speech towards Mrs Russell and delivering it in a charming, if slightly patronising, tone. He then turned his attention to Edward and began to talk about the more experimental chemotherapy regimes available to treat cancers of this type. Throughout this part of his explanation he spoke over the bed and did not look once at Mrs Russell, discussing her cancer as if it were entirely unrelated to the woman below him.

Edward nodded attentively as he listened to the bewildering jargon concerning technological advances, but Tess noticed the slight crinkling at the corners of his eyes as he concentrated on the doctor's words and recognised the face of someone desperate to hear good news. The expression revealed a need for hope. The helplessness was further evident as he leaned into the side of the bed and squeezed his mother's hand.

"Please, Mum." He spoke urgently, his voice breaking slightly. "It's got to be worth a try? Please, please consider it?"

Tess was suddenly reminded of the crumpled face of her own mother, sitting beside her granny in a scenario not unlike this, and had to swallow hard in order to dislodge the uncomfortable sensation in her throat. She had been so caught up in her own hurt feelings about Edward and his wordless rejection, but it wasn't his fault that he couldn't remember her. He hadn't treated her badly. The exact opposite, in fact. He'd been the perfect gentleman that night five years ago, probably knowing that he could have taken advantage of her obvious infatuation if he'd wanted to. And so what if he'd been rude and dismissive yesterday? He didn't owe her anything and her own feelings paled into insignificance beside this looming spectre of grief. His pain was on an entirely different scale to hers at the moment. It was swamping him, and she suddenly felt an almost overwhelming urge to reach out and touch him, to share some of this burden.

Instead she stayed where she was, tucked in the corner, bearing witness. The oncologist diverted his gaze, clearly uncomfortable in the face of such raw emotion. He left the room, quietly murmuring that he would be available on his mobile if they had any questions, and it seemed that the combined forces of professional pressure and filial guilt won out. The decision was made for Mary Russell to be transferred back into hospital the following day and Tess assumed that Edward would disappear from her life once more, although, as the television host was at great pains to remind her, he'd never really been in her life in the first place.

———

That night she called her mum. Seeing Edward and his mum had left her feeling as if she were on the brink of tears for the remainder of the day, and even though she'd seen plenty of grieving families since starting at the hospice a few weeks ago, she still wasn't entirely comfortable in the face of it.

"You sound a bit flat, pet. Everything okay with work? Busy is it?" She could hear her mum bustling about in the background and pictured her, phone tucked into the crook of her neck as she tidied.

"No, Mam. Not too bad. The pace is a bit easier actually. It's not like when I was tearing around Casualty."

"Ooh God, yeah, d'you remember that job? They ran you ragged. I were worried sick, every night. Thought you were going to get beaten up by some smackhead."

"That's how I feel when you're doing shifts at the off-licence."

"No, you don't need worry about me, pet. For a start, our Jake's only at the end of the phone. He'd be round the like clappers if he thought owt were kicking off. And then Big Colin's got me back. He wouldn't let any bugger give me aggro."

Tess laughed. "I'm not surprised. I don't think even the most hardened criminal would be tempted to chance it where Big Colin's concerned. You do know he fancies you, right?"

"Oh, away with you, you daft mare. He knows I'm a good worker is all."

Tess snorted a laugh. "Knows you could run that place single-handed, more like. You still doing all the invoices for him?"

"I enjoy it. Better than staring at bottles of Strongbow all evening and it keeps me mind ticking over. I'm not like you, love. Didn't have the chance to put me brain to good use, did I? Not with you and Jake coming along when you did and me being on me own. I would've liked to have gone to college, you know. If the situation had been different, like."

"I know, Mam. You have mentioned it." Tess supressed a smile. It didn't take much to get her mother started on the injustices of life, and particularly the root of all evil: men who didn't hang around to support their offspring. She was used to it by now, although it still hurt occasionally to hear her father dismissed as a feckless bastard. Still, it could be worse; her mother was far more scathing about Jake's dad.

"It's not too late, you know," Tess said. "You could still get into further education. They've got courses even for ancient people like you."

"Pfff. Don't be ridiculous. Me? A student?" Tess was sure she could hear a tiny note of yearning beneath her mother's dismissal, but she didn't push it.

"Anyway, I've got you, haven't I? You're the one flying the flag for higher education in this family. It makes me right proud, you know, having a daughter who's a doctor."

Tess smiled and rolled her eyes which involved some fairly impressive facial gymnastics. "I know, Mam. You tell me often enough."

"You still keeping up with your studying, like? No distractions?"

"Boyfriends you mean?" She thought of Ryan and his feet. "No. Nothing to worry about there."

"Good. More trouble than they're worth. Bright girl like you'll want to stay focussed. Keep your eye on your goal."

"I know, Mam."

"Like that Scott. Look how that turned out. Gay or straight, lying toads the lot of 'em. Other than our Jakey of course. Speaking of which, when are you next home? He's missing you. We both are."

"I know. I spoke to him a few days ago. He's got a new girlfriend, sounds like?"

"Hmmm. When hasn't he got a new lass on the go? Too handsome for his own good, that boy of mine." There was pride mixed in with the disapproval in her voice. Jake's endless string of girlfriends had been a source of amusement over the years and it never seemed to occur to Tess's mum that she had one set of rules for her son and an entirely different one for her daughter.

"I'll be up in a week or so I reckon."

"You'll be bringing that naughty Kathleen up with you?" Her mother's voice was fond. She adored Kath and the feeling was mutual. Kath rarely saw her own parents who were back in Ireland, largely oblivious to the antics of their youngest daughter. She had often accompanied Tess on trips home during their student years.

"I might do, although she'll probably just try and cop off with Jake."

"I thought she was seeing someone now?"

"Yeah, I was only joking. She is seeing someone. And very happy too. It's the most settled I've ever seen her."

"Well, I'm happy for her, but it's a shame to see that career go to waste. I've always thought she'd make a fine consultant doctor, that one."

"Mam, it is possible to have a boyfriend and climb the professional ladder. Ravi's nothing but a support to Kath.

He's been brilliant. No complaints about her crazy hours or her, you know, erratic temperament. He's perfect for her. And let's face it, Kath would kick him to the kerb if he ever tried to even suggest that she rein in her ambition."

Tess could hear her mum pause at that. "You're right. She's got a good head on her shoulders. Still, give it year or two, she'll have a toddler running about, baby on the way, and that Ravi who's being such a support at the moment, he'll be sniffing around the next piece of skirt. You mark my words."

Tess laughed in spite of herself. "There's no persuading you, is there? All right. I'll see when she's next free and tempt her with a night out on the tiles in Sheffield. As long as you promise not to fill her head with stories of doomed romance."

Her mother chuckled good-naturedly. "I promise. And it'll be lovely to see you whenever you can come. I miss you."

"I miss you too, Mam." Tess's voice caught in her throat for a second as an image of Edward and Mary flashed into her head. "I love you."

Chapter Six

Despite receiving her treatment elsewhere, Mary continued to make use of the outpatient facilities at St Martin's and Tess saw her a few weeks later emerging through the sliding doors of the main entrance, deep in conversation with a tiny birdlike woman who was supporting her weight on a stick.

"Morning ladies." Tess wandered over and greeted them both, "Lovely scarf, Deirdre," she said to the woman with the stick, and gestured to the fabric. "Is it silk?"

Deirdre looked pleased. "Yes, it is – a present from my granddaughter. My favourite colour, and so soft."

Tess rubbed the fabric between her fingers appreciatively. "You're right, and mauve really suits you. Was it a present for any special reason, or just because she knew you'd look fabulous in it?"

"You are sweet. Yes, it was my birthday two weeks ago. Seventy-four."

"Well, frankly I refuse to believe that. You look about forty."

Deirdre grinned and Tess turned her attention to her companion. "And Mrs Russell, it's lovely to see you too. How have things been going? Have you both been out for one of the wellness walks?"

"Oh, you must call me Mary," said Mrs Russell. "Yes, Deirdre and I have been put through our paces by your physiotherapist, James." She nudged her companion.

"We're both quite happy to let James put us through our paces," Deirdre said with a giggle. "He's very easy on the eye. I guess he works out a lot."

"So that's why you've got your best scarf on, Deirdre! That's outrageous. Although, you're not wrong. Who else was in the harem today then?"

"Pam was here for a short while," said Deirdre. "She got as far as the flower beds which was what she wanted, to see some of the spring bulbs coming through. So nice to see the back of winter. There's blossom on the cherry trees; new life everywhere you look. Even in a hospice garden!" She paused, counting the other walkers off on her fingers. "Clive. He did quite well, although the wheelchair's difficult in the mud so there was quite a lot of swearing involved. Belinda lost one of her shoes, but she didn't seem too troubled by it. She kept tight hold of her hip flask though, you know, the one with *coffee* in it." Deirdre made a noise that sounded suspiciously like 'vodka' as she coughed into her hand before continuing. "And William was there. Full of beans, competitive as ever – broke into a spontaneous bout of star jumps when we got to the lake, but I think he was showing off for Mary's benefit, and he was a bit wheezy afterwards. Couldn't talk for at least twenty minutes."

Mrs Russell laughed and Tess noticed that despite the new chemotherapy regime, there was more colour in her cheeks.

"Well, I have to say, you're both looking very invigorated. Seems the fresh air has worked wonders even if it is a bit nippy out. Nice hat, Mary," she said. "Suits you."

"Thank you. Yes, I'm getting to the point where I need to start experimenting." Mary lifted the brim of the hat in partial explanation; Tess could see a couple of patches where the hair was thinning, her pink scalp showing through.

"I knew it was going to happen," Mary said. "But it's still a bit of a surprise to see huge clumps of hair falling out, blocking up the shower. Anyway, I am really looking forward to my wig fitting; Deirdre has given me plenty of ideas, some more practical than others." She looked fondly at her new friend, "I'm not sure that the full Tina Turner would be appropriate, although I'd love to see Edward's face if I turned up in it! Speaking of which, I think he's waiting for me in the café. I'd better go and let him know I haven't fallen in the lake."

"I'm just heading there myself," said Tess, falling into step beside them as they walked, Deirdre fractionally slower but determined not to be left behind.

They arrived in the café to find Edward Russell seated at the Formica table nearest the serving hatch.

"Dr Carter," he said, rising to stand and she felt the

thump in her stomach again. When was seeing him going to get a little easier?

"Mr Russell." She nodded and swallowed hard. "Good morning."

She couldn't think of anything else to say and turned to the serving hatch before her cheeks became too florid and blotchy. She spied a portly figure stacking mugs on a tray and called over, "Dave, any chance I could have one of your flapjacks? They haven't sold out yet, have they?"

Dave reached below the counter, his apron straining across his considerable girth. "They have..." he said in broad Bristolian, "but I knew you'd be wanting one, so I put this aside." He pulled out a brown paper bag with a flourish, placing it triumphantly on the counter. "Although it does mean if either of these lovely ladies are after one, they'll have to fight you for it."

Tess looked across to Mary and Deirdre. "I'm not sure I'd fancy my chances; these two seem to be at the peak of physical fitness. If either of them wants the last one, I'd back down pretty quickly."

"The Chelsea buns also come highly recommended," Dave said to Mary, gesturing towards the tray in front of him. "You have a look, my love, and tell me what you're after." He moved his attention back to Tess. "Cup of tea is it, doc?"

"Absolutely." She opened her purse.

"Will you have a little sit down with us?" Mary asked. "Do you have time?"

Tess darted a look at Edward who was pulling out a chair for his mother. Deirdre patted the seat beside her for

Tess to take. She paused. Was she crossing a line here, or was it just a simple interaction with a couple of her patients? The television host was muttering about professionalism and inappropriate behaviour but she decided to ignore him.

"Okay." She looked at her watch as she handed her coins over. "I've got ten minutes, so that would be lovely." She sat down, noticing that Deirdre was wincing and holding her side.

"Are you all right?" she asked. "Can I help?"

"Don't be daft." Deirdre lowered herself gingerly onto her chair. "You're supposed to be having a break. We haven't asked you to sit with us for a consultation. Nooo. We want gossip, don't we, Mary? News from the youth of today. Edward, you too, young man. Your mother tells me you work in the City – whatever that means."

Edward's expression was alternating between amusement and alarm at the prospect of having to deliver gossip.

"Well, I'm not entirely sure that I'm the best representative of 'the youth of today'," he said. "Being thirty-one almost certainly counts me out."

He glanced in Tess's direction, looking slightly to the side of her. "Dr Carter's probably much better suited to answer any questions you may have about youth culture, but yes, I do work in the City. I'm a lawyer for a large bank, basically. It's a bit dull, corporate clients, you know."

Deirdre nodded wisely. "Fat cats, you mean. Yes. I suppose there's a lot of events and entertaining goes on? I've seen *The Wolf of Wall Street*, champagne and dancing girls, speedboats, casinos… snorting lines of cocaine off the thighs of strippers and suchlike?"

Edward nearly spat his coffee across the table and Tess stifled a giggle as she caught his eye. "Well, not recently," he said.

Deirdre looked sceptical. "You probably wouldn't want to let on in front of your mother though?" She nudged Mrs Russell who was sitting next to her, smiling broadly. "You should see that film, Mary, honestly, that DiCaprio fella. The shenanigans, you wouldn't believe it."

She stopped suddenly, turning her attention to an elderly gentleman making his way steadily towards the table. "Stanley!" She gave a girlish wave. "Come join us. We were just talking about class A drugs and general debauchery with these lovely youngsters."

She whispered across the table to Edward, "He's deaf as a post my husband. I could be yelling my head off for all he'd know."

"I can't imagine that, Deirdre." Edward stood to offer his hand to Stanley who had at last made it as far as their table. "Hello, sir. I believe you have the good fortune to be married to this fine woman?"

Stanley shook Edward's hand with a wry smile and looked down at his wife. "Here you are," he said. "I thought you'd absconded with your gorgeous physiotherapist! Come on, girl, I'm illegally parked in the disabled bay."

"Well, I hardly think you'd be done by the Trade Descriptions Act for that." She turned her face towards her husband's ear, raising her voice. "You with your arthritis and me with metastatic liver cancer. I'd like to have a word with anyone who'd refuse us a blue badge."

"Rubbish, woman! You'd be bloody furious if someone suggested you had any type of disability. Come on, shift yourself. I'll get started now and you'll have caught me up by the time I get to the door." He smiled at the group as he turned, waved to Dave in the kitchen, and began the slow shuffle back across the floor.

"He's not wrong." Deirdre gathered up her coat and stick. "Mary, I'll see you on Thursday, same time, same place? Race you to the lake and see if William attempts any more star jumps?" She turned to Edward. "Lovely to meet you, young man, and I don't care what you say, thirty-one is no age at all. You should have seen what I was getting up to in my thirties. And Dr Carter, I'm back in tomorrow for a chat with one of the counsellors, so I might see you then. Cheerio!" She galloped off after Stanley, the pain in her side forgotten.

"Well," Edward relaxed back into his chair, "she's certainly a character, isn't she?"

"She's wonderful," said Mary. "A real live wire. Although how she has the energy for it, I just can't imagine. She never seems to stop. I suppose you know her quite well, doctor?"

"Mum," Edward leaned across. "Dr Carter can't tell us whether she knows Deirdre well or not."

"Oh, goodness, yes of course." Mary put her hand to her mouth. "Sorry. It must be terribly difficult for you, all this blurring of boundaries, what you can and can't say. I'm sure I'd trip up all the time."

"It's not too much of a problem," Tess said carefully. "Usually it's only an issue when I see someone out of context."

Mary was nodding.

"So, say I'm at the supermarket," Tess said, settling into her explanation. "I might see a mother and toddler coming towards me, waving, and I'm racking my brains as to where I know them from and whether it's in a professional or social capacity."

She could see out of the corner of her eye that Edward was listening and almost wished she hadn't noticed. Being anxious always made her particularly talkative.

"And the mum recognises *me* because a year ago her child was critically ill in hospital and maybe I clerked him in, or took his bloods, or saw him once on a ward round. Whatever it was, I'm associated with a really significant time in her life and she expects me to remember it as clearly as she does. So, she says, 'Oh, Charlie's doing so much better now.' And I say, 'That's great,' whilst trying desperately to remember what Charlie had been in with. And then she says, 'Could you just take a look at this rash on his arm. Do you think it's related to the medication?' or something. And I say, 'Which medication?' or, 'What rash?' or I say, 'I'm sorry, I'm really not sure. Remind me about Charlie's history.' And she looks at me all disappointed because she was hoping I'd remember her, or remember her son at least, and she's realising that I don't know who either of them are. And so, she starts to feel stupid and the whole thing ends up being a bit awkward." She paused to catch her breath, aware that her explanation was unravelling in an entirely different direction to the one she'd started with.

"And you're just doing your shopping," Mary said gently.

"Exactly. I'm trying to think about what I'm going to cook for tea or whether I need more toothpaste and now, out of the blue, I'm in this weird charade where I'm trying to be professional and make a diagnosis whilst trying to make this woman feel less awkward." She took a sip of her tea in an attempt to stem the torrent of words pouring from her mouth but the seconds of silence yawned like a chasm beneath her, one that she had to fill. Off she went again, like an unstoppable train.

"I'm not complaining," she said, "just in case you were thinking that. And I'm not saying that each individual patient isn't special in their own way. Sometimes you can get really attached to people who you see a lot of or whose story really touches you. But there is this conflict between when I'm in doctor mode and when I'm just, I don't know, Tess buying fish and chips." Edward's eyes seemed to be boring a hole in her face as she entered the final furlong.

"I mean, now, for example, I'm starting to question whether even this was an appropriate conversation to have with a patient. Do you see? The last thing I would want is for you to be feeling awkward about asking me a medical question because I'm on my coffee break."

Mary nodded, looking slightly relieved that Tess had finally finished. "I do see, absolutely. The relationships must be very hard to navigate."

"And I suppose," Edward began, his deeper voice

somewhat startling for having been silent so long, "that because these people have shared so much with you, maybe they think there's some kind of special connection. So, they see you as a friend, someone they've bonded with, more than a professional?"

"Yes!" Tess looked at him, surprised enough by this observation to momentarily forget her inner turmoil. "Exactly that. It's kind of flattering, you know. It makes you feel special, like you've made a difference in someone's life, but it also makes things a bit tricky. There's a blurring of boundaries and sometimes that's the thing that's hard to navigate, as you said, Mary."

She shifted in her chair.

"The confidentiality is much less of an issue because although I like to chat, I also know when to keep my mouth shut – not that you'd know it now. But it's the keeping a professional distance I find hard."

She took another sip of tea, knowing that this was the best way to pace herself, to give herself a bit of thinking time. "Maybe it's because I'm still quite junior, from a medical point of view."

"Or maybe it's just the type of person you are. You like to get involved," Edward said. He was looking at her intently, as if he was trying to work something out.

Tess felt a flush creeping up from her neck at the idea of being assessed so acutely and the reality of who exactly was making the assessment.

"Perhaps you're right, Mr Russell. Maybe I get a little too involved." She cleared her throat and looked down at the table. There was silence for a moment until, suddenly decisive, she scrunched up the paper wrapper from her flapjack and tucked it into her empty mug.

"Anyway! Tea break over for me. I've got to get to clinic. I'll probably see you in a couple of days, Mrs Russell. That is if Deirdre doesn't drag you off on another adventure."

She turned to Edward. "Mr Russell."

He inclined his head. "Dr Carter."

As she walked out of the café, she silently remonstrated with herself about this tendency of hers to overshare, to fill silences with meandering nonsense. She felt exposed and foolish, briefly thinking back to a time when she'd spoken to Edward in a different way, when his presence had made her feel comfortable and confident instead of this gibbering wreck. Was it him who had changed, or was it her? Either way, she really must rein it in. It was horrifically unprofessional for a start.

"Unfortunately, in one's desperation to appear agreeable, it is entirely possible to instead resemble an amiable fool," said Jane Austen as the door shut behind her.

"You just made a bit of a tit of yourself, didn't you, Tess?" the television host added more succinctly.

Chapter Seven

S he was determined to be more guarded when she saw Edward a few days later, back in the café. The thought had occurred to her that he might be in there waiting for Mary to return from her walk, but it would have been an exaggeration to say she was stalking him. She just happened to want a cup of tea after the ward round. That was all.

The plan had been to casually nod in his direction, acknowledge his presence, and move on to another table but in the event, all the other tables were occupied. As he saw her returning from the serving hatch, a flapjack balanced precariously on her mug and a newspaper tucked under her arm, he gestured in an off-hand manner to the empty chair beside him, clearing his papers and moving his laptop to give her some space to set her things down.

"Thank you," she said. Her mug wobbled as she lowered it, spilling the tea onto her paper. "Oops! Sorry.

Basic manual dexterity was never my strongest point." She dabbed at the spillage with a napkin.

"No plans to be a surgeon then?" Edward said.

"What?" She'd just taken a bite of her snack and her voice was muffled. "Oh, I see. No. A vascular consultant at medical school once said he'd rather be sewn up by a blind amputee than subject himself to my cack-handed attempts." She registered the expression on his face and laughed. "I know! He saw my sutures – on a bit of foam, not an actual patient – and asked why I hadn't paid more attention in embroidery lessons." She brushed a crumb off her chin. "He was a complete arse, mind you."

"Sounds it."

"Maybe I should have pursued a career in cardiothoracics just to spite him."

"Might have been a bit extreme." Edward smiled and looked back down to his laptop screen. "Just doing some work," he explained. "The office has been pretty understanding about everything."

Tess nodded. She flicked through her newspaper, pausing at an article on page four about the recent anti-austerity protests. Seeing Edward looking over to what had captured her attention she pointed to the headline, "A couple of my friends went on this march."

"Oh yes? You didn't want to go?"

She was still looking down at the article, scanning through the details. "I was working. Otherwise I might have."

He nodded. "Hmm. I'm not sure I've ever been on a protest march."

She looked up at him, a tiny smile on her lips as she recalled the Edward of five years ago. She wouldn't have imagined that he'd have been big into protest marches either. "Not really your thing?" she said.

"That amuses you, does it?"

"A little."

"And what exactly is so hilarious?" he said, smiling. "The idea of me on a march or the fact that I conform so much to a stereotype?"

"Hmmm. I'm not sure. A bit of both." This was more like it. She felt as if she were back on familiar territory with him now. A bit of banter. A flirtatious undercurrent perhaps?

"Fair enough." He looked back at his screen and there was silence as she skimmed through the rest of the paper until she reached the crossword. She snuck a look at him, worried that she'd misjudged it again. Had she been too bold in assuming a shared understanding? After all, she felt like she knew him. But he didn't know her.

"I wasn't trying to be rude," she said. "Just to clarify."

He turned his attention away from the screen, amused. "I realise that. You're not someone who enjoys making people uncomfortable."

"Well, quite. I just don't have a very good poker face."

"And I guess it's a bit of a struggle to imagine that I might want to protest about unequal wealth distribution, given that I work for a bank?"

"Umm. Possibly."

"And the idea of me slipping into my combat gear, pulling on a beanie, and brandishing my placard probably feels a little unlikely as well?"

Tess laughed. "It does a bit, although I'm not sure the dress code is mandatory."

There was another pause as she drank her tea. Edward scrolled back down his screen before he spoke again. "You know, I'm not completely comfortable with what's going on in the country at the moment," he said eventually. "I do see the poverty around me, but big City firms aren't all as corrupt as everyone thinks. Our bank spends a lot on charity projects and the tax generated by the City probably supports the entire NHS."

Tess nodded. "I guess I hadn't really thought of that. It doesn't fit with the tabloid image, does it?"

He smiled. "No. It does get a bit irritating when people assume you're a corrupt, mercenary bastard just because you work for a bank – a bit like everyone assuming all doctors are Harold Shipman or all benefits claimants are scroungers."

"I'll consider myself suitably corrected," she said. Her tone was light and he laughed.

"Sorry, I wasn't meaning to be so defensive, I know you weren't really being critical. And you're right. I suspect I'd feel desperately uncool on a march."

"Whereas I'd fit right in?"

The smile broadened. "You're clearly much cooler than I am."

"Are you basing that on my cardigan and sensible shoes, Mr Russell, or the fact that I work in a hospice, both of which give me massive street credibility?" She gave him a wry look. "Anyway, I hate to break it to you but I don't think people use the word *cool* anymore. I do believe the current parlance is either *lit* or *savage*."

He raised a single eyebrow. "I can see that you are quite well informed for one who claims to be so out of touch, what with your cardigan and all."

"Only because of my brother. He's a teacher and therefore contractually obliged to have some rough understanding of what's being said when the kids are *throwing him some shade*."

"Stop it. You're just showing off now."

"Ha! Yes, you're right. I am." She was enjoying the combative tone again. "My other source of intelligence is my housemate. She works in Casualty and knows the slang name for every street drug and sexually transmitted disease in the UK."

"How very useful."

"Surprisingly so. It's like the medical equivalent of The Knowledge for London cabbies. I expect she had to sit an extra exam."

"No doubt. She must be the very pinnacle of *lit* or *savage*, or indeed both." He gave her a sardonic smile, his eyebrow still raised in amusement.

"I see what you've done there," she returned his look, "but sadly we both need to recognise that we're massively past it. Any attempt from either of us to enter into this type of conversation unironically is likely to trigger off some kind of alarm."

He laughed. "And we'll be whisked back to the 90s where we belong."

"Indeed. I expect it's only Deirdre who thinks either of

us might have a clue about the zeitgeist, what with her having watched *The Wolf of Wall Street* and all."

"You're right. She's probably the best qualified of any of us."

"Probably."

Edward turned back to his screen still smiling. "Just read your paper," he said. "And do let me know if there are any articles you need help interpreting, particularly regarding popular culture, teen slang, youth-speak, *whatevs*."

"I'll be sure to do so," she said. "And likewise, with your report. Any long words you want explaining, I'm right here."

He shook his head, chuckling appreciatively.

She took another sip of her drink, watching him out of the corner of her eye as she read through the crossword clues. He was evidently capable of cutting out the distractions of the café and focussing on his work, and as she sat quietly she was able to continue her covert study. He seemed entirely disciplined, sitting with his elbows resting on the table, his tall frame and long limbs cramped by the rigid plastic chair and his tanned forearms laid flat either side of the screen in front of him, the extensor muscles flexing and contracting beneath the skin as he jotted notes or drummed his fingers. Again, she remembered holding his hand that night, arms stretched across the woollen rug, her on the sofa, him on the floor. What was it that had made him reach for her? What had they been talking about at that point? She couldn't remember, but she knew that his touch had soothed her somehow and that they had drifted into an hour or two of sleep with their fingers still intertwined.

Tess continued to stare at Edward whilst pretending to look at her newspaper. She took in his profile, which was just as she'd remembered: the slight bump at the bridge of his nose, the firm jaw, the lower lip occasionally chewed in concentration. There was a pulse beating at his temple and she wanted to reach out and touch it, feel it throb under her fingertip. Without any conscious intent she found her hand moving fractionally towards him and he became aware of her gaze, sliding his eyes in her direction, catching her stare. The hint of a smile flickered across his mouth as she blushed and looked away, pretending to be engrossed in a difficult section of the crossword. He leant across and looked at the clue.

"Embarrassment," he said confidently, tapping Eight Down with his finger.

"How very apposite," said Jane Austen.

Chapter Eight

As the weeks passed, Mrs Russell continued to attend the wellness sessions, and Edward continued to drop her off at the designated time, waiting in the café until she returned. There developed a routine of sorts whereby Tess would often happen to be wandering through the café for what was becoming a fairly regular mid-morning break at about the same time as Edward was laying out his paperwork or scrolling through a case report on his computer. She never questioned herself about her timing on these occasions, but the television host usually had a lot to say about it.

Edward was similarly casual, often barely looking up to acknowledge her presence. Instead he would continue to focus on his screen whilst wordlessly clearing a space for her and sometimes they would merely sit together in companionable silence, each occupied with their own activities. Despite the apparently chance nature of their meetings, it seemed that he was as much a creature of habit as her because one evening when Tess arrived for her night shift, Dave was in the kitchen eager to impart information.

"That nice-mannered chap you sit with, Mary's lad?" he said leaning his considerable bulk through the serving hatch, "Well, he looked proper confused this morning with you not pitching up. Kept looking at his watch and then at the empty chair. I was going to tell him you were on nights but I says to myself, 'Dave,' I says, 'you mind your own business.'" He regarded Tess with obvious glee. "I've even caught him checking how many flapjacks there are left on the counter some mornings before you get here. I want to say to him, 'Don't worry, sir, I'll make sure there's one for her,' but I stay quiet and he sees me put one in a bag and tuck it under the shelf and we smile at each other. You'd be surprised the things you pick up by just going about your business, watching the world." He looked shy for a moment, lost in his own thoughts as he wiped the surfaces down with disinfectant. "I do love this job," he said, handing Tess her sandwich. "You meet all sorts."

Tess was finding herself looking forward to her encounters with Edward with a level of enthusiasm that she couldn't really justify. It wasn't that they discussed anything of enormous significance, and it wasn't just that he was devastatingly handsome – although this helped, obviously. Being with him, simply being in his presence, was exhilarating in a way she couldn't really put her finger on, although she was sure it felt similar to the night they'd met, all those years ago. She anticipated their chats with a degree of excitement that one might better associate with a child waiting for Christmas, checking her watch repeatedly as the hour approached, nipping into the ladies' toilets for a quick look in the mirror and perhaps to add a touch of lip gloss. Even Kath had noticed that she seemed to take more care with her appearance on a Tuesdays and Thursdays. She would subconsciously make a note of things during the week that might amuse him – films she'd seen or books she'd read – and one day, just as she was about to return her mug to the counter and get back to work, he reached into a bag and pulled out a paperback.

"I thought you might want to read this," he said. "It was recommended by a friend of mine. He's an ENT doctor."

"You mean Dan?" She said it without thinking. He looked confused and she realised her mistake.

"Yes," he said slowly. "How did…?"

"Umm…" She tried to style it out. Made a dismissive gesture with her hands. "I think maybe you mentioned him a few weeks ago. Said you had a friend in ENT, used to work in Bristol, I think you said?"

She looked at him closely, aware that she was shamelessly fishing; hoping desperately that he would respond in a sudden flash of clarity, *Yes Dan, I went to visit him once, stayed over at his after a party, met this amazing woman… Oh my God, it was you…*

He didn't say that. He just looked back down at the paperback in his hands and nodded and said, "Yeah, well, anyway. This book…" He held it out to her.

She looked at the cover, reading the title, "*This is Going to Hurt*. Oh! That's the Adam Kaye one, isn't it? I've been dying to read it. Thank you."

"No problem. It's absolutely hilarious. You'll love it. My girlfriend, Clara, got it me for Christmas."

"Oh!" There was a pause as Tess looked back at the book to mask some of her surprise and, in all honesty, crushing disappointment. "Will she mind? Your girlfriend? Would she mind you lending her present to someone else?"

Unaware of this inner turmoil, Edward replied, "No, she won't be fussed. She's not much of a reader. I mean, she can read, obviously. She's just not really into fiction, or medical memoirs for that matter. She only got it for me because I'd been going on about it since Dan recommended it. And as you can see, I've read it a few times now." He pointed to the slightly dog-eared corners.

"Oh, I'm much worse," she said, composure recovered, at least superficially. "Books I read always look like they've been run over by an HGV or survived some sort of nuclear apocalypse, but then I think it's nice to see they've been well loved. I never trust someone who claims to have read and enjoyed a pristine-looking paperback. And I just can't get my head around downloading them. I like to hold a book in my hands, read it in the bath, fold the corners of the pages down..."

"I bet you break the spines as well," he said, shuddering comically. "And frankly it's that kind of cavalier attitude to rules that leads to anarchy and chaos, which would be nothing more than I'd expect from you. But as vices go, it could be worse." He tapped its cover. "Feel free to abuse it any way you wish, but I think you'll enjoy it."

He started to tell her about another book he was now reading, and no further mention was made of Clara. Tess tried not to analyse her own response too closely. She shouldn't have been surprised. The fact that Edward hadn't remembered her from their first meeting had been disappointment enough – deep down she had probably known that he was already attached. Why wouldn't he be? He was handsome and, when he put his mind to it, utterly charming: *"A most eligible match"* as Jane Austen kept putting it, no matter how many times Tess asked her to be quiet or mentioned that these opinions were extremely unhelpful.

In the days following the revelation, she succumbed once more to the ritual binging that had characterised her winter months. It wasn't simply that her blossoming friendship with Edward had bolstered her confidence. She had started to feel attractive again, and had made the mistake of paying renewed attention to her appearance. As always, the television host was on hand and eager to point out her error.

"You should have known better really, shouldn't you, Tess? I honestly don't know what you were thinking."

He sighed, waiting until she had assembled the biscuits and chocolate in front of her before he resumed.

"The sad truth is that fat, ugly girls are simply not appealing to attractive men like that."

Tess felt a single tear trickle down her cheek and angrily brushed it away.

"And in addition to your physical disadvantages, consider your background," he said, using his patient, explaining-to-a-small-child voice. *"Girls from broken homes where paternity is questionable, money is tight, and aspirations are narrow, well,*

girls like that, girls like you, *don't end up with wealthy men. Not classy ones like your posh Edward Russell anyway."*

He paused as she unwrapped her second Twix.

"It doesn't matter how clever you think you are, how many books you've read, or how much you've shrugged off that coal-miner accent, sweetheart. Men don't like clever, dumpy, boring girls and they don't like working-class trash."

His voice continued to drip the litany of abuse into Tess's ear, filling her up with poison faster than she could stuff in the carbohydrate antidote.

"It's for your own good, Tess. I'm only telling you what you need to hear. Aiming too high is dangerous. Let's face it. Don't make the same mistake again."

She wouldn't, she told herself. She wouldn't aim anywhere; high, low, subterranean. In fact, she convinced herself that, in a way, it was something of a relief to learn about Edward's girlfriend. It meant that whatever was happening (*"Um, there's literally* nothing *happening,"* said the host, who was bored now) was entirely and absolutely platonic. Maybe it took the pressure off. She had, after all, sworn herself off men for a while and Miss Austen had made her views clear in the late hours of the evening when Tess lay on her bed feeling bloated and ugly.

"I do not wish to appear indelicate," she said. *"But after the unfortunate episode with your previous match, the indiscretions and unpleasantness and so forth… I do wonder if it may be advisable to guard your heart a little more carefully, my dear? Perhaps such a maelstrom of emotions is best avoided for the immediate future, and instead of tormenting oneself with missed opportunities, one might instead draw a veil across the experience*

and focus on the companionship of friends, the pleasures of the mind, and the rigours of academic study?"

"You sound like my mother," Tess had grumbled, but she knew that Jane Austen was right. The episode with Scott had left her bruised to say the least. She was reluctant to invite someone else into her life, and if she did, she'd have to be pretty certain that they were a safe bet. And Edward, with the charged atmosphere that surrounded him and the giddy excitement he induced, did not seem like a safe bet. News of the girlfriend acted as the perfect deterrent, patrolling her emotions like a guard dog, forcing her to acknowledge that what she had with Edward was nothing more than platonic conversation with someone she bumped into now and again.

Their meetings continued with the same regularity and frequency but Tess's guard, which had been melting away as she basked in Edward's attention, had now returned. The television host kept her in check if she started to daydream, constantly reminding her that Edward was way out of her league, that he had no recollection of ever meeting her before, and that she was still probably too fat, too ugly, and too common to get a boyfriend anyway. Such pronouncements were generally accompanied by replayed footage of discovering Scott in bed with Luke and a great deal of signposting towards various confectionery items. Jane Austen gave up on forcing a match that had no real future and instead devoted her time to gentle rebuttal of the television host's more unpleasant commentary, averting her eyes when Tess scoffed an entire tray of mini-muffins, whispering faintly, *"I'm sure this unhealthy obsession with sustenance was not 'a thing' back in my day."* Tess didn't feel able to point out to her that Georgian ladies of quality had had even more elaborate means with which to torment themselves.

Comfort-eating aside, life continued much as usual and she still enjoyed seeing Edward – probably a little too much. They avoided discussions regarding Mary's health or prognosis and Tess was initially cautious about revealing too much regarding her own family, feeling that there were enough chinks in her armour already. However, one morning she did mention a trip back to Sheffield she had planned for the weekend and Edward looked up from his laptop. "You going to see your parents?" he asked.

"My mum," she corrected him, "and my brother. Well, half-brother strictly speaking, but we never say that. It's always felt like we were peas in a pod, other than the fact that we look very different."

"Oh?"

"Jake's dad was Jamaican," she explained. "Mum was completely bowled over. Thought he was the man of her dreams. She fell pregnant at nineteen, ruined all her plans, but she didn't see that at the time. Not until he buggered off a year later." She sat back in her chair. "So, we're a variety of shades in our house, flying the melanin tricolour for multi-cultural Britain. Mum's white, Jake's half Afro-Caribbean, and I'm half Italian. She obviously had a thing for exotic blokes, at least by Yorkshire standards."

"And your father's not around either?"

"No. I mean it's no big deal. Same for a lot of families I knew growing up. Mum clearly had a thing not just for exotic-looking men but ones with a tendency to leg it as soon as the babies arrived. To be fair, Marco, my dad, stayed until I was five. I do have some memories of him, and he sent presents for a while after he left. He ran off with a girl from Barnsley called Jolene. Mum still can't listen to Dolly Parton."

"That must have been tough."

"Well, yes. Everyone should have a bit of Dolly in their lives now and again."

"No. Obviously, I meant your mum, being on her own, with two small children. You're right; it's not an uncommon scenario but still, doesn't mean it's easy?"

"Oh, it was fine. I imagine it was a bit different to your pampered existence. But no, we managed to eke out a living, Jake narrowly escaped being sent down t'pit for coal, I avoided a life of servitude and prostitution—"

"You don't need to be flippant about it. I'm interested." He leaned in towards her.

"I'm not being flippant." She cleared her throat and looked away.

"I'm sorry, I didn't mean to upset you."

"I'm not upset. Really, I'm not. It's just, sometimes I wish… I don't know. I wish I'd got to know him just a little better before he left. It's hard not to take it personally when your own father runs out on you and never makes contact again. I mean, it's one thing to walk out on your partner and some other bloke's child, but to abandon your own flesh and blood without a word of explanation? It's a bit pathetic but I'd like to have the opportunity to ask him what I did wrong."

"If it's any consolation, growing up with a father who is emotionally unavailable can be just as damaging as not having one at all," Edward said.

Tess raised her eyebrows, glad to have had the attention shifted away from her own mixed feelings about Marco. "D'you mean in general or…?"

Edward shrugged. "My father was never what you would describe as a 'hands-on' dad," he said. "He wasn't cruel, and it's not like he was some kind of tyrant or anything. He was just… never there. Physically or emotionally. He wasn't part of my life. I feel like I never knew him and then suddenly, bam, it's too late. He keeled over with a heart attack and that opportunity for anything approaching a father–son relationship died with him."

"I'm sorry," said Tess. "That must have been really tough. And you're right. My idea of what it might have been like to have my dad around is optimistic at best…" Her voice trailed off as Mrs Russell entered the café, leaning on the arm of an athletic but concerned-looking physiotherapist.

"We couldn't quite get there today," James the physio explained to Edward as Tess stood to offer her seat to her patient. Mrs Russell looked shattered. "It's. Nothing. Just. Pain."

Edward reached out to clasp her arm, "Where Mum? Where's the pain? Is it in your back again?" He picked up his phone. "We'll talk to them about some more radiotherapy, see if we can book it in for tomorrow." He swiped across the screen, still holding onto his mum's shoulder as he stood above her waiting for someone to answer.

Tess, meanwhile, thanked the physio and crouched down to Mrs Russell's eye level. "Mary, is this pain new? Would you like me to see if we've got a bed free for a few hours, somewhere you can wait quietly while we look at your medication?"

Mrs Russell nodded, her face contorted in a grimace. "Yes," she breathed. "That would. Be good."

Tess consulted with Dr Fielding and managed to find Mrs Russell a side room and some diamorphine. As the medication coursed through her system Mary's breathing eased and the colour returned to her cheeks. Edward bustled about the room, trying and failing to be useful. Eventually he slumped into a chair by the window and put his head in his hands. Seeing his mother was now sleeping peacefully, he looked over to where Tess was altering the drug chart to allow her patient better pain control. She was focussing all her attention on getting the calculation right and her eyebrows were screwed together in concentration. A lone strand of hair had worked its way loose from her ponytail and was dangling in front of her face despite repeated subconscious attempts to tuck it behind her ear. The sky beyond the window was darkening with cloud and she had turned on a lamp in the corner to avoid the stark phosphorescent glare of the overhead lights while she worked. Edward, sitting in the corner, could see the warm glow glinting off Tess's skin, her dark hair a halo of fiery brunette. Her features were soft in the lamplight, a frown of concentration smoothed by golden shadow, the curve of her lips outlined as she brought her pen to rest there while ratios and dilutions danced through her head. The hypnotic sound of opiate-induced breathing – a soft inhalation followed by longer whispered exhalations – coming from the bed, somehow added to the intimate atmosphere.

Edward cleared his throat, breaking the spell. "She's had a dose of radiotherapy to try and shrink some of the tumour. Do you, I mean, in your experience, does that help, usually?" His tone was casual but it was clear that he wanted her approval. It was quite endearing.

"Sometimes it can do." Tess nodded.

He moved forward in the chair and his face emerged from the shadows, his expression betraying a need for further reassurance. She wished she could give him more and almost reached out to touch his hand but stopped herself just in time.

"It's often a good option," she said instead, keeping her voice level and practical. "Worth considering for symptom relief, certainly." There was a pause before she spoke again, "What's the response to the chemotherapy been like?"

Edward exhaled, the sigh a mixture of despair and weary resignation. "It's been bloody awful, to be honest, but we're hoping to see some good results. Dr Hamilton-Jones, you remember? He thinks she's got a chance. I mean, he really seems to think that there's a possibility it might cure her entirely."

"Really?" She tried and failed to keep the surprise out of her voice and Edward acknowledged it with a defensive look. Tess could almost see the barriers coming up, battle lines being drawn. While his mother's condition was stable he had been able to relax and perhaps persuade himself that something miraculous was going to happen. Clearly, the state of Mary's health was inextricably linked to his emotional wellbeing, and now it seemed she might be deteriorating again. This didn't bode well.

"It's a long shot," he said. "I know that. I'm not an idiot."

"I'm not for one minute implying—"

"But if there's any chance at all, no matter how remote, we've got to try." He looked across at his mum's now peaceful face, her frail shoulders cradled by the pillows. "I feel bad for…" He sighed. "I know she finds it hard, but we have to keep trying."

Chapter Nine

T ess was crossing the foyer from room four, where she had just been checking on a patient's syringe driver. It was mid-afternoon and the May sunshine was filtering through the skylights, forming bright patches on the linoleum. Vases of flowers stood on the reception desk, their heady scent filling the room. Janice, the receptionist, took it upon herself to ensure that the flowers were always fresh, arguing that the last place for the depressing sight of dying blooms was a hospice. Many of the bouquets were donated by families inundated with funeral flowers or gifts from well-wishers, and Janice often had a lot to work with. Tess suspected that the ability to indulge her aptitude for floristry was what kept Janice at St Martin's, because her customer service skills were questionable. Still, she had been busy this week, because the foyer smelt like a boudoir and looked like the hothouse at Kew Gardens.

Dave was wheeling a large trolley of rattling mugs through from the industrial dishwasher to the café and narrowly avoided colliding with Edward Russell as he hurried through the main entrance. Edward caught sight of Tess standing in a patch of sunlight as she turned to see the source of the commotion. She waved and made her way to the nurses' station to begin writing up her notes as he went through to check on his mum. Mary Russell had been for another dose of radiotherapy to her lower spine yesterday but had opted to come back to the hospice rather than stay on the private ward at the hospital. Tess continued to write up her notes, leaning back in the swivel chair every now and again to catch the rays of sunlight that continued to glint through from the top windows. It was a glorious day. One of those English spring afternoons, perfect for a wedding or a fete if you could predict with any certainty that the weather would last, which of course you never could. She thought fondly of her friend Golda's wedding a few weeks ago, when the heavens had opened, depositing their April showers, and Golda had spent the majority of the day with a muddy hem and damp confetti down her cleavage. It hadn't reduced the radiance of her smile though; she had been a beautiful bride, and her husband Tom had looked as though he couldn't believe his luck.

Over the edge of the desk she could see Janice working on reception trimming stems and stepping back to admire her latest creation whilst she answered phone calls and directed porters to their designated sites. After a while, Tess became aware of raised voices coming from Mrs Russell's room. She startled as the door was flung open and Edward stalked out in a thunderous mood. He seemed unsure of what to do with himself; his teeth were gritted and his hands were balled up in fists as he paced over to the nurses' station and slammed his palms down on the raised countertop right at Tess's eye level. She pushed her seat back in surprise.

"Can you speak to her?" The volume of his voice jarred in the quiet foyer. "The next round of chemo begins tomorrow and she's saying she won't go. I've told her that it's just this last course and then it's done – but if she won't go, well then it definitely won't work, and what's the point in having started it at all, and... Bloody hell! What is she thinking?"

Tess tried her best to be placatory. "Okay. I will talk to her – and see what she wants to do..."

The visible tension in Edward's jaw eased and his shoulders began to drop. "Good," he said. "She'll listen to you."

"But," Tess said quickly, "it is *up to her*."

"Yes, of course it is, but she's not thinking straight at the moment. You'll be able to put her right."

Tess hesitated. "Mr Russell, your mum has the capacity to make these decisions, and if she doesn't want to go ahead with any course of treatment then I am not going to be able to change her mind..." She waited again before adding more quietly. "And neither would I want to."

There was a loaded pause and she could virtually see the red mist descending over Edward's face.

"Right," he said. "I see."

"I just wouldn't want her to feel forced into—"

"Forced into *being cured*! Of course, you wouldn't," he slammed his hands down on the desk again. "What kind of bloody doctor *are* you? What's the point in going to medical school and doing all that training if you're just going to preside over death all day? Surely you're supposed to *preserve* life! Not just let it trickle away without a whimper. That's this place *all over*, isn't it? Why bother trying to *actually cure* anyone? Just give them some bloody morphine and let. Them. *Die!*"

Tess tried to remain calm, but the shouting was now starting to attract attention. Dave had come back out of the kitchen with a tea towel in his hands and was keeping a wary eye on proceedings as he dried a plate. Janice had paused midway through her gerbera arrangement and was looking as much like a coiled spring as it is possible for an overweight receptionist holding a pair of secateurs to look. What was worse, the new lady in room three had also poked her head round the door and was regarding the outburst with obvious distress.

"May. I. Remind. You"—Tess pulled herself up to her full height and placed her hands on the desktop in front of him—"that there are sick patients here." Her cheeks were flushed and her volume was now starting to increase to match his, "And that this is *completely* inappropriate behaviour." She cut across his protestations, "I understand that you are finding this difficult, Mr Russell, but if you carry on upsetting our staff and patients like this I will have to ask you to leave." She could feel her nostrils flaring and her arms were rigid on the desk as she held her ground. Edward removed his hands from the raised platform, conceding territory but still glowering at Tess.

"Oh, don't worry," he said. "I'm off! Sooner I get out of

this bloody mausoleum the better." And with a turn on his heel and a few angry strides he was out of the door.

Tess sat back down on the chair, her hands shaking slightly as she tried to steady her breathing. Dave sauntered over from the direction of the café, tea towel still in hand. "Well done, love," he said. "You handled that just right. Got to nip that sort of chat in the bud pronto." Tess looked up, grateful for his words.

"He'll be kicking himself now, mind. Always a nice polite fella that one. Loves his mum." Dave continued drying the plate despite the fact that there was clearly no water residue left anywhere on its surface. "Quite keen on you an' all, I shouldn't wonder. Blown it now though, ain't he?" He wandered off again, taking his plate with him.

Janice had also moved across from reception with surprising speed. Once Dave had said his piece she came around to the back of the nurses' station and wrapped her arms around Tess in an enormous matronly hug.

"No need for that sort of behaviour. I'll give him a piece of my mind if he tries that again, honest to God I will."

Tess allowed herself to be comforted for a few moments before taking a deep breath and pasting a watery smile to her face.

"I'm okay, Janice," she said. "Honestly, it could have been worse. I'm sure he didn't mean to be so... well, so bloody rude."

She looked back down at the notes she had been writing and saw where her biro had scrawled off the paper when she had pushed her chair back so fast. Ripping out the page, she scrunched it into a ball and pulled a fresh sheet onto the desk, putting her energies into producing a neat cursive script. She thought Jane Austen might have the good grace at this point to comment on her fortitude in adversity, or at the very least the beauty of her impeccable handwriting given the circumstances, but that particular voice was ominously silent.

Instead, the television host tutted slowly. *"Oh dear, oh dear, oh dear. What a nasty little scene. And how exactly did that make you feel, Tess? A bit low? A bit… hurt?"*

She carried on writing.

"Still," he said. *"I know just the thing to make you feel better…"*

Edward was as good as his word, and no matter how many times the click and slide of the main doors caused Tess to turn her head towards them that afternoon, it was never him. On the way back home that evening she stopped in at the corner shop and began her soothing ritual: freezer cabinet for the ice cream, grocery shelf for the biscuits, and chocolate bars in their usual place next to the cashier.

Accompanied by her bag of therapy, she returned to an empty house, the television host's voice in her ear, the studio audience loudly munching on their popcorn, and not a peep out of Jane Austen.

Chapter Ten

In an attempt to regain a professional focus on the situation, Tess decided to try and establish what Mary Russell really wanted. After all, maybe she had got it wrong and Mary *did* want more treatment. There was no point in stoking up a family confrontation if it didn't exist so she went to see her straight after the ward round the following morning.

Mary smiled as she looked up and saw Tess but faltered at the serious expression on her face.

"Oh dear," she said. "You look like someone has died."

"Well, it *is* a hospice." Tess closed the door behind her. "Sorry, that's not remotely amusing. No, I didn't mean to look so preoccupied. I just wanted to get to the bottom of what happened yesterday. It all seemed to get a bit heated?" She moved her chair alongside the bed where Mary was resting against her pillows, her face drawn with fatigue. "If you don't want to talk about it, it's fine. I'm a terrible one for expecting people to overshare. Some call it nosiness; I prefer to call it 'being interested in people's lives'."

"That can't be considered a bad thing, surely?"

"You're right, but my housemate, Kath, suggested that asking somebody, 'How do you feel about this situation?' until they burst into tears is not necessarily an approach that works for everyone, so do just let me know if you want me to leave you in peace."

Mary laughed and looked down at her hands which were resting on top of the starched hospice linen.

"I would welcome having someone to talk to about it," she said after a while. "Someone who is not directly involved. It's hard to have a rational discussion with friends and family because they are all so affected by the outcome. And I know you care about what happens to me, but it's a different type of care, a professional one."

"Absolutely."

"So that does make it a bit more straightforward, to perhaps say things to you that I wouldn't say to others. It's just… it's difficult to know where to start. Edward is finding this all so hard. He doesn't mean to get angry and I… I just don't know what to do for the best."

She looked so anguished. Tess started to feel the indignation that Edward's outburst had roused in her yesterday coming to the fore again, but Jane Austen's voice in her ear cautioned her to remain detached and professional.

"How about we avoid talking specifically about this round of chemotherapy for a moment and just maybe focus on the more general stuff," she said, and Mary nodded. "I know your main concern is your son and I get that. But this isn't about him. Not really. This is about you and what you want. And I can understand why you might want to stop treatment if it's making you feel dreadful."

There was a pause before Mary started to speak. Her voice was soft but she had the same authoritative tone as Edward, albeit with a gentler edge.

"The thing is, Dr Carter, it's all well and good to say that this discussion isn't about my son, but that's not strictly true when you're a mother. I take it you're not?" Tess shook her head. "I'm sorry, I didn't mean to be presumptuous. It's just that I need to think about what this scenario means for my children. If I do stop treatment, then my chances of dying sooner are probably increased, although I know it's impossible to predict. Yes?"

"Possibly. Okay, probably."

"So, let's say I stop the chemotherapy because I want to feel a bit better in these last few months. I'm still making an active decision to end things more quickly, aren't I?"

"Ye-es."

"Okay, so I've made that choice and it's over for me. But the problem is that Edward and Madeleine will still be here, dealing with the consequences for the rest of *their* lives. Do you see? It's not over for them. I need to think about what happens after I've gone."

"But surely neither of your children would want you to have treatment that is making you feel worse, just through some misguided attempt to keep them happy?"

Mary interrupted her: "I'm sorry, doctor, it's not misguided." Her voice was firmer now. "Edward doesn't need to know that I am doing this for him. He sees I'm struggling at the moment, that I'm finding the therapy difficult, and he doesn't perceive it as a weakness. He just can't understand why I wouldn't want to do everything I possibly could to stay alive. There is a part of him that feels let down even by the notion that I might give up. Subconsciously I think it is causing him to question his value: would I try harder if he was a *better* son? You see? I'm sorry... I just need a moment..."

She dabbed her eyes and Tess reached out to hold her hand.

"But Mary, if you told him, if you said exactly what you've said to me, that you're fed up of it all and that the treatment is making you feel unwell, then surely he'd understand? He wouldn't think it was a reflection on him? I mean, would he? Obviously, he's your son. You know him, but..."

Mary was considering Tess's words. "I think on a rational level, yes, of course he'd listen to what I had to say – although he's doing a spectacular job of turning a deaf ear to it currently – but yes, I could really force the issue and he would presumably see the logic. What I'm more worried about is how he feels deep down, and of course he's absolutely hopeless at sharing that with anyone."

"I can imagine," said Tess.

Mary's forehead was wrinkled in a frown. "I'm worried that in the long run Edward might blame himself. Maybe what I need to do is just pull myself together, continue the treatment, and show him that I want to survive at all costs. That he is someone worth fighting to be alive for?" She leant back into her pillows with a groan, "Ugh, I hate this battle talk in the context of illness. I can't believe I'm resorting to it myself. The notion that people who die from cancer haven't fought hard enough. It's so unhelpful."

A tear trickled out of the corner of Mary's eye and she looked exhausted. She obviously didn't want to have any more treatment, and Tess was just going to have to nudge her into making the right decision.

"I think you should stop the chemo," she said. She had observed her senior consultant, Dr Fielding, approach the subject of ending treatment in a diplomatic and non-judgemental way, so she was confident this was the right thing to do, although the television host in her ear suddenly seemed delighted, as he often did when he sensed she was about to screw things up.

"Or..." she tried to back-pedal, "... how about as a compromise, you delay the current round of treatment at least? Give yourself a bit of time to think, to talk to Edward again, to explain?"

There was a pause. Mary looked thoughtful. The television host was quiet, and Tess pushed her advantage.

"That way, maybe you can see how you feel whilst not on treatment and, I don't know, at least it kicks the decision into the long grass for a while?"

"It's all a little dependent on how much long grass there is though, isn't it?" Mary smiled. "But you're right, a break does seem a very appealing prospect, and it couldn't do much harm. I think certainly missing today's session feels like a good idea. I've been dreading it, to be honest." She sat up a little more upright. "I'm going to make an executive decision. Today's chemo is cancelled. There. I feel better already."

"Well, get a load of you! Let's hang out the bunting!" Tess made a little trumpeting noise which masked the sound of the television host hitting his forehead with the heel of his palm, and Mary giggled.

They were both laughing when Edward entered the room. The sudden noise and cold draft of air startled them, and Tess's smile faltered as she looked towards the door.

"Mr Russell. We were just catching up, weren't we, Mary?"

His movements were brisk and businesslike as he removed his jacket and folded it over the back of a chair.

"Evidently. Although I can't really imagine what you might have to catch up on. Don't mind me; you carry on with whatever was so amusing."

"Edward." Mary sat forward. "Don't be so snide. Dr Carter and I were just having a little chat. Is it against the law to laugh occasionally when one is terminally ill?"

"Not at all. God knows you should find your moments of entertainment where you can." He turned to Tess but did not make eye contact. "Dr Carter. I must apologise for yesterday's outburst. You were right. It was not appropriate given the circumstances and the potential audience. It will not happen again."

Tess could feel a blotchy rash prickling at her neck but reminded herself that this was her turf. Edward's apology was necessary, and although delivered with bad grace, it was an apology nonetheless. She acknowledged it with a cursory nod and forced a smile onto her face.

As she left the room she saw Edward pulling up the same chair she had been sitting in a few moments earlier and heard him say, "So, Mum. Ready for this afternoon's session?"

Tess felt an ominous lurch in her stomach.

"Oooh!" said the television host happily. It sounded like he was clapping his hands. *"I think this might really kick off!"*

Chapter Eleven

Tess had cancelled the ambulance transfer to the hospital and had just put the phone down when Edward emerged from his mother's room and crossed the foyer in five long strides to come to a halt at the desk.

"So! It appears that my mother is *not* going to be having today's session of chemotherapy," Edward said. "I suppose I have you to thank for that?"

She could see a pulse beating at the base of his neck near his shirt collar.

"It's not really anything to do with—"

"In fact, it seems she has decided to stop it altogether. The entire course of treatment. I hope you're happy now?" His fingers were back to their angry tapping on the counter and Tess could see Debs, one of the nurses, look over from the drugs trolley.

"Mr Russell, I think we are both in agreement that this is not a suitable location for this type of discussion. Would you like to accompany me to the office where we can have a little more privacy?" She returned his stiff nod of agreement and led the way down a corridor, past a concerned-looking Janice, to an empty room where she gestured for Edward to take a seat.

"Actually, I'd rather stand," he said firmly.

"As you wish," she replied, matching his tone and his stance.

He took a deep breath. "I'm really unhappy," he began, "with the way that you are influencing my mother. She's not well. She's vulnerable. You're giving her the wrong idea about what's best for her, and I think you're letting your own agenda dictate her treatment choices." He folded his arms across his broad chest.

"My agenda? Right. I see."

"Yes, Dr Carter, your agenda."

"Are you… joking?"

"I am most certainly *not* joking. It seems it's just you and my mother who think this is a laughing matter."

"Okay. Mr Russell, the only reason she was so chipper earlier is because she was relieved not to be having today's session of chemo. I understand that you have concerns, but you've got this the wrong way round. I'm trying to help."

"And I'm not?"

"Well," Tess paused. "I don't think this *is* terribly helpful, to be honest. Have you actually talked to her about it, or asked her what she wants?"

"Do you have any idea how patronising you sound?"

She ignored his comment and tried to maintain a dignified air. "I can see that you're angry but maybe you need to speak to her again, and listen to what she says. Your mum and I had a good chat this morning. I can't share the details due to confidentiality—"

"Well, that's mightily convenient, isn't it?"

Tess felt her temper start to rise, his absolute refusal to see reason was exasperating. "It's not *convenient*, Mr Russell. It's actually the law. Which I thought was supposed to be your field of expertise? I think it is pretty obvious that *my agenda* is not the issue here. I don't even have one, and I'm certainly not the person most guilty of coercion."

There was a moment of silence and Tess knew she'd gone too far. Doctors were absolutely, categorically *not* supposed to get drawn into arguments with patients or their relatives. Edward looked furious.

"What are you saying exactly? Do spell it out for me. Despite it being so spankingly obvious, I haven't quite grasped your point."

"Okay." She might as well just spit it out. "I think you're bullying her."

They stared at each other for a few moments, both of them arms folded, pulled up to full height, neither wanting to be the one to drop eye contact. The words *bullying* and *coercion* sat there like verbal grenades, waiting to explode.

When he next spoke, Edward was cold and controlled, channelling his anger into every syllable. "You know nothing about me. And you know *nothing* about my family. You seem to think that because we've shared a bit of small talk over the weeks, you know about my life."

"I don't think anything of the sort." She tried to keep her voice level but his comments had shaken her badly because he was right; she *did* feel like she knew him. More than he realised.

"You do. You've made your little judgements already, caught my mother in a few moments of weakness, and jumped to conclusions that fit with what you've already decided, don't you see?"

"Now, hang on—"

"No! I will not *hang on*. You're busy painting a picture that supports your view of how my mother should choose to live her life, or end it, and you don't even know her. You accuse me of bullying, Dr Carter? Well, I accuse you of wilful misrepresentation of the facts."

Tess snorted in disbelief. He really was the most pompous, arrogant individual she had ever encountered. What on earth had she been thinking? Drifting about in a daydream of shared understanding and mutual regard. The gulf between them widened in that moment, and any semblance of a cool, professional demeanour was abandoned (not that there had been much of one to begin with).

"Oh, that's great that is," she said. "Wilful misrepresentation of the facts! You don't intimidate me with your legalese, Mr Russell. I'm just as clever as you, but I choose to use my knowledge to help people rather than, I don't know, find gaps in the law that make money for bankers."

He laughed at her then, a short derisory noise that seemed to come from a well of contempt he had stored up just for her. She realised she was being ridiculous, allowing this to deteriorate into a slanging match about their respective occupations. She had relinquished any moral high ground or advantage she may have possessed.

"And there we go." Edward's tone was almost triumphant, as if her words had confirmed all of his worst suspicions. "That says it all. You find me and my career choices somehow morally repugnant; as if it's only you who understands about life being tough, you with your clichéd gritty-upbringing chip-on-your-shoulder. It's pathetic, frankly."

"That's simply not true."

"Isn't it? Really? We've talked about this before. I don't see why I should have to defend my financial situation or my career choices to you, but your prejudice is obvious. And it demeans you."

Tess felt a flicker of self-doubt but quickly dismissed it. He was in the wrong here and his accusations of inverted snobbery were just further evidence of his bullying behaviour. Classic deflection. She was doing the right thing sticking to her guns, she felt sure of it.

"This whole notion you seem to have about my life being somehow easier than yours," Edward continued, "is so *embarrassingly* unimaginative. You think you have this broad worldview, a knowledge of hardship and suffering, but you don't understand any of it."

"I'm not sure how this is relevant. You're just being rude now."

"And you don't think it's rude, the way you've spoken to me? Not to mention incredibly unprofessional. I think it's fair to say you've overstepped the mark."

"That's completely—"

"No. Let me finish. You have already made your feelings about me and my family abundantly clear and I want you to have *nothing* further to do with my mother's care. I will be requesting that she sees a different doctor in future."

He turned and walked towards the door but waited on the threshold, his voice quieter and somehow more dangerous: "If she decides to stop the treatment – treatment that we know could cure her," he paused, "and if that decision is down to you and your misguided advice... then you will have to live with the consequences. And you will have to consider whether it's appropriate to continue practising medicine with her death on your conscience."

Rage was etched into the lines of Edward's face and he glared at her for a moment before letting himself out of the office, leaving a stunned Tess to crumple into her chair like a beaten dog. What *had* she done?

Chapter Twelve

Edward had just finished his phone call to Dr Fielding and was feeling a little calmer when the alert beep came through on the hands-free set and his sister's number flashed on the central screen.

"Eddie, it's me." Her voice cut through the static with a slight delay.

"Madeleine. You all right?"

"Yes, you driving? Okay to talk?"

"No problem, I'll just pull over. What are you doing up? It must be the crack of dawn."

"Six in the morning, to be precise, and I'm completely exhausted. Annabelle's being a little beast; she was up at five wanting to choose outfits for a party. Don't laugh. I'm bloody furious."

"You sound it."

"I've plonked her in front of the telly now, dressed in some frightful combo. Given up trying to get back to sleep. Thought I'd call you instead. How's Mummy getting on?"

"Oi! That was my space, you bastard… Sorry Mads, give me a minute. I'll just slip in… here. Good. So, yes. Mum. Well. Long story. She's decided to give up on the chemo, at least for now."

"Oh!"

"Quite."

"Given up? What, completely? Why?"

"Well. I suppose because it makes her feel like shit, but I reckon this Dr Carter, who seems to be on some sort of moral crusade, has had a hand in the decision. Just exactly the sort of misguided, clumsy approach you'd expect."

"Sorry darling, reception's shocking. Is this the doctor you talked about before? I thought you rated her? Mummy thinks she's wonderful."

"That's part of the problem, isn't it? They're too close. There's not enough professionalism. She's admitted it herself, this doctor. She's already said that she's not good at keeping her nose out of other people's business or understanding professional boundaries, and she's proved her own point nicely. It just happens to be at Mum's expense."

"Really?"

"She's got this bee in her bonnet about Mum's *right to choose*. And it's all terribly earnest and patronising. You can imagine."

"Well. Ye-esss. But, Mum *does* have a right to choose, Eddie."

"I am well aware of that, thank you, Madeleine, but she's not exactly in a good place to be making those decisions at the moment, is she? She doesn't feel well, it's all a bit overwhelming, and so she's really susceptible to persuasion."

"And, you what... you think she was persuaded?"

"Well, yeah. I'm sure this doctor thought she was doing the right thing, but her interfering has caused real problems. You know as well as I do that if Mum doesn't carry on with the chemo then that's it, we might as well hold our hands up and admit defeat, game over."

"Umm... Is it really that cut and dried? I don't know, maybe if she doesn't want to do this then perhaps we should listen to her?"

"Christ, Madeleine. I'm just trying to keep her alive, for God's sake."

"All right! Calm down. I just meant that maybe we ought to consider letting her take a bit of a break, if that's what she wants?"

He sighed. "A bit of a break could make a massive difference. You weren't there. You didn't hear what the oncologist said, but the stats aren't good if she stops now."

"The stats aren't good full stop, though, are they, darling?"

"No, but at least there's a chance. He seemed to think it could cure her entirely if she continued the treatment."

"Is... is that actually what he said? Because I was under the impression that a cure was extremely unl—"

"Sort of. He implied it. God! Why am I the only one who seems to be interested in Mum's actual survival here?"

There was a pause broken only by static.

"That's not fair."

"I know," he said. "I'm sorry. Look, I understand it's

hard for you stuck over there on the other side of the Atlantic, but the trouble is, you aren't seeing this first hand like I am. She's… she looks so bloody *ill*." He smacked his hand against the steering wheel. "If you could see her you'd think differently. I mean it. I keep feeling like she's a ticking time bomb and if we don't do the right thing, don't make her see what's happening, she might just sleepwalk her way out of life altogether. We can't let that happen. I just don't know what to do."

"How about if I speak to her?"

"Yes, that would be good. I think she's a bit pissed off with me. Not as pissed off as she's going to be when she finds out I've shouted at her favourite doctor though."

"You didn't really lose it, did you?"

"No! I did not *lose it*. I was very calm and collected actually. Don't worry. Anyway, she needed putting in her place. She's got a massive chip on her shoulder."

"Well, if you're sure. I can't help but think it's not going to be terribly useful if you end up alienating the very people who are looking after our mother though."

"For God's sake, Madeleine. I'm having to make all the decisions at the moment and I really don't need a telling off from someone who is *not actually here*. It's not that long ago you were giving me loads of shit about not being involved enough, and now it feels like—"

"All right, fair point. Although could you keep a lid on the language, darling? I've just put you on speaker-phone so I can help Annabelle with her feather boa."

"Her feather what?"

"Don't ask. Look, I'm trying to arrange flights so that the

kids and I can all come over in a few weeks, take some of the pressure off you for a bit? Are you going to be able to manage until then?"

"I suspect I'll have to, won't I?"

"Eddie…"

"Sorry." He sighed.

"We've talked about this before. You know how guilty I feel about not being there. Please don't make it worse."

"Madeleine, to be fair, you were the one dishing out the guilt trips until recently, making out the whole thing was my fault, as if I could have prevented Mum getting cancer by popping in to see her more often."

"I know. I've said I'm sorry. And I meant it. There is no sense in either of us doing anything but working together on this, so *please* let's not rake all that up again? I'm worried about you as well. It doesn't sound as if you've got any way of offloading this. Are you talking to Clara about it all?"

"It's not really her thing."

"What the fuck's that supposed to mean? No, Annabelle, ignore Mummy, I was just sneezing. How can it not be her thing, darling? It's not really anybody's *thing*, for God's sake!"

"No but she… she doesn't like talking about it. Says I'm dragging her down, being morose. She's right too. I am a proper grumpy old bastard at the moment."

"Even more than usual?"

"Even more than usual. Yes. Thanks."

"Well, please call me if you want to talk about stuff, or maybe think about speaking to a counsellor or something?"

"This isn't America. We don't all need to see therapists."

"Oh, good grief! You are utterly impossible. Look, I'll call Mum later today. Maybe you should leave things for a bit?"

"Let me guess, you're worried I'm going to make things worse?"

"Don't be ridiculous. I just know how upset you are, and I expect she does too. I'll talk to her and we'll go from there? And how about you see if you can avoid further alienating any of her doctors, particularly her favourite one? Sounds like it might be better to have this Dr Carter onside?"

"Too late for that. Sorry. She's going to hate my guts now. I mean, I probably was just a little overbearing, but she needed to hear it. I'm certainly not going to apologise to her."

"Okay, whatever. Tell Mummy I'll call her later, okay? I love you, Eddie. Take care."

———————

Tess meanwhile, had been called in to have a conversation with her boss. Dr Fielding made them both a cup of tea and sought to reassure her that she was not in any trouble. He had a calm voice that soothed Tess's frayed nerves as he outlined the conversation he had already had with Edward Russell.

"He's very distressed, Tess, but he's an eloquent and articulate man," Dr Fielding said, peering over his wire-rimmed spectacles. "I wonder if you caught the sharp end of his tongue somewhat. Hmm?" He leaned forward and steepled his fingers together on a desk piled high with old journals.

The gentleness of his tone and the level of understatement about exactly how sharp Edward Russell's punishing tongue had been overwhelmed Tess and she began, in spite of her best efforts, to cry. She still couldn't reconcile the man she thought she knew with the one who had accused her of those awful things.

"He's horrible," she spluttered through her tears. "He's horrible to me; he's horrible to his mother. He's forcing her to undergo treatment that she doesn't want and his response to anything other than total obedience is to bully people into submission. He's rude," she continued. "He's arrogant. He's obnoxious."

"And he's clearly upset you a great deal. Yes?"

She nodded miserably, wiping her tears away with the back of her hand.

"He may indeed be all those things you describe," said Dr Fielding. "I have to say that I found him to be polite and quite considerate, but I know that people behave in different ways according to audience and scenario." He paused. "But – and here is the crux of the matter – he is grieving. He is going through the angry phase of his bereavement process a little prematurely, and he is lashing out."

"Yes, but I know all that," Tess blurted out before she could stop herself. "Sorry, with the greatest respect and all, I *know* that. And if it were just me he was being vile to, I could absolutely take it on the chin. My concern is for my patient, his mother. His behaviour is having a negative impact on her and he is bullying her into decisions about treatment." She leant forward in her chair. "I think this is potentially a safeguarding issue. Mary is vulnerable and he is coercing her. It's simple. And it's not on!"

Dr Fielding strove to avoid a patronising tone. "Tess. This is your first job in palliative care, yes? And you enjoy it, you like the patient contact, the holistic nature of the role?"

"Yes. I really do."

"The thing is, palliative care is not the pink and fluffy creature that our surgical and medical colleagues like to suggest. You need balls of steel for this job, forgive the euphemism. I suspect there is a gender-neutral alternative but I can't pluck it out of the air at the moment."

She smiled, this time a genuine, although shaky, one.

"You need to be tough. Really tough. These are not insignificant decisions; they are literally life-and-death decisions. These are not minor feelings we are encountering; they are right out of the top drawer of high-intensity emotions, the strongest, most basic of instincts we are dealing with here: grief, anger, hurt, loss, pain." His fingers relaxed out of the steeple and he placed his hands flat on the desktop. "I can't tell you how much it irritates me when people assume that end-of-life care is all about aromatherapy and mood lighting," he said, and Tess laughed. "That's better. Now, I know that you are coming from a good place on this. And I applaud your dedication to your advocacy role, I really do. But you are too invested in this particular case and it will be more destructive for you than you realise if you don't detach yourself a little. Does that make sense?"

"Yes. Of course. I understand." She continued to look troubled. "He said that if she died, he would blame me and suggested I shouldn't be a doctor anymore. Could I be accused of negligence or I don't know...?"

"What is it you're worried about?"

"It wouldn't be my fault if she died, would it?" she asked in a small voice.

"Tess," he peered over his glasses again. "You know that you're not responsible for the death of this patient. She's already dying."

She nodded.

"However, I cannot promise that her son will see it in the same light. He may well hold you personally accountable for his mother's death, however unreasonable that may seem. There is very little you can do about it. Grief is not reasonable."

There was a brief silence as they both mulled this over and Tess shifted in her chair. "Thank you, that really helps. And you're right, of course. I need some distance from this entire case."

"Another thought, Tess." Dr Fielding gestured back at the chair. "Mr Russell does not strike me as a man who enjoys having his vulnerabilities exposed."

She gave a snort of agreement as she sat back down.

"No. Indeed," he said, "it occurs to me that the reason you may have been on the receiving end of the majority of his animosity is because perhaps you have witnessed him in moments of what he would perceive to be weakness? Yes?"

"I suppose so."

"And that's not your fault. But when someone has opened up to you, there's often a bit of fallout if they subsequently regret lowering their guard."

He leant back with an air of conclusion and gestured towards the door. "Now, you go and enjoy your bank holiday weekend. Next week, a fresh start, and I would suggest that whilst you attend to all of Mrs Russell's medical needs, you perhaps avoid lengthy existential conversations for the time being. I think I can persuade her son that intervention on a purely clinical level, as provided by yourself, will be entirely suitable and appropriate."

Tess had her hand on the door before she spoke: "Dr Fielding, thank you. You're really very… wise."

He smiled broadly. "Thank you, Tess, but rest assured, we all doubt ourselves from time to time, and whenever I'm feeling too smug about my own staggering genius, my wife, who is a professor of astrophysics, disabuses me of the notion fairly rapidly. Now off you go."

Chapter Thirteen

Tess made the journey home to Sheffield the next morning and brought Morris, who was happy stretched out across the parcel shelf in the sun. She was really looking forward to seeing her mum and felt that it could not have come at a better time, given recent events. She felt completely wrung-out and Kath, who had known something was amiss, approached the topic with her usual candour.

"Tess, babe," she'd said. "It's pretty clear there's something kicking off at work. At least, I'm assuming it's work because let's face it, there isn't exactly a whole heap of other stuff going on in your life at the moment."

Tess pointed out that being alerted to the shoddy state of her work–life balance was not the most helpful in terms of cheery reminders but Kath remained unabashed.

"It must get a bit draining, is all. You're there all the bleedin' time and it's a pretty intense job anyways. You need to get yourself home, bit of quality time with your mam and that gorgeous brother of yours – well, I mean, he is, you can't deny it – anyways, you'll be grand."

Tess had to admit Kath was probably right. The strain of attending to other people's needs was starting to take its toll, and as she left the motorway and joined the meandering A-roads, she opened the windows to let in the bracing air, taking a couple of deep breaths and feeling the tension in her neck and shoulders ease. Even her forehead relaxed and she realised that she had grown accustomed to a perpetual frown for the past few days, which was most unlike her. Every time she came back to Yorkshire she enjoyed the freedom of vast open space; even when in the centre of the city, you could often see glimpses of dramatic natural landscapes if you raised your eyes to the skyline and took in the surrounding hills. It seemed that on this occasion the further north she went the less constrained and suffocated she felt, a sensation that was odd given the fact that the reverse had been true when she initially left home at eighteen and headed south for the broad horizons of university life. She supposed she had been escaping in a different way at that time, and perhaps the geography was immaterial; what mattered was the getting away, the putting of physical distance between herself and a problem. Either way, although her family home was neither grand nor picturesque, the faded ex-council house set in a terrace of identical stone-clad properties looked so welcoming as she pulled up outside that she almost wept.

Jane Austen sighed contentedly. *"The comforts of home are truly a restorative salve for the troubled soul,"* she said as Tess dropped her bags in the cluttered porch and released Morris who was wriggling under her arm. He padded off to rediscover his favourite haunts and Tess found him in the kitchen, purring loudly as he rubbed up against her mother's ankles.

"Mam." They hugged and Tess breathed in the scent of hairspray and clean washing.

"Perfect timing, pet." Her mum reached up to take two mugs off the shelf. "I've just put the kettle on. You'll be needing a brew after that journey."

"Yeah. Ta." Tess sank into one of the kitchen chairs and propped her elbows up on the table, exhaling loudly.

"You sound a bit tired." She looked more closely at her daughter, this time noticing the groove at the top of her nose where a worry line was forming.

"*Are* you all right, love?" She pulled up a chair opposite. "You're not quite yourself? Is it Scott?"

"God no! It's nothing to do with him. I haven't given him a second thought." As Tess said this the truth of the statement hit home. She really *hadn't* thought about Scott and Luke for ages. "It's difficult to explain. I guess work has been getting me down a bit."

Her mum paused in stirring her tea for a moment, the spoon held in mid-air. She had never heard Tess complain about her job before. "Do you want to talk about it?"

"Actually, no. Just being home makes it better. It's nothing specific anyway." Tess picked up her mug, blowing across the surface and staring into the distance. "Can I do anything? Help with lunch or something?"

Her mother went to the breadbin and brought her over a pack of rolls. "You could butter those bread buns while I get the soup on," she said, seeing that her daughter needed an activity to occupy her before she would start talking. She opened up a tin of soup from the cupboard and poured it into a saucepan. "I'll do us something nice for tea," she said. "Viv and Gina are coming over later, your Aunty Gee's looking forward to seeing you, and Jake'll be here too. He's bringing that new lass with him – nice girl, sounds like. Another trainee teacher. Met her at college." She paused again. There was silence and then, as predicted, Tess began to unburden herself.

"It's just... this guy," she said.

"Go on..." Her mum raised her eyebrows in a question.

"No! It's nothing like that. *Really*, it isn't. There might have been a time in the past, I mean, I sort of knew him before and I thought... But it was a long time ago, and people change, and if anything, it's the complete opposite now." She continued to butter the rolls, aware that she wasn't making much sense. "He's not a patient, but his mother is, and she's dying – obviously – it's a hospice, so no surprise there, but he's not accepting it."

Her mum started to open the cutlery drawer, removing items with as little noise as possible, like a middle-aged cat burglar with a penchant for teaspoons.

"I guess he blames me for not doing more," said Tess. "She's had enough of all the treatments and she wants to stop. I told him that and he got angry, said some stuff about me having a chip on my shoulder and being a crap doctor. He's making out like I don't care, or I've got my priorities wrong, and really, it's him, he's the one who's in the wrong." She looked down at the rolls. "Mum, this butter's way too hard to spread. Has it been in the fridge? You got any marge?"

Her mother silently handed her a tub.

"But then of course he's grieving, and I spoke to my consultant and he said he's bound to be confused and lashing out, but he... Oh, I don't know... It was just so horrible." She raised the back of her hand to her eye.

Tess's mum was not one to offer unsolicited opinions, particularly where the world of medicine was concerned. She weighed up her words carefully. "Right. So, this lad... he really loves his mum and he's proper cut up about her dying."

Tess nodded.

"He's furious with everybody. Including you, yeah?"

"Particularly me."

"But you're doing your job properly, like, and presumably this happens all the time in the hospice. So... why the bother? Why are you hauling yourself over the coals about it, pet?" She sat back down in front of her daughter and took her hands in her own. "He obviously had a right go at you, but people say all kinds of daft stuff when they're grieving, love. D'you remember that earful I gave the nurse looking after your gran? I were a proper cow to her." She smiled. "I did go back and apologise afterwards, mind. You never know, this lad may do the same?"

"I think that's pretty unlikely. He's not really the type to admit he was wrong."

"So... why d'you care? He don't sound like someone whose opinion would matter to you." There was a pause while she regarded her daughter, a curious expression on her face.

Tess shrugged. "I don't honestly know, Mum. I agree, it doesn't make any sense. I guess, to start off with, I actually *did* sort of value his opinion?"

"I see."

"God knows why. I mean he clearly has no regard for me or my professional judgement. But… we'd chatted a bit over the weeks and kind of got to know each other better, and I thought perhaps… As I said, I knew him before, sort of, but he doesn't remember me and that in itself kind of hurt my feelings a bit. I don't know. I'm being stupid letting it get to me like this."

Her mother gave her a shrewd look, sensing a lot of what had been left unsaid. She poured the soup into two bowls and brought them to the table with a tiny frown. "Right, love, let's get this down you and then how about you go have a nice bath and a kip upstairs?" She put her arm back round her daughter. "Sounds like you just needed a bit of time back at home with your mam, and Jake of course, whenever he gets here – we'll be like three amigos again! Oh, I've missed you both!" She gave Tess a squeeze. "After you've had a snooze maybe we'll head over to Meadowhall for some shopping, buy yourself something nice?"

"That sounds good." Tess started ripping up her bread roll with a decisive action and dropping sections of it into her bowl. "I'll be fine, honestly. This bloke… it's nothing I haven't had to deal with before. I've just got to be professional about it, you're absolutely right."

After lunch, Tess took her bags upstairs whilst her mum ran her a bath. Once wrapped in her towel she entered the bathroom, followed by Morris who seemed to have no natural feline aversion to water and often chose to sit in the sink drinking from the tap. Crossing the floor, she stubbed her toe on the set of scales poking out from beneath the cabinet and swore under her breath, thinking back to the times she had stood poised above them, half looking at the dial and hoping they were broken.

She avoided the temptation to get on the scales now, taking the stubbed toe as fair warning. The last thing she needed was tangible evidence of weight gain to whittle away at her fragile self-esteem. The television host had been more vocal these past couple of days, capitalising on her insecurities around work, and she had already decided to allow herself one more binge when she returned to Bristol. The thought calmed her.

She forced herself to drop her shoulders and relax into the bath, to enjoy the sensation of being back on home territory, because whilst there were reminders of youthful angst here, there was also comfort and familiarity. The tiny room was filled with the perfumed steam of her mum's favourite bubble bath, the water was hot and soothing, and a cup of tea had been left next to the splayed toothbrush and soap fragments along with a rolled-up copy of *Marie Claire* magazine wedged behind the tap. It was as close to a spa as her mother could make it, and Tess felt suitably pampered by her little gestures. She made a conscious effort to drown out the voice of the television host and clear her mind of negative teenage memories, along with all traces of Edward Russell and his cruel words, as she closed her eyes and sank beneath the soapy suds.

———————

Later they went shopping, Tess buying herself a new top and treating her mum to a pair of shoes. There was the usual wrangle over payment, her mother predictably embarrassed to have her daughter feel it necessary to fund her wardrobe, but Tess could see as soon as her mum tried on the shoes that she was hopelessly smitten with them. She had even responded with a flirtatious giggle to the sales assistant who insisted that of course she wasn't too old for them. "After all," he said, "it's not everyone who has a fine pair of legs like that, miss. It'd be a crime not to show them off to their full advantage and those shoes look right classy. See, even your sister thinks so."

Tess rolled her eyes at this blatant sales patter, but her mum, usually so vigilant against flattery, blushed and told the young man that, actually, this wasn't her sister but her daughter, a comment that was predictably greeted with disbelief. It was evident from this point on that she had to have the shoes and eventually Tess managed to persuade her to accept them as an extra birthday present. She felt a glow of happiness in her stomach to see her mum so overjoyed with her new heels. She knew how much she loved a little touch of glamour; it was just that she could so rarely afford it.

"You deserve a treat sometimes," Tess said, "and I'm not having any arguments. Just consider it payback for all the support you've given me over the years, all those hours of extra shifts at the garage and the off-licence to get me through medical school. Basically, these shoes are just interest on your initial investment."

"Don't be daft, love. Seeing you graduate was reward enough. All the strappy heels in the world couldn't compete with that." Her mum reached into the bag and opened the shoe-box a fraction, smiling at the contents. "Although, they are proper classy, aren't they? Like that fella said. Silly bugger going on about me pins."

"Well. They are pretty hot for a woman your age – or even half your age, it would appear."

"Thank you, pet." She squeezed Tess's hand. "And that new top looked lovely on you too," she indicated the carrier-bag on her daughter's shoulder. "Although I did wonder if it was a bit low around the neck-line? A bit revealing? You'll probably be after a little scarf or a cardie or something to go with it."

Tess sighed. She knew where this was heading. "Maybe you're right, Mam. Anyway, let's get back and see if Jake's home yet."

Chapter Fourteen

J ake arrived later that afternoon, bringing his new
girlfriend, Rini, with him. He introduced her shyly, with
a hand pressed in the small of her back, prompting her
forward as if he were displaying a new prized possession.
Tess was thrilled to see him and greeted Rini with equal
warmth. Jake's girlfriends had previously arrived in the house
with no ceremony at all, so this was clearly someone special.
She managed to get some time to chat with her brother on his
own whilst Rini helped their mum prepare dinner. They made
their way out to the lean-to, optimistically referred to as the
conservatory, pulling the door shut tight behind them, which
was as close to privacy as anyone ever got in this house.

"So," Tess squeezed up next to him on the wicker sofa.
"Rini seems nice? Is she the one you were talking about on
the phone?"

"Few weeks back? Yeah. I didn't really know whether
she were into me at that point."

"And she is?"

He smiled. "Obviously. How could she not be?"

"Fair point. You are a gorgeous human being."

"Exactly."

"You're pretty taken with her as well? It's nice."

"Glad you approve."

Tess turned awkwardly in the tight space and looked at her brother. "I do. Mam seems to like her too."

"She's always been okay about whoever I brought back. Never that fussed. As long as they weren't too rough like. Not like that Karen, d'you remember her?"

"God yeah. She was a belter, wasn't she? I was bloody terrified of her." She sat back in her seat to face the window and the broken fence beyond. "D'you remember that time she tried to teach me how to put make-up on and I looked like a prostitute?"

Jake smiled. "Well, that were what Mam said. You looked all right really. She just weren't used to seeing you with a bit of lippy on." He stretched his arms above his head and yawned expansively. "D'you know, that were the only time I ever saw Karen be a bit gentle with anyone. I think she felt sorry for you, shut up in here with your baggy jumpers and your books, like."

Tess looked back at her brother. "God, that's depressing."

"No, she just didn't get it. Didn't know why you weren't out there knocking back vodkas in Yates's with your mates."

"I didn't have any mates."

"That's not true. You did. They were just all a bit like you."

"What? Square and minging?" She smiled.

"No, don't be daft, I didn't mean that. I meant, more interested in school than in drinking and lads, like."

Tess gave a short laugh. "Well, being interested in lads wasn't really an option, was it? Far as Mam was concerned."

"No. You're right." He stretched his legs out with a sigh. "Sometimes I think she were bang out of order."

"What for?"

"Well, the way she had different rules for me and you. I know I were older, but she were totally mental about you, fretting about keeping you away from trouble, and you were, like, no trouble at all, ever. Always the golden girl you, with your exams and your doctoring and that." There was a trace of bitterness in his voice.

"I didn't ask to be wrapped in cotton wool, Jake. It wasn't easy actually."

"I know. Ignore me. I'm never sure who should be more pissed off about it, me or you." He peered over her head into the kitchen to ensure that their mum was immersed in conversation with Rini and not eavesdropping.

Tess wrinkled up her nose in consideration, remembering her struggle, and indeed failure, to navigate the sexual politics of her school days under their mother's watchful eye while Jake had been at liberty to exploit his charms, drawing girls to him like moths to a flame. She had always been jealous of his freedom, but could also see that their mother's unequal treatment of her children could have led Jake to believe that she just didn't care as much about him.

"I've not really thought about it," she said honestly, "or at least, not until today. Something Mam said when we were out shopping reminded me."

"What about?"

"You know, clothes and that. You're right – I suppose it was pretty claustrophobic when I was living here, but once I got out it was easier."

"I guess you must have really needed to get away."

"Maybe. Coming home for holidays and that, sometimes it'd trigger it all off again. I'd not ever mention boyfriends, or nights out and stuff. It was like my other life." She looked thoughtful. "But I never resented her for it, I don't think."

"No. You're too nice to think a bad thing about anyone, you."

"That's certainly not true. You should see what I used to write in my diary about you."

"I've seen it. Used to read it all the time. It were always right boring."

"Hey! That was private." She shoved him hard, laughing, and her mum looked up from inside the kitchen, distracted by the noise. Jake was still chuckling to himself.

"Mate, sorry but it was! Proper tedious. In fact, only good bits in it were when you were slagging me off."

"You are so bloody annoying!" She threw a cushion at him just as Rini knocked on the window and gestured them inside. "We will continue this. Later."

Much as Tess was inclined to shrug off Jake's comments, something about the idea of her mum keeping her away from boys stuck in her head. Jake was right; she'd never been allowed to wear make-up or pluck her monstrous eyebrows. Even shaving her legs had had to be done in secret, her mother's argument about the hazards of razors sounding somewhat hollow when she allowed Jake to wield his blade with impunity, despite his "beard" at the age of fourteen amounting to little more than a few strands of fluff. The more that Tess thought about it, the more the spectacular lack of gender equality in their household rankled, and by the time her mum's friends, Viv and Gina, had arrived there was a low level of tension in her jaw and the feeling of being on edge had returned. She tried to ignore the sensation and to enjoy being at home surrounded by her family but she knew she was being a little oversensitive and Viv's bragging about her new grandchild didn't help.

"So, you're still single then, are you, love?" she asked Tess. Viv's features were small and squashed in her pale, doughy face; she had always looked like an underbaked Cornish pasty, but the years of weight gain had made it worse. "Of course, that was what yer mother always wanted though, weren't it?" She nodded in her mum's direction, "Always thought you were summat special. Too good for settling down with someone from round here."

Tess was feeling an irritating twitch near her eye that suddenly reminded her of Edward Russell.

"I don't know, Viv, I think Mam just wanted me to have options, not be stuck with babies like she was." She smiled thinly but there was an edge to her voice and Gina looked over in concern. Gina had been her mum's friend since they were teenagers and had always treated Tess like the daughter she'd never had. If anyone was alert to uncharacteristic behaviour, it was her, and she followed the conversation with a wary curiosity as Viv blundered on regardless.

"Yeah, but she doesn't know how *special* it is to have grandchildren," she said. "I've been *so* blessed, and our Kayleigh's made up to have a little girl now after the three boys. They're all angels of course, but so nice to finally have a little princess too."

Gina raised her eyebrows so high up her forehead, Tess thought they might just fall off. It seemed that Viv's grandsons were anything but angelic, and the idea of having four children by the age of twenty-six was frankly terrifying, but Tess forced a conciliatory tone. "You're right Viv. You must be proper proud."

Her mum piped up from the other side of the table. "She's still got to qualify as a GP yet, Viv. She'll not be wanting babies to slow her down until then."

Jake caught Tess's eye. He gave her a knowing nod as if to say, *See? She still wants final say on what you do with your ovaries.* She pulled a face back at him and rose to clear the plates.

"I've just got to go and check something on my phone," she said quietly to her mum, who looked up from her conversation with Rini.

"Oh, that's fine love," she said loud enough for Viv to hear. "Are you expecting a call from work?" She shook her head, smiling, and looked across the table.

"It never stops, being a doctor and all. Everyone wants a piece of her. I'm so glad that she's doing something important with her life though, really fulfilled her potential. I wouldn't have it any other way."

Viv pursed her mouth up, looking more liked the crimped edge of a pasty than ever as she felt the sting of the retort.

Tess knew that the pair of them could carry on like this all night. She left them to it and climbed the creaking plywood stairs up to her old bedroom. Despite being surrounded by people, she suddenly felt very alone, and seeing Jake's easy intimacy with Rini made it worse. She missed having a partner, someone to keep an eye on her during evenings out, someone to plan trips away with, to join in the small triumphs and disasters of daily life. And particularly at the moment, the argument with Edward still fresh in her mind, she needed someone to share things with and distract her. Kath had been right; there wasn't anything much going on in her life outside of work, and therefore if her job was not going well, there was little else to fall back on.

Viv's comments had wound her up and the television host was in her ear again. She had the impression he'd been building up his routine.

"Humble beginnings!" he said. *"Nothing to be ashamed of, folks."*

Tess took a large gulp of her wine, the acidic taste of the

cheap chardonnay stinging the back of her throat. The host was getting into his stride.

"As always, it's lovely to have one of our favourite guests on the show... drum roll... Tess! Or Dr Carter as she's known now. How very la-di-da! All these airs and graces!"

He paused for dramatic effect. *"But we know where she came from, don't we, folks? That's right! The rough side of town!"* Another pause. *"And it's a pretty rough town to begin with!"*

The audience chuckled appreciatively as the host settled into fond reminiscing mode. *"And she'll always be fat, geeky little Tess to us, won't she? Raised on benefits..."* another pause *"and chips by the look of her!"*

The audience started to chant, *"Benefits and Chips! Benefits and Chips!"* but he hushed them. He was on a roll.

"Mum's been on the show before of course, one of our best features: 'Up the duff at nineteen by a Yardie who left me!'"

The audience clapped and cheered but the host lowered his voice again. *"And that's where the problem all started isn't it, Dr Carter?"* he hissed. *"Once your mum's been on the show it's only a matter of time before you end up here. Doesn't matter how much you polish your accent, how many diplomas and degrees you get. If the tree's rotten to begin with then so is all the fruit. Can't escape it. It's what we're all about. Family."* The volume increased again. *"What's this show all about? Come on, everybody!"*

"FAMILY!" the audience shouted in unison.

Tess knew she was not in the right frame of mind to be drinking alcohol this quickly. The rational part of her brain told her she needed to get back downstairs and force herself into a more sociable mood. The other part of her brain, where the television host lurked, was intent on self-punishment. She began to scroll through her phone, initially just checking her messages and alerts for anything new but then delving deeper until she was scouring her social media networks for news about Scott.

She had unfriended him from her own accounts as soon as his status had changed from "In a relationship with Tess Carter" to "In a relationship with Luke Foster" – the speed with which he shrugged her off had almost been more upsetting than the betrayal itself. But on nights such as these she couldn't maintain the discipline, and trawled the internet for painful reminders of her past life and what could have been. Because even though *she* was no longer friends with Scott Wickham, it didn't mean all of their shared acquaintances had lost contact with him; in fact, many of their mutual friends had surprised her by taking his side. She didn't mind the lack of support, didn't expect them to shun Scott out of respect for her feelings, but she hadn't expected them to revel in it all quite so much either. When she looked back, most of these individuals had been more Scott's friends than hers from the beginning. They had tolerated her in their social circle but didn't feel an enormous sense of obligation to rally round when it all fell apart. She continued to keep in touch in a limited capacity on social media, but she had deliberately withdrawn from the group's activities when it became apparent that she was no longer an established member, and probably never had been.

It was these people who had the most recent photos of Scott on their Instagram accounts, his handsome face caught seemingly unawares, raising a glass to his lips, dancing exuberantly in a club, or draping his muscular arm around an equally handsome Luke. It was irritating how good-looking they were as a couple; Tess was sure there were no photos like that of her and Scott in existence.

She had just stumbled on a recent shot of the two men hand-in-hand on the beach of a Balearic Island with a caption that read "Mr and Mr Wickham-Foster?" surrounded by heart emojis. Her face was screwed up in concentration as she tried to process whether this was indeed evidence that Scott was now engaged, or possibly even already married. Jane Austen's voice was suddenly audible.

"Well!" She was clearly angry. "All I can say is that he has used a fine young lady most abominably ill and I wish with all my soul that his new husband will plague his heart out!"

Tess smiled at her narrator's uncharacteristically feisty tone and was trying to establish exactly how she *would* feel about Scott getting married, when she heard a thud on the landing. The door creaked open to reveal Jake holding the half empty bottle of Viv's wine. He crossed to Tess in a single stride – the combination of minimal floorspace and his long legs meant he could traverse the house in a couple of steps. Seeing the picture on her phone his eyebrows creased in drunken concern.

"What you playing at, Tess?" He seemed unable to articulate any further and squeezed his large frame onto the floor beside her, lifting the phone out of her hands and skimming it across the carpet out of reach.

"Why are you wasting your time looking at pictures of

that loser?" he asked, shaking his head in disgust. "He were a total prick. You are so much better off without him."

Tess raised her glass of wine into the air between them. "I know," she said. She finished the drink off with a long swig and poured another. "But, loser or not, it seems he may have discovered matrimonial bliss far earlier than I'm going to."

Jake scrunched up his nose and made a derisory noise. "Well, sod him. No really, Tess. He were a prick even before you caught him in bed with someone else. He were never good enough for you. He didn't treat you well even before he cheated." He turned to face her. "Do you remember that time he forgot your birthday and then made out like you were just being a massive whinger for mentioning it? Or when he took the piss out of Mam for listening to reggae, like she weren't allowed to because she's white?"

He took a swig straight from the bottle. "*And* that time he couldn't be arsed to come to Granny's funeral because he had some grime thing he needed to DJ at instead?"

"Oh yeah!" The memory registered with Tess. "Like he was Stormzy and the music world might collapse if he didn't lay down his tracks!"

"Jesus. Even I'd forgotten what a twat he was. I'll tell you what, good luck to his new husband if that's what he is – there's not many lads who'd put up with that sort of bollocks."

"No. You're probably right."

"Tessie, you don't need to be spending your evenings rose-tinting that crappy relationship. You need a new bloke, someone who'll be good to you."

Tess leant into him, pondering for a moment. She had forgotten some of those incidents, and actually Jake was right; there had been times in the past when Scott had taken her for granted, made comments that were less than complimentary about her family, her clothes, her appearance, even the money she was bringing into the house to subsidise some of his more expensive habits. He had often implied that she was deliberately making him feel guilty for not earning as much as her. The idea of finding someone who might support and value her as an equal was appealing. She rested her head against her brother's side; the warm bulk of his arm felt comforting.

"Yep, well, you might be right, Jakey. Maybe I do."

He closed his eyes, "It's Mam's fault you know, a bit of it anyway." His voice was quiet, either surprised by this moment of clarity or simply drunk and tired. "It's like we said earlier: she never made you feel good about yourself unless it were to do with exams. Maybe... I don't know. I should've said something to her. It weren't right..."

Tess poked him with her finger. "Christ, Jake. This thing with Rini's got you properly in touch with your softer side. Bugger off and rescue your girlfriend. Go on. Viv'll be busy persuading her to fall pregnant and furnish Mam with the blessings of grandchildren as soon as possible otherwise – what with babies being *so special* and all."

Jake's eyes opened wide and he hauled himself up from his seated position with a lurch. "Bloody hell – you're right!" he said, lumbering out of the door. He threw a quick look over his shoulder to his sister.

"I'll be down in a moment," she called after him and

then heard a crash on the landing followed by a, "Fuck's sake! Who left that there?" She followed the noise and found Jake holding up a shopping bag.

"Near broke me neck!" He waved the bag at her.

"Mam's new shoes," she said, holding out her hand to take them. "Give 'em here. I'll put them in her wardrobe."

Jake made his way back downstairs, mumbling something about women and their bloody shopping, and Tess went through to her mum's room. The wardrobe door was ajar and there were a variety of bags and boxes crammed into the lower shelf. It looked as though Tess could squeeze the new shoes in if she stacked them in a less haphazard fashion, so she removed a couple of older, more battered-looking containers from the deep recess at the back to make some space. One of them was particularly ancient – she wasn't sure that Dolcis Shoes even existed as a high-street brand any longer. Curious as to the contents, she lifted the lid, but the vintage footwear she'd hoped for turned out to be an assortment of letters and cards. She pulled the box onto the carpet, ignoring the whisper of "Pandora…" from the television host, and began to separate the bundles of paper from the other items, lifting them out to see the writing more clearly. Except, she couldn't focus. The words swam in front of her eyes. She steadied herself, clutching at the wardrobe door as she sat back on her heels. Many of the envelopes were addressed to Tess Carter, and they all had the same distinguishing feature: an Italian postmark.

Chapter Fifteen

I n a daze, Tess tipped the contents of the box out onto the floor. There were some objects that made no sense at all: tickets for a gig at The Leadmill, a champagne cork, a wire bracelet, a postcard from Jamaica with a scribbled "Sorry" on the back. But most of the items were cards and letters. So many letters. She began to pick through them at random, not really understanding what she was seeing or doing. The majority were from her father, Marco, and a few dated back to the late 90s. There were some things she had seen before: a card for her seventh birthday that she remembered had been accompanied by a leather purse, and a box containing a locket with a faded photo of a handsome man and a five-year-old Tess, both pulling silly faces to the camera. She'd seen that locket, but thought she had lost it years ago. She realised her hands were shaking.

There was a letter from the year that she'd qualified as a doctor. Lines jumped out at her:

So proud to hear your news… always knew you'd do well… such a kind little girl.

He recalled how quickly she had learned to read, how much she loved looking at books and being told stories. He said that he'd always known she'd be a "clever little thing". There was mention of a time where she had looked after her big brother when he'd fallen out of a tree, held Jake's hand, reassured him. Tess couldn't recall much about the incident but welled up at the fact that her father had stored this information away, treasured those memories and stacked them up as evidence as to why his daughter had become a doctor. It was as if, through his letters, he was trying to prove that he knew her, that he remembered moments which had shaped her future course. After a while the lines began to blur into one another, but all the letters, from the earliest to the most recent, ended with similar words:

Miss you so much.

Think of you often.

If you ever want to get in touch…

She leant her head back against the wardrobe door, a letter dated from last year in her hand. It was the year she had discovered Scott in bed with Luke. She wondered what her father would have made of that. She wondered what he would have made of a lot of things. Growing up, she had never been particularly troubled by his absence. Jake's father hadn't been in their lives either, and many of her friends had very limited contact with their own dads. She'd always assumed this was normal; that her father had simply grown bored of his family and gone to make a new one. While this assumption hurt, and sometimes made her question her own worth, it remained an abstract concept. She knew her mother loved her; she knew Jake loved her. That was enough. At least, it had seemed enough. But now to discover that Marco *had* been interested, that he *had* cared what was happening to her and clearly wanted to maintain a relationship with her... This was new, unexpected knowledge and raised more questions than it answered.

As if on cue, the door creaked open and her mum stuck her head around the corner. She, too, was looking a little worse for wear and it took her a while to register what was going on.

"What you doing up here, pet?" she asked, her accent, like Jake's, becoming more pronounced with the alcohol. "You still frettin' about that fella from work? What's all that stuff on your lap...?" Her eyes narrowed as she focussed on the debris scattered around Tess's hunched figure, the mascara-stained tear tracks on her daughter's cheeks. And suddenly the realisation hit her, and she froze. It seemed to Tess that her mum couldn't work out whether to be furious or contrite; both emotions were evident on her face, working against each other. She raised a hand to her mouth.

"Oh, God. Tess..."

Tess clutched the letter in her hand. There was so much

to say but the words wouldn't seem to come. "Mam?" The noise was strangled in her throat. "The box… I was just… Your new shoes…" She gestured to the letters and cards – artefacts of the crime. "Why?"

Her mum crossed quickly to where Tess was seated and started to gather up the envelopes, but Tess pushed her away, "No!" Tess was feeling a righteous indignation burning up through her body. She jumped to her feet, clutching the letters to her chest. "These are mine. They're addressed to me!"

Her mother's hand went limp; the paper she had gathered dropped from her fingers to the floor. She searched her daughter's face for a way in, a way to make herself understood. "Tessie?" Her voice was tentative, unsure. "I can explain. I didn't mean for it to be like this. I was going to show you…"

"When, Mam?" Tess thrust a handful of paper towards her mother's face. "Some of these letters are almost twenty years old, for Christ's sake! When did you think you might get around to it?"

Her mother reached out towards her but Tess batted her away.

"I *did* show you. I did, to start off with. Look…" she plucked the birthday card from the edge of the bed where it had fallen. "See? I showed you this one? This was out on the mantelpiece for months after your birthday. And… the locket… Where's the locket…?" Tess opened her curled fist to reveal the tarnished silver nestled in her palm. Her mother pounced on it, "There! See? That was for your eighth birthday." Her eyes were imploring, "And you loved it, remember?"

Tess did remember. She had adored that locket, worn it every day she was allowed, tried to take it to school, to swimming lessons... "But you hid it?" She was incredulous. "I loved it and you took it away? I thought I'd lost it. I cried for days..."

"And then you forgot about it." Her mother was nodding along with her words, trying to push the understanding into her daughter by sheer force of will. "Do you see? You were obsessed with it, obsessed with everything he sent, every mention of him. And it hurt you so much that he wasn't here. You don't remember it now, but you spent hours just gazing at it and crying, it was like a constant reminder, the two of you frozen in time inside that locket. That photo, you were five; it was one of the last times you saw him..." She broke off and her face crumpled in on itself. "I couldn't bear it. I couldn't bear to see you hurt, like I'd been."

"But it wasn't about you." Tess's voice was faltering. "He wanted to see *me*. He wanted to... He could have been there for me. He could have helped." She brought her hand to her forehead. The effort of rational thought was suddenly overwhelming. A few moments passed before she spoke again. "But instead, you hid all of this," she gestured to the debris scattered around them. "You lied and lied. You built up your wall, told me that Dad didn't want to know, that men were best avoided. 'Stay away from everyone other than Jake,' you said. 'He's the only good one of the lot.' You were consumed by it, this fixation of yours, hiding me away."

"I just didn't want you getting hurt." The phrase repeated again, like a mantra, and Tess felt the fury rise up once more. Her voice exploded out of her, ringing against the windows and the tinny surface of the dressing-table mirror.

"The trouble is, Mam, I *did* get hurt. And the reason I got hurt was because I didn't understand men. I didn't understand relationships *at all*. I mean, I lived with Scott for a year without realising he was gay! Do you know how embarrassing that is?"

"Tessie, love—"

"No, you don't know. You have no idea what that felt like. You were so worried about me making the same mistakes as you, falling for the bad boys… whereas I end up with someone who *doesn't even fancy girls*." She was shouting now, aware that her voice would be echoing through the walls and floorboards and not caring. "If I'd had just the tiniest bit more knowledge of men then I might have known, might have sensed something wasn't right. As it was, all the experience I had came from a whole load of drunken one-night stands when I started med school – screwing around to see what all the fuss was about." She felt a vicious stab of satisfaction, seeing the shock register on her mother's face. "That's right. I shagged everyone I could get my hands on. Surprise you, does it? Your good girl behaving like that?"

"Tess… I…"

"And predictably, none of those one-night stands was

134

especially fulfilling or made me feel good about myself. Just confirmed what you'd always told me. And then I met Pete and I thought, perfect; he's solid, stable, dull. I'll stick with him. I won't risk it. I won't do what Mum did. And I was bored rigid. I didn't realise that I didn't have to settle for that either. I didn't *know* anything." Her voice quietened. "Don't you see? I was so bloody naïve, and it was your fault. You took your bad experiences with relationships out on me and you kept me away from my dad, the one man who might have been able to help me understand how life works; what I should look out for, what to avoid."

"Oh, Tess." Her mother's face was distraught. "I just wanted to protect you. I did what I thought was best, for you and for Jake. Just like I always do. You don't know how difficult it was. You don't know the half of it…" She was concentrating on her words, knowing she was in the wrong but not being used to having to navigate conflict with her daughter.

"If I did try and steer you away from making a mistake, what of it? Look where you are now. A doctor. I wrote to your dad about that, I did. I sent him a photo of your graduation and all. You were happy. You didn't need him. All your training, all your hard work paid off; you didn't have to watch it trickle away. You didn't have your dreams shattered."

"They were your dreams really, Mam." Tess's voice had quietened. She sounded more sad than angry now. "You were the one with something to prove. That pressure, it was hard to live with sometimes. And keeping me away from lads like you did… well, I felt ugly. *You* made me feel ugly."

"Oh Tess. I never thought—"

"Jake knew. And Gran. She always told me I was beautiful, even when it was patently untrue, even when I was a total minger. She was always kind. Always."

She gulped back a sob and her mother took a step towards her, distress written across her face. "Oh, my love. I miss Gran too. You know I do. And you were never a minger. What a daft thing to say." She cupped her daughter's chin. "You were always beautiful. Always. From the moment you were born – it were terrifying." She sniffed. "Can you imagine? Can you? I can't explain it, that fear. Not wanting you to end up like me."

She brought her other hand up to stroke her daughter's hair; the dark strands damp with perspiration had stuck in tiny curls and tendrils to her forehead. She recognised the blotchy flush on Tess's neck as matching her own, the histamine response to stress that she had passed on to her daughter. Every other external feature was Marco's: the dark eyes, the high-arched cheekbones, the full voluptuous lips, a face that drew glances from passers-by.

"Some men, love…" She spoke earnestly, willing her daughter to understand. "Some fellas – they're like animals. They can't help themselves. If you'd had your head turned by one of them when there were so many better things ahead of you… I'd never have forgiven myself. But I didn't mean to make you feel ugly, my love. Never. What mother would do that?" She pulled her daughter close. "You," she said, "you and Jakey, you're my pride and joy." She held Tess out at arm's length, wiped her tears from her face and pulled her back into an embrace. "And I've been selfish.

And it was wrong. But you were mine, both of you…" She squeezed Tess possessively. "*Mine*. I thought we didn't need anyone else. I'm so sorry."

The television host allowed mother to console daughter a little longer. *"Family,"* he said happily. *"That's what keeps this show on the road."*

Chapter Sixteen

A little later Tess heard her mum ushering her friends out of the house, Viv's flattened vowels drifting up to the window as she whispered loudly to Gina, "Well! I never knew the Italian had kept in touch. She kept right quiet about it. And I'd never've guessed that our Tess would've ended up with a poof. Poor lass. There's a lot more of 'em down South of course..." Her voice disappeared into the waiting taxi and Tess smiled despite herself, the outcome of her failed relationship clearly confirming Viv's suspicions about southerners. She curled up on her bed, folding her body around Morris, who had sought her out and was now purring loudly, nudging her chin, making her feel needed. She knew that she should go downstairs but wanted instead to be alone with her thoughts.

She was still furious with her mother for keeping the truth from her, especially as the lies about her father had simply led to lying about men in general, making them something to be feared, something to keep her daughter safe from. In perpetuating this myth, she had made Tess's situation potentially much more confusing. The attempts to kerb her social life had only resulted in a reckless attitude to men and sex as soon as Tess had escaped, and it was more luck than judgement that had stopped her falling into exactly the situation that her mother had tried so hard to prevent.

In spite of her distress, Tess smiled as she remembered that first term; like a butterfly emerging from a chrysalis composed of baggy jumpers and bad hair, by Christmas she had been slimmer and wearing clothes that suited her new shape. Her skin had improved, the eyebrows were tamed, and she had exuded a self-assurance that increased almost daily. Her first visit home had proved a shock to her mother, and she had reverted to the loose-fitting clothing of her childhood to avoid confrontation – but as soon as she returned to Bristol in the new year, the heady combination of teenage lack of responsibility and a wide playing field had proved irresistible. She had enjoyed the attention, felt desirable for the first time in her life, and her confidence had grown and grown.

Tess rolled onto her side and caught sight of her sad face in the mirrored tiles tacked to the wall. What had happened to that liberated, free spirit of a girl? Since uncovering Scott's infidelity, the self-loathing had crept back. She realised she was just as paralysed with fear and confusion about men now as she had been as an innocent fresher waving goodbye to her mother at the halls of residence. She sat up in bed suddenly determined. If she could rescue herself at eighteen then she could certainly do it again now;

she could go back to being the Tess of her medical school days. *That* was the girl she needed to find, to blow away the cobwebs and shake some sense back into her. She stuck up two metaphorical fingers to the daytime television host who was now muttering about the new spin-off series featuring Tess's dad – he could sod off. She was going to be wild and carefree. She was going to start dating again.

Seized by the conviction that she somehow needed to act now, capitalise on this burst of self-belief, she reached out of bed to where Jake had discarded her phone hours earlier. She closed the photo of Scott and unfollowed the account that had featured it. A plan was forming in her mind; she recalled from some distant part of her memory a conversation with Ravi, Kath's boyfriend, about a schoolfriend of his who was single and potentially interested in a blind date. She had initially dismissed the idea out of hand but now, at one o'clock in the morning with a bellyful of cheap wine and revelatory shock, the notion did not seem quite so ridiculous. In fact, what better time to find a new man? It wasn't as if her life could become much more melodramatic.

She thought perhaps Ravi had sent her this guy's number but couldn't remember his name. She scrolled through… There it was, Simon Collins, contact details texted over from Ravi's phone. Tess stared at the screen for a few seconds, and before she could interrogate her motives too thoroughly, she tapped out a message asking him if he'd like to meet up some time. There, that had done it. Too late now. Tess sank back into her bed, emotional exhaustion overtaking all sensible thoughts of cleaning her teeth or taking her make-up off. She shrugged out of her jeans and lay for a moment with Morris noisily kneading her hair. As she dozed, the soothing voice of Jane Austen echoed in her head:

"It had been a night of nonsense and folly, of agitation and excess of feeling, and yet our heroine felt the approach of resolution. For, once the mind of a young woman is fixed upon a decisive course of action, there is little that can be done to dissuade her. Particularly in matters of the heart."

Tess smiled in her sleep.

———————

Simon responded to Tess's text within a couple of hours, and on the Sunday morning she awoke bleary-eyed and groggy to a message in her inbox asking if she'd like to go out the following Saturday. She scrunched her eyes against the daylight and struggled up onto her elbows, propping her head up with another pillow as she tried to focus on the screen. Wincing at her headache she replied in what she hoped was a suitably cheerful, but not too desperate, tone and then stared at the phone in her hand for a few moments, contemplating the implications.

She didn't mention the blind date to her mother, feeling that conversations about potential boyfriends were best avoided, but they had a long hug in the kitchen before her mum wrinkled up her nose and said, "Did you sleep in that top, you grubby mare? Go get yourself in the shower. I'll get breakfast on," and no reference was made to the previous night's argument or the letters that were now stashed in

Tess's rucksack. Jake looked contrite when he returned later that morning without Rini and Tess apologised for embarrassing him in front of his new girlfriend.

"It's hardly the picture of domestic harmony, is it?" she said when they were back in the privacy of the conservatory. "And I know how thin these walls are. You'll have heard all of it."

"Oh, look Tess, some of it were my fault," he said, staring down at his open palms. "I started you off fretting about Mam, and then for you to find them letters… To be honest she needed a few home truths."

"Yeah, but maybe screaming them around the neighbourhood was not the best way to do it."

He leant back and laughed. "No, it were grand. Should've seen Viv's face when she heard you talking about all them lads you'd shagged at university."

"Oh my God! I can imagine." Tess put a hand to her mouth in horror.

"But don't worry about Rini. Her family's way more messed up than ours."

"Oh, well that's reassuring, I suppose." She patted him on the arm. "Thank you."

"Nowt to thank me for. Don't be daft, woman."

And that was the end of the conversation.

When she got back to Bristol, she found that Simon had texted her again and suggested The Garage as a place to meet up on Saturday. It was a bit townie for Tess's taste, but maybe this was all part of her reinvention – before she could change her mind, she replied that she'd see him there. She sat back on the sofa, Morris pawing at her lap.

Well, she'd done it now. She was going on a date. An actual blind date. She didn't know whether to be excited or terrified, but one thing was certain: she'd taken charge of herself again. She hadn't bought anything other than petrol at the motorway service station, ignoring the television host as he pointed out the array of confectionary items.

"It has been a very eventful few hours, Tess, are you quite sure you don't need a little pick-me-up? After all, your mum's been lying to you for years and years. That's gotta hurt, hasn't it? And your dad. What must he have thought? Probably that you just didn't care... It's all such a mess."

Past the super-size bars of chocolate she'd walked, swinging her keys. Past the grab-bags of crisps and the multipacks of biscuits, past the freezer cabinet with its tubs of ice cream. The host's voice became increasingly frantic.

"You know I'm right, Tess. Because I understand you better than anyone else. I know about that emptiness inside of you and the best way to fill it... It's all here, look! Here's your sugar rush, your own little shot of comfort wrapped up in shiny foil. There's even those little puddings you like. I mean, they're so small they barely count!"

Still she'd walked on, straight up to the till, past the shelves of groceries and barely given them a second glance.

"Don't make the mistake of thinking you don't need it, Tess, because you do!" he'd screeched as she paid and walked back to her car. But this time, Miss Austen's voice had been louder and it had drowned him out.

"The evidence of a parent's love is a balm to the soul, sir, no matter how shocking the manner of discovery. I think you might

find that Tess is, in fact, already in possession of everything she requires."

It was true. The feeling from last night remained strong within her; she was in control. Maybe she was closer to rediscovering her confident former self than she had thought. She pulled the sheaf of her dad's letters out of her rucksack and pressed them to her face for a moment, breathing in the scent of warm dust before carrying them upstairs and tucking them away safely in a drawer, for now.

Later that afternoon, Kath returned from her shift. Tess was making herself a cup of tea when her housemate came in and dropped her bag and keys with a noisy clatter on the work surface. She opened one of the cupboards and started searching for food while enquiring as to Tess's weekend. Tess filled her in about the row with her mum and the discovery of Marco's letters.

"Shit." Kath gave a low whistle. "What are you going to do?"

Tess admitted that she didn't know. The information was just sinking in and she didn't want to make any rash decision about attempting to forge a relationship with a father she hadn't seen in twenty years. "It was a massive shock," she said. "I mean, my mum, you can imagine. I'm still completely livid with her."

"But you can sort of see why she did it?"

"Kind of. No. Not really, to be honest. I get that it was out of some misguided attempt to protect me. She still maintains that he was an absolute bastard and I'm sure he wasn't perfect, but she's basically guided my opinion of him by lying, or at least, hiding the truth. Now, it's like I found these letters, I realise he did want to know me and I have to readjust my idea of him. It all feels like a complete…"

"Head-fuck?"

"Yeah."

"Totally. I mean, if you've been told often enough, like, that your father didn't love you, I guess it's hard to suddenly believe that he did?"

Tess's eyes filled with tears and Kath rushed to put her arm around her. "Shit, I'm sorry. I wasn't trying to be, you know…"

Tess sniffed. "No, you're right. It's exactly like that." She gave a watery smile. "And in a way, that's what makes it more bearable. It's finding out a nice thing rather than a horrible thing, and in recent years I feel like I'm only ever stumbling across really crappy surprises."

"Sure, you're not wrong. Walking in on yer man Scott in bed with another fella is, like, right up there with the crappiest."

"Yeah." Tess laughed. "Given my luck recently, I'm just amazed that I didn't discover that my real father's actually an axe-murderer or that I'm about to be deported or—"

"An envelope full of anthrax…"

Tess laughed. "Exactly."

Kath leant back against the cupboard. "So, what did Gorgeous Jake say?"

"Well. He's was just Jake, you know. Gorgeous or not,

he's so matter-of-fact about everything, it's hard to tell if he's bothered either way. I'll call him later, once I've got my head straight. I know he'll be cross with Mam and he's probably worried about me – not that he'd show it particularly. I don't know, though, whether he's upset that it's my dad who's been in touch and not his."

"You don't think she's got another bloody shoebox squirrelled away somewhere full of letters from Jamaica?!" Kath hooted with laughter and then put her hand over her mouth. "Sorry, that was me being inappropriate again."

"You're fine. It helps, you being so... you know."

Kath nodded. "Well, grand. Any time you want to chat about it, you let me know. If you want someone with you when you go through the letters, like, or...? No. Sure, you're right, that would be weird. Well, I'm here if you need." She moved to the cupboard. "Now, I am half-starved. What paltry offerings have we here?"

Tess meant what she'd said about not wanting to make any rash decisions; she just needed to let the information sit with her for a while. In the meantime, the blind date was a more pressing concern and something she definitely wanted Kath's opinion on. "I texted that guy Simon last night," she said, feeling quite proud of her extreme bravery.

Kath was bent over searching in the furthest depths of what was essentially an empty cupboard, so Tess's voice was muffled. "What?" she asked, backing out carefully.

"Simon Collins? That guy Ravi was talking about? I texted him."

Kath still looked none the wiser.

"The blind date? Possibly the only man in England who might want to go out with me?"

A flicker of recognition crossed Kath's face. "Ah…" she said, starting to nod, but then shook her head. "No. He wasn't called Simon. You mean Leon."

"Who?"

"Leon. Leon Marshall. He's the friend of Ravi's who was interested in a blind date. Mind you, you'd have to be blind. He's no ride, that fella. Face like a bag of spanners. That's why he's had no luck on Tinder." She bent back down and continued to forage in the cupboard, smiling in triumph as she pulled out a dusty pack of noodles.

"But… No. It was Simon." Tess reached for her phone and started scrolling through to Ravi's message. "Simon Collins. Not Leon Whatever…" She paused. "See?"

Kath peered at the screen. "Ah well, maybe all of Rav's mates are keen on hooking up with you, God knows. Certainly, the one he'd mentioned to me was Leon… What? What is it?"

Tess's nose was screwed up in confusion as she looked at the message immediately above Simon's contact details. The text from Ravi said: *"E. Agent info"*, with a smiley emoji.

"E. Agent? What does that mean?" Tess was staring at the screen, willing it to make sense.

Kath took the phone out of her hand. "Estate Agent, I guess. Oh! It'll be that time we thought we might look for a flat nearer the hospital, d'you remember? Rav had the number of that guy who'd found Dion's place, the one with the balcony… Wait, so this is the… Holy Christ! You total arse!"

Tess's face was frozen in horror as the realisation dawned. "Oh. My. God. I've texted the wrong guy."

Kath was lost for words. They both looked at each other for a few seconds and then exploded into laughter.

"So. Just to re-cap," said Kath wiping her eyes, "you're going on a blind date with a complete and utter random."

Tess nodded, "It would appear so. Christ, what must he have thought when he got my message? And what kind of person agrees to a date with a total stranger who texts him at"—she looked back at her phone—"at one-thirty in the morning, especially when it's not even come through a dating app?"

"Well, I guess you're going to find out." Kath was shaking her head in a combination of astonishment and admiration and they both burst out laughing again.

Kath suggested a thorough trawl through the internet. They didn't have to look for long. Information about Simon Collins's life and opinions was easy to find, due to his regularly updated posts on every social media platform available, including some Tess had never even heard of.

"Sure, he likes to let everyone know what he's up to." Kath laughed as they looked at a picture of him lifting weights that morning.

On Simon's LinkedIn page he described himself as a "Residential and Commercial Property Retail Executive" and away from the polyester-suited splendour of his business profile, his extensive photo collection indicated that he was quite good-looking. There were many images of him in a pair of shorts, top off, revealing a toned torso and what might have been a fake tan. Tess groaned. "He's clearly a complete narcissist. Oh God, what *am* I doing?"

Kath was studying a shot of Simon in his jeans and muscle vest. "He's got a pretty decent reason for being a narcissist though. I mean, he's in good shape, isn't he. I wouldn't say no – if I wasn't going out with Ravi, obviously."

Tess picked up her mug and moved to the dishwasher. "I must be out of my mind," she said. "D'you think I should just cancel? Explain the mistake."

Kath folded her arms. "Babe," she said. "Don't cancel. It'll be an adventure. It doesn't matter if he's not Mr Perfect, and it's not like you've suggested meeting in an abandoned shack on the Downs. You'll be in the centre of town, and if he's a dick, or you feel unsafe or whatever, you just get an Uber straight home."

Tess didn't look convinced but Kath continued, "It'll be good to go out, get a new outfit, get back some of that sass? You've had a crappy time at work. You need some fun, flirt a bit, you know. It's never going to be easy, after Scott, but you've got to get back on that horse sometime." She looked back at the phone. "And that sure is some horse."

"Show pony, more like. But yes, you're right. I've got nothing to lose."

"And who knows – you might even make it to the Instagram hall of fame, if he decides there's space on there for anything other than his pecs."

Chapter Seventeen

A week later and Tess was standing on the pavement outside The Garage Bar feeling nervous. The television host had been in her ear for the whole taxi journey contemplating his list of possible show titles for her night out.

"I've had some ideas, Tess, see what you think... How about: 'Fat Girls Dating Fit Boys – When It All Goes Wrong!' No? What about: 'I'm Dating an Ugly Doctor, Get Me Out of Here!' Not keen? It's a bit derivative, you're right. We could try: 'My Mum Was a Lying Tart, Am I One Too?' It's up to you," he said as she shut the taxi door and stepped out onto the pavement. "After all, you're integral to the creative process here. Without you, there'd be no show!"

She had decided to wear the top she'd bought at Meadowhall the previous weekend, and suddenly she was reminded of her mum's words about the low neckline. Resisting the urge to tug at it and make herself more decent, she took a deep breath and pushed against the glass doors of the bar, where she was met by a wall of noise. The posters proclaimed that happy hour was in full swing and the place was packed. Gangs of scantily clad girls tottered around high bar stools with improbably named cocktails. In the corner, a large screen was showing the end stages of a Champions League match and a group of men were gathered beneath it, feet planted widely apart, taking occasional swigs of their designer cider as they gazed, mesmerised by their team's progress. It was clear that this was not a place for couples; gender lines were well defined and the groups of males and females would not mix or mingle until significant quantities of alcohol had been consumed. It was one of those venues where the primary objective appeared to be getting as loaded as possible, stumbling around the sticky dance floor and eventually toppling into the arms of a stranger, either going on to indulge in a night of erotic adventure, or fall over on the pavement and vomit on your shoes. Which way it would go for each individual was anyone's guess at this early stage of the evening, but Tess thought she could already identify a few girls for whom the latter option seemed most likely.

Amid these circling packs there were one or two lone wolves, and up at the bar Tess could see a razor-sharp hairline cut into a broad neck and shoulders that seemed to fit with the extensive profile of images she now associated with Simon Collins. Her suspicions were confirmed when she saw him turn his head towards the mirrored glass behind the bar and surreptitiously groom his eyebrows with a forefinger. *That's my man,* she thought to herself as she made her way through the throng and tapped him on the shoulder. He was a bit shorter than he looked in his photos and, in her heels, Tess matched his height.

"Simon?" she said as he turned to her with a wide, friendly grin.

"Tess?" There was a momentary look of doubt on his face, or did she imagine it? Then a flicker of his eyes down to her cleavage and back, and the smile was just as wide again. He leant in to give her an air kiss on both cheeks and then held her out at arm's length to admire her.

"Well, you're a proper stunner, aren't you? What'll you be having, gorgeous?"

His Bristolian accent was partially hidden beneath a more gentrified tone but she could still hear it, and his warm manner made her smile, disproportionately gratified to be called a stunner by someone who held physical appearance in high regard.

"Thank you. I'll have a gin and tonic, please."

He relayed the order to the pouty barmaid with whom he appeared to be on first-name terms, and then handed Tess her drink.

They made their way across the crowded bar, found a table, and settled into some small talk, shouting to make themselves heard above the competing noise from the hen party on the table next to them and the football fans arguing with the TV referee above their heads. Tess explained about her mistake regarding the text message and how she'd come to have his number. Simon admitted that he had been a little bemused by her offer of a date. "But, you know, I'm single. I just thought, why not?" He gestured to Tess with a smile. "And now I'm glad I did." He drained his bottle of cider and thumped it down on the table.

"Tell you what, it's a bit loud in here, isn't it?" he said as an inflatable penis whizzed past his ear, thrown by the neighbouring hen party and accompanied by howls of delight. Simon turned to them. "All right girls! Ain't you seen enough of the real thing lately?" He picked up the lurid pink balloon and carried it over to them. "Bit small, I'd say."

He handed the inflatable penis to the L-plated bride-to-be with a suggestive wink and she asked him to take a few photos of the party, finishing with a group selfie featuring Simon himself, grinning up at the screen amidst an ocean of cleavage, pink glitter, and feather boas. Tess observed all this from her table where she sat quietly sipping her drink and trying not to feel too awkward. She had a smile fixed to her face that she hoped suggested she was entirely used to her date being so obliging and attentive to other women, but she did have to concede that Simon knew how to work a crowd. He was very personable and his cheeky charms were having the desired effect on this particular bevy of beauties. The television host had to shout quite loudly to make himself heard over the din.

"I've thought of another one, Tess. How about, 'Being on a Date with Me Is as Boring as Watching Paint Dry – How Will I Ever Get a Man?'"

Tess muttered an expletive into her drink.

Once the girls were happy with their pictures and Simon had taken a few with his own phone and uploaded them, he returned to Tess with an apologetic shrug as if to say, *What can you do? The girls love me.* Tess acknowledged the look with a smile and shrug of her own. She could hardly begrudge him the female attention he so enjoyed; she didn't know him well enough to monopolise his time and he was only being friendly.

"Quite the paparazzo," she said.

"Ah well, happy to help." He looked down at Tess's drink, which was still half-full.

"Shall we go and eat then?"

Not wishing to be a spoilsport, or to hang around to witness the further deterioration of the hen party, Tess picked up the rest of her gin and knocked it back in a few gulps. Simon waved to the girls on the neighbouring table.

"You enjoy yourselves, ladies. Don't do anything I wouldn't do!" he shouted over his shoulder as they squeezed back through the crowd and out into the cool evening air.

They ended up in a small Italian chain restaurant at the top of Park Street. Tess's jeans were already feeling a little snug so she settled on a small salad which consisted of warm iceberg lettuce, four slices of over-ripe tomato, and a scattering of cheesy rocks that she presumed to be croutons. Simon, who tucked into his own Vesuvius Pizza with gusto, had nodded with understanding when she placed her order.

"Probably a wise decision. Not that you need to watch your weight at all," he said quickly. "That's not what I meant – you're just about perfect as you are. Just thinking maybe I should have followed your lead. I'll have to spend an hour at the gym tomorrow to shift this bad boy. Knock out a few reps. It's not easy staying in shape."

She had resisted the urge to contradict him, or to overshare the exact nature of her issues with food. Instead, she eyed his pizza jealously and, after almost cracking a molar on a crouton, she had to admit that she had made a poor choice. A bit of bloating would be preferable to gnawing hunger, particularly given the fact that the wine she was drinking was so vinegary she had almost mistaken it for salad dressing. Undeterred, she drank it steadily through the meal, the limp lettuce doing little to line her stomach as Simon regaled her with stories of life as an estate agent.

"I've been promoted to the more high-end properties now," he said, "which is nice. It's where the money is. I mean, obviously."

Tess picked up another crouton and eyed it warily as Simon continued.

"Some of these people though. They got more cash than sense. You wow them with a bit of a flash interior and they don't even ask about the square footage or the plumbing. They'd barely notice if the place was falling down as long as it's got a nice touch of Farrow and Ball on the walls. It's crazy; they're desperate for that perfect look. I'm just selling them the lifestyle, telling them what they want to hear."

"Do you not have to tell them about any major problems, structural issues, things like that?"

"Not really. I mean, I try not to lie about anything. I

want them to like the place at the end of the day – it's a good feeling if you know you've helped someone find their dream home. But I've also got an obligation to the vendor; I want to get them the best price too, so it's about balancing those two things. It's basic sales technique, just some of us are better at it than others."

"I imagine you're pretty good at it." She smiled. She really could imagine him in full pitching mode and suspected he'd charm the pants off most buyers. He told her that he had recently won a local sales team award for total number of properties completed in March.

"I was shortlisted a few years ago for the regional scheme but Shanice Voden in the Portishead branch won it." He looked at Tess, smiling. "Not that I'm bitter or anything."

"Bloody Shanice and her reasonably priced terraces," said Tess, and he laughed.

"Too right. But yeah, I do okay. I like meeting my targets, which sounds a bit sad doesn't it? But I enjoy it, enjoy the challenge and clients pick up on that. You must see it at work, people know if you hate your job or if you love it – whatever you're feeling, it sort of transfers to them, I guess."

Tess thought about this for a moment. "Yeah, I guess so. It's nice to hear about someone enjoying their job. A lot of people just seem to hate work. Maybe we're both pretty lucky."

"I certainly feel lucky tonight, sat here with a gorgeous woman." He smiled broadly at her. "And a doctor and all. Is it as glamorous and high-adrenaline as it seems on the telly?

Everyone having affairs and bonking in cupboards and the like?"

She laughed. "It's not really like that at all – sorry to disappoint. I guess it's the same as any other job. Probably no more salacious than being an estate agent."

"Oh!" He pulled a face of mock disappointment. "D'you mean you're not all at it like rabbits the whole time? Maybe it's only the surgeons then," he said, taking a sip of wine and grimacing. "God, this stuff's a bit ropey, isn't it? You not a surgeon I take it, Tess?"

"No," she replied. "No, I want to be a GP. I like a bit of variety."

"Yeah, I get that. It's like a mixed property portfolio, I suppose. So, you working in a practice now then?"

"No, still training. I'm in palliative care at the moment." She saw his look of confusion. "In a hospice? I work with people who are dying."

"Right. I see."

"Yes. People often have that reaction. I don't really know why. Bit of a taboo, I suppose."

"Yes." He was thoughtful for a moment and she wondered if he was about to launch into a story of bereavement. Telling people that she worked in a hospice usually went one of two ways: they were either uncomfortable and didn't want to discuss it any further, or they had an experience they wanted to share. With Simon, predictably, it was neither.

"So," he said seriously. "You work with people who are dying, hey?"

She nodded.

"Well, I guess that would explain the lack of shagging then."

Tess began to laugh. "Yeah, I guess it would."

Chapter Eighteen

I t was just after eleven when they left Little Italia, their waitress wiping down the PVC checked tablecloths and mopping the floor with greyish water. They hit the fresh air outside and Simon suggested that they move on to another bar. As they headed down Park Street, a place caught Tess's eye. It was an old pub but had been given a facelift, and the subdued light filtering through the leaded windows below the new signage triggered a memory. She pointed over the road to the bar.

"Can we go there?" she asked, stepping out into the road and narrowly avoiding a taxi which was pulling up with its fare. Luckily Simon grabbed her just in time.

"Oh thanks!" she said. "Farida at work mentioned it. It's new, but supposed to be quite nice. Authentic feel, you know?"

Simon knew all about authentic feel; it was one of his favourite estate agent phrases. He was less impressed by the idea of going somewhere that had been recommended by one of Tess's hospice colleagues and voiced his reservations.

"Don't worry. I promise if anyone from work is there we won't talk about death," she said, and he laughed as they stepped through the doorway and into the throng.

The atmosphere in this bar was markedly different from The Garage. The main room was smaller, there was no wide-screen television on the wall, and no obvious hen parties or inflatable penises, which was a bonus. It was still noisy and people were enjoying themselves, but there was a more relaxed atmosphere compared to the frenetic alcopop-fuelled hysteria of The Garage happy hour, and the clientele were varied, with some smart city types surrounding a high table, a group of students sitting in the large bay window, and a family with teenage children poring over a theatre programme in the corner. The two of them had to squeeze together to make it through to the bar and the room was warm after the relative chill of outside. Tess slipped her jacket back off her shoulders and slung it over her arm. As she did so, her heel stuck into a gap between the intentionally rustic floorboards and she fell against Simon who mistook her stumble for an attempt to get closer to his manly physique.

"Steady on, Tess!" he laughed, but his confidence was bolstered and he slipped his arm round her waist to steer her through the crowd. They reached the bar and Tess was just beginning to wonder whether she was entirely happy with Simon's arm being placed so proprietorially around her middle when she felt her eyes drawn to a familiar figure to her right.

Oh God. The evening had been okay up to now, but things seemed to be taking a turn for the worse when she realised who they were sharing the bar space with. It was Edward Russell. And some tall, sculpted, elegant creature who looked as if she might snap in half at any given moment. Tess turned her face away and pretended to be fascinated by Simon's thoughts on pub renovation.

"Dr Carter?"

She tried to ignore his voice behind her. His tone was measured as opposed to loud, but there was a natural authority that was hard to avoid. Clearly the bartender responded in the same way because immediately he piped up, shouting over the throng to Edward, "What can I get you, mate?" and Simon nudged her, "That bloke's trying to get your attention, love!"

Tess turned very slowly and looked up into those deep-blue eyes. Edward gave her a tentative smile and she responded with the slightest of nods to acknowledge him.

"Mr Russell," she said with obvious distaste.

He did at least have the good grace to look a little awkward and it seemed that they were both recalling the events of the previous fortnight, because an almost imperceptible expression of regret flickered across his face in the same moment that Tess's mouth set into a hard, defensive line.

Simon could not help but notice the waves of hostility radiating off his date and the way that her body had stiffened in response to this man. He attempted to break the ice by thrusting his hand across to Edward. "All right, mate?" he said. "I'm Simon, Simon Collins. How d'you know Tess then?"

The barman had moved his attention elsewhere and Edward Russell flickered his gaze across Simon in a way that seemed to find him lacking. Simon was either blissfully unaware of this evaluation of his deficiencies or genuinely didn't give two hoots; either way he went up in Tess's estimation.

"My name's Edward Russell," said Edward, "and this," he gestured to the girl beside him, "is Clara Delaney. Clara, this is Dr Carter, she has been involved in the care of my mother."

"Oh!" exclaimed the gazelle, looking momentarily interested. She was the embodiment of what Tess's mother would have described as a *posh bint*.

"Are you the oncologist?" She extended a perfectly manicured hand whilst giving Tess a thorough appraising stare, taking in the cheap handbag, the tight jeans, and the low-cut top. Evidently Tess did not fit the bill of what Clara thought a doctor ought to look like.

"No. Not me. I'm just one of the palliative care doctors. Nobody important. Isn't that right, Mr Russell?" She looked across at him with an artificially bright smile.

"That's not strictly what I…"

"Nonsense. I know how you feel about my particular branch of medicine." The cool, detached sarcasm Tess was hoping for was sounding a little more hysterical than she'd anticipated. "Doctors like me just tend to, what was it? Oh yes, 'Preside over death all day.' That, and give people morphine. I'm more of a glorified pharmacist really."

"Dr Carter." Edward's attention was focussed entirely on her. "I'm so sorry if what I said caused you offence. It really wasn't my intention."

She looked straight at him, her eyes locked with his, and for a moment it was as if nobody else was in the bar. She felt herself drawn back to that first meeting in the kitchen of Dan's flat. The spark of electricity. Yet again she was trying to read his facial expression, searching for a sign of recognition. Did he feel it too? Out of nowhere, Jane Austen piped up:

"The evidence of the gentleman's agitation is clear in both his countenance and bearing, Tess dear. He too is struggling for the appearance of composure."

But just as suddenly the connection was lost, crowded out by the memory of his wounding words. She turned her back on both him and his girlfriend, aware that she was being rude but finding the feeling strangely liberating; it was not often that she deliberately forgot her manners. "I'll wait over at the table," she said to Simon and, ignoring the little sniff of outrage from Clara behind her, she strode away as confidently as her heels would allow.

A few moments later Simon came over with their drinks, looking confused. "What's the score there then?" he asked. "Did you two used to go out or something?"

"No, nothing like that. We just don't really get on, that's all."

"Oh, okay. I have to say he seemed all right up at the bar. We had a bit of a chat about the housing market. He's got that moneyed look, hasn't he? I offered to show him a place over on the waterfront – great space. He wasn't interested but I gave him my card just in case." He put a hand to her cheek. "He must be a tosser if he's upset you though. Don't look so angry, sweetheart; it don't suit you. Give us that nice big smile again. That's better."

———————

Clara had turned to Edward at the bar as they watched Simon walk back to the table with the drinks.

"Quite extraordinary! That doctor…" she said, "she was so rude."

"She was a little."

"More than a little, Edward. I mean, it was just so unprofessional. And she was clearly drunk."

"Maybe she doesn't want to have to act like a professional the whole time."

"What? You're not trying to defend that obnoxious little display, surely?"

"I just mean, she's out with her boyfriend. Maybe she doesn't want to be constantly being a doctor. Maybe she's trying to draw a line between her life and her work? I don't know."

"Edward, surely you can see that her comments were inappropriate? I'm baffled you think that behaviour is somehow acceptable – even if one has issues with work–life balance, there's never any need to be that unpleasant. It's just so passive aggressive."

"I think it's quite out of character."

"Oh?" Her nostrils flared. "And you know her character

pretty well, do you? She's not normally a rude little madam, I take it?"

"No, she's not. She must have her reasons."

"Really? What is it you're not telling me?"

"If you must know, I upset her a few weeks ago. I accused her of… well, let's just say she's got every reason to be pissed off."

"And what exactly do you mean by that?"

He sighed. "Nothing. Look, Clara, I don't want to talk about it. And if we're honest, neither do you. Let's just leave it."

Clara folded her arms across her narrow chest, noting the distracted look on her boyfriend's face. She quietly fumed as she sipped her white wine. "I see," she said eventually. "No further explanation then?"

"No. Have you finished that drink?"

Tess was starting to find Simon Collins significantly more appealing as the alcohol kicked in and the night wore on. His chivalrous attempt to protect her feelings made her warm to him even further. Out of the corner of her eye she could see Edward and Clara still at the bar, both exuding entitlement in their posture and their haughty assessment of the remaining clientele. She was also aware of Edward's eyes on her and subconsciously she wanted to demonstrate to him that his opinion meant nothing, that his comments had had no impact on her whatsoever. She moved closer to Simon and pulled her hair back from her neck, leaning a little into the table and resting her fingertips near the edge of her top to draw his gaze downwards. She knew it would have the desired effect. Simon got an eyeful of ample bosom and responded by putting his hand back on her waist and letting it rest there while they continued chatting. She intensified the flirting in tiny increments, laughing ostentatiously at Simon's jokes, which seemed to be getting funnier as the night wore on – all the time aware of Edward's eyes boring into the back of her neck. She knew she was drunk and being more than a little ridiculous, but she wanted to convey a message in the most obvious terms: *See? There are people here who think I'm worth being with. You forgot me and then you misjudged me, more fool you.*

Eventually Simon got the hint and his face moved closer and closer to hers until at last he pulled her into an embrace.

"God, you really are gorgeous, love. D'you want to come back to my place?"

Tess toyed with the idea for a few moments and then whispered in his ear, "Yes. Go on then. Why the hell not!"

She kissed him lingeringly on the cheek as she rose to gather her belongings and made a point of completely blanking Edward and his girlfriend as she and Simon left the bar with their arms around each other.

———

Much later that night, she was tucked up in her own bed, having got a taxi back from Simon's modern and tastefully furnished apartment a little earlier. He was very good-looking and she was definitely attracted to him, but despite a lengthy period of kissing on his sofa she had found that her attention was flagging, and he noticed it too. He had asked her whether she was okay, made her a cup of tea, and been most chivalrous, but they both knew she wasn't going to be leaping into bed with him that night. He called her a cab just after midnight and they had agreed to go out again the following week – there wasn't any harm in seeing him again, after all. He was nice enough, he made her laugh, and he was the first man she'd kissed since Scott. And maybe that was part of the problem. Whenever Simon's hand had strayed too far under her clothes, she had tensed with the knowledge that the last man who'd seen her naked had ended up in bed with someone else. This, it turned out, was not a particularly solid foundation for getting her kit off in a confident manner.

However, the upshot of all the snogging on the sofa was that she was left in a semi-aroused, slightly drunken state now that she was back home on her own. She moved her hand to between her thighs, thinking of Simon and how it had felt to kiss him, the firm pressure of his lips against hers. This worked for a time, but she was a little numbed from the alcohol and needed to move her focus. In her head she scrolled through the usual suspects: brooding actors, literary heroes, her orthopaedic registrar from medical student days, but no joy. She then turned her attention to the events of the past few weeks, trying to light on something, anything, with an erotic undercurrent. Suddenly, unbidden, an image of Edward resting against the bar earlier that evening sprang into her mind – the sensation of feeling his gaze on her, knowing he was watching her – and it took her back to that first night they met, their hands entwined, and the morning after when he'd kissed her and the world had stood still.

All at once she was there, the familiar rhythmic waves rolling up from her pelvis and a sense of relief that finally she could let go. A short but perfectly satisfying orgasm later, she lay on her back and pondered the idiosyncrasies of the human brain. She had dreamed of Edward before, of course. In fact, following their first encounter she had been able to think of little else, day or night. Her boyfriend, Pete, had realised that something had changed. She was distracted and listless, going through the motions, until she felt unable to maintain the charade any longer. She felt guilty every time Pete kissed her, every time she slept with him. Because she no longer wanted him. In fact, she wasn't sure she'd ever wanted him, or anyone else, in the way she now wanted Eddie.

During those months she'd gone through every moment of that kiss in her mind, reliving it over and over again. She had woken that morning to find her hand entwined in Eddie's and felt an exhilaration, a lightness in her chest that had never been there before. She had watched him sleeping, and when he woke a few moments later, he had pulled her towards him so that she slipped from the sofa down onto the floor, her face inches from his. Without a word, her mouth met his and within seconds their hands were scrabbling for each other's clothes and pulling at blankets and bedding in a thirst to get their bodies closer together and then, just as suddenly, she had pulled away. A memory had echoed in her ear, a comment floating through the smoky air on her way to the toilet last night, from another person at the party, another friend of Dan's, something about "Eddie being on the prowl again", and the familiar doubt entered her mind – is he going to hurt me? Not physically – she had never felt safer or more certain of what her body wanted than at that very moment – but emotionally; she knew she was vulnerable, that she'd always be vulnerable. And she couldn't bear it. Couldn't bear the idea of him doing exactly what her mother had told her most men did: take what they wanted and leave without a trace. He had sensed her withdrawal almost before she'd had time to process these thoughts and had searched her face for clues.

"I have a boyfriend," she said, pulling herself up to a seating position, readjusting her clothes. "I can't do this."

Eddie chewed his lip. "But this," he gestured between the two of them. "This is different. Isn't it? I mean, this is different for me. I thought maybe we could spend the rest of the day together and then..."

"Then what?" she said. "You're going back to London."

"It's only London," he said. "It's not like it's the other side of the world. We can't just leave it like this. I can't. I don't want to."

She'd pulled on her boots, unable to look at him. She'd had to get back to Pete. What was she thinking? "I'm sorry," she'd said as she left the flat. "Tell Dan thanks for the party and tell Donna... I don't know, that I had to get home. I'm sorry, Eddie. I'm sorry." And she'd stumbled down the steps of the Georgian terrace, mascara streaking her cheeks.

The sense of regret, of having missed out on something vital, only increased as she crossed the streets of Bristol, oblivious to the Sunday morning traffic trundling past her, and as she crashed into her own bed, her last waking thought was of him, of Eddie, and whether she might have just made the biggest mistake of her life.

Chapter Nineteen

Tess continued to see Simon over the next few weeks. They went out for dinner on two or three occasions – to nicer restaurants – and he was good company, even if she sometimes found her attention wandering. She knew they made an attractive couple, and together they drew admiring glances from passers-by, but she couldn't help feeling that there was something missing. She confided in Kath one evening when they were tucking in to a takeaway.

"I have slept with him," she said, "before you ask. Because I know you will." She gave a sideways look towards Kath who was trying and failing to maintain a casual expression. "It was okay, but it wasn't amazing, you know."

"Got you. I know exactly what you mean. I've had my fair share of mediocre shags."

"You've had more than your fair share of every type of shag, my friend."

"Harsh, but accurate."

"It's just, it's difficult to say why it wasn't great. He's nice-looking, he's… he knows what he's doing."

"Well, that's a good start. No weird kinks or fetishes? Did he want you to wrap him up in cling-film and beat him with a frying pan?"

Tess laughed and shook her head. "No."

"And he's not one of those blokes who totally loses their shit when they realise that women have pubes?"

"No, the existence of my pubic hair didn't seem to be a problem – although he clearly waxes. There's a fair amount of manscaping going on."

"And he didn't want you to do anything weird with your stethoscope?"

"No. Wait. What? No!" Tess choked a little on her egg-fried rice.

"Okay. Just asking," Kath said breezily.

"It was perfectly normal, vanilla sex," said Tess. "He's technically proficient. Not terrified by the presence or distribution of female body hair. Adequately endowed. All fine."

Kath tipped her chow mein onto a plate. "And he likes girls, as opposed to boys, which is a giant leap forward."

"It is. Although we both know that it's perfectly possible to enjoy both. But I wonder if that's part of the problem." Tess poked at a bamboo shoot.

"What, the fact that he's *not bisexual*?"

"No!" She laughed. "The fact that my last boyfriend left me."

"Ahhh." Kath twirled her fork into her noodles, looking thoughtful. "Right you are."

"It's just, it's hard not to think that I must be really rubbish in bed if I, you know, if sleeping with me isn't *enough* for someone."

"Tess." Kath's voice was firm. "It's not your fault that Scott left you. It's not about you being unattractive or somehow *bad at sex*, or any of that shit. You do know that, right?"

Tess wrinkled up her nose. "I do know that," she said slowly. "But it's difficult to get it out of your head when you've finally got your kit off and it's all getting a bit hot and heavy."

"So, you were overthinking. Classic inhibitor to female arousal."

"Yes. Yes, I probably was. But it wasn't just that. I don't know what the problem is. He's handsome and he's charming and he makes me feel good about myself, but there's something missing. We don't quite, you know, click."

Kath helped herself to more noodles. "Ahh. I get you. So, it's more like you just don't fancy him enough. He's a bit like Pete – nice and safe, but didn't have much about him. Like he's got the emotional range of a paving slab?"

"Kind of. Except he seems a bit more resilient. I hurt Pete, I think; he really was sweet and he made me feel like some kind of princess. But, yes, you're right, there wasn't *enough* to keep either of us interested long-term. I just realised it before him. In fact, I realised it after that night with Eddie."

"Who? The fella whose mum was in the hospice?"

"Yeah."

"The one who had no recollection of your night of romance? The same one who kicked off with you about work and that? I know you didn't give me any details about what happened a few weeks back, but it was clear that he'd got under your skin something fierce."

"The same. He's the reason I dumped Pete. I realised I needed something more. Not Eddie, as it turned out – a relationship with him would have been way too much of a rollercoaster. But being with him, just for that night, made me feel, I don't know, different."

"He was a challenge?"

"Yes, but a challenge I felt I could handle, at least initially. Those few hours made me braver; they made me feel that I was entitled to a bit more excitement in my life, a bit more passion, I guess. My mistake, because the next bloke I fell for properly after Pete was Scott, and look how that turned out. Maybe safe and steady is the way ahead. Either that or stay single." She flopped back onto the sofa. "I can't be doing with the drama."

Kath looked up from her food. "Oh, you say that, but we all know that's a load of old bollocks. Everyone needs a drama. Everyone needs a bit of passion, a spark of electricity. You're just as entitled to it as the next girl."

"Yes, but…"

"No. Hang on there." Kath jabbed her fork in the air to make her point. "Safe is fine. I mean, safe is good. We don't want actual danger now, do we? But boring – boring is *not* fine and *not* good. You do not want to be looking back at your life thinking *Sweet Jesus, I've ended up married to a risk-free lump of lard.*"

Tess laughed. "No, you're right. I do not want that. And to be clear, I don't think Simon could ever be described as a lump of lard. Lump of chiselled marble maybe; he's kind and he makes me laugh but... I know it sounds awful, but sometimes I'm wondering if I'm laughing *at* him, not with him?"

"Oh, I've been there. Remember that numpty from Cornwall I went out with? Greg? Always playing the arse with everyone, clowning around, and you think to yourself, *Sure, but he's a great craic* – right up until the moment that you realise he's a complete tit who's driving you up the feckin' wall."

Tess chewed on a prawn cracker for a moment, letting it fizzle against the roof of her mouth. "Oh, God, no. He's not like Greg. I mean, he really *was* a pillock – no offence."

"None taken."

"No, Simon's good company. It's just sometimes I ask him a question about something I'm interested in or, I don't know, what his opinion is on anything other than house prices, and his face just goes blank." She turned to Kath. "Do you know what I mean?"

"You're after an intellectual then?" said Kath, opening up yet another carton of food.

"No. Well, maybe. I want someone clever, sharp, you know? Someone where I can catch their eye across a room and know that they've spotted the same thing I've noticed, and that we'll both laugh about whatever it is later, and he'll be witty and insightful and..."

"And devilishly handsome, and great in the sack?"

"Well, yeah, obviously!"

"Good luck with that then!"

Kath flicked the television on and loaded up the film they had chosen. "You don't think maybe you should just keep sleeping with him?" she asked after a pause. "See if things improve? Take the bull by the horns, so to speak, and come at it the other way, so to speak."

They both started to laugh. "Maybe," said Tess. "I'll give your plan some serious thought."

Kath shrugged. "It's less of a plan and more of a general guide for living, I'd say. Either way, I'm glad you're finally getting a sense of what you want. It doesn't have to be a straightforward choice between 'boring old Pete' and 'exciting, yet confused and unfaithful, Scott'. There is a middle ground, you know."

They both watched as the opening credits rolled.

"And it's also done you no good hiding from men since then." Kath turned from the screen to look at her housemate. "Cowering away like Rapunzel. You had me wondering if we were ever going to get you back to your former glory days. But when you walked in with that new hairdo and your spendy lipstick, I thought, *yes, here's my girl*."

Tess hid a pleased smile behind a forkful of food and surreptitiously plumped up her hair with her other hand. Since her visit home and her dates with Simon she felt a lot better about herself, despite the quite literal anti-climax in the bedroom department. She thought she looked okay. Not amazing, not beautiful, but not repulsive either, which was progress of sorts. Her eating was under control, and she'd managed to avoid all temptations to binge. Instead she and Kath had treated themselves to a spa day and booked a July trip to the South of France. She had bought some new clothes, had her hair cut, her nails done. All the little things that added up to a change in outlook and a boost to her self-esteem. Maybe being with Simon really was doing her some good.

She still had to decide what, if anything, to do about her dad, but there was no hurry and somehow the knowledge that he had continued to care about her was enough in its own way. She'd read through his letters, taking her time with each one, reading and re-reading until she had wrung every last drop of meaning from his words. She had spoken to Jake about it, feeling that he was probably the only person who could understand some of what she was going through, and he had been his usual pragmatic self. Advising her to take her time. "Them letters ain't going nowhere Tess. Ain't no rush. Just see how you feel. You'll be reet." And he was right. She was doing okay.

Later that evening Jane Austen had a quiet but firm word with the television host:

"Dr Carter is a young woman of considerable capacity and application. Your treatment of her to date has been most vexatious. You have filled her head with scandalous falsehoods regarding her coarse features and limited means. What say you, sir, in your defence?"

The host whistled tunelessly. *"La, la, la, not listening."*

Miss Austen summoned up her most imperious tone. *"I*

will suffer this nonsense no longer, sir. I must have your word. Dr Carter is not to be trifled with."

The host gave a long and mirthless laugh. *"Jane. Janey. Jazza – can I call you Jazza? Appreciate the pep-talk, love, but you and I both know that there's a lot more trifling to be done before this story is through. Vexatious or not."*

Chapter Twenty

Tess was working nights when she next saw the Russell family. Mary had been admitted to the General Hospital a few days earlier when she had become breathless. Fluid had been drained from her chest and sent to the laboratory, but rather than recuperate there she had chosen to be transferred back to the hospice, knowing that she had a better chance of recovery in familiar, peaceful surroundings with staff who knew her.

Tess knew that Mary was expected to arrive during the early part of her shift. Rob, who was working that evening, had handed over with characteristic efficiency, despite the fact that ever since Tess had come into work with her new haircut he seemed to have even more difficulty meeting her eye. She was aware of the recent changes in Mary's clinical condition and was steeling herself for further awkwardness from a wounded Edward, who she hadn't seen since the night of her blind date with Simon.

However, her first thought on seeing Mary that night

was how dreadful she looked. Her breathing was shallow and the process of shifting air in and out of her lungs seemed to be exhausting. Her lips were a greyish blue and her cheeks were drawn with the effort of communicating even a few words. Edward, who accompanied his mother, gave Tess only a fleeting glance. He too looked shattered, worry etched on his face, his focus entirely on the trolley as it was wheeled into Mary's usual room. Tess made only one veiled reference to their previous argument, asking Edward whether he was happy for her to try and make his mother more comfortable or whether he wanted her to find a different doctor to attend. She knew that finding a replacement would be almost impossible on a night shift, but had to at least feel she'd given him the option.

He looked at her, bewildered. "Just do whatever you need to do," he said. "I don't care who sees her as long as they make things better."

"Absolutely. Of course."

She returned her attention to her patient.

"Mary, I know this is frightening. I'm going to need to ask you a few things, but you can just nod or shake your head; there's no rush. Okay?"

She reached out to hold Mary's hand.

"Do you have any pain?"

Mary shook her head.

"Do you feel sick at all?"

She shook her head again and Tess could see in her face that her breathing difficulties were being exacerbated by anxiety. She needed to act decisively.

"Good. Now I'm going to move your pillows and prop

you up a little, good. And, um..." she looked towards Edward. "Could you just turn that electric fan on in the corner? Great, and maybe point it a little more this way? Thanks." She turned back to Mary. "I want you to just close your eyes and think about your breathing for a moment. Can you do that for me? Great. I want you to concentrate on the out breath. Make it as long as you can. Fantastic."

She sat, keeping a tight hold of Mary's hand and watching her face closely.

"You're doing brilliantly. Nice short breath in... And lovely, long, slow breath out... Good."

They sat for five minutes in a silence broken only by the rattling breaths and the occasional word of encouragement from Tess until she was reassured that Mary's panic was subsiding. She was aware of Edward's gaze from the far corner of the room but did not look back at him, keeping her focus on Mary.

"You're doing really well. You're going to be fine. We just need to concentrate on that breathing, nothing else. Yes, that's great. Well done."

Mary squeezed Tess's hand and opened her eyes.

"You see now, does it feel a bit easier? Don't worry, you're doing great. Keep going exactly as you are, okay?"

She stood and Mary's hand slipped from her grasp. She stroked the back of it gently.

"I'm going to pop out now and get a few things sorted. I want you to keep focussing on that breathing. I'll be back in ten minutes but if you need me press the buzzer and I'll come straight in, okay?"

"I'd been wondering if I should write her up for some

sedation to calm her breathing down a bit, but I think she just needs some rest," she said a little later to Edward as they both stood either side of Mary's bed, watching her chest rise and fall peacefully and her eyelids flutter to a close. He nodded, still looking at his mother, his face betraying little of his own internal conflict. He knew from their last meeting in the bar that Tess continued to have residual ill-feeling towards him, and yet in spite of this she had been able to act in an entirely professional capacity, soothing and calming his mother with her kind and practical demeanour. He wanted to convey his gratitude, but didn't trust himself to speak without breaking down, so he simply nodded again and, taking his mother's hand, bent to sit beside her. As Tess left the room, he managed a hoarse, "Thank you," which she acknowledged with a thin smile that didn't quite reach her eyes. She could see the emotional turmoil he was in, and knew how hard he was trying to keep himself together, but she wasn't quite ready to forgive him just yet.

For the remainder of the night, Tess was kept busy with another patient, Mr Gardiner, who was in his final hours of life. She sat with him until his family arrived and once she had finished answering their questions and made sure Mr Gardiner was comfortable, she popped her head round the door of Mary Russell's room to find her fast asleep – with Edward, still awake, hunched in the chair beside her and looking wretched.

"Do you want me to see if one of the porters can bring a camp bed down for you?" she whispered over to him. As much as her feelings for this man were confused and complicated, she could not help but be moved by his distress. She wouldn't want to see her worst enemy in this much pain.

"No." His voice cracked and faltered, "Don't worry. It'll be morning soon; there's no point."

Tess looked at her watch. He was right; it was five o'clock and the sun was starting to filter weakly through the curtains. "Okay, if you're sure."

She held his gaze for a few moments before she left to make an emergency referral to the respiratory physiotherapist who held clinics at the hospice. She knew that Mary would benefit from his expertise, and when she left for home, she passed the message on to Farida to ensure that the referral had been picked up.

"Madeleine? It's me. It's Edward."

"Hello? Sorry?"

"It's me. I'm just outside the hospice. I'm trying to keep my voice down. People's windows are open, you know. I don't want to disturb anyone. Hang on, I'll walk down to the lake, see if the reception's a bit better."

"Outside the hospice?"

"Yeah. Mum's been transferred."

"Oh good. Glad she got a bed. How's she doing?"

There was a pause.

"Eddie? You still there?"

"Yes." Edward's voice caught in his throat. "Yes, I'm

here. She's not doing well, Mads. Past few days, it's been pretty tough, her breathing and everything."

"Because of the fluid?"

"Yes. It's been drained off so she can breathe a bit easier, but they had to whack a massive needle in her chest to do it. It all looked pretty brutal. She was brilliant of course, so brave, barely flinched. Probably just didn't want me being upset."

"Sounds like Mummy."

"And she can definitely breathe more easily, so it was worth it. She's also much happier now she's back here. They've been really good with her, to be fair."

"You've changed your tune. Time was, you couldn't wait to get her out of the hospice and onto active treatment."

"I know. I haven't necessarily changed my mind. I just want her to feel better, and they seem to be pretty good at that here. They know her. They know what to do."

"And how are you?"

"Okay. Just a bit knackered, you know." He paused. "It's hard."

"Oh, Eddie! I know. I so wish I could be there to take some of this burden off. Is Clara stepping up a bit?"

"I haven't seen her much. She's busy with work. Trying to make partner and, well, I remember being in that position. She can't just drop everything. And I'm spending so much time in Bristol now. She's come to visit a few times."

"What? To visit Mummy?"

"No. She's not… I don't think she'd be comfortable with that."

"Hmm. Your office still being good about everything?"

"Yes, they've been great. Told me to take as much time as I need. I'm doing little bits here and there for clients – online, over the phone, you know. I need to take my mind off things now and again. But the reality of taking Mum to all these appointments and being there for all the treatment… I don't know how people manage if they can't take time off work. Must be a nightmare."

"Yes, I suppose I've never thought about it before. How the other half live and all that. Anyway. You won't be on your own for much longer. Flight's booked for Monday."

"Great. Can you text me the details and I'll pick you guys up from the airport? Assuming nothing more dramatic has happened in the meantime."

"God, don't say that. She is stable, isn't she? I mean she is going to still be… Do you think I should change the flights? Bring them forward? I could, you know."

"No. It's fine. She is stable. I'm sorry, being melodramatic." There was a pause. "I'm really looking forward to seeing you."

"Oh God, me too. And the kids. They've been getting so excited, packing and repacking their bags. Annabelle's already chosen and discarded at least fourteen outfits for the plane, let alone the rest of the trip. She's decided she wants to go to Harvey Nicks. Heard me telling Shalini about the fact that they've opened one up in little old Bristol."

Edward spluttered a laugh. "I'll take her. Get her something glamorous."

"Oh, she would love that, Eddie. That's a great idea. Look, I'll see you in a few days. Hang on in there, okay? You're doing a splendid job. Give Mummy a big kiss for me."

"Will do."

"Love you."

"You too."

Edward walked back into the hospice, a smile on his face as he contemplated the prospect of a shopping trip with his niece. By the time Tess arrived for her night shift he was sitting talking to Mary, who had colour in her cheeks and was more animated than she had been in days. The physiotherapist had visited and they both thanked Tess for arranging the referral; it was clear from their faces how beneficial it had been.

Tess was gratified to see the improvement, but there was little in terms of additional medical input required for Mary that night and she remained cautious about maintaining a professional distance. She had not forgotten Dr Fielding's advice and knew that she could not face another harrowing re-run of the previous altercation, which had left her feeling so bruised.

So she avoided sitting and chatting too long with Mary, even though she wanted to find out how much her patient knew and how she was coping. She avoided pressing her on how she felt about the impending results of her recent investigations and instead focussed on purely clinical support; doing the jobs that were necessary for her patient's comfort and ease, but not engaging in any real sense. Edward and Tess's exchanges during the night were polite and courteous, but they were both wary of each other. However, Tess reflected, it was a giant leap forward from open warfare.

Chapter Twenty-One

The next day was Saturday and Tess was looking forward to completing the week – this would be her last night-shift for a while, and she had the luxury of two days off to recover afterwards. Kath had been working days like a normal human being, so their paths had crossed infrequently at home, and as a result Morris had been receiving twice the usual amount of cat food, each housemate feeding him before she left for her shift. That morning Tess noticed the bag of food was a lot lighter than it should have been and, realising their mistake, omitted his breakfast.

The weather was unusually warm for June and she left the windows wide open in every room to encourage what available breeze there was into the house while she went upstairs to sleep. A few hours later Morris pushed his not inconsiderable bulk through the sitting room window and headed towards the uncharted territory and gastronomic delights of the wheelie bins at the front of the house next to the main road.

By the time Tess arrived at the hospice that evening, some of the day's heat had abated, but it still felt muggy in the foyer. Janice on reception had spent most of the day complaining bitterly about the polyester tabard she was forced to wear, and by early afternoon the hospice manager had finally relented and allowed her to remove it. When Tess arrived, Janice was fanning herself extravagantly with a flyer advertising commodes and muttering about workers' rights for menopausal women.

Tess first went to check on Mr Silvy, a retired geography teacher with motor neurone disease, who had regaled Tess with stories of his previous rugby triumphs when she had clerked him in the night before. Before she started her evening ward round, she looked in on Mary Russell, having seen Edward leave the building a few minutes earlier. She found her patient sitting by the window where a gentle breeze was bringing in some welcome freshness.

"Do you have a minute, Dr Carter? I wonder if you might be able to help me get over to the bed? Edward has gone out for some air and I've started to feel a little fatigued. I wonder if another one of my extended sleeps is in order. It's all I seem to spend my time doing at the moment."

"Of course," Tess said. "It would be lovely to catch up with you anyway. I've been wondering how you've been getting on. I know we haven't talked much about it all recently. I thought it best to, you know, keep a low profile."

"Oh?"

"I just didn't want to make things more complicated for you…" She stopped herself, remembering Dr Fielding's advice. "Never mind, let's get you back into bed."

The process of transferring out of the chair and walking the few steps across the room was slow and arduous. As Tess supported her patient's weight, she noted how frail Mary had become, the sharp ridges of her shoulder blades poking through her thin cotton nightgown and her wrists fragile, like fine porcelain resting in Tess's hand. Mary told her, in short staccato bursts, how much easier her breathing had become since the physiotherapy assessment and how glad she was that the doctors at the General had been able to drain the fluid off her lungs.

"It felt like I was drowning," she said. "Such a relief to be rid of it."

"They didn't manage to slip you some extra chemotherapy while you were in then?" Tess asked.

Mary shook her head and smiled as she sank into the bed.

"Oh, that's better. No, no more chemo, thank goodness. I think Edward is slowly coming around to the idea that further noxious chemicals may do more harm than good. Dr Hamilton-Jones has been very kind but I worry that he might have given my son unrealistic expectations in the beginning. To be honest, I always feel a sense of alarm when I see him now, wondering what horrific treatment plan he has come up with this time."

"Do you want to hear my favourite oncologist joke?"

"Go on then."

"Admittedly, it's from a limited repertoire: why do they nail coffin lids down?"

"No idea."

"To stop the oncologists delivering one more dose of chemotherapy!"

Mrs Russell snorted a delicate laugh through her nose.

"Sorry." Tess looked sheepish. "Not at all appropriate. Make sure you don't tell your son about that joke – he'd be appalled. Probably have me escorted off the premises!"

"Actually, it seems perfectly appropriate given the circumstances. And I don't think Edward would necessarily disagree." She looked sidelong at Tess, "His views have changed somewhat."

"Mary, we don't have to talk about this. Your son's opinions are his own business. He has made that abundantly clear on several occasions."

There was a pause as Mary found a better position in the bed. "I can imagine. And I am sorry if he upset you. He has a fierce temper on him, that one. He's learnt to control it but goodness, it did cause havoc when he was young. He was a bit of a terror really – never malicious but he could get so fired up! Always so fixed on what was right or wrong, outraged by anything he perceived as injustice – against himself, his friends, or even complete strangers."

She told Tess about several occasions when Edward had intervened in fights between much older children. "He was always fearless. He'd wade right in, often ending up being hurt in the process, but he'd be completely unfazed, standing there with a bloody nose, scraped and bruised, explaining patiently to his teachers how the situation had arisen and what he thought needed to be done to sort it out."

"He sounds a bit like my brother," said Tess. "He was always getting into scrapes on behalf of other people, looking out for the underdog, you know."

"Exactly. I think that's why Edward ended up studying law: he had this very clear idea of doing the right thing. Well, that and the fact that his father was completely determined he should follow in his footsteps. Edward actually wanted to be a vet for a long time, but sometimes a parent's wishes have a way of encroaching on their children's choices, don't they?"

Tess smiled to herself, thinking of her mother and her secrets. Mary's comments also chimed with something Edward had told her that first night together, about his reservations regarding his current choice of career. Hearing Mary's take on Edward was interesting. His mother's opinion fit better with Tess's earlier recollections and made her wonder whether her initial assessment of him had actually been correct.

"Still," Mary said, "he's a good lawyer and his clients certainly seem to appreciate him."

"He's very driven? Focussed, I mean? Only, from what I've seen of him working in the café…" She was aware that she was treading a fine line between allowing her patient to talk and get things off her chest, whilst also wanting to probe a bit further for her own self-interest.

Mary was nodding in agreement. "He works very hard. Too hard, but at least it keeps him busy. Takes his mind off things. And his office have been very understanding about him needing time off at the moment. I think because he's put so many hours in over the years. And they can't afford to lose him; he's so good at what he does."

She shifted position in the bed and took another slow breath that rattled through her chest. "But I still see that expression on his face sometimes, that outraged little boy, determined to make things right. He's really struggling with this"—she gestured to herself—"because he can't make it better. Obviously. And it drives him up the wall. Hence the outburst. Or rather, series of outbursts."

She looked Tess directly in the eye. "He does feel bad about the things he said, Dr Carter, I can tell. He actually holds you in very high regard, although I appreciate that may be a little hard to believe."

There was a pause and Tess patted her hand. "It's okay," she said. "Honestly. These things are sometimes more complicated than any of us realise."

Mary sighed and Tess could see she was starting to look tired, so she took her cue and rose to leave. "Is there anything you need? Can I get you a drink of water?" She pulled the table closer to the bed and poured some iced water into the plastic cup, holding it out to Mary who pursed her mouth round the straw and took a couple of gulps.

"Delicious, thank you," she said. "One forgets how lovely a cold drink is on a hot night."

Tess rested her hand briefly on Mary's shoulder before making her way out of the room, bumping into a returning Edward who was holding a worn paperback in his hand.

"Oh, I've read that," she said looking down at the book.

"*The Song of Achilles* – yeah, it's great. In fact, I think that one might be mine. Was it from the library shelf? Yes, it's one I brought in."

"Oh, I'm sorry, should I not have taken it?"

"No. I mean obviously, it's a library shelf; I brought it in for people to borrow. That's the idea. It's a good read anyway. I think you'll enjoy it."

"Well. Thank you. Did you get a chance to…?"

"Oh, to finish the Adam Kaye you lent me? Yes, I did. It was fantastic wasn't it? I laughed so much, but it was also just so poignant."

"I know. That bit where he casually mentions the effect the job has had on his partner…"

"Oh, God, yes, and the bit where he says, 'You saved the wrong one.' I was in pieces. Anyway, I suspect you might be wanting to immerse yourself in a story tonight. It looks like your mum's settling down to sleep. You can always sit in the relatives' room if you want? Or the offer of a camp bed still stands? Just let me know."

She remembered Mary's words about him holding her in high regard and in spite of herself, smiled at him genuinely for the first time in a long while.

It was close to midnight when Tess's mobile rang. She was re-writing a patient's drug chart when she felt a buzzing in her pocket and saw an unfamiliar number on her screen. She answered impatiently, suspecting that at this time of night it was probably a call centre based in Delhi trying to sell her insurance.

"Hel-lo?" She was only half concentrating as she continued writing the chart in front of her.

"Oh. Hello there." The deep voice on the other end of the line was gruff and there was traffic noise in the background. "I'm sorry to trouble you. Do you own a ginger cat?"

"Yes?" replied Tess. Suddenly on high alert, she held the phone closer to her ear. "Yes, yes I do. Morris. He's my cat. Is something wrong?" She tried to stop the alarm creeping into her voice.

"I'm terribly sorry, miss." The man's voice softened into a Bristol burr. "Your cat, he, um, well, he just came out of nowhere. Shot out from behind the bins and, well, he was under my wheels before I knew what!"

Tess felt her throat tighten and gave a little sob as she pressed the phone to her ear. "Is he, is he alive?"

"He is, miss. He is indeed. He's in a pretty bad way though. He'll need to see a vet, I reckon."

"Oh, thank God!" Tess almost wept with relief. He was alive. But what was she going to do now? Her shift didn't finish for another nine hours.

"Where... whereabouts are you?"

"Just at the junction by Cranbrook Road," he said. "Near your house, is it?"

"It is, but I'm at work at the moment," said Tess. "I'm just thinking... Could you give me a minute to see if I can get hold of a friend to collect him? I'll call you straight back? Thank you so much, if you could just stay with him for a little longer I'd be really grateful?"

"Of course, my lovely. I'll stay right here with him for now. I've got to get on though. I can't stay all night. But you see what you can sort out. Call me back on this number – I'm Chris, Chris Tyler."

"Thank you so much, Mr Tyler. I'll, I'll get back to you as quick as I can."

She rang off and went to dial the landline at home but remembered that Kath was in Bath with Ravi. "Shit!" she said under her breath. She tried Simon but the call went straight to voicemail, so she started scrolling through her phone contacts trying to work out who might be around and able to help. Of course, it was nearly midnight on a warm Saturday in the city, and most of her friends who weren't working or sleeping would be in noisy pubs and clubs. Every number she tried either went straight to voicemail or just rang out.

"Shit, shit, shit!"

She thumped the palms of her hands down on the desk and stared at her phone, willing it to offer up a solution. She thought of Morris, hurt, bleeding by the side of the road, and put her head in her hands. What on earth was she going to do? She couldn't leave work; there was nobody else to cover the end of her shift and she couldn't expect Mr Tyler to stay with Morris until eight in the morning.

At that moment Edward emerged from his mum's room and strode over to the desk.

"I thought I'd take your advice," he said quietly, waving

the paperback in his hand and then he caught sight of Tess's face.

"Are you all right? What is it? What's happened?"

Tess, trying to keep her composure, explained in stilted breaths what had happened to Morris.

"I know it's ridiculous," she said when she'd filled Edward in on most of the details. "He's only a cat, but I can't bear to think of him hurt and alone, and, and, I can't get hold of anyone. God! What am I going to do?"

Edward passed her the box of tissues from the top of the desk and waited while she wiped her eyes and blew her nose loudly. He looked thoughtful.

"Okay. Here's what we'll do. *I'll* go and collect your cat. No, no…" he interrupted her as she began to protest. "No. Mum is fine. She's sleeping. I've been with her all day. She won't even know I've gone and I assume"—he looked at Tess to verify—"that you'd call me if her situation changed anyway?"

"Of course, but—"

He held out his hand for her to stop, "I'll sort it out. Give me this chap's number."

"But how are you…? What are you going to…? Where are you going to take him? How is this going to work? I… I don't… It's really kind of you but I just don't…"

"I will sort it," Edward said. "What other option have you got? Now, just let me have the number and don't worry."

Tess slid the piece of paper with Chris's number scribbled on it across the desk.

"Are you sure? I, just, well, thank you *so* much. I don't know what to say. Thank you."

Edward took the paper and pulled out his phone.

"It'll be okay. Despite all evidence to the contrary, I happen to be excellent in a crisis..."

He gave her an ironic smile and strode out of the foyer, dialling Chris's number on his way. Tess heard him as the sliding doors closed, "Hello, is that Mr Tyler? My name's Edward Russell..."

Tess was busier than usual for the rest of her shift, the heat was causing people to feel agitated and patients who couldn't sleep were in pain and distressed. She texted Edward repeatedly after finding his number on Mary's notes but there was no response, and as a result she was frantic by the time her shift ended, not knowing what had happened to Morris and whether he was even alive. She shared her concerns with the day staff after she had completed her handover.

"I hope everything's all right," Jill, one of the ward sisters, said as she gave Tess a little squeeze. "You let us know. It's horrid when something happens to a pet. I remember when those bloody foxes got one of our hens. My favourite she was too, Agatha, always a good layer." Jill paused, gazing into the middle distance before returning to focus on Tess. "Anyway, my love, we all understand. I'm sure he'll be right as rain." She patted Tess's arm. "Don't you fret. Home you go and get some sleep."

Tess was tense as she drove, alert to any flash of colour darting in the corner of her vision, any movement that could be an animal, a pedestrian, a cyclist. What had Morris been doing going as far as the junction with Cranbrook Road? He never went that far. *Anyway*, she sighed, *too late to question it now.* Cats were always a law unto themselves; even fat predictable lumps like Morris could surprise you. Another tear rolled down her cheek and she wiped it away angrily. Honestly, she dealt with death and serious illness all the time. People all around her at work were struggling to come to terms with real bereavement and grief. She needed to get a grip.

Chapter Twenty-Two

Back at home the house was silent with no welcoming miaow or writhing bundle of fluff to greet her. The armchairs with their little mounds of matted ginger fur all reminded her of Morris's favourite places to snooze in the sun, and her eyes filled with tears again. The television host's voice was back in her ear:

"I've gone for another audience poll, Tess. Try and help you out a bit. Here it is: 'Has Morris succumbed to the inevitable and shuffled off this mortal coil? Text DEAD now. Or has he only sustained life-altering injuries? Text MAIMED now. We'll be back with the results after this short ad break. Don't go away!' What d'you think?"

She phoned Edward on the way upstairs to the shower, increasingly desperate to find out what had happened. There was no answer, so she left a message and texted him again. While she was in the shower her phone rang, but by the time she reached it, the message had gone to voicemail. It was a sleepy-sounding Edward. He apologised for not calling sooner but the reception had been patchy and her texts had only just come through. He reassured her that Morris had needed emergency surgery but was now doing well. He left the address of the vet's, apologising that he had used the veterinary practice nearest his own home, as they were the only ones he knew would be open at that time of night, and suggested that she head over there as soon as she had a chance.

The sun was beating down on the pavement as she got into her car and the tree-lined streets were dappled with bright light. She made her way through Clifton and crossed the suspension bridge with the water of the Severn twinkling below. The roads were more shaded as she followed her satnav and headed out towards Clevedon, past Ashton Court and the golf course. Halfway down a winding country lane, as instructed she took a turning down a narrower track and crossed a cattle grid, following a sign for "Rosings Veterinary Practice". She drove on, passing a large outdoor manège with a stable block and a sign indicating the equestrian hydrotherapy unit to the right. Another sign pointed to the rehabilitation unit where Edward had said Morris would be. The size of the place took Tess's breath away, and whilst part of her was smiling to herself at the idea of her non-pedigree RSPCA moggy being treated in this centre of excellence, another part was panicking enormously at the costs she had already incurred. She was certain that her budget pet insurance would not cover emergency surgery and a recovery package in what appeared to be the veterinary equivalent of The Priory.

The reception area was cool and clean, with squeaky

linoleum underfoot and a medicinal smell of disinfectant that reminded Tess of some of her previous hospital placements. She walked up to the teenage girl sitting behind the main desk and asked to see Morris Carter, feeling faintly ridiculous as she always did using her pet's full name. The girl, whose badge identified her as Flo, had been expecting her and led her through a key-coded door to the side of the desk.

"He's pretty groggy at the moment," she said, "but it'll be nice for him to see you, and hear your voice. Henry, our head vet, was in theatre with him for most of the night and one of our orthopaedic specialists came in to assist with his surgery, so he's had the absolute best."

Tess found herself welling up again. She was so anxious to see him, although alarm bells were ringing at Flo's words; two surgeons called out in the middle of the night would be incredibly expensive. How on earth was she ever going to be able to pay for it? She was briefly distracted until they approached a door on her left and she heard a familiar miaow. Flo led her into a small white room and Tess could see Morris through the grill of a narrow crate.

Tess walked over to the crate and poked her fingers through the grill, "Hey puss!" she said as Morris nudged his nose against her hand, hampered by the neck collar he was wearing that kept knocking into the grill. She put her face down towards him and he came as close as possible, purring loudly and butting the plastic against the bars while she reached her fingers in to just behind his ears. Flo laughed.

"Well, he's certainly perked up now. I might try him

with a bit of breakfast. You can stay in here with him for a while, if you like? But he'll have to stay in the crate, sorry."

Half an hour later Morris had wolfed down his breakfast with breathtaking speed and was trying to work out how to get the last specks of cat food off the periphery of his head collar, when Henry the vet arrived. He introduced himself with a vigorous handshake, although Tess had heard him well before she saw him, his booming voice reverberating off the walls of the corridor as he greeted various animals like old friends. He was wearing a tweed jacket and had the complexion of a man who spends the majority of his time out of doors; his russet cheeks were sprinkled liberally with greying whiskers that met in an extraordinarily impressive moustache. This item of facial hair bobbed up and down as Henry spoke, dancing across his upper lip as if it had a life entirely independent of its owner.

"Well, young lady!" he bellowed. "You've got a very lucky mog there. Used up eight of his nine lives in one fell swoop, I should say. Not that he seems to have suffered enormously for it."

"No, he seems to be doing really well. Your assistant, Flo, said—"

Henry roared with laughter as Morris tentatively poked a paw through the grill and caught his jacket.

"Aha! My friend. You can smell the sprats hey?" He pulled a tiny dry fish out of his top pocket like a magician and posted it through the grill to Morris who couldn't believe his luck.

"Got to keep the boy's strength up," he said to Tess. "Although, he is a bit of a porker to be honest, dear.

Carrying a bit too much timber currently. You might have to keep an eye on him, food-wise. He won't be very mobile with that hip, and it's tough to keep the weight off. I should know! My old hip's an absolute bugger."

"I'm sorry to hear that."

"Don't you worry, dear girl. I'm not about to regale you with tales about my own ailments. I know you're a medic and I bet you're sick to the back teeth of ruddy old fools like me banging on about their arthritis."

"Oh, how did you—?"

"Yes, yes, yes! Eddie told me. I know all about you, my girl." His bushy eyebrows were high on his forehead. "His mother speaks very highly of you – favourite doc, I think. Talks about you every time I see her out with those daft dogs! Of course, she can't manage walking them now. Smashing lass that Mary. Ruddy shame, the old Big C and all." He frowned as he foraged in his pocket for a handkerchief. "Still, back to your cat, my dear. He's fixed up a treat now. Had to call Jumbo in at two. Think we woke up the wife, but she's used to it. He's done a cracking job – titanium plate and whacked a few pins in, nice and tidy."

"Thank you," said Tess. "I can't believe how much you've done for him."

"Pah! No bother. I enjoy a bit of drama in my old age. Keeps me on my toes."

"I know it sounds ridiculous but, I don't know what I'd have done without him. He's one of my favourite things in the world."

"Oh, I know exactly how you feel. Not ridiculous at all. I'd be the same if anything happened to my Bert or Ernie.

Anyway, I knew we had to get it sorted when I heard from young Edward last night. He ran in here carrying that cat like a baby. Not the first time he's been here frantic about an animal, mind, but he hasn't done it for a while, not since he's all grown-up and a big-shot lawyer at any rate. Now – where was I? Ah yes, this cat of yours, he'll need a bit of rest now, so let's us head back to ground control and I'll talk you through what needs doing."

Tess gave Morris a last scratch behind his ears and reluctantly left him pawing at the corner of newspaper in the crate. She walked back to the main desk with Henry, who was limping slightly on his aching hip. He told Tess more about the younger Edward. How he had spent hours helping out in the practice during his holidays from boarding school.

"Enjoyed school, he did, Edward. At least I never heard anything to the contrary, but back home most of his friends lived miles away and he didn't know any local lads. Father working all the time, Mary running the house and the estate, not much for him and his sister to do, so he and Maddie were always down here, walking the dogs, mucking out the stables, larking about. Maddie split her time between here and the riding school down the road – fantastic rider she was, natural equestrian. Her brother, fearless but not quite so graceful on a pony. Ha!"

Henry paused to poke his head through a window in the corridor and gave a cheery "Morning Marge!" to a woman sitting at the desk before making his way back to the reception, still chatting to Tess and enjoying the sound of his own voice.

"Loved them though, Eddie did. All those horses that came in lame or colicky, he used to head off on his bike as the sun was setting, and he'd be back here at the crack of dawn the next day, finding out how they'd fared overnight. And if he wasn't here he'd be at home, just up the hill, looking after his own little zoo. Mary used to spoil him rotten with whatever animal he wanted; of course, she was left looking after the whole menagerie when he was boarding, so she put her foot down about the snakes, but they've had all sorts up there: lizards, llamas, goats, parrots, an axolotl at one point, I think? You'd have to ask him. Audrey, he called her, as I recollect... Hmmm."

They had reached the main desk some moments ago and Tess had opened her handbag to get out her credit card. She was stood politely, waiting for Henry to finish talking whilst becoming increasingly anxious to establish exactly what the damage to her finances was. Henry finally noticed her open purse.

"I'm terribly sorry," she said, "I might not have enough in my account to cover the bill all at once. Do you have a payment scheme or something similar?"

Henry put a calloused hand on her purse and closed it firmly. "Oh no, dear girl," he boomed. "No need for that. All paid for. You've got young Edward to thank for that. Which reminds me..." He reached behind the counter top and pulled out a blue cashmere scarf that was covered in dried blood. "You might want to return this to him." He handed it to Tess.

"He'd wrapped Morris up in it I think, judging by the

look of it. Not sure as it'll ever recover. But if you're heading over to the house then you could maybe pop it in?"

"Of course. But can I just check… He's paid for *all* of it? I, um, don't know what to say…"

"Yup!" said Henry. "Every last prescription and dressing, emergency call-out fee – even the physio, all sorted." He smiled broadly. "He's up at the house now, getting it ready for when Madeleine and the kids arrive this week. You pop along there now; you should catch him."

He gave Tess the directions to the house, advising her that she couldn't really miss it, and suggested she try the back door because, "Nobody ever answers at the ruddy front in those types of houses – mainly just for show! Oh, and watch out for the dogs. Pack of lunatics, but terribly friendly."

She nodded and listened but in the back of her mind she was totting up the various expenses that Henry had outlined. She must owe Edward Russell a fortune.

Henry thought it likely that Morris would only need a couple of days on the rehabilitation unit and then Tess would be able to take him home.

"I can't take him now?" Her face fell. "Or maybe a little later today?"

"No can do, I'm afraid. We'll need to keep a close eye on him for the next forty-eight hours. You can pop in and see him whenever you like though. He'll be fighting fit and back home before you know it. Flo will talk you through all the post-operative care protocol when you collect him. For now, I suggest you head off and enjoy the rest of this sunny Sunday, hey?"

Tess was suddenly overwhelmed with emotion and gave Henry an enormous hug. "Thank you so much for everything you've done," she said, her voice muffled into his tweed blazer which smelt reassuringly of horses and hay.

"Steady, old girl!" Henry laughed, patting her on the shoulder. "Absolute pleasure, no bother at all."

He showed her back out to the car with a promise to call her if there were any further developments.

Chapter Twenty-Three

Tess was entirely unprepared for the view of the Russell residence, which was indeed just up the hill from the vet's practice. As she cornered round the leafy lane that circumnavigated the estate she caught a glimpse of the main house, a Georgian manor in mellow stone nestled amongst smaller outbuildings, including a carriage house and stable block. She pulled to a stop on the gravel drive, half expecting a butler from a Merchant Ivory production to emerge from the main portico and open her passenger door. She sat for a moment in the car just gazing in awe at her surroundings: the lawn rolling down away from the house towards a thicket of trees, the neatly trimmed box hedges that bordered the drive, the sash windows reflecting the early sunlight and lending a cheerful openness to the façade.

"I know, Jane. Don't say a word," Tess murmured under her breath.

Although the house was beautiful, something about its

splendour, along with the acres of prime land it sat in, bothered her. It wasn't normal. Who could actually live somewhere like this and not grow up to feel that they ruled the world? It smacked of elitism, public schools and old boys' networks, and further underlined some of the reservations she had about Edward Russell – although interestingly, she reflected, not about his mother, who always wore her wealth lightly. Tess had encountered a few extremely rich characters at medical school, often failed Oxbridge applicants who had been on the receiving end of extraordinarily expensive educations and who surrounded themselves with a peer group of identical friends. Medicine, however, was a great leveller, and most of these individuals, if they could hack it, were brought down to earth when faced with the realities of the lives of working people. They learnt how hard it was for the majority to make ends meet and started to claw back some of their humanity as they realised that their careers were dependent on helping those less fortunate than themselves. But people like Edward, she thought ruefully, never had to mingle with the proletariat. She stared again at the house, comparing it briefly with her own family home, and feeling that she would in all honesty much rather be there.

However, she realised that the longer she sat there pondering the class system, the more intimidated and nervous she was going to feel about speaking to him, so she picked up his scarf and got out of the car, closing the door behind her with a decisive slam. She made her way round to the back of the house, where she found a weathered rear door with iron boot scrapers at either side.

She knocked hard against the door panel and found that it was ajar. With some trepidation she nudged it open and called out, "Hello?" Almost immediately there was a cacophony of noise from within the house – barking and the scrabbling of claws across tiles – and she was nearly knocked off her feet by a pack of dogs hurtling into her, tails wagging. The first three dogs were rangy setters, their knobbly heads knocking into her thighs as she fussed over them. A few moments later an elderly cocker spaniel with cloudy eyes shuffled into view and the setters backed off to allow the senior member of the party to greet the visitor.

"Hello?" Edward's familiar voice shouted through from the next room. "I'm just in here. Come through."

Tess made her way into the kitchen accompanied by the enthusiastic canines and discovered Edward, clad in damp running gear and holding his ankle behind him with one hand to stretch out his quads whilst supporting himself on the back of a chair with his other hand. He looked up at her in surprise.

"Dr Carter! How nice." He was smiling, although she couldn't tell if it was genuine pleasure at seeing her or more of a grimace as his muscles relaxed into the stretch. He released his right ankle and repeated the move with the left whilst trying to fend off the dogs who were all trying to get involved in the warm down. Tess was mortified.

"The door was open… Sorry, you're clearly busy. I'll just…" She started to back out of the house and walked into a stack of metal dog bowls, which fell to the floor with a crash, causing the dogs to tear across the room towards her.

"Oh God, I'm so sorry!" She put her hands in front of her face; her cheeks were burning.

Edward did not appear flustered by her presence. "I've only been for a run," he said. "Do I really look that alarming?"

She composed herself, deliberately looking at his face and not at any other part of him. Somehow, finding him clad in his T-shirt and jogging shorts with a sheen of sweat over his upper arms and neck seemed terribly intimate, and thoughts of that body pressed up against hers on another sunny morning five years ago flooded into her head.

"I am sorry, honestly. I had absolutely no intention of catching you unawares. Henry suggested I come to return your scarf"—she gestured to the stained garment in her hands—"and I wanted to thank you, and also organise paying you back for the vet's bills. I should have waited until I saw you at the hospice. I am sorry – I'll leave now, and we can sort this out some other time."

She placed the scarf down on the work surface to her right and turned towards the exit but he called her back.

"Dr Carter? No need to be embarrassed. I expect in your line of work you've seen people looking hot and sweaty before. Take a seat. I'll go and hop in the shower – give me two minutes."

She turned back towards him. "Oh, no, I really…" but he had already returned to the hallway and she could hear footsteps disappearing up the stairs.

Jane Austen appeared to be hyperventilating. *"Goodness! A most peculiar sensation. Whilst I am certain that the strange flutterings in my breast are merely related to this dreadfully hot weather we are having, which keeps one in a continual state of inelegance, I must confess it is hard to remain entirely indifferent in the face of such a fine specimen of manhood."* She gulped for air. *"I am sure that I am quite undone."*

Tess took a deep breath. She suddenly felt exhausted and dropped her bag on the sofa next to the larger dogs, who had arranged themselves in a general morass of paws, jowls, and thumping tails. The cocker spaniel was perched on a neighbouring floor cushion, maintaining a distinguished air as he sniffed in Tess's direction. She pulled up the kitchen chair nearest the smaller dog and rested her hand on his head, absentmindedly stroking his nose while she looked around the room. The long table she was sitting next to was warped and roughened with age. There were deep scratches in some areas and a chewed table leg at one end that looked as if an errant puppy had nibbled on it in the past. The floor was made up of large, smooth flagstones and was surprisingly clean, given the number of resident canines. The kitchen surfaces were also clean, although cluttered with tins, spices, potted plants, spoon rests, coasters and piles of books and letters.

The room was warm and her eyelids were starting to droop when Edward re-emerged a few moments later in a clean T-shirt and shorts, his damp hair tousled and his feet bare. She jumped up out of her chair. "Sorry, I…" She wasn't entirely sure what she was apologising for.

"Please. Do sit down. Would you like a cup of tea?"

She shook her head as a yawn escaped. "No, look, I'd really rather not bother you. I only wanted to say thank you and bring the scarf back. I'm so, so grateful. I really don't want to put you to any further trouble."

He turned to her, holding the kettle in his hand.

"I am about to make myself a cup, so it would be absolutely no bother whatsoever," he said. "And you have just finished a night shift. Let me at least get some caffeine into you before you head back off in the car. I think we've all had enough traffic accidents in our lives for one day?"

She conceded that he was probably right and muttered something about, "Just one quick cup then," as she sank gratefully back into the chair.

Edward was clattering around one of the deep cupboards and emerged brandishing a blackened frying pan, which he set on the hotplate of the large cast-iron range in the corner, clearly intending on making himself some breakfast. He moved a chipped brown teapot off the trivet at the side, glanced at the contents with a frown and poured the old tea down the sink.

"Pauline," he said, "she's the housekeeper, and the reason this place hasn't fallen into total disrepair while Mum's been ill, but she cannot seem to leave a building without a pot of heavily stewed tea festering in a warm corner somewhere." He rinsed the teapot out and put two fresh bags in.

Tess felt she had to say something. The whole scenario was beginning to feel a bit surreal in her sleep-deprived state.

"Mr Russell."

"Edward, please."

"Edward. How much do I owe you for Morris's

treatment? I am very grateful, but I do really need to know."

He turned to her, leaning against the range.

"No, honestly, it's fine. I've paid for it. You've really no need to worry. I thought that, seeing as I was making the decision about where to take him, I couldn't expect you to foot the bill, and I don't think Henry charged for his time anyway – he's done all of our veterinary work on the horses and dogs and the assorted animals on the estate for years, so he did it as a favour. Please, don't trouble yourself about that. I only wish I could have got hold of you sooner to put your mind at rest. I knew you'd probably be going out of your mind with worry, but I didn't have your number until your texts came through."

The kettle on the other side of the hotplate started to whistle and he poured the boiling water into the pot. Tess shifted in her chair, resting her forearm on the edge of the table.

"I'm so grateful, I can't tell you. But... I cannot possibly let you pay for that treatment. For a start, I suspect it's a vast amount and I don't want to feel indebted—"

"To someone like me?" he cut in before she'd finished her sentence.

"It's not like that. Honestly, it's not; there's no need for you to pull that face."

"Okay."

"I just don't want to feel beholden. To anyone. It's not how I run my life. I've always been self-sufficient. It's important to me. Well, to be honest, it's been drummed into me: do not get into debt, ever, with anyone. I probably should have had it tattooed on my forehead."

"You might have looked a bit odd."

"Yeah, you're right. And I don't have a massive forehead." She smiled. "But no, seriously, I just have a bit of a thing about it."

"And I imagine that there could be little worse than owing money to someone who 'finds gaps in the law to make money for bankers'?" He raised his eyebrows but his voice was light as he recalled her words.

"There's no need to bring that up. We both spoke out of turn on that occasion."

"Yes," he conceded. "We did. We haven't actually discussed it since, have we? I do want to apologise properly for the things I said."

"Thank you." She smiled at him. "I think it's fair to say that both of us may have been guilty of misjudging each other." *On many levels*, she thought to herself. "I am very grateful, really. It was such a kind thing to do and honestly this isn't to do with any moral high ground. I'd feel the same if somebody on minimum wage had paid for Morris's treatment. I just don't want to be in debt."

"Fair enough. Look, how about we leave it for now?" he said, looking in the fridge for the milk. "Consider it a long-term loan? I really do think that I should absorb some of the cost anyway. It was my decision to bring him to Henry. You could almost certainly have got him cheaper treatment elsewhere."

"It wouldn't have been the five-star emergency surgery

he's received, would it, though? If I had taken him to someone else?"

"Oh, that's not necessarily true. It's like healthcare for humans: expensive isn't always better. Although I have to say in Henry's case it probably is. He's very good."

"Yes, well. He speaks very highly of you too. You clearly go back a long way."

"Hmmm, I can imagine. Did he recount endless tales of my childhood? I'm sure that's the last thing you needed."

"No. Actually it was quite *interesting*."

"I would have thought there was very little about me that would be of interest. I'm pretty dull really."

"I'm not sure as I'd agree with that," she said.

He smiled and turned back to the range and poured some oil into the frying pan.

"Right. I am about to make some breakfast. You are more than welcome to have some too; there's plenty. I don't know if it would be against your self-sufficiency principles and I don't want to burden you by making you feel any more indebted, but it would just be some bacon and eggs?"

Tess shrugged. This day was getting stranger by the minute. In fact, it was starting to develop that timeless quality that she'd remembered from the night she'd spent with him. "Why not," she said, "if you're sure."

"Excellent."

He brought a bottle of milk and two chipped mugs over to the table with the teapot still in its wonky cosy knitted from violently pink wool.

"One of Madeleine's craft projects at school," he said, gesturing to it as he poured. "It's almost twenty years old and she's mortified that Mum still uses it, so I always pull it out of the cupboard when she comes to stay, obviously."

"Yes, I can imagine. Very brotherly."

He smiled. "There are various other examples of her work dotted about the house: macramé plant hangers, crocheted doilies, badly embroidered handkerchiefs, all disastrous."

He crossed back over to the range and cracked a couple of eggs into the pan as Tess watched him. "Sounds like me – my craft activities were never up to much. Although Mum didn't mind as long as I had my head in a book."

He turned and looked over his shoulder towards her.

"Ah," he said. "Well Maddie didn't really enjoy reading either. She never was one for indoor pursuits, always wanted to be off riding her pony or racing around with me."

"Sounds like you were close?"

"Yes, at times. We got on well when we were together, but we were at different schools, so for vast stretches of time I didn't see her at all. Quite an odd set-up, I guess. You have a brother, don't you? Jake, was it?"

He continued to prepare breakfast, adding the rashers of bacon to the eggs as Tess talked about the sibling dynamics in her own household, surprised that Edward had remembered she had a brother, let alone that he recalled his name. Especially given that all the evidence to date seemed to point to his powers of recall being pretty abysmal.

"I guess our relationship was more conventional in some ways," she said, "given the fact that we spent all our time under the same roof, went to the same school, you know. But sometimes things were tough. Jake being mixed-race caused issues – you can imagine, the usual, a bit of casual racism – although he was pretty good at just shrugging it off."

"And I can imagine it must have been pretty difficult for your mother too? Ouch!" The bacon was spitting in the pan and he rubbed his hand.

"You okay?"

"Yes, fine." He ran his hand wrist under the tap. "I know you got all prickly before, last time I asked about it, but clearly money has been tight in the past, hence your attitude to debt? Which is admirable, by the way."

"Thank you. I know it probably seems a bit odd to someone who has grown up with"—she gestured to indicate the luxury of their surroundings—"all this. I guess it's hard for you to imagine. I wondered whether you thought I was being ridiculous."

"Not at all."

His interest seemed genuine and Tess relaxed a little. "Well, yes, money was always tight, space even tighter. I mean, our entire house would fit into this kitchen." She looked around the vast room. "And Jake was like some sort of man-mountain from the age of about thirteen. It was like keeping a giant in a shoebox, but we were happy and well looked after – well loved, you know."

Edward nodded, smiling as she continued.

"Not having a dad around meant that Jake was the man of the house, I suppose, but he never seemed to feel the pressure of that. Mum decided quite early on that I was the one who would take on the burden of being the perfect child."

"What do you mean by that?"

"Nothing really."

He raised an eyebrow.

"No. Enough with the meaningful looks. Don't you try and casually cross-examine me. I know your tricks." She wagged a finger at him.

"All right! I'm only asking." He put his hands up in a gesture of surrender.

"I'm too tired to think straight, and you know how my mouth runs away with me. I'll just end up blathering on… There was something that happened a few weeks back, family-wise, about my dad and…"

"I thought you didn't have any contact with him?"

"I don't. Well, I haven't. It's complicated."

"Okay."

"It was just a bit of a surprise. I'm still not quite sure how I feel about it and I'd rather not…"

"Of course. I'm not going to pry. Although I quite like it when you blather on, to be honest. I never know what you're going to say next." He crossed to the table and cleared a space for a plateful of toast, bacon, and eggs in front of her.

"There. Eat up; you must be starving – it's nearly eleven o'clock."

Tess realised that she was indeed ravenous. She hadn't been able to stomach the thought of food earlier that morning when she came home, racked with anxiety about

Morris. She helped herself to extra toast and Edward threw a couple of extra rashers of bacon in the pan.

Although they chatted easily over breakfast, Tess remained wary of lowering her guard and was keen to ensure that she did not outstay her welcome; as soon as she'd cleared her plate away, she picked up her bag and thanked him again. She asked if he would like her to take his scarf to the dry cleaner's, an offer he declined politely, and then she repeated her request for a total bill outlining how much she owed him. He assured her that he would arrange it and asked when she would next be in work.

"I'm not sure how much longer Mum will be with you," he said. "But if she is still at St Martin's on Tuesday, I'll see you then."

"Okay. Thanks again." She made her way towards the door but he called her back.

"Dr Carter?" He was leaning against the sink, a thoughtful expression on his face. "As you're here, do you think I could ask a favour?"

"Well, I'm really not sure." She smiled and put her hand on her hip. "I mean, it's not as if you've done anything for me, is it? Other than rescue my cat in the middle of the night and then cook me breakfast. On balance I'd say you can probably risk asking me a favour. Depends what it is, mind."

He laughed and brushed a crumb off the table. "You've done paediatrics recently, haven't you?"

"I have indeed."

"So, you'd know what children of different ages might

like? As in, you'd have an idea about what would be fun and what might be desperately boring?"

"Your niece and nephew?"

"Yep. Would you mind…?"

He walked towards the door without further clarification but she followed him into a large, high-ceilinged hallway with a sweeping oak staircase leading to the upper floors.

"My mother has warned me about going upstairs with strange men," she said as they climbed towards the first floor.

"I just want to show you something; it won't take long."

"Heard that before."

He laughed but both of them had flushed cheeks when they reached the top and it wasn't entirely due to the exertions of getting there.

Chapter Twenty-Four

They made their way along the landing to a large south-facing bedroom. The sunlight was streaming in through the sash windows onto a double bed with a blue-striped duvet cover and a large orange teddy bear sitting upon it. A poster of a sports car was tacked at a jaunty angle on the far wall.

"What d'you reckon? Too babyish?"

Tess was flattered that he wanted her reassurance. "The bear? For a five-year-old boy? No. It's perfect." She looked around the rest of the room. "Have you got a football about, or some Lego?"

"Yes. Up in the attic. I'll get them later. Good idea."

In the adjoining room he gestured towards a newly purchased Disney princess duvet covering a single bed with rails down one side, propping up two rag dolls. He raised his eyebrows, again awaiting her verdict.

"How old is she?" Tess asked.

"Annabelle's three. Behaves more like a forty-something CEO of a large corporation, but amazingly only three."

"Perfect again," she said. "I mean, I'm no expert, and they're your family, but I think they'll love sleeping in here."

"Great. That's a relief. Thank you."

Tess caught sight of a range of framed photographs displayed on the chest of drawers and walked over to them.

"Now that"—she pointed to a picture of a small boy in orange trunks, brown hair flopping across a scowl, arms folded—"is a strong look."

Edward smiled. "It certainly is. I was known for my mean and moody poses in my youth."

"Not keen on joining the Instagram generation then? Or have you mellowed in your old age? I can't imagine you're big into selfies."

"No, not really my thing." He glanced across at her. "And I can't say as I've mellowed – I'm still a grumpy bastard who takes himself too seriously. Anyway, you're not exactly an active Instagrammer yourself. I'd had you pegged as a massive exhibitionist, but it seems not."

"Have you been online-stalking me, Mr Russell?" Tess was pleased to see a flicker of embarrassment cross Edward's face as he realised the trap he'd set himself.

"Nothing of the sort," he muttered and crossed the room to look out of the window. She went to join him, seeing the gardens sweeping down in a gentle roll to the copse beyond.

"Your niece and nephew are going to have a brilliant time. I mean, how could they *not* love being here?"

"I know. It is beautiful, but I just want them to have fun." He turned to look at her.

"I don't want to be the out-of-touch uncle, you know? The last time they came to visit I was working so much I think we just had one family meal together in a completely inappropriate restaurant that I'd booked, not having any idea about high-chairs or why a toddler and a pre-schooler might not be ecstatic about a seafood platter or steak tartare. I think my mother gave them fish-fingers as soon as they got home, but by then I'd gone to meet a client."

"I wouldn't be too hard on yourself. It's not easy to automatically know what to do."

"No, I know, but I'd just like things to be different this time, now that I'm virtually living back at home, and also because their granny might not be around for too much longer." He looked back out of the window, leaning his hand on the frame. "Sorry, dragging the mood down."

Tess reached out to touch his arm, but stopped herself. "Look, I'm sure they'll really enjoy themselves, and make lots of happy memories. I know it's a bit trite but you don't have to do anything special, just be around and spend time with them, and, I guess, be honest about the fact that your mum is unwell. You don't need to give them too much detail, but kids can smell secrets a mile off."

He turned and their eyes met briefly in an acknowledgement of previous difficult conversations. Edward seemed to be about to say something in response, but thought better of it. Tess found herself wishing that he had shared whatever he was thinking at that moment. As always with him there was so much left unsaid. So many undercurrents and questions she wanted answered. But there had been a significant easing of tensions. In a way, the fact that they had both said such upsetting things to each other in the past few weeks freed them up to talk now with impunity. She no longer felt the low-level anxiety that one of them might misunderstand the other or over-react, she had much less fear of offending him here in his home surroundings, and wondered how much of the strained, tense demeanour she had witnessed in the hospice sprang from being in that environment. Usually it was the opposite; people often commented on how relaxing the hospice was, using words like "haven" and "sanctuary", but perhaps for Edward it was none of these things. It was somewhere way out of his comfort zone, a place he didn't understand, and his confusion put him on edge.

She decided to capitalise on this new, easier atmosphere. "Did you want to talk about anything regarding your mum?" she said. "I mean, if you did, I am very happy to. I'm not sure if you feel it would help or…?"

He shrugged. "It's okay," he said. "It's quite nice not to have to think about it today. But thanks for asking."

"No problem. Anytime."

They went back downstairs and Edward asked Tess if she wanted one more cup of tea before she headed home. He suggested they sat out on the terrace, it being such a lovely day, so she made her way out to a stone bench just beyond the back door where the cocker spaniel, Toby, was stretching out in the sunshine.

She slipped her feet out of her canvas shoes and idly stroked the dog with her toes, resting her head back against the warm yellowed stone of the house and feeling the sun beat down on her face and arms. After a few moments she became vaguely aware that in the kitchen a mobile phone was ringing. At the fifth ring she wandered over to the back door to investigate – perhaps Edward hadn't heard his phone, and given the precarious state of his mother's health it may well be urgent. But when she poked her head through from the cool shade of the utility room she saw him with the mobile in his hand, staring at the screen whilst it continued to ring out. Her eyes adjusted from the glare of the bright afternoon sun outside and she could see a tense expression on Edward's face as if he were steeling himself to answer. He still hadn't noticed Tess and she was about to say something when his expression changed, he gave a decisive nod, swiped the phone, and put it to his ear to answer. "Clara?"

Tess backed away from the door, not wanting to alert him to her presence now that she knew who was calling. Her feet were still bare and she tiptoed across the cool flagstones of the utility room, past the coats and wellies and out onto the warmer, rougher surface of the garden terrace. She resumed stroking Toby with her toes whilst trying not to eavesdrop, although at one point she heard him say, "Look, I can't talk about this now. I'll call you later." After this, she assumed he had ended the call because there was a silence broken only by the clinking of china and Edward swearing at one of the dogs who had clearly tried to snaffle an entire plateful of biscuits, before he emerged carrying a metal tray, closely followed by one of the setters, Gladys, who had the remains of a Jammy Dodger in her mouth. He placed the tray, with two mugs of tea and the plate of biscuits, down on a small wrought-iron table and glared at Gladys who was circling optimistically.

"Clara called," he said as he sat down next to Tess and passed her a mug.

"Oh. Right. All okay?" She leant forward and took a bourbon biscuit from the plate while the setter eyed her resentfully.

"She's a bit stressed," he said, looking over at Gladys. "Clara, I mean, not the dog. Although this one doesn't like getting a telling off either." He made a little gesture with his hand and Gladys trotted over to receive a conciliatory pat.

"She's got a lot on with work and she struggles a bit with the situation with Mum, to be honest. I told her you were here," he said, looking sideways at her as he picked up his mug.

"Okay."

There was a pause before he spoke again.

"I just told her about Morris and, you know, what happened, and that you'd come round to say thanks. I didn't really need to have said anything at all. She's back in London. She'd have just assumed I was here on my own." He turned to look at Tess again and held her gaze with his clear blue eyes. "But I don't want to feel I'm having to watch what I say. I like things to be straightforward, out in the open. It's not fair otherwise, is it?"

Tess wasn't entirely sure what he was asking her but made another murmur of agreement anyway. He leaned forward, rubbing the bridge of his nose.

"Look," Tess said. "I can see why she'd be a bit put out,

strange woman in your house, you know, especially given my behaviour the last time she saw me, it would make me a bit mardy. Maybe give her a call back later and explain? You've been really kind, with everything you've done for Morris; I'd hate for that to cause problems between the two of you. She'll understand."

"I'm not so sure about that!" He gave a terse laugh. "She's not the most understanding woman in the world." He looked down into his mug as if the tea might hold the answers. "But you're right. There's a perfectly reasonable explanation, and nothing for her to be concerned about. It's not as if there's anything untoward going on, is there?"

"No. Exactly." She had a sudden flashback to their bodies squeezed together, his lips on hers, their feverish attempts to remove each other's clothes, and her cheeks went crimson. "Nothing untoward at all."

A companionable silence fell between them as they both lifted their faces to the sun for a few moments and then, almost reluctantly, he extended a long arm and looked at his watch.

"It's almost two," he said. "I haven't seen Mum since yesterday evening, and I said I'd pop in today. I'd better head off."

Tess leapt up off the bench. "Oh God! Of course. I feel terrible." She started gathering the mugs and putting them back on the tray with the biscuits. "Of course, you need to go and see her instead of providing me with a constant supply of food and drinks. I'm so sorry. You should have said earlier..." She broke off mid-sentence as Edward took the tray from her. The brush of his hand against hers seemed to startle them both and they paused, looking down at their still-touching fingertips before she released the tray.

"Don't be ridiculous," he said. "Mum spent most of yesterday asleep. She is constantly on at me to go out and get some fresh air; she's always worried that I'm looking peaky, or depressed, or stressed. When I tell her that I've had a lovely morning here with you and that the house is ready for Maddie and the kids, she'll be overjoyed, honestly. I think me loitering by her bedside all day is not necessarily doing either of us much good."

Tess visibly relaxed and she slipped her shoes back on. "Well, when you put it like that," she said, "it's clearly me who's doing you the favour."

"No need for the default sarcasm; it's actually true – you have done me a favour. Today's the first day in ages that I've felt, I don't know, like a normal human being. Not worried about work, not worried about Mum..." He stopped and chewed his lip. "I mean, it really has been *ages*!"

"Good!" she said. "And I've had a lovely morning, too. A little surreal, but lovely. Thank you."

They looked at each other for a few moments, smiling and squinting a little into the sun, both reluctant to move, but then the spaniel gave a noisy yawn from beneath the bench and the spell was broken.

"Tess!" The television host was in her ear as she drove home. *"We haven't chatted for a few days, have we? It's fabulous*

to see you're doing so well." He couldn't keep the disappointment out of his voice. *"That fella from the blind date still seems keen. At least he seemed to find you moderately attractive? And now it looks like the amnesiac Adonis who barely registered your presence, other than to criticise your medical skills, is back on side? Although honestly, 'surreal but lovely'? What were you thinking? Isn't that a line out of a film?"*

Tess ignored him as she approached the suspension bridge.

"Shame he still blames you for his mum stopping chemo though. He won't have forgotten, you know. If anything goes wrong, it'll be you he'll hold responsible and all that gallant 'pet rescue' stuff will disappear."

She pulled up at the traffic lights and stared resolutely ahead.

"And he's got a girlfriend, so it's not as if it makes any difference anyway…"

She hummed a happy tune to herself, determined not to let the host get to her. She was tired, true; the night shift and adrenaline of the past few hours had caught up with her, but as she waited for the lights to change, she smiled, her thoughts drifting back to some of the conversations she and Edward had shared.

"I just don't want you making a fool of yourself, Tess. That's all. I'm only thinking of you. After all, he's bound to discover what a shabby little individual you are in the long run, isn't he?"

"Come on, Jane." Tess spoke through gritted teeth. "Help me out here."

The lights changed and she started to make her way across the bridge, the Georgian townhouses of Clifton looming into view. Jane Austen gave a sigh of satisfaction. *"So glad you called, my dear. I simply can't abide your having to indulge the company of that odious little man a moment longer than necessary. He is exceedingly unpleasant."*

"I couldn't agree more. It's no picnic having him in my head, believe me."

"Now, the other gentleman, Tess, dearest. He is an entirely different matter. One finds his company extremely tolerable. In fact, one finds oneself in quite a fever of admiration."

Tess wasn't completely sure whether she meant Edward or Simon. She'd had multiple text messages from the latter enquiring as to Morris's health, and he clearly felt terrible about not having been available to help last night. She suspected that he would have enjoyed playing the knight in shining armour, although that was a little unfair. He was really kind.

"Far be it from me to presume to know how best to proceed." Miss Austen's voice was barely audible over the rhythmic beat of the tyres on the bridge. *"Such matters are complex indeed and one must be prudent when considering potential obstacles and prior attachments. One must weigh up character, suitability, affection, admiration, and the potential for enduring love."*

Tess raised her eyebrows at this and glanced down at the swirling depths of the Severn below.

"However," Jane continued in a murmur. *"None of us wish to be in calm waters all our lives."*

Chapter Twenty-Five

Simon took Tess to collect Morris from the vet's a few days later, and as Henry had promised, he was much more mobile, although not very nimble on his feet. He didn't appear to be in any significant pain though, and she followed Flo's instructions to keep him away from stairs. She put a soft bed for him in the kitchen along with a litter tray that he tended to use with disdain, waiting until everyone else had vacated the room first. Kath thought it was hilarious: "Who knew the little fella would be so fastidious?" she laughed as Morris hovered near the tray and glared at her to leave.

Edward had been true to his word and there was no bill to pay when she went to collect Morris. Flo was adamant that the account had been settled, although she was very grateful for the flowers and chocolates, and said that she would pass the cards and bottles of whisky on to Henry and Jumbo when she saw them next. Tess knew that she was going to have to push Edward into revealing how much she owed him. She suspected, having seen his family home, that a few hundred pounds was nothing to him, but for her it felt like a weight she had to remove.

She had always been scrupulous about her finances; growing up they had counted every penny, and it was only the hardship fund through school that had allowed her to even consider applying for medicine. Had she known quite how complicated the issue regarding the vet's bills was due to become, she might have pushed harder, but the next time she saw Edward he was with his young niece and nephew and she felt embarrassed to mention it. As the television host said, *"It would be a bit vulgar Tess, and believe me, I make a living from vulgar."*

Edward was looking relaxed and happy when he arrived at the hospice with his sister Madeleine a few days later. Tess was on the phone and she waved as they trooped by, the little boy, Harvey, dressed in smart cargo shorts and a polo shirt, his younger sister, Annabelle, wearing an interesting outfit of winter tights, swimsuit, and fairy wings, her face smeared with chocolate. Madeleine was tall and imposing, like her brother, but she had a capable, down-to-earth manner and, perhaps because of her young children, she seemed a less intimidating figure. She looked anxious as they walked past and Tess realised that this would be the first time she'd have seen her mother looking quite this ill. It was bound to be a shock, and she wondered whether Edward had prepared her.

In the event, it seemed that the children were an ideal distraction from the grim realities of the situation, and if Madeleine was distressed she hid it well. After a while,

Edward stuck his head out of the door and asked Tess if maybe she could come in, as Mary was keen to introduce her to the grandchildren. Both kids were perched on Mary's bed when she walked in and she went straight up to them and shook their sticky hands.

"Well! I know exactly who you two fine, upstanding citizens are. Your granny has told me all about you, and I have to say your photos do not do you justice. I had no idea we were going to be visited by such a handsome gentleman and a proper fairy princess today – I love your outfit, by the way," she said as an aside to Annabelle.

"I'm Harvey," the little boy said, "and this is my sister Annabelle."

"Well. I'm Tess and I am very pleased to meet you!" she said, dropping them a small curtsy.

"Uncle Eddie has told us about your cat!" piped up Annabelle from the foot of the bed where she was balancing an unused disposable sick bowl on her head.

"Ah yes, the brave and valiant Morris. Your uncle came to the rescue and no mistake."

"Like a fireman?" Annabelle wanted to know.

Tess nodded slowly and looked sideways at Edward who was smiling. "Kind of, yes. Like a fireman," she said.

Annabelle beamed at her uncle and patted him proudly on the hand.

Tess turned her attention back to the little boy who was playing with the edge of the blanket on his grandmother's bed.

"And I understand that you like animals too, Harvey? Granny tells me you ride horses? But of course, I said to her,

'No, five-year-olds can't ride horses!' And I think, looking at you, that she must be wrong, because surely you are seven or eight at least?"

Harvey smiled shyly. "No," he said. "I am really five *and* I do have a pony! I ride her every day. And we have two cats and three dogs and, well, a lot of hens. They are noisy but I like them. Daddy's looking after them at the moment." He returned to plucking at the edge of the blanket. "I miss them."

"He's just like you were, Eddie," Madeleine said to her brother. "Obsessed with everything that barks, clucks, neighs, whatever."

"Hi," she reached out a hand to Tess. "I'm Madeleine. Mum has told us about you, and how much of a difference you've made to her. It's nice to meet you." Her voice was brittle; she was maintaining a brave front for the children, but her concern was evident in her eyes.

Tess shook her hand. "Likewise," she said. "I hope your journey was okay?"

"As good as a transatlantic flight with small children ever can be." She had picked up none of the American intonations of her children; her accent was exactly the same refined English as her mother and brother's.

"Hmm! Yes." Tess rolled her eyes in what she hoped was a knowing manner despite never having been on a transatlantic flight herself, let alone accompanied by children. "Now," she said, "I've got to crack on." She turned to look at the children again. "Would you like to see if we could make that into a fairy crown for you?" she asked

Annabelle, pointing to the sick bowl still on her head. "I expect I can find you some crayons?"

"I'll draw a picture of your cat," said Harvey in a serious voice.

"Good thinking," said Tess. "He would *love* that, and it might help him get better. He's a ginger tomcat, so I'll make sure we get you an orange crayon."

"Will it make Granny get better?" Harvey asked Tess. "If I draw her a picture too?"

"It might make her *feel* better, and that's very important. Why don't you find out what her favourite thing is and draw that?"

"Well that's easy." He smiled as he looked back at Mary propped up on her pillows. "Her favourite thing is me!"

"There you go then," said Tess as she opened the door. "I'll see what I can find."

A few hours later she was presented with an approximation of an orange cat lying in a hospital bed with a bandage on his head, and a stick figure wearing a pink dress standing next to him that was clearly supposed to be her.

"Now that is *fantastic*!" she said. "You've got my hair just right! Morris is going to love this." She leant down and kissed Harvey on the cheek. He blushed.

"Bye-bye Tessie," said Annabelle, running around the foyer in circles with a hand holding her crown in place. Janice had managed to locate some glitter in the relatives' room, and a fine trail of pink sparkle was settling on the linoleum.

"I suspect a lot of that is going to end up in your car,"

Tess said to Edward as he passed by the desk, laughing as he watched his niece.

"She appears to have inherited her mother's dubious craft skills. But we're off to Pizza Express anyway; I expect my car's interior will be trashed after that, if Annabelle's previous form with ice cream is anything to go by."

He and Madeleine waved as they left the building, and Tess reflected that she had not seen him looking so carefree in the entire time that she had known him. Any underlying concerns he might have had about his sister blaming him for not doing enough to support their mother seemed to have been allayed, and Tess recognised the relief of having a sibling to share some of the burden that he must be feeling.

Mary was predictably exhausted by the visit, but was beaming when Tess saw her later that day. She explained that it had been six months since she had last seen her daughter and grandchildren, having flown out to visit them for Christmas at the end of last year. The trip had been marred somewhat by Mary having to reveal her diagnosis. Madeleine had been particularly hurt that her mother had known about her cancer a full two months before telling either of her children, but Mary had downplayed the prognosis even then, not wanting to spoil her family's festive celebrations with the knowledge that the tumour had already metastasised. She had begged Madeleine not to tell Edward when he called to wish them a happy Christmas, and asked instead that she be allowed to tell him face to face when she returned. The memory of that conversation was painful: seeing the realisation dawn in his eyes, the knowledge that he may in fact have missed the last

Christmas he could have spent with his mother because he'd been too busy to leave the firm for more than the obligatory bank holiday. It had been a freezing January morning, and Edward had driven over to Bristol to collect Mary from the airport, having no inkling of the catastrophic information she was about to unleash.

"He just didn't seem to understand it at all at first," she said. "I wondered if he was being deliberately obtuse, but with hindsight it was clear that he just couldn't process the information."

Tess nodded. "Yes, I think that's quite a common reaction."

"And then of course when he did understand he went into overdrive, researching every possible treatment option, arranging second and even third opinions from private specialists in London and Manchester."

"Gosh, that must have been exhausting – for both of you?"

"Well, yes, but he needed something to *do*. Eventually he realised that I had a serious, untreatable cancer, but even then he refused to entertain the notion that I might actually die. And that is about the point when we first met you. As I'm sure you remember."

"It rings a bell." They shared a knowing smile. "He seems… I don't know, a little more accepting of it now?"

"I do hope so." Mary sighed. "I do wonder if he's just putting on a show for me though, or whether he remains completely in denial. It's interesting what the human brain can do, isn't it? He's a very rational person, but once he realised I wasn't going to pursue that last course of chemotherapy, it was almost as if he stuck his fingers in his ears and pretended he couldn't hear me."

"I guess he just didn't want it to be true?"

"Quite. Edward's a devil for repressing his feelings. He had to learn to keep his temper in check, but he applies the same control to all other emotions now, which I suspect is not terribly healthy. You never know quite what he's thinking."

"Stiff upper lip and all that."

"Yes, exactly. It was the same when his dad died. Although they weren't particularly close, which maybe makes it worse? I don't know. There's no easy way to lose a parent, is there? Let alone two."

"No. People do manage, but it is hard."

"Still, let's not dwell on that. It's been a perfect afternoon and those two are such little angels, aren't they? Tell me it's not just grandmotherly bias – they bring me so much joy!" She showed Tess the picture Harvey had drawn her – the whole family with Mary taking central position in her hospital bed.

"That certainly needs to go in pride of place."

Tess propped it up on the windowsill next to Mary's collection of photos.

"Quite the artist!" She grinned at Harvey's depiction of his uncle Edward, long and thin with enormous hands and feet, but her expression turned to one of concern as she saw Mary clutch at her stomach and take a sharp intake of breath.

"Mary?" she crossed the room back to the bed and put a hand to Mary's shoulder. "What is it? Are you in pain?"

Mary nodded. Her eyes squeezed shut and she scrabbled around with her hand on the table in front of her, reaching a sick bowl. She grabbed it and brought it under her chin just in time. She heaved and winced as she vomited up a small amount of bile and blood. Tess handed her a tissue to wipe her mouth and they both looked at the contents of the bowl.

"Good thing Annabelle had already made her crown," she said, as she rubbed Mary's back and brushed a wisp of hair out of the way.

"Hmm, yes. I don't think she realised what these are actually for." Mary pushed the bowl away. "You won't tell them, will you? Or at least, don't call them back today. I want them to be out enjoying themselves. And besides"— she dabbed her mouth with a tissue—"I'm feeling a lot better now."

Tess eyed her sceptically, seeing her hands clutch again to her stomach. "I'll get your drug chart," she said. "Let's see if we can give you something for the nausea."

Later that evening, Tess phoned her mum.

"Tess? You all right?"

"Hi, Mam. Sorry it's late. I didn't wake you, did I?"

"No, love. No bloody chance; I'm at work. Hang on, I'll get Colin to keep an eye on the till. Col! Would you mind, love? It's our Tess on phone." There was a rustling as her mum relocated somewhere more private. "There. I'm in the store cupboard now," she said. "Are you all right?"

"Yeah, sorry. I didn't mean to bother you at work. I just wanted a chat."

"Of course, pet, any time, you know that. Just a catch-up was it, or did you have summat particular on your mind? Coz if you didn't, I can tell you all about idiots we've had in this evening. That'll keep you entertained and no mistake. Colin's surpassed himself – caught a group of lads trying to nick three packs of Doritos and a bottle of Cinzano. A bottle of Cinzano, would you believe?! Gave them such an earful he reduced them to tears! And then there were—"

"Mam. I just wanted to say… I know I was mad at you about the letters."

Her mother's voice hushed slightly. "Oh, right. D'you want to talk about this now, pet?"

"It's just that, I know I was angry, but I do get it. I know why you did it and I just wanted you to know… that it doesn't matter. Well, it does, but I'm okay with it, and in the grand scheme of things, it's like… seeing patients of mine in the hospice at the moment and it just makes me think about… I don't know."

Her mum stayed silent at the other end of the phone.

"I just wanted you to know how much I love you," Tess said in a rush. "And that's the only important thing. I keep seeing people who've left it too late and they think, 'Oh, it's okay, they know I love them,' and then they're gone and the person is left wondering if they should have done more or said more or… I just wanted you to know. That's all."

There was a loud sniff from the other end of the line and a rummaging noise as her mum found a tissue. "Thank you, pet," she said. "That means a lot. I thought, I really thought

242

I'd blown it. Jake's still furious, and to be honest, I wondered if you'd ever forgive me... I can't tell you how much it means to know..." She broke down and started to cry.

Tess was crying too. "Shit, Mam, sorry. This wasn't the plan. We'll have a proper chat okay? Over the weekend maybe? I could pop home for a night?"

"That'd be lovely."

"But it was just for now, I wanted you to know I love you and it's all okay. I know you've only ever wanted the best for me and Jake. He knows it too."

Her mother sniffed again. "Got to sort me bloody face out now. Give customers a scare otherwise. Not to mention Colin."

"Oh, I think it'll take more than some streaky mascara to put Colin off, Mam. You finish your shift. I'm going to head off to bed. But I'll give you a ring tomorrow, and I'll pop up in few days' time. See if Jake's about too?"

Her mother took a deep shaky breath. "Grand. That'll be grand. Right, I'll get back to shop floor."

"Love you, Mam."

"I love you too, Tessie. So much."

"I'll see you soon."

"Yep. And Tess?"

"Yeah?"

"Thank you, pet. You don't know how much this means to me. Thank you."

Chapter Twenty-Six

The heavy clouds thudding across the sky gave the hospice an ominous grey glow the next morning and Mary was unusually subdued. Today they would get the cytology results and find out whether the cancer had spread to her lungs, and Tess wasn't sure whether her drawn expression was a result of anxiety or nausea, or both. Edward, however, seemed cheerful as he accompanied her to the ambulance. He'd brought another of Harvey's pictures and a bag of his mum's favourite sweets for the journey to their appointment at the General, and didn't appear to notice that she left them untouched. Spending time with his sister and the kids had clearly been just what he needed and Tess was glad to see him smiling and jollying his mother along, even if it seemed to be having little effect.

By the time they returned it was late afternoon. Mary smiled bravely at Tess as the paramedics helped her back to her room, but Edward did not look at her, focussing only on getting across the foyer. Tess wasn't sure whether this was deliberate; his face was impassive and she couldn't read anything into his blank expression, but she was worried. Although the atmosphere between the two of them had mellowed considerably, she had not forgotten his chilling words from their row a few months ago. If there was bad news, he would likely hold her responsible. Sure enough, the television host was around to remind her of the potential challenges ahead by muttering about medical negligence claims and charges of manslaughter.

When she went to check on them later, she found Madeleine sitting at the far end of her mum's bed. Her cheeks were red and blotchy but she looked up with gratitude as Tess entered the room, seemingly hoping that an additional person may help deflect some of the emotional burden she was struggling with. Edward was sitting by the window, studiously ignoring her. It was not her imagination; he wouldn't look at her. Instead he rose out of his chair, a tall shadow against the grey light of the window. He cleared his throat and spoke to his mother and sister.

"I'm just popping out for some fresh air."

"Really Edward? It's chucking it down out there!"

"I won't be long."

Tess moved aside as he brushed past her. His eyes were averted but she could see that they were tinged with red, and his hand shook as he opened the door to leave. She went to take his seat, still warm from his body, the atmosphere around it still smelling faintly of him.

"Now." She leaned forward. "What did the doctors tell you?"

Mary took a deep breath. "It's not the greatest news."

Madeleine muttered something into her tissue.

"Dr Brown was very kind but, yes, the fluid they took off my lungs does contain some cancerous cells."

"So, it's spreading." Madeline's bald statement was barely audible.

"Yes, dear. It's spreading. But I knew that." Mary smiled bravely at Tess. "It's fine. I feel much better and that's the important thing. I've tried telling these two"—she gestured round the room and to the door to indicate the absent Edward as well as her daughter—"that what matters now is making the most of the time I have left."

Madeline stifled a sob, her hand twisting into the tissue and shredding fragments of it over the bed. Mary ploughed on valiantly. "The staff were very kind. And the doctor was honest, which is what I wanted. He said likely weeks. Possibly months, but more likely weeks. Which I think came as a bit of a shock. Not to me so much. But Edward... I think he was still hoping I'd been miraculously cured."

Tess realised that Edward would have had to break the news to his sister, who hadn't attended the appointment. He would have heard what the consultant said and had to sit through the remainder of the appointment turning the information over in his head and working out how best to frame it for the ears of his sibling. This whilst supporting his mother and dealing with his own shock. Her chest felt tight at the thought of it.

"He's trying not to show it, but there is a part of him

that really thought more chemo might cure Mum," Madeleine said to Tess. "I did try to tell him that it seemed unlikely, but he was pinning his hopes on her carrying on with the treatment and…" She turned to her mother. "I think he blames himself for not persuading you to keep going."

Mary sighed. "Dr Brown said there was little evidence another course of chemotherapy would have made much difference, darling, but even if it had, I wouldn't have wanted endless months of feeling dreadful." She reached out to take her daughter's hand. "Far better to have had a shorter time with my family and felt well enough to enjoy it. I did try and talk to Edward about it but once he'd heard the words 'possible cure' it was like he couldn't hear anything else."

"Mummy," said Madeleine, "to be fair to Eddie, I suspect he just didn't feel qualified to have that conversation with you. He maybe thought he wouldn't be able to do it justice."

"Perhaps. But he shouldn't get cross if there is someone else around, someone professional, who will listen and give me an honest view. He thinks I was somehow talked out of further treatment, but he has to learn that I am a grown woman, capable of making my own decisions."

"I know, but I think he associates Dr Carter with so much of what is going on here… And he's upset. It feels like nothing makes sense anymore."

Madeleine had started twisting the tissue in her hand again. Tess resisted the urge to offer her another, not wanting to draw attention to her obvious distress. "How are *you* both feeling about the results?" she asked.

"Oh, I knew already," said Mary. "From the moment I saw the doctor's face, the one who drained off the fluid. He said something to his colleague about it being bloodstained and they gave each other a look and… I've seen that look before, on other doctors' faces. So, no surprises for me today, I'm afraid. Much harder for you, darling." She looked towards her daughter.

"I have to be honest." Madeleine looked down at her hands again. "I am frightened." She rubbed at a patch of dry skin on her wrist. "Mainly by the timescale. I mean, weeks… It seems so very short."

She raised her eyes in silent appeal to Tess, as if she might be able to extend the prognosis, prolong the stay of execution. Tess nodded but looked away; she could offer nothing, and she didn't want to fall into the very easy trap of providing false hope.

"I think it's worse because we don't know what to expect," Madeleine carried on. "I've never seen somebody… I mean been with someone when they are…"

"Dying?"

Madeleine nodded, her lips pressed together in a thin white line.

"Would it help," Tess looked back at Mary, "if I asked Dr Fielding to talk you through it? I mean, he can't give you an exact timetabled sequence of events, but he knows an awful lot about the usual pattern."

Mary nodded emphatically and Madeleine spoke again,

"That would be really helpful. And I think it would be good for Eddie to hear too."

"Of course. I expect he'd find it easier coming from Dr Fielding anyway. I'll see if he's free. Maybe sometime tomorrow?"

"I think Edward said that Clara might be popping in tomorrow as well?" Mary looked at Madeleine, who gave a derisory snort.

"Madeleine! Whilst it's nice to see you more animated, please do be kind. It's not easy for her either. She barely knows us, and she's been saddled with an awful load of emotional baggage. It's not easy for anybody, is it?" Mary looked back at Tess.

"No," she said. "You're right. It's not."

"It is hard to navigate a clear path when assailed by rumour and suspicion," said Miss Austen as Tess pulled the door shut behind her, *"but candour and truth are a promising beginning. And it was a wise choice, Tess, to involve those with greater experience and expertise; for as one observes good practice, one learns, and as one learns, one grows and—"*

"I know, Jane," Tess interrupted. "I know. But I've only got a few weeks left working here before I start general practice, and there seems to be a ridiculous amount of learning and growing I still need to do in that time."

Chapter Twenty-Seven

That evening, Tess went out to the cinema with Simon. They watched an action movie, which wouldn't have been Tess's first choice, but it was strangely soothing to be able to switch off from everything else that was going on in her life and simply concentrate on good guys and bad guys, interspersed with weapons-grade explosives. After the film they walked out onto the riverside in the warm July air and Simon held her hand. Tess felt oddly calm. She never really spoke to Simon about work, and he had no idea of the current tensions, or indeed attachments, between her and the various members of the Russell family – just as he didn't know about Scott, or her dad, or any of the other baggage she was currently lugging about with her. His lack of curiosity was helpful in this instance. Simon listened when she needed him to and asked no questions. He was uncomplicated. Life was easy with him: no volatility, no moods to interpret or strong opinions to grapple with, no crimson flushes of embarrassment or moments of nervous anticipation. He was a straightforward, nice, dependable guy, and if being with him wasn't particularly exciting, well, neither was it stressful – and she had plenty of the latter on her plate already.

"How's that pussy of yours?" he asked, turning to face her with a cheeky grin on his face.

"Morris is fine, thank you very much," she said. It wasn't the first time he'd made this joke, although he still thought it hilarious. "Thanks for offering to have him when I'm in France."

"No problem, although probably best that your mum's going to have him, thinking about it," he said. "Especially with the litter tray and everything. The flat would never recover. I always say when I'm showing clients round places, you can tell when someone's had a pet, even if it's only a budgie. Never smells the same after."

"Yeah, you're right. Anyway, Mum loves having him. She'll spoil him rotten. He'll come back even fatter, if that's possible."

They crossed over the footbridge, navigating their way between other couples and families out enjoying the light evening.

"I've only got one more week at the hospice after I get back," she said as he swung her arm back and forward in time with their walk. The action reminded her of Harvey and Annabelle swinging arms as they raced around the hospice courtyard. "From France, I mean. It'll be weird not working there. I'm going to really miss everyone. All my patients, all the staff. They feel almost like family."

They carried on further up the riverside walk, watching

the gulls swooping down to the water and back. "And I've got a pretty full-on day tomorrow," she said. "Tricky conversation to have with relatives first thing, the ward's already really busy, Rob's on annual leave, and we've got medical students coming for teaching in the afternoon."

Simon nodded and looked to be deep in thought. She wondered if he was going to offer some insight into how to manage her current workload, or advice about how to adapt to the transition between different working environments when she left the hospice at the end of the month.

"Chips or curry?" he said eventually.

"What?"

"Which d'you fancy? I'm thinking curry. I could murder a balti and a Peshwari naan."

She nodded in agreement. "Throw in some poppadoms and you're on," she said, smiling as they pushed open the door to The Star of India.

"Good Morning, Dr Carter. I'm not sure whether you know Edward's girlfriend, Clara Delaney?"

"Oh yes, thank you, Mary. Miss Delaney and I have already met, very briefly. Hello again." Tess reached out a hand in greeting, a little embarrassed by the memory of her rudeness at their last meeting.

Clara was standing near the window with Edward. He was dressed smartly as usual, but she outdid him for sophistication, wearing an expensive tailored suit with elegant heels and clutching a designer handbag as if her life depended on it. Indeed, it seemed to take an extraordinary force of will to peel her fingers away from the clasp and return the handshake. Her skin was damp and cold, her hand bony and fragile in Tess's grasp, and she felt a twinge of sympathy for the woman. The veneer of poise was only just masking her obvious and rising anxiety at being in a building of this type and in such close proximity to the terminally ill. She was clearly very uncomfortable in these surroundings and Tess was reminded of Edward restlessly drumming his fingers against the countertop when he had first arrived in February. For most people, the first visit to a hospice was not easy and she tried to speak kindly when she addressed Clara.

"Mrs Russell had asked to have a chat about the likely sequence of events over the coming weeks and months. Specifically, to talk about the events leading up to dying."

She noticed both Clara and Edward flinch at the word but continued: there was no point in pretending that she or her consultant were going to be anything other than honest during today's discussion. She owed Mary that at least.

"Dr Fielding is just finishing off a patient in clinic. Sorry, unfortunate phrasing. He's just finishing *with* a patient, and then he'll be right along."

She paused, noticing a tiny smile at the corner of both Mary and Madeleine's mouths and, feeling that she may start giggling herself, she turned her attention to Clara.

"I realise that this may be a tricky conversation to hear, and if anybody would be more comfortable leaving the room and maybe approaching him, or me, or indeed any of the other doctors later in the day, that would be fine."

Clara breathed an audible sigh of relief as she moved towards the door; she appeared to be on the verge of breaking into a run.

"I'll wait outside. I'm terribly sorry but it's not really my thing. A bit too um… you know."

"That's completely understandable." Tess held the door for her, wondering whether this woman could really not bring herself to be outside her comfort zone for a few moments in order to support her boyfriend.

"You could always take a seat in the relatives' room? Or the café does some nice cakes and biscuits…" Tess called after her.

"Sounds delightful…" Her words were disappearing across the linoleum as she scuttled away.

Tess noticed Edward direct the tiniest of smiles to the floor. The door swung to a close and the atmosphere lifted almost immediately.

"I don't think cakes and biscuits are really 'Clara's thing' either," said Madeleine. "Too much in the way of carbs, I suspect."

"Madeleine!"

"Sorry Mummy. But they're not, are they Eddie? I simply meant that she doesn't like baked goods very much. Nothing more."

Mary gave her daughter a warning look. Tess glanced at Edward. "Mr Russell, would you like a seat? I can get another from the desk?"

He shifted back towards the windowsill and leant

against it. "No, I'll be fine here," he said, still unable to meet her eye. "Thank you."

There was a knock at the door and Dr Fielding entered. He peered at the assembled crowd over the top of his glasses.

"Morning all! Tess, dear, would you like to get another chair from the relatives' room?"

"Oh, no, it's okay, Dr Fielding. I'll stand." She positioned herself in the opposite corner from Edward, focussing her attention on the bed and the people gathered round it.

"Right." Dr Fielding pulled his chair closer to the bed. "Excellent. Mrs Russell, you're looking well. Tess – Dr Carter – mentioned that you had a few questions, things on your mind? Is that right? She thought perhaps you might have some specific concerns, things I could help with?"

"Yes, there are questions." Madeleine said, flipping to page one in her notebook, but Mary interrupted her.

"What I want to know, Dr Fielding, is what will actually happen. How will I die?"

Edward gave a sharp intake of breath from the other side of the room but said nothing.

"Okay," Dr Fielding began. "I'm guessing that you haven't been with someone who is dying of a similar condition to yours? Maybe you haven't seen anybody die? Most people haven't."

"Only my husband," Mary said. "And I wasn't even there when it happened. He was on the coronary care unit. I'd popped out to make a phone call and the next thing I knew there was a sign on the door saying 'Do not Enter'. He'd had the entire cardiac arrest team and two coronary care nurses trying to resuscitate him for twenty minutes. I didn't even get a chance to say goodbye."

Tess slid the box of tissues along the table towards Mary.

"Thank you, Dr Carter."

Dr Fielding waited until Mary had finished dabbing her eyes.

"Well. That is not an uncommon scenario with a death in hospital. People can feel quite distanced from their loved one at the end. The doctors intervene and become the conduit for that experience, so it is not shared by those who perhaps need or want to be involved."

"Yes, it did feel like that. But it also felt as though that was normal. As though it was best that he had died surrounded by doctors and nurses."

"Well, in a way, it probably was. Because his death was unexpected and therefore most families want to know that everything to potentially reverse it has been tried. But with you we can plan better, try to make it as comfortable as possible for you and those around you."

Edward's shoes squeaked as he shifted position but Tess did not turn to look at him. She was watching Dr Fielding, trying to commit his words to memory.

"Now, people who have similar conditions to you, and who are being managed by a specialist palliative care team, do not tend to die in this traumatic way. It is often peaceful. There is rarely pain, but if that becomes an issue, we can deal with it."

"Well, that's a relief."

"Yes, I know. It worries patients a lot, but the reality is that most people simply become tired, they spend more time sleeping, and as they get closer to the end they may sleep very deeply, and even lose consciousness every now and then."

There was absolute silence in the room.

"Are you happy for me to go on?" he asked, and Mary nodded.

"So, when and if you do become unconscious, it is not painful or distressing, it's basically just being in a coma. And if you are in a coma, we wouldn't want to wake you up just to give you tablets or medicine, so we set up a syringe driver to allow you to have those medications through a tiny tube beneath the skin. That means we can control your pain and any other symptoms without needing to disturb you. You can choose whether you want additional sedation, or whether you want to be as alert as possible right until the end, but either way your body will need to rest and your energy will reduce... Still okay, Mrs Russell?"

"I'm completely fine with it, doctor. Thank you."

"Everyone else, all fine for me to continue?"

Tess could see Edward look over to the consultant and nod for him to keep talking. He was chewing his lip. Dr Fielding resumed.

"So, you will be spending less and less time awake each day until eventually you will slip into a coma for the last time. We don't know when that will be; there are clues sometimes, patterns of breathing that alert us. Often patients seem to know themselves, but it is rarely a Hollywood-style eloquent speech that we hear. Last words are usually brief because most people in your situation have had ample opportunity to say everything they wanted to say to their loved ones in the preceding days and weeks."

"Yes, that's one of the advantages, I suppose."

"Exactly. It's not like it was with your husband. There's time at least for people to become acclimatised. It's still just as upsetting of course, but less sudden and dramatic."

"Yes, okay."

"So, you see, there's no mystery really. People create an idea about dying based on what they see on television, or maybe things they've heard in the papers about violent crimes or death during war or famine, and it's a million miles removed from the normal process that we see occurring here every day. People are frightened about losing their dignity, or being in pain, but as I've said, most of that can be controlled, and if you discuss your fears then we can usually address them and provide reassurance." He peered over his glasses again and tapped his hands against his thighs. There was a momentary silence.

"Well, you've certainly done that," Mary said. "I really appreciate your taking the time to explain it all."

"Good." He smiled. "I'm glad it was helpful. I'd better get back to clinic now, but if you have any further questions just let one of us know."

Tess snuck a look at Edward who was still resting against the window ledge, his expression impenetrable. "Do you want me to ask Miss Delaney to come back in?" she asked. Edward nodded but did not look up. "Thank you," he said.

Clara was perched on a wooden bench outside the main entrance, flicking through her phone. She cut an isolated figure, unable and seemingly unwilling to show solidarity with the tight little family unit currently gathered in Mary's room. She regarded Tess warily. "Finished, are they?"

"Just now. I think they found it quite helpful."

"Good, good." She gave a long, slow exhalation with her eyebrows raised; clearly this day was going just as badly as she had expected. "I've got to head off soon actually, get to a meeting… you know how it is." She looked back at her phone.

Tess toyed with the idea of saying something more but limited herself to a, "Whatever you think is best," before heading inside. The woman seemed to have no comprehension of how to behave, but it was not Tess's job to tell her.

Clara stood, almost reluctant to move back into the building, but once Tess had returned inside she seemed to gather herself and clipped back across to Mary's room with more confidence. She didn't remain in there for long, emerging twenty minutes later to ask Tess to call her a taxi.

"Your chat appears to have worked wonders," she said tightly. "They're certainly very impressed by your consultant, and Edward has always, well – almost always – spoken very highly of you. But then I suspect this is all very familiar to you, isn't it?" She gestured vaguely towards the patients' rooms. "I think it's remarkable that some people would choose to spend their working life doing this. I simply couldn't. I find the whole thing terrifying."

It seemed to Tess that Clara was not trying to be rude, just honest. If she had known her better, she would have advised her to swallow her pride and admit to the family, rather than to her, that she found the scenario difficult. She could reach out to her boyfriend who so desperately needed support, even if she felt unable to shoulder the practical burden. But Tess didn't know her, and she was not in a position to give her that sort of advice; she suspected that it would be taken very badly and then probably ignored or dismissed as meddling and interference. Instead she replied that she enjoyed her job in spite of its challenges and suggested that Clara ask Janice on reception about booking a taxi because she had to go and see a patient.

"*Do not seek to judge the poor woman too harshly,*" murmured Jane Austen as Tess gathered the notes for the new admission. "*For seldom have I witnessed a figure more discomfited by mere proximity to grief. And whilst her honesty is refreshing, her command of the situation and her own reaction to it is stretched so thin as to be almost entirely absent.*"

Chapter Twenty-Eight

B y the following week it had become clear that Mary
Russell was deteriorating rapidly. Madeleine had
returned on several occasions, bringing the children with
her, but since the weekend she had attended alone,
concerned her mother would find them exhausting. She and
Edward took turns sitting with Mary or staying at home
with Harvey and Annabelle. Mary was, as predicted,
spending more time sleeping, drifting in and out of
consciousness, and Dr Fielding had been in to have another
frank discussion with the family regarding planning for an
end that now appeared to be imminent. Tess also had
conversations with Mary during her lucid periods, where
she stated a clear desire to die at home. She often drifted
into mild confusion and would describe the Georgian
manor house at length, forgetting that Tess had seen it
already, a fact that had delighted her when she'd initially
been told. Tess found Mary's ramblings soothing and her

obvious love of the house, the grounds, and the memories they held for her made Tess more determined to help Mary achieve her wish of returning. At some points she clearly thought she was already there, back on the estate; she would advise Tess of lists of instructions for the groundsmen and housekeeper, and her face would light up as she described the large oak trees she could see from the window, the smell of the flowers, how the dogs barked and the horses whinnied in the fields beyond. For her children, though, her confusion was becoming more distressing. Tess often found Madeleine in tears, holding her mother's hand and whispering, "But Mum, it's me. It's Maddie," when Mary was at her most disorientated and thought her daughter a stranger.

Once the medical team were confident that Mary's symptoms were well controlled, arrangements were made to transfer her back home the next day. Tess went to check on her during her evening shift and was pleased to see her sitting upright, much more alert and orientated than she had been. Mary patted the bed. Her voice when she spoke was a whispery thread.

"Come and talk to me, Dr Carter. If you're not too busy?"

"Of course," said Tess. "I'd love to." Rather than sitting on the bed, she pulled up a chair. "Don't want to squash you. Now, are you after small talk, or big, deep, and meaningful? I know I'm not likely to get you on your own again."

"Oh, just hearing a happy voice is enough; everyone is

being so terribly gloomy. Tell me about you – what are you up to this weekend? Or is it the weekend now? I'm losing track."

"Well, today's Wednesday, but actually I'll be spending most of the weekend packing to go on holiday. Do you want me to tell you about it, or will it make you mad with jealousy?"

"No, no. Do tell me. I love to believe you have a life outside of here, away from all of this."

Tess told Mary about the planned trip. She was going to the South of France with Kath for a few nights, and it would be the first holiday she had been on in over a year. She was excited, but also aware as she was talking that the chances of Mary still being alive when she returned were low, which added a certain poignancy to her description. Still, she told Mary about the hotel they had booked and what she was going to wear on the flight, where she was getting her nails done, and how she was hoping to keep Kath on the straight and narrow.

"She's a bit of a wild card, my housemate. Which makes for excellent entertainment but is not the most conducive to relaxation."

"I can imagine."

Mary's eyes were sunken but still bright and her eyelids fluttered as she struggled to keep them open. She reached out a hand to Tess who took it in hers, Mary's sallow skin, fragile and thin as parchment, contrasting with the healthy warm olive tone of her own. Mary looked down at them, "You have beautiful hands. Kind hands."

"Thank you. That's a very lovely thing to say."

"No ring on there?" She tapped Tess's fourth finger lightly. "But of course you're far too young to be married. Still, it would be nice to know you had someone who cares for you as much as you care for others."

Tess could feel her throat tightening and a sharp prickling at the backs of her eyes. The last thing she wanted for Mary to endure was more of someone else's tears, so she swallowed the sensation away.

"Mrs Russell, please don't let your final words be asking me why I'm still single," she said with a shaky laugh.

But Mary was pushing herself up in the bed to sit a little straighter. She clearly had something she wanted to get off her chest.

"Dr Carter," she began, "what I really wanted to say was thank you. No…" she batted away Tess's protestations and continued. "Thank you for putting your feelings to one side when it came to dealing with my family." She took another slow rattling breath and Tess did not interrupt her. "Thank you for all that you've done, and I'm sure will continue to do for many others after me. It eases my passing from this world to know that there are people like you left in it."

"That's, well, of course it's…" Tess gave up her composure at this point and let the tears flow. She was aware of how lucky she was to be present for one of Mary's rare moments of clarity and hoped that her son would make it in time to see his mother like this again. As if intuiting her wishes, there was a brisk but gentle knock at the door. It opened, and Edward entered the room. He stood for a moment, taking in the scene. Tess stood to leave, but knowing this might be the last time she had the chance, she bent and whispered in Mary's ear, "It's been a privilege – honestly. You take care." And with that she left the room, her tears distorting the image of Edward's concerned face as he held the door for her.

It was nine-thirty and Tess had completed all her tasks on the ward, all of her patients were comfortable, and she was due to finish her shift in half an hour. She felt drained by her recent conversation with Mary Russell, so made herself a cup of tea and curled up on the sofa in one of the sitting rooms, preferring this to the more remote office that the medical team used for their handovers. She turned the television on and idly flicked through the channels, not finding anything that took her fancy but needing some distraction. She settled on a wildlife documentary and was watching a family of otters in their river habitat when there was a knock on the open door and in walked Edward Russell. She could see straight away that he was a mess. His handsome face was contorted in pain, almost crumpling in on itself; his shirt was untucked and looked as if he had slept in it. She had never seen him looking more dishevelled.

"I'm sorry. I just had to get out of there. I can't let her see me like this."

He sank heavily into the chair on the opposite side of the room to Tess. She rose to leave.

"It's fine! That's what this room's here for – exactly that

reason." She was gabbling, knowing how much he would hate having been caught at such a vulnerable moment. "It's certainly not meant for junior doctors to be learning about the behaviour of otters!" She moved towards the door.

"No. Stay." He cradled his head in his hands, his fingers curled into his hair as if he were about to rip it out at the roots. His voice became muffled by his shirt. "Please. I don't want to be on my own."

He started to cry in earnest then, sobs wracking his body. Tess was torn but she couldn't possibly leave him there like that, and not when he had specifically asked her to be with him. She closed the door to give him some privacy as one of the porters crossed the foyer beyond. In any other scenario she would have been across the other side of the room like a shot, soothing, consoling, offering a shoulder to cry on. She didn't believe in standing on ceremony with patients or families; they needed to know that their grief was normal, and that they could share it with her. Edward Russell was different though; she was still wary of getting too close.

She walked tentatively over to the armchair, in the way that one might approach a wounded tiger. There was a box of tissues on the table and she held them out in front of him as she placed a cautious hand on his shoulder. She could feel the heat of his skin through his shirt as his muscles contracted in shuddering sobs. They stood that way for a few moments as his grief forced its way out of him, like an animal clamouring to escape. Eventually, the tension beneath Tess's fingers seemed to ease a little; she could feel all the muscles of his shoulder and neck start to relax as his breathing slowed. He lifted his head; she kept her hand where it was and bent to look at him.

"I know how hard this must be. I really do. But you have done such a great job of looking after her – and taking her home is the right thing to do. She'll be happier there."

She could see the conflicting emotions play out on his face: sorrow, helplessness, indignation, outrage. Without warning he stood and turned towards her.

"*How* do you know? You don't understand how this feels." His breath was hot on her face.

"I simply meant…"

Tess was against the wall and Edward's face was inches from hers. His distress was raw and would have been frightening if it had not been for the look of panic in his eyes. She reached out to touch his arm gently and he moved back a fraction, realising even in the midst of his anger that his posture was intimidating.

"I don't need your platitudes. You don't get it, do you?" His voice quietened and cracked with emotion. "There is a part of me that wants to blame you for your role in this, but then there is another part of me that doesn't know how we would have got through it without you."

"Edward, please. Sit back down. Let's talk about this…"

He shook his head as if trying to clear the fog of confusion and his eyes fixed back on hers. She couldn't look away. His pupils were dilated and all that remained of the irises was a halo of blue. The lashes were fringed with tears, which he angrily wiped away as he continued.

"It is *so* hard, having to deal with my feelings for you on top of everything else. All this being raked up again. And I know it's not fair, but then the whole thing is unfair. This entire situation… there's nowhere for me to go with this. I can't deal with it, I just can't, I don't know—"

He broke off, unable to complete the sentence. She could see the frustration in his face and went to speak again but suddenly his mouth was on hers, hard and insistent, his tears wet against her skin. He placed both his palms to her cheeks, the power of his need for her overwhelming both of them. But she didn't push him away. Without knowing what she was doing, her body responded to him automatically, slipping back in time. Five years ago; Dan's sitting-room floor; the two of them pressing together. Although, this was different. This was ferocious. She was caught up in his rage, as angry as he was. She wanted to punish him in the same way that he wanted to punish her, both needing to purge themselves of these violent emotions, to transfer them to the other and be rid of them. His mouth was hot against hers and she had her hands around his back, clutching at him, forcing him closer until there was barely breath left in her body.

And then, just as suddenly, he pulled away, still holding her face in his hands but tenderly now, a look of utter bewilderment in his eyes. He stroked his thumb against her cheek and then dropped his hands to his sides.

"I am so sorry," he said, squeezing his eyes shut. "Oh Christ. I am such a fucking mess! I'm so sorry."

He put a hand to his own face, covering his eyes, but warding her off with the other hand as she came towards him. She stayed back then, pressed against the wall, still breathing heavily as he turned and left the room, the door slamming and disturbing the peaceful twilight of the foyer. He stumbled across it, through the double doors and out into the night air.

Chapter Twenty-Nine

Tess stood looking at the door in disbelief. Her face was flushed and a warmth had spread down her throat. She sank into the chair that Edward had been sitting in only moments earlier. Her legs felt weak and she put her hands on her thighs to stop them shaking. Her head was a whirl of mixed emotions, but beneath that there was a fire in the pit of her stomach. The adrenaline was pumping and she was certainly not going to be able to switch it off. She felt as if she could run a marathon to burn up all the energy, but deep down she knew what she needed.

She ran her tongue over her bruised lips and stood, decided. Her shift was over. She checked in with Rob who was working nights; he was happy everybody was stable. Tess didn't feel particularly stable herself. She felt unhinged.

"You all right?" Rob asked.

She nodded, mutely.

"You sure? You look a bit... feverish? There's a bout of summer flu going round; two of the nurses are off with it."

"No, Rob, it's okay. I feel fine. Just want to get home, you know."

"Yeah, of course."

She turned to leave.

"Um, Tess?"

"Yeah?"

"Um, I was wondering, if, well, if you weren't busy, I don't know, over the next few weeks, maybe, if you, um, wanted—"

"Rob, sorry. I've got to head off. If you want to talk about swapping shifts or something we can do that tomorrow maybe?"

"Oh, yes, of course. Sorry. Absolutely. Okay, well, drive carefully." He continued to watch her as she left through the foyer, swinging her bag onto her shoulder and she didn't see him aim a tiny kick of frustration at the door to the coffee room.

She emerged into the warm July night. The sun had recently set and the darkness was not yet impenetrable. Tess knew Edward would be here, in the gardens. She suddenly felt so feral that she could almost sniff him out. And after all, she *knew* him. She really did know him. That first night together had meant something, she was sure of it. Even if he'd forgotten, part of him had been imprinted on her ever since. And she was so sick of being passive. All the rage that had built up since discovering Scott in bed with Luke was bubbling up and exploding out of her. She was fed up with being the reasonable one, the kind one, the amenable one, the one who had always done as she'd been told. It was astounding that she had waited so many years to confront her mother about her stringent rules. Their argument in May had proved to be so cathartic, she wished she had vented her feelings much earlier. So why hadn't she thrashed things out with Scott as she had so recently with her mum? He was much more deserving of her anger. She should have responded in the moment, rained blows upon him, hurt him as he had hurt her; should have yelled at him, railed against the injustice of it, but instead she had been calm, sad, sensible. Numbed into an acceptance that she didn't truly feel or deserve and then left with useless fury.

And now Edward, letting her slip from his memory as though she meant nothing, forgetting those moments that she had cherished for years, and when he finally had acknowledged her existence, treating her as dispensable, using her as an emotional punching bag whenever he needed. She seemed to be forever the recipient, letting things be done to her, words said to her, insults and accusations hurled at her, just for her to absorb them. He had made the same mistake as Scott, confusing her compliance with weakness. Well, he was wrong. He had sought her out tonight; he had initiated that encounter. He had kissed her, brought all these feelings to the surface again, roused her blood. And then he had run away from what he'd started, leaving her with no outlet for this restless, febrile energy. Enough. No more submission.

"Life should not always be weary resignation and acceptance.

Always prudence and honour and duty. Examine your heart. You are the mistress of yourself."

Jane was right. Tess felt a surge of defiance: she was in control; she was going to find Edward.

"A note of caution though, Tess, dear." She sounded a little alarmed. *"These violent feelings and passions are apt to —"*

"Miss Austen," said Tess, "I am going to have to ask you to absent yourself for a moment. This may prove to be a little too much."

A path led off to her right, round the back of the building and deep into a wooded copse, where there was a cabin for patients and families to escape the more clinical environment of the hospice. The walking group also used it as a base for a warming drink at a halfway point, but she knew it would be empty at this time of night, and she suspected Edward may have found his way there. She followed the path, like a predator – all of her senses were heightened: she heard the snap of twigs underfoot, the rustle of leaves as she entered the copse, the smell of warm pine from the floor, and the chill of a breeze lifting the hairs on the backs of her arms. The cabin door was ajar and he was sitting outside on the edge of the veranda. She couldn't see his face clearly but his posture was wretched, his shoulders hunched up round his neck. The desire to relieve some of his pain and suffering, to jolt him back to life, matched her own need for release. He looked up as he heard her approach and went to speak but she shook her head. She could see that the hunger was still in him, battling with the despair. Taking hold of his hand, she led him into the cabin.

Once inside, keeping hold of his hands, she kissed him hard on the mouth. He seemed to understand that no words were required, that to try and explain or rationalise what was about to happen would be impossible. He surrendered to her, his mouth yielding as she pressed hers against him. Her fingers were unbuttoning his shirt and she laid her palms flat across his chest, feeling his heart thudding beneath. They looked at each other for a moment, breathing hard, pausing, checking that they both knew what was happening. And then their bodies were drawn irresistibly back together. She started unbuckling his belt, forcing his clothes down, all the while kissing him and not letting him speak. She didn't want to think; she just wanted to feel. Feel him. The drive was overwhelming. She was dizzy with the power of it.

She pushed him down onto the bench so he was seated in front of her and slipped off her underwear, climbing up to sit astride him where she could feel how much he wanted her. She guided his hands to her thighs, increasing the pressure down onto him until he was inside her. He drew a sharp intake of breath, but before he could make another sound, she silenced him again by putting her mouth back on his and kissing him feverishly. His hands gripped her tightly and she could feel waves of heat rippling through her body from where she was pressed against him, until at last she was lost, gasping into the beams of moonlight filtering through the window.

She held him like that for a few moments, cradled into her, his face against her chest, her arms around his shoulders, every part of her in contact with him as their breathing slowed and then, without a word, she pulled her clothes back on and slipped out of the cabin. She had no remorse; she was without shame. Their desire had been mutual and equal, she was sure of it. Instead, she felt strong, and so very alert, like an animal woken from hibernation – aware of the blood pumping through her veins, the warm air entering her lungs, every inch of her skin tingling with satisfaction. It was true what they said about sex and death, she reflected as she got into her car. Never had she needed more proof of her own vitality, and here was her body giving her that reminder. You are here. You are alive.

———

Edward meanwhile made his way home in a daze. The emotional turmoil of the past few hours had tipped him to a point of nervous exhaustion and he was relieved, on returning to the house, to find that Madeleine and the children were already in bed. Maddie had left a note to say that she would do the early shift at the hospice and hopefully accompany their mother home that morning. He poured himself a drink and went to sit out on the terrace, the warmth of the evening sun still radiating back from the flagstones as the bats wheeled in the darkness. He closed his eyes and leant his head back against the rough stone of the house, slowing his breathing. What had happened with Tess? he hardly knew how to frame it into words. And yet, it had seemed at the time to be the most natural thing in the world, as if of course this was where they would end up.

But now he was going to have to put things right. He could not ignore what had happened; he was not one of those men who could breeze in and out of the lives of multiple women, and the prospect of spinning a web of deceit was as exhausting as it was repellent. He knew enough of life to understand that good people did bad things, and that the mark of a man was how he responded in the aftermath. With this in mind, he placed his glass on the floor beside him, pulled out his phone, and dialled Clara's number.

Chapter Thirty

K ath was already asleep when Tess got home that night and for once she was relieved, feeling that she wanted to get what had happened straight in her mind before sharing any of it. She felt invincible as she lay in bed. It was as if a fire had been ignited deep within her. She wanted to be with Edward again. She was not used to feeling out of control, and it was not a sensation she had ever sought, but her body had seemed to act on impulse alone. Emotionally and physically exhausted, she slipped into a deep, heavy sleep and that night she dreamed of him – his mouth on hers, his hands on her skin.

She woke the next morning drenched in sweat, tangled in her sheets, and feeling utterly wretched. The euphoria had drained away and the enormity of what she had done hit her hard; a fistful of guilt punched into her stomach. She was not remotely surprised to find the first voice in her ear was the television host.

"*Tess!*" he crowed. "*What. Have. You. Done? You naughty girl! You've scared old Jazza off, you know. She's still having an attack of the vapours. Most unimpressed at the indelicate situation you've put yourself in. And don't think it's been easy for me either. I've had to reschedule an entire week for this. The, 'I banned my prostitute sister from our grandmother's funeral because she's a thief' episode is on hold.*" He was barely able to contain his joy at this, her most recent – and perhaps worst – fall from grace. "*But really, SO great to have you back on the show. Give Tess a warm welcome everyone!*"

The applause was deafening but this time was also accompanied by jeering and taunts. The baying mob turning nasty.

"*What about Simon? Lovely, kind, attentive Simon?*" he hissed. "*How could you do this to him? When he's been so understanding about your reluctance to 'get too physical'? Didn't see you having any qualms about getting too physical last night!*" The audience booed. "*And what about Clara? I mean, we all know she was a chilly bitch, but did she deserve this?*"

He was right. She hadn't been fair to Simon, and as for Clara, it didn't matter that her only encounters with the woman had shown her to be cold and snooty. Tess had certainly never liked her, but she didn't deserve to be on the receiving end of a betrayal. Nobody did. She lay for a few moments as the remorse caught up with the memory of last night, the strong emotional re-connection she had felt with Edward gradually tainted by the shame of her actions. She cried quietly to herself, the tears running in tiny rivers and pooling in her ears and her hair. She realised that she wanted him even now, wanted him here in her bed, to hold her and tell her she wasn't a bad person after all.

But she was; the cold, hard facts were that she had been prepared to destroy someone else's relationship to get what she wanted. This in itself disgusted her. She was not a selfish person. She was not *that* woman – was she?

She got up and dragged herself around the house, getting reading for work, having no idea what she was going to say when she next saw Edward. She was torn between wanting desperately to be in his physical presence and anxiety about how they could behave normally after what had happened. The guilt pressed in on her from all sides as she approached the hospice building, suffocating her, making her want to take strangers to one side and confide in them, just to relieve herself of the burden. But when she arrived, there was no sign of him, and the realisation resulted in a combined sensation of disappointment and relief. She saw that Madeleine was there instead, sitting in the foyer waiting for the ambulance to arrive to collect Mary and take her home. She saw Tess and smiled but her attention was elsewhere, and Tess was grateful to be able to slip away without having to maintain a brittle veneer of composure.

Mary Russell left the hospice for the last time at ten o'clock on that sunny Thursday morning. Many of the staff came to wave her off, all aware that they were unlikely to see her again. People had become accustomed to her gentle good manners, and her kindly attentions to those who were looking after her. She knew the names of every nurse, cleaner, porter, and doctor in the building, and for many she knew important little details about their lives that had made a difference to their day as well as hers. Most patients spent only a brief time at the hospice and whilst every effort was made not to have favourites, those who were regulars were bound to have a closer attachment to the staff than those whose stay was fleeting. Dave came out of the kitchen, Janice waved from reception, and Farida gave Mary's hand a squeeze as she said goodbye.

As the trolley was wheeled out by Bill, the same paramedic who had first brought Mary into the hospice five months ago on that cold February day, Tess, who had been waiting by the sliding doors, asked if they could stop for a moment. She bent to kiss Mary on the cheek. "Goodbye," she said, smoothing the wispy strands of Mary's remaining hair back from her forehead. They shared a look; there was nothing more to say.

Madeleine, who was walking alongside the trolley carrying Mary's suitcase, embraced Tess quickly. "Thank you so much," she said. "We'll keep you posted." She said a louder thank-you to the others assembled, and then they were gone.

Again, Tess was grateful for a busy shift that day and ward work kept her occupied until the early afternoon when things began to settle down. She was sorting through paperwork at the desk when she recognised an elegant woman walking purposefully towards her. Something about the set of Clara's jaw made her skin prickle with anxiety.

"Dr Carter," Clara began in a neutral voice. "I was wondering if I might have a word?"

Tess's throat tightened. The guilt was suddenly as crippling as it had been when she had woken that morning. She felt as though she may as well have been wearing a banner that said "I slept with your boyfriend – I am an appalling individual." She tried to keep her face and tone impassive to match Clara's. "Miss Delaney, of course. What can I do for—"

"I was hoping to speak to you about how you tried to seduce my boyfriend last night?"

Tess gave a sharp intake of breath and prepared for the verbal assault.

"Particularly about the appropriateness of the attempted seduction taking place here," Clara gestured around the building, "in a hospice!"

Tess's heart thudded against her chest painfully. She felt sick. Surely no more drama today?

"Miss Delaney." Her voice carried none of the gravitas she had hoped. "I wonder if we could discuss this elsewhere?"

"I don't think so. This seems ideal. After all, if it's a good enough venue to conduct your tawdry affairs then I'm sure it's perfectly suitable for a pleasant little chat between us girls?"

"Please. This is *not* an appropriate venue for this kind of conversation. Could we just move into the relatives' room or the office for a—?"

"Not appropriate? Really?" Clara was obviously furious but, looking closely, Tess could see that her eyes were tinged red and she had clearly been crying. "I'll tell you what's not appropriate, shall I? Insinuating your way into the lives of grieving families to tap into their money."

"I beg your pardon?" Tess's surprise at the comment was evident.

"And while we're on the topic, how appropriate is it for a medical professional to be rolling around town drunk, dressed like some streetwalker? Or responding with completely unnecessary hostility to a patient's relatives when they try to engage you in polite conversation?"

"Dressed like what?" She spluttered the words, incredulous.

"Sniffing out wealth and ingratiating yourself with a grieving son who just happens to be due to inherit a whole pile of money when his mother dies, and *she* just happens to be dying *under your care*! What could be less *bloody appropriate* than that?"

"I didn't... I'm sorry, what...?"

Tess's tongue felt like it was stuck in the back of her throat and her mouth simply wouldn't form the shapes needed to articulate coherent sentences. She was trying to remain professional but the combination of guilt and shock made it incredibly difficult in the face of such a barrage of personal insults, and Clara wasn't finished yet.

"Don't think I don't know how this works, *doctor*." She spat the word out in disgust. "I'm a lawyer. I know about probity and the regulations regarding professional behaviour. I think the GMC would be interested to know that you've been accepting expensive gifts from patients, don't you?"

"Gifts? Sorry?" Now Tess was genuinely confused. She had been prepared for a confrontation but this didn't make any sense. "What? Nobody has given me any gifts!"

"Don't play the innocent with me. I'm talking about the thousands of pounds of vet's bills you conned out of Edward. He admitted it all to me last night."

"*Thousands?* Oh my God."

"Yes, thousands of pounds. Don't pretend this is all such a shock. He explained that he felt responsible for upsetting you, the argument you had, the time you were trying to persuade him to let his wealthy mother die – you recall?"

"I didn't try to persuade—"

"That's what led to all of this: he felt guilty; he was worried he had caused you *tremendous offence*, and he must have felt the need to make up for it by stepping in to help when you got yourself into a predicament."

She paused, watching the effect her words were having. Tess was so riddled with self-loathing already that she appeared to be incapable of defending herself against the unrelated accusations now coming her way.

Clara lowered her voice a fraction. "Whilst I obviously don't think you arranged to get your cat run over, it's a neat coincidence that it ended up being treated in a state-of-the-art facility, while you plead poverty. Edward said it was terribly awkward. He felt he had little option but to offer to pay, and of course that would have just confirmed your suspicions, wouldn't it? Easy money."

"No! I—"

"And you then just happen to stumble across the Russell estate on the same day."

"That was just… Henry had said—"

"Bit of a step up, I expect? Thought you'd try and get yourself a piece of that, did you? That's why you kissed him. Here of all places." She gestured again around the room.

"How could you do that?" Her voice cracked. "I suppose you were desperate, weren't you? Knowing that his mother was leaving today, last night would have been your one remaining chance to snare him. Well, your little plan didn't work."

"There was no plan. Miss Delaney, I never meant to… I'm so sorry."

"You disgust me. Just a nasty gold-digger. Abusing your position, targeting vulnerable people for your own ends. Well, it's over. You are in all likelihood getting struck off, if I have anything to do with it. I will be writing to your medical director and the GMC later today."

"What? No. Really, please—"

"I will be suggesting that you are suspended immediately pending an investigation, and that you are never allowed back into a position where you can take advantage of susceptible patients and families again."

She smiled thinly, but a tear had escaped from the corner of her eye and Tess watched it trickle down her cheek as if mesmerised. "Good day, Dr Carter."

Clara smoothed down the barely rumpled sides of her jacket, tilting her chin upward and turning to walk with poise and precision across the foyer and back out of the doors to the car park without a backward glance, leaving Tess reeling in shock.

An hour later she had a call from Dr Fielding. He was very apologetic, but clearly Clara had been as good as her word and had contacted him already, outlining her concerns and making what Dr Fielding described as "significant allegations". He suggested that he came in to cover the rest of Tess's shift and, while he made no reference to active suspension, he did mention that the timing was somewhat fortuitous given that she had annual leave already booked. He recommended that she gather her things, take the rest of the day off and contact her medical defence union.

Tess sat in the car and tried to steady her breathing and her shaking hands.

"*For once, even I'm speechless,*" said the television host. Of course, he wasn't. Far from it. "*He can't have thought much of you, can he? That Edward. Sold you down the river, hasn't he?*" He paused, contemplating. "*What do you think, Tess? After all, you're a clever girl. Did you wonder if… he might've actually had feelings for you? I mean, it's not as if you haven't made that mistake before! Seems there's no limit to the number of times you can make a fool of yourself with this man. Maybe you should just face facts: he doesn't care about you at all.*"

Tess screwed her eyes up and put her hands over her ears but she couldn't block him out. "*It's gotta hurt, hasn't it?*" His tone was sorrowful. "*He's played away but keeps the girlfriend and you're the one who might lose her job. But you've got to learn, Tess. There's no white knight coming to rescue you. You're stuck down here in the murk and the shit with the rest of us. And you always will be…"*

As she began to cry, the host returned to presenter mode. *"Now! Coming up after the break, we speak to Clara and Edward, and learn how infidelity has made their relationship stronger than ever…"* The opening chords of Tammy Wynette's "Stand By Your Man" could be heard in the background.

She drove home in a daze, trying to process the events and the implications of what Clara had said. As it was, the knowledge of what she had done twisted like a knife in her guts, but prior to seeing Clara, her main concern had been guilt about sleeping with someone else's boyfriend. Now she realised that there were potentially much wider repercussions. Was it true? Could she be struck off for not having declared the vet's bills? Who should she have declared them to? It probably did look like a gift. It *was* a gift, and it was a significant amount of money – thousands of pounds, Clara had said. It could look like she had been taking advantage. Clara was right. Had she actually made it awkward for Edward to say no? Had she put him in an unreasonable position? Her memories of that morning at his house were so jumbled that now she wasn't sure.

He had been the one who kissed her last night. He'd instigated that, hadn't he? He'd said he had feelings for her, she was sure of it. But what if she'd misinterpreted that too? Just like she'd overestimated the significance of their first meeting, maybe she'd interpreted his grief as something else, feelings for her that he didn't really have? What if Clara, and the television host come to that, were right?

He had been vulnerable. He *was* vulnerable. Of course he was. He hid it well, that was all, but everyone who was experiencing bereavement, in whatever form, was defenceless and exposed in a way. She knew that. For God's sake. She *knew that*. Why hadn't she been more careful? More cautious. She cringed as she went back over the events of last night. What if that hadn't been what he wanted? What if her need for him had blinded her? The feeling had been so overwhelming, but Clara was right: she had a responsibility; she shouldn't have used her power in that way, wielding it over him, using him to fulfil her own desires.

She squeezed her eyes shut for a second to try and block it out, but a loud beep from the driver pulling out in front of her brought her to her senses and she gripped the steering wheel hard to correct the direction in which she had been drifting. She must focus. Do what she used to do when driving back from a horrific night shift: clear her head entirely and just concentrate on the road. Eyes on the road. That was all.

But she couldn't ignore the siren call of the television host as she drove past the petrol station and found herself doubling back and pulling onto the forecourt. She knew she needed to fill this void opening up within her, to soak up the panic. She piled chocolates, biscuits, and milkshake into her basket and paid with the shaking hands of an addict, making it home as if on autopilot. The bag of food sat on the passenger seat, taunting her almost as much as the host's voice. *"You know it makes sense, Tess. It's the only thing you've got left, isn't it? No man, likely no job, and certainly no self-*

respect… *But at least you can still do this, hmmm? At least you still have this in your life, a way out, a way to ease the pain."* He gave a soft chuckle of satisfaction as she carried the bag of food into the house.

The first thing she saw walking through the front door was Morris, sitting in the hallway casually licking a paw, the bald patch and scar still visible on his flank. She scooped him up gently, burying her face in his soft fur as she let the tears come, and at last she heard Jane Austen's voice in her ear.

"You do not need to do this, Tess dear. The gentleman— No, I cannot call him that. The vile abomination who has your ear when I do not, he deals in falsehoods and his lies are legion. He does you great wrong."

Tess looked at the bulging bag of food. It was sitting squatly on the tiled floor. Jane Austen seemed to sense her hesitation and spoke again. *"Remember, Tess, you are the mistress of yourself."*

She placed Morris gently onto the step and picked up the bag.

"There are trials and tribulations ahead, but you will conquer them, for I know you to be of strong heart and true character. This monster within you… he can be overcome."

Jane's voice was rising in volume as Tess crossed back to the open front door, stepped out to the wheelie-bin… and dropped the bag of food into it. She slammed the lid for good measure.

"It's a bit of a waste of money, Jane," she said. "And Kath would almost certainly have loved the milkshake – but everyone needs a symbolic gesture in their lives now and again." She clenched her fists and strode back into the house. "Now, enough self-doubt, and enough indulging of anxieties. Time to face up to my mistakes and see what I can do to rescue what's left of my career."

Jane Austen gave a sigh of deep satisfaction.

"I simply could not have put it better myself," she said.

Chapter Thirty-One

Tess spent the remainder of the day speaking to her defence union and her GP trainer to clarify her position, should a complaint make it as far as the GMC. The following morning she phoned Dr Fielding, who advised her to take her annual leave as planned and try as hard as she could to put the situation out of her mind. This was going to be a lot easier said than done.

She also bit the bullet and arranged to meet Simon during his lunchbreak. She explained to him that there were all sorts of things going on in her life that were becoming increasingly confusing and that she had no desire to involve him in them. She wanted to remain friends but she didn't want to string him along. Simon was surprisingly relaxed about being dumped.

"It's funny, isn't it," he said. "We're both good-looking, we're both nice people, and we have a laugh, don't we? But I agree. There's something missing." He gave her a chaste peck on the cheek. "Friends it is. I'm okay with that, Tess.

And I appreciate the honesty. There's some birds would've kept a bloke dangling, not sure if he was coming or going. You're a straight talker. I appreciate that."

They parted on good terms and agreed to keep in touch. She knew that she would always be grateful to him for getting her "back in the game", as Kath would have said, but she also knew that she'd done the right thing. And his reaction only confirmed it.

Later, when Kath came home, she felt able to fill her in on recent events. Kath was by turns amused and appalled. She conceded that Tess had behaved badly, but she was always staunchly loyal to her friend, even if it meant turning a blind eye to her faults, and she laid the blame squarely at Clara's door. She was on the verge of tracking her down and giving her a piece of her mind until Tess reminded her that this would only serve to make the situation much, much worse.

"Yes but… what a nightmare! I just can't believe it. What a bitch… Sure, she's pissed off, but to do this? To try and wreck your career? It's that boyfriend of hers she wants to be talking to. What a feckin' spiteful, vindictive cow." Kath went on until the level of expletives reached epic proportions and they both began to laugh. She put her arms around Tess and squeezed her tight.

"Cheer up, babes. Sure, you've been a silly tart, but you'll be grand, so you will. You just hang on in there, and in a couple of days' time we'll be in the South of France without a care in the world. I think it's fair to say we need a bloody holiday."

She paused and looked at Tess more closely. "But, just

for one moment, can we backtrack a little here? Are you seriously telling me that you shagged this guy in a garden shed, in the grounds of a hospice?" She shook her head, "Mate, even I think that's pretty mental."

The holiday, it turned out, was exactly what Tess needed. On their first morning they made straight for the beach. Kath slathered herself in factor fifty and found two sunloungers with a good view of the male volleyball team who were practising down by the water's edge. Huddled beneath her parasol, she flicked through a magazine, leaning over to show Tess photos of various footballers' wives and Love Island contestants.

"What in God's name does she think she's doing getting a tattoo of that eejit's name on her buttocks, I'd like to know... Christ, will you get a load of that! Another boob job? They look near to exploding... I despair, I really do..."

She folded the magazine in two and lifted her sunglasses to peer over at Tess. "Are you thinking about work?"

"Mmm. A bit. I'm trying not to but..."

Kath looked at her more closely. "Or, are you thinking about the fella, this Eddie?"

"God, is it that obvious?"

"Well, sure, I know you're anxious about the complaint and that, but you're mooning about like a lovesick puppy. D'you want to talk it over?"

Tess propped herself up on an elbow and adjusted the

brim of her hat to shelter her eyes from the glare of the sun as she looked towards Kath. "Would you mind?"

"Not at all, babe." She settled her face into attentive listening mode. "That's what I'm here for."

"It's just, I keep trying to clear my head of it," Tess said. "I know I should be focussing on whether I'm going to get struck off, or the fact that I slept with someone else's boyfriend, which I always swore I'd never do. But all I can think about is him... and why he's hung me out to dry." She slumped back into her sunlounger. "I thought he... Oh, I don't know."

Kath nodded wisely. "Okay. So, the thing that's really weighing you down is the fallout from the night in question? As in... what in the name of Holy Christ actually happened?"

"Indeed. Beautifully put." Tess smiled but still looked troubled. "D'you think I could have just completely misread the situation? Like I have before. I mean, he started it, but maybe he didn't want to take it further."

Kath gave a derisory sniff. "Well, sure it would have been a biological impossibility for him to have, shall we say, 'participated against his will'?"

"That's very coy for you."

"I know. I've come over all demure for a moment. It must be watching all these hot lads in their tight little trunks." Her eyes drifted momentarily to where one of the more athletic members of the volleyball team was stretching up to take a shot. "Sorry. Look, I think we can assume he didn't feel physically violated by your wanton actions. He probably just felt guilty afterwards, about being unfaithful, like?"

"I guess."

"And then overcome with remorse, he sees the girlfriend, unburdens himself, and paints you as the cruel seductress." She adjusted her bikini strap. "He tells her enough to make himself feel like he's been honest, but maybe not so much as to make him look like the bad guy?"

"How d'you mean?"

"Well, you know, he spins it in his favour? So, he tells her that *you* tried to kiss *him* – he neglects to say that he was the one who tried to kiss you – and he doesn't mention so much as a dickie bird about the fact that you then shagged each other's brains out." Kath rubbed at a streak of sun lotion on her thigh in contemplation. "I mean, doesn't it strike you as odd that she didn't include it in her complaint? It's not illegal – it's not like *he* was your patient – but it could look pretty bad for you: 'sexual relations with a vulnerable family member' and all."

Tess groaned. "Oh God. It sounds dreadful when you put it like that. I've been such a bloody idiot."

"No, no, shush. I'm not trying to make you feel worse." Kath shook her head impatiently. "I'm just looking for the most rational explanation. And I don't reckon she knows you slept with him."

Tess took a sip of her drink. "The thing is… I know him."

"You sure do, in the biblical sense."

"No, I mean I *know* him. He's not the cowardly type. I just can't see him blaming someone else for something he'd done. He's really principled about fairness and justice. Doing the right thing. It doesn't make sense."

"Maybe you don't know him as well as you think? I mean, I don't want to state the obvious here, but didn't you think you *knew* him last time and it turns out he had no recollection of you?"

"Yeah, maybe." Both girls contemplated this for a moment.

"Or…" said Kath, "to be fair to the fella, he's about to lose his mam, perhaps he just couldn't cope with the idea of losing the girlfriend at the same time. Even if she is a cold-hearted weasel."

"I guess."

"Either way, I'm sorry to say it but he's looking out for number one. I think you maybe have to accept he's thrown you under the bus."

"Great. Thanks."

"I'm just looking out for you, babe. You're your own worst enemy sometimes. The funny thing is," Kath picked up her magazine, "I reckon that despite all this shite, if you had the chance to do it all again, you would."

Tess pulled her sunhat down over her face and refused to comment, but Kath was right. If she had been given the chance to rewrite history, she knew that she would still have chosen to follow Edward that night; even now she did not regret what had happened. She firmly believed that in some way it had been necessary, essential even, for both of them.

July 15th 2018

~~Dear Dad~~

~~Dear Signor Fratelli~~

Dear Marco,

I have been struggling to think of the best way to contact you. A phone call would probably be a bit of a shock, and I don't have your number. An email just feels too casual and I don't have your email address, so I'm writing, and to be honest, I think this is the best way. I know that when I found your letters there was something really nice about being able to go back and re-read them and physically hold them in my hand. It also means I can send you a couple of photos. I thought you might like to see one of me on my first day at work and this one of me and Jake. I bet he's grown a bit since you last saw him! Mum took this picture last Christmas. Jake's wearing the new coat she bought him. She had to work so much overtime to pay for it, but you can see from his face how much he loves it.

Anyway, you're probably wondering why you haven't heard from me until now. I'm not sure if Mum has been in touch to let you know what happened. I guess probably not, so I'll start at the beginning. A few weeks ago I was at home and I discovered your letters. I had no idea you'd been sending them and as you can imagine, it was ~~a bit of a shock~~ quite a surprise.

~~Mum had hidden them from me~~

~~Mum had kept them secret~~

Mum had wanted to protect me and had therefore never told me that you'd been in contact. As far as I knew, the last communication we'd had was the day you left when I was five. Growing up, I knew that Jake's father had done the same, so I guess I didn't question it – it seemed "normal" and just something that dads tended to do. I wasn't unhappy and I'm not trying to make you feel guilty. Mum did a great job of raising both me and Jake. She has done the work of two parents in terms of providing for us and loving us, and I wouldn't want you to think otherwise. But, having said all that, it was still really amazing to discover that you had in fact been trying to get in touch.

I've had a lot of time to think about how things could have been different; if I'd known you'd written, it would have been lovely to have had contact with you growing up, but we can't change it now, and there's still plenty of time for us to get to know each other, if you'd like to?

~~You might not want to~~
~~Your current family~~

I'm not sure what your current situation is and I have no intention of making your life difficult if you have other children, or maybe a partner who would find the knowledge of my existence a bit of a challenge? But if you would like to get in touch at any point, my number and email are on the bottom of this letter.

~~If you are ever coming back to the UK~~
~~I've always wanted to see Italy~~
I would love to hear from you but understand if you
have moved on and would prefer to leave things as
they are. I just wanted to explain the reasons for my
silence over the past twenty years, and to let you know
that I have now read all of your letters and cherish them
dearly.

~~Lots of love~~
~~Your loving daughter~~
Best wishes,
Tess x

P.S. I've also got the locket. You probably don't
remember, but it's the one you got me for my eighth
birthday. I thought I'd lost it, but then I found it again.
I'd forgotten how pretty it is. Thank you x

Chapter Thirty-Two

The girls returned from their break rested and refreshed. Tess had deliberately not checked her emails whilst she'd been on holiday, but there was a message on her return asking her to come along to the hospice for a meeting with Dr Fielding. He informed her that, in the absence of contact from the GMC, he could see no reason why Tess should not complete her hospice placement.

"Clearly there will be no further clinical contact with the Russell family whilst you are working here," he said, "because, as I suspect you are aware, Mary Russell passed away last week."

Tess's expression immediately indicated that she had not been aware of that fact, and Dr Fielding was quick to realise his mistake. The reality was that although Tess had been expecting the death of Mary Russell, she had not been prepared for it emotionally. Her overwhelming concern over the past week had been herself, her job, and her own feelings of rejection. Putting all of these issues to one side, she realised how much her own relationship with this particular patient had meant to her, and how saddened she was personally by the loss. She struggled to hold back the tears, being aware that every time she encountered Dr Fielding in this office she seemed to be an emotional wreck. He may have reservations about recommending her as suitably qualified for the provision of palliative care if she was unable to handle the news that one of her terminally ill patients had actually died.

Dr Fielding, however, was entirely familiar with the concept that some patients affect doctors more than others, and was wise enough to see this case had further-reaching consequences for Tess than most. He let her absorb the news in her own time, and when she had wiped her eyes and composed herself he handed her an envelope edged in black, addressed to Dr Tess Carter.

"We received a general one addressed to the hospice, but it seems that Mrs Russell and her family particularly wanted you to attend," he said.

He went on to explain that Madeleine had called the hospice to inform them, and had asked to speak directly to Tess herself.

"One of your colleagues was a little unguarded in their discussions and advised Mrs Russell's daughter that you may in fact be facing suspension because of a complaint coming directly from her family," Dr Fielding said with a small frown. "Although, I suspect Farida knew exactly what she was doing, because we immediately had a follow-up phone call from Mr Russell putting us very clearly in the picture and absolving you of any shred of responsibility for whatever financial misunderstanding might have occurred."

He peered over his glasses at her. "The very fact that the poor man saw fit to concern himself with the allegation during the immediate period of mourning his mother speaks volumes."

"Yes." A frown of confusion clouded Tess's features as Dr Fielding continued.

"So, you will see from your letter that the funeral is scheduled for next Friday afternoon."

"I'm not sure that I want—"

"Tess," he cut in, "I understand that you may have reservations about going to this funeral, and I share some of those reservations. But I also feel that you need closure in this case, almost as much as the family do. Your patient very clearly wanted you to be there."

Tess nodded. "Yes. I see."

"I understand that Mrs Russell knew nothing of Miss Delaney's complaint, and went to her death unencumbered by that potentially distressing news. She wanted you to be there. I know you were close, and I think if you feel able to attend then a discreet presence at the ceremony, accompanied by a few of your colleagues, including Farida, would be appropriate and appreciated."

"Okay," she said, deep in thought. "Thank you."

Dr Fielding, noticing her expression, let her mull it over for a few moments before continuing. "While we are on the subject of being close to patients, I think there are potentially important issues to address regarding your future career."

Tess looked up in alarm; did he know more about what had happened with Edward than she thought?

"Nothing at all to be worried about, Tess. Only that I am fearful for your sanity working as a GP if you let yourself get this attached to patients. I have seen colleagues of mine burn out, and I need to reassure myself that this will not happen to you. You will remember my advice when we spoke about the Russells in May? About giving yourself some distance?"

"I tried. I tried to back off. But events sort of conspired against me. I know it sounds lame."

"Not at all. None of us is capable of heeding advice to the letter, especially when it concerns our own wellbeing. You only need to look at half of our patients to see that."

"True."

"So, no, it's not a telling off, or an 'I told you so'. I just wonder whether the way in which events have developed has made my point for me, perhaps a little more forcibly than I would have hoped."

Tess nodded in agreement, relieved that the conversation had not taken a very difficult turn. She left the hospice clutching the black-edged envelope and did not open it until she got home. Inside, on stiff card, she found an invitation to both the formal service being held in the church at two o'clock, and to the family home for refreshments afterwards. On the back of the invitation there was a scribbled note saying:

Please come – Edward x

She chose not to read too much into the kiss next to his name; it had clearly been written in haste, and the man was still in shock. However, she suspected Clara hadn't seen it. She traced her finger along the words, wondering how he was coping, how the loss of his mother would be affecting him. She wanted desperately to hear his voice or just to catch a glimpse of him, to reassure herself that he was okay, but she knew that she owed it to Clara to not make further contact. Tess could not be involved, no matter how much she wanted to be.

Chapter Thirty-Three

Friday morning dawned bright and sunny, a beautiful day to celebrate the life of Mary Russell. Tess and Farida deliberately coordinated their arrival with the latecomers and squeezed into one of the back pews. The church was packed to the rafters and rays of sunlight poured through the stained glass, throwing patches of colour onto the sombre clothes of the people gathered beneath. The heady scent of lilies and stocks filled the cooler air of the stone interior and Tess thought briefly of Janice arranging her flowers back at the hospice, and smiled. She couldn't see Clara but guessed that she must be nearer the front, out of view. Once Tess had established that there was little danger of either woman observing the other, she relaxed. That was until she saw Edward.

As the doors closed and the entrance music began, the slow tread of the pallbearers caused a hush to fall across the congregation. Tess had her head bowed but looked across just as they passed her section of the aisle and saw him supporting the leading edge of the coffin on his shoulder. She felt as if someone had taken a baton to the backs of her knees and she jolted, having to steady herself with a hand on the pew in front.

"*Hold firm, my dear,*" Jane Austen murmured quietly. "*Courage and fortitude.*"

Farida took her arm to steady her, mistaking her reaction for anxiety about potentially bumping into Clara. Tess did not allow herself another look until she had the reassuring solidity of the pew beneath her, but she could just about make out Edward right at the front, sitting next to Madeleine. Even from this distance she could see that he had lost a little weight; his face was drawn as if he hadn't slept for days. Her heart ached seeing him like this. It was ridiculous to speak of love, but the rush of emotion she felt for him was more than just sympathy and compassion. It felt much stronger, as if she wanted to take his pain and break it, to protect him from ever being harmed again. She had felt something similar when her grandmother was dying, a sense of her own hurt being intrinsically linked to that of another. Seeing Edward at that moment she felt real grief, not only for Mary, but for the loss of what might have been.

When he stood for the first reading and came to the lectern, she could see him more clearly. He didn't falter, delivering the words in a clear, precise voice, but she could hear the sorrow just beneath the surface. As he finished the reading, he seemed to scan the people arrayed before him, searching the faces in the congregation before sitting back down and taking Madeleine's hand.

Finally, it was over. Tess wanted to leave before there was any possibility of running into Clara, but it felt unseemly to bid too hasty a retreat from a funeral, and Farida wanted the family to know that she had been there, representing the hospice. They stood a little way back from the crowd, in the shade of a large tree, as the congregation made their way out of the church. Edward was occupied with an elderly couple, the man gripping his hands and the woman dabbing her eyes whilst talking to him, but Madeleine spotted them immediately and headed straight over, flinging her arms round Tess as she reached her.

"Tess! I'm so glad you could make it. And Dr Grainger"—she turned to Farida—"you too. It means a great deal to us as a family to have you here."

"Oh, that's fine," said Farida, and Tess added, "We really wanted to come."

Madeleine smiled her gratitude. "St Martin's was such a tremendous support to Mummy over the past few months. She wanted all donations to go there, so you'll probably be getting a big cheque soon. There's quite a few of her friends with very deep pockets!"

The last thing Tess wanted to be involved with was a conversation about the Russells's financial dealings, particularly in the context of gifts to the hospice, a fact that Madeleine suddenly realised. She grabbed Tess's hand.

"I'm so sorry. That was insensitive, given the recent issues. I've never been the most diplomatic of people, always putting my foot in it, and now I seem to be even worse than ever!"

Her words were tumbling out of her mouth and she

stopped to take a deep breath. Tess could see that she was tense, strung with a nervous energy, and likely drawing on her very last reserves to get through the funeral.

"It's okay," she squeezed Madeleine's hand back. "People understand; you've got a lot on your plate. It can't be easy having to organise all of this when you've got the kids with you and are still going through your own loss. You must make sure you get a break at some point."

Madeleine nodded, tears were shining in her eyes, but she blinked them away. "Just got to get through today! And then we're back to America next week. Eddie's coming with us. He needs a rest just as much as I do, maybe more so…" She smiled. "Secretly I'm hoping he'll stay for good. There's nothing to keep him here anymore, and he can just as easily work out there; he'll slip into a job like *that*." She clicked her fingers. "He's got a great reputation, very much in demand. The Chicago office is already lining up projects for him, but he's been very clear about wanting a proper break first. Where is he anyway?" She peered over her shoulder. "Oh, with the Barnetts. He'll be a while."

She turned back to Tess. "He really wants to see you. You are coming to the house afterwards? And you too, Dr Grainger? There's a mountain of food. Goodness only knows how we're going to get through it all, and many of Mum's friends will want to meet the people who looked after her. She talked about you a lot…"

Farida explained that she had to get back to work; her shift did not finish until later that evening and Dr Fielding was covering until she returned. "But thank you for the offer and for your kind words about the hospice," she said, taking Madeleine's hand. "I will relay them to the rest of the team. They loved looking after your mum. She was an absolute treasure."

She turned to Tess. "I'll see you soon? Pop in and let us know about the world of general practice, won't you? I know Rob would love to see you too. Maybe we could meet up for coffee? I'll call you."

She headed off to her car, leaving Tess standing with Madeleine.

"You'll come to the house though, Dr Carter?"

"I really don't want to cause a scene." Tess fiddled with her handbag. The news about Edward going to America had hit her harder than expected. "I'm not sure Miss Delaney would be thrilled to have me there, and I can't bear the idea of some kind of public slanging match on a day like today. Maybe it's better if I just pay my respects here and leave?"

Madeleine looked nonplussed. "Clara won't be there. She and Edward split up a couple of weeks ago." She registered Tess's look of surprise. "Sorry, I thought you knew. The timings are all a bit muddled. I think it kicked off the night before Mummy came home. It seems he and Clara had a frightful row and I imagine it was absolutely the last straw. As far as I could tell she'd been absolutely no support whatsoever, and I'm amazed she hung around for as long as she did."

"I'm so sorry. I didn't know…"

"Clearly she was more hindrance than help, because straight away it was like a weight had been lifted off Eddie's shoulders." Madeleine smiled. "Mummy came home and he was much better able to cope; he really enjoyed his last few days with her. It's an odd thing to say, but we all did. She was surrounded by family and we could see how much happier she was at home. It made everything easier, just like you said it would."

She went on to tell Tess about calling the hospice to let them know about Mary's death and finding out about the complaint. "Eddie was absolutely livid. We knew it must be Clara, but I guess we were all a little surprised that she would be so vindictive."

"Perhaps she didn't mean—"

"Oh, she knew what she was doing all right. I think maybe she was jealous of you in some way... she saw you as a threat? I don't know..." She paused, looking at Tess carefully, "There is *something*, isn't there? I can't put my finger on it, but I'm not stupid; there's something about the way he looks at you. I expect Clara picked up on it before me."

"I'm not really—"

"Anyway, the upshot was that Eddie got on the phone to them immediately and put the record straight. He was completely devastated about the fact that this might have all had a negative impact on your career. Held himself responsible – you know what he's like." She looked at Tess shrewdly again. "I mean, you really *do* know what he's like. Not many other people see who he is, but I think perhaps you do."

Tess was careful not to give too much away, but she could easily imagine how Edward would have beaten himself up over something like that. She let Madeleine carry on.

"So, I thought it might plunge him back into the gloom again, but your boss, lovely chap, said that he thought everything would be all right and that Eddie had really helped give some clarity to the situation. He still blames himself for the entire fiasco, but what can you do?"

"Very little, I imagine."

"Long and short of it is, Dr Carter, he'd really want to tell you this himself. Please do come to the house. I'll make sure you get a chance to talk properly whilst I man the vol-au-vents and sherry."

Tess thanked Madeleine for the invitation and said that she would do her best to get there, buying herself some time with a fabricated excuse about something she needed to do in town first. Madeleine explained that she and Edward would be going to the crematorium with immediate family members and then back to the house, where Pauline and a small army of helpers were currently preparing some sort of Sandwich Armageddon, alongside entertaining the children. She pressed Tess's hands between hers. "Please, please do come," she said, before releasing her and moving off into the assembled crowd of mourners who were showing little sign of dispersing.

Tess was increasingly feeling the need for a bit of space to clear her head. She saw Henry, the vet, from a distance and returned his wave but managed to slip away otherwise unnoticed, driving back into Bristol just as far as the Downs and pulling up beside one of the grander houses of Sneyd Park before walking the short distance to the viewpoint where she could see the suspension bridge and the Avon Gorge. Here she took a few deep lungfuls of air, feeling the welcome breeze gusting off the Severn and bouncing up the walls of the gorge to the people above. She could see the odd climber dotted across the cliff face, their hard hats reflecting in the sun, and behind her a group of kids were playing a loose game of football, the end of term still recent enough for the sense of freedom not to have yet been overtaken by boredom. Mums and nannies were queuing by the ice cream van nearby, and it felt to all intents and purposes like an ordinary summer's day. Except that to Tess, it was anything but ordinary.

Over the other side of the gorge, beyond the scrabbled shrubbery clinging to the sheer edges, preparations at the Russell residence would be well underway. Edward and Madeleine would be arriving home shortly, and Tess allowed herself to imagine the house in its glorious splendour, opening its doors to all those who wanted to pay their respects and bring condolences to Mary's family. And, extraordinarily, it seemed that amongst the gathered assembly, there would be no Clara Delaney. The source of Tess's angst over the past few weeks was gone, an enemy vanquished, and suddenly she was overcome by her previous sense of shame and guilt. The television host was back in her ear, and this time she could almost picture him, perched jauntily on the stone wall, his teeth white, his tan mahogany, his hair highlighted and oiled, everything about him oozing fakery and malign intent.

"How does it feel, Tess? To know that you destroyed a relationship?" In her mind's eye she saw him take a slow,

languorous lick of his ice cream. *"After all, you've been on the receiving end of betrayal. You know how it feels when the man you thought you loved no longer wants you."* He swung his legs against the stone, humming to himself as he watched the children playing on the green. *"That Edward fella could have been happy with his classy bird if you hadn't come grubbing about like a nasty little whore. And why did you do it?"* He leaned his face in and she could almost smell the sickly vanilla on his breath. *"Just to boost your own self-esteem!"* He leaned back and laughed to the studio audience. *"She thinks she's better than us, this one. But she's not. She's just like her mother – a cheap tart!"*

The audience booed loudly and the host returned his attention to Tess. *"You listen to them, doc,"* he whispered. *"You'll be hearing that noise again and again. D'you know what that is? The sound of judgement!"*

Tess began to walk away but she could still see the faint image of him sidling along the wall to keep up with her.

"And don't think them splitting up changes anything, Tess! He doesn't have feelings for you. He knows what you are, and he won't be in any hurry to replace his posh totty with an ugly trollop! Why d'you think he's going to America? Better skulk away now while you've got your dignity… Oh, wait, I think you left that behind in the hospice shed!"

Tess stopped and turned to face her imaginary host, this manifestation of all the negative thoughts that had plagued her over the years. Jane Austen's voice was suddenly so powerful and present that it was almost as if she too had taken on a physical shape.

"You have no further need of this particular gentleman's

services, Tess, dearest. He has no power over you. Perhaps we should now take our leave of hi. Bid him adieu." And with those words the host toppled back off the wall, plummeting into the gorge below, his malicious stream of invective trailing after him, becoming fainter the further he fell.

Chapter Thirty-Four

Tess arrived at the Russell estate an hour later and tucked her Fiat Punto in amongst the Audis and Range Rovers in the cordoned-off area near the stables. As she crossed the gravel, approaching from the side, she could hear the sound of voices coming from the rear garden. She felt a momentary rush of anxiety and wished that Farida had accompanied her, but she settled her nerves by remembering how insistent Madeleine had been that she attend. Her fingers gripped firmly the invitation in her handbag as if fearing that someone might stop her and ask to see identification, proof that she was not just an imposter intruding on someone else's wake. She supposed that there might actually be people out there who would contemplate such an action, a chance to nose around a wealthy estate, pick out a couple of heirlooms to come back for later. She shuddered; the thought was unsettling.

Suddenly, from out of Tess's range of vision, there came a shriek of laughter and a small child hurtled around the corner almost clattering into her. Tess saw a blur of blonde hair and bright-pink taffeta, and as the child whirling in circles in front of her came to a halt she realised it was Annabelle, wearing a tutu, large brown wellingtons, and a scarlet poncho. She beamed up at Tess and clapped her hands.

"It's Dr Tessie!" she cried in delight, sliding one of her hands into Tess's and guiding her round to the back of the house and the gardens. The sun was still relatively high in the sky, despite it now being late afternoon. The terrace was bathed in light and teeming with guests, all balancing wine glasses and tiny plates of sandwiches in their hands, lifting them occasionally to avoid impeding the progress of a small child or large dog tearing across the flagstones. The laughter and chinking of glasses gave the event an air of a garden party or wedding breakfast, and it was only the sombre clothing that provided any indication as to the true nature of the occasion. Annabelle continued to grip Tess's hand tightly as she steered her through the crowd until at last she found Harvey, sitting next to a large stone urn examining pebbles. She presented her trophy and was gratified by Harvey's smile.

"Hello Dr Tess! It's very nice to see you. How is your ginger cat?"

He was so endearingly serious. Tess crouched down as low as modesty would allow in her dress and looked him straight in the eye.

"Marvellous, thank you Harvey," she said, "but certainly all the better for having your picture on the wall. I stuck it up with tape next to his bed and he looks at it every day."

Harvey smiled shyly and his cheeks went pink. He showed Tess one of the stones he had been looking at.

"See?" he pointed to a crenulation in the surface. "I think it might be a dinosaur."

Tess was just about to reply when she became aware of a presence behind her. She was still crouched down and almost lost her balance when she turned to see Edward looming tall over her. He held out a hand to help her up and she wobbled to an upright position.

"Whoops!" Her laugh was a fraction more hysterical than she would have liked.

"Whoops indeed. How lovely to see you, Dr Carter."

Tess realised that the last time they had been in this close proximity she had been astride him in the cabin at the hospice. Her thighs squeezed together and her mouth went dry with the memory of it, but she managed to speak.

"It's Tess, please, not Dr Carter today. I'm not here in a medical capacity. Well, I mean, I am, if there's an accident or something, I can help out. Um, and clearly I'm here because I was your mum's doctor, so I guess—"

"Tess," he interrupted her. "Of course."

"Doc-tor Tes-sie!" sang Annabelle as she skipped off into the crowd to find one of the dogs.

Edward looked fondly after her. "They've been an absolute godsend," he said, taking Tess by the elbow and steering her away from the garden towards the house, seemingly unaware of the effect the simple contact of him was having on her.

"I don't know what we would have done without them. There's nothing quite like having to discuss the merits of various breakfast cereals, or dig for worms, or explain that wellingtons and a tutu aren't necessarily appropriate for a funeral, to take your mind off bereavement." He gestured towards Annabelle. "As you can see, we lost the last argument. She's a law unto herself in the fashion stakes."

"I hear you're heading back to America with them next week?" Tess asked as casually as she could manage, although her heart was hammering in her chest.

He looked at her for a beat or two. His hand was still on her arm and the pressure of his fingers increased a fraction before he nodded.

"Yes. Madeleine suggested it and the idea seemed sensible at the time, although now that it feels a bit more imminent I'm not so sure…' His blue eyes were fixed on her and he chewed his bottom lip in the way she had seen him do many times before.

They were nearing a set of large French doors that opened out from a beautiful drawing room and he stopped just on the threshold and turned to look back out over the terrace.

"Look, there are heaps of people here that I still need to speak to and I'm sure they'd all like to meet you too. Most of them will have heard Mum talk about you and the others – well, you know how the older generation love to chat to a doctor. Do you mind if I commandeer your social skills for a while, to make up for my own deficiencies? I'm starting to run out of things to say to everyone."

"Oh! Well, that would be fine, I suppose. I'm not sure my social skills are worth, um, commandeering but I should be able to manage a bit of small talk. Lead the way."

He had remained lightly holding onto her arm throughout, and now moved her towards one of the smaller crowds gathered within the drawing room, pausing next to a large sideboard to pour her a drink. "Just a half glass please," she said, watching the liquid rise up inside the crystal. "I'm driving."

"Of course," he said and then hesitated, eyeing her curiously. "Do you think you might be able to stay a little later? Until the other guests have gone? I think we need to talk."

His eyes were unreadable but there was a twitch at the corner of his mouth. She dragged her gaze away from his face, thinking of how those lips had felt pressed hard against hers and imagining them moving across hers now. Her mouth went dry again and she took a quick sip of the wine, feeling the tingle of it on her tongue.

"Sure, I can stay for a bit."

They made their way around the room, greeting guests and sharing stories about Mary. Tess recounted some of the conversations they'd had over the months; she talked about how much Mary had enjoyed the walks in the hospice grounds, how kind she had been to the staff, and how her room had been filled with pictures of her family. She often referenced Edward, who was standing beside her throughout, sometimes offering up additional comments but mainly just watching her, entertained by her easy familiarity with complete strangers.

"This has certainly got a lot more enjoyable since you arrived," he murmured as they moved between groups.

Occasionally he touched her, brushing his fingers

against her wrist as he took her empty glass, slipping his hand to her waist in order to edge her past a couple who were leaving, and the reminder of his physical proximity made Tess tremble.

When they had spoken to everyone in the vast room, they made their way back towards the terrace and Tess excused herself to go and find the bathroom, more to have a moment to herself than anything else. The children were sitting on the floor in the main hallway surrounded by a huddle of exhausted dogs, who wagged their tails in unison at her approach.

She crouched to pet them, "Oh, it's a hot day to be a dog, isn't it?" she said as she scratched one behind his ears. Annabelle was lying next to her making angel shapes on the cool tiled floor and Harvey was focussed on building a tower out of his stones.

"They miss Granny. That's why they're sleepy. They feel a bit sad."

"Hmmm. You're probably right, Harvey. Lucky they've got you guys around, hey?"

He smiled but then frowned again. "But we're going home soon," he said, "and then they'll be lonely."

A clipped Scottish voice echoed out from the kitchen: "They won't be lonely, my darlings. They'll still have me to pester, won't they?" A short woman holding a tea towel emerged through the doorway, extending a hand in greeting to Tess who introduced herself.

"Oh! The doctor." She took Tess's hand in a firm grip. "I'm Pauline. I was hoping to meet you; I wanted to say thank you for all that you lovely people at the hospice did for Mary – I know she felt very well looked after there."

Pauline had known the family for years and she had often driven Mary to her appointments in those early months before anyone else knew the diagnosis. It was clear that they had been very close and she was affected a great deal by her loss.

"I've kept myself tucked away in the kitchen for most of the day, to be honest."

"Oh, okay. I can imagine it's less manic in there?"

"Absolutely. I couldn't face lots of chatter. Much prefer being surrounded by sandwiches than people, but I do feel a bit bad about landing it all on wee Eddie and Maddie; they've been through so much, poor lambs. I think a good trip away will do Eddie the world of good, but it's certainly going to feel a bit empty here, come next week."

She looked down at the children. "You'd better phone your Auntie Pauline now and then, so I can tell you what these hounds have been up to."

She turned her attention back to Tess. "Now, would you like a quick cup of tea, doctor? You could come and have a quiet sit down with me?"

Tess welcomed the opportunity to return to the less formal surroundings of the kitchen, where Pauline poured her a mug of, admittedly, stewed tea. She smiled as she remembered Edward's comments when she'd last been in this room, only a few weeks ago. It felt like an eternity. Pauline was a woman of few words, but seemed to expect few in return, and Tess found the silence comfortable, closing her eyes at one point and leaning back in her chair.

This was where Edward found her moments later. He pulled up a chair beside her.

"That's what I need to do," he said, bringing his elbows to the table and yawning expansively. Pauline pinched him fondly on the cheek.

"You're exhausted, wee boy. Why don't you take this lovely girl for a walk around the garden now it's cooling down a bit? I'm sure you've done as much socialising as would be expected, and probably a good deal more than you're comfortable with. A bit of fresh air is what you need."

Edward looked across at Tess, his eyebrows raised in a question and she nodded, following him through the rear kitchen door back to the south terrace where the guests were dispersing. They walked out across the lawns towards a wrought-iron gate set into a high boundary wall to the left side of the property. Once through, Tess could see that they were now in a walled garden with raised beds and a sheltered pergola at the far end. It was here they headed, their feet crunching across the pea shingle that ran between the borders. Edward took a sidelong glance over to Tess, smiling at her reaction. "It's nice, isn't it? Peaceful. Mum loved it in here."

They sat on a stone bench under the cover of a climbing rose and he told her about those last few days before Mary died. How Pauline had gathered flowers from this garden and placed them in vases all around Mary's room to fill it with scent and colour, how the windows had been opened to their full extent to allow the noise and air from the grounds to filter in. That the hospice nurses had sat with them, explaining what would happen as the end approached, the flickering in and out of consciousness, the rare moments of clarity when she told them she loved them, that she was proud, that they had been the best children a mother could ask for.

"It was, okay, I suppose. We were prepared and so was she. It's funny, I had anticipated it being a shock, but of course, it's not shocking at all. Dying, I mean." He looked over at Tess.

"No," she agreed, stretching out her legs in the sun. "It shouldn't be a shock to any of us. It's one of the only certainties in life, and we all avoid talking or thinking about it, so it becomes frightening." She turned towards him. "From what I've seen, most of the deaths in the hospice have been peaceful and comfortable, often a release.

"Of course," she looked away, "you were right, that evening, when you said that I didn't know how it felt. I don't. I've seen death, and I lost my gran a few years ago, but the thought of losing a parent..." She considered the absence of her mother, the future rolling bleakly out in front of her without the comfort and reassurance of that familiar face and warm, maternal solidity. Her voice tightened. "Well, I can't imagine. As you said, no number of lectures on empathy will change that, and you were right to pull me up on it."

He put a hand out to her cheek, turning her face back towards his and looking straight at her. "I *wasn't* right to do that. Not right at all. I was in a state, I didn't know what I was saying, and you were only trying to help."

His hand remained on her cheek for a few moments, the

warmth of it comforting, and she thought he might lean in to kiss her. Much as she wanted him to, she felt that there was still a lot more to say, and he seemed to share her view, because he broke eye contact and moved his hand away, stretching his arm out behind her to rest on the back of the bench. Still, she was aware throughout their remaining conversation that his body was close to hers, the crook of his elbow lying just behind her neck, his fingers almost brushing her shoulder. The position was protective but casual, as if he could pull her into an embrace at any moment, but might also choose not to.

They talked for a while longer, discussing the house and what would happen to it when they left for America on Monday. Tess tried to hide her own feelings regarding his imminent departure. She knew he needed a break, and that he was addressing this in the most practical way that he could, so she found herself saying things like, "Hmm, seems sensible," and, "What about the dogs?" and, "Do you have a burglar alarm?" when really all she could concentrate on was the feeling of a chasm opening up beneath her as he detailed the steps the family had taken to ensure their absence would be managed. In the short-term, Pauline and the gardener could take care of the day-to-day running of the estate, just as they had been to all intents and purposes for the past year whilst Mary had been unwell, but there were issues regarding what would become of it in the future.

"It's difficult to know what to do," he said. "This place has been in the family for generations, but there's no way Maddie will be living here; her home is in America for the foreseeable future. I've got my flat in London – that'll be easy enough to rent out – but I just don't know how long I'm going to be away for. I suspect it might be some time."

"What are you going to do about work?"

"Oh, they've been great. I guess putting in all the hard graft over the past few years has bought me a bit of leeway. They're happy for me to take an extended sabbatical and there's always the potential to work in one of their American offices, if I decided to stay."

"Oh." Her voice was a little wobblier than she had intended. "And do you think you might stay? Do you think you might"—she shifted her position—"emigrate?"

He looked at her closely. "I just don't know," he said. He seemed to realise that she was asking about more than his career intentions, but the topic of work was a safer one to address at the moment. "It's a possibility. If I want to continue in the same field, I can certainly transfer there easily. Or I might decide I want to do something entirely different with my life."

"Yes? Like what?" Honestly, she could kick herself. What did she think he was going to say? *I might decide I want to do something entirely different with my life, like staying here with my burden of grief, waving goodbye to what's left of my family as they head off across the Atlantic and making a go of a relationship based on an extraordinarily volatile set of circumstances with a completely unprofessional nymphomaniac?*

Unsurprisingly, Edward did not say this. "I'm not sure," he said instead. "It's a dreadful cliché but what happened with Mum, and to a lesser extent my dad, I suppose, it does really make you think life is too short to be spending it doing something you don't enjoy. Being in the wrong job, being with the wrong person, it's just wasting time. And that time, as everyone always says, is really precious."

He stretched his long legs out in front of him, focussing his attention on his feet.

"I look at Harvey and Annabelle; they've changed so much even in the past year, and I don't want to miss all of that – I don't want to be the distant English uncle, like something out of a Dickens novel. They and Maddie are my only family now."

"Yes." She nodded a little sadly to herself. "I get that."

"I've got to make sure I don't just keep on making the same mistakes." He scuffed at the gravel with his shoe. "My father was a case in point; he thought success was all about financial gain and professional recognition. I don't want to be like that."

"Okay."

"I mean, don't get me wrong, it's nice for people to think you're doing well in your job, to think of you as a high-flyer, and there are aspects of my work that are really rewarding." He turned to Tess. "But I think at the start of my career, the cut and thrust of it was somehow more exciting, whereas now, the constant adrenaline, it's stressful. Maybe I'm getting too old for it." He smiled and looked back out over the garden to the tops of the trees, deep in thought. "I wonder if I'd rather do something less financially orientated and go back to practising law in a more meaningful sense, maybe some pro bono work, or perhaps something that allowed me a better balance in my life – it's not like I do anything *good*, is it? Not like you. People aren't going to think back and say, 'Ah yes, Edward Russell, he really made a difference, he really got us out of that financial loophole using his precise understanding of the current legislation – what a hero', are they?"

"And do you want to be a hero?"

Her leg was now resting up against his and she was gradually acclimatising to the physical closeness of him without having a minor heart attack every time he brushed against her.

"No. I don't need to be a hero. I just don't want to feel that life has passed me by. I want to enjoy it, to feel content, rather than this constant, restless dissatisfaction. I haven't been properly satisfied for a long time."

There was a pause.

"Well, maybe that's not strictly true." He didn't look at her, but his tone had changed, "There was an *extremely* satisfying episode a few weeks back…"

Tess studied her knees, squeezing them together. She could feel a trickle of sweat at the nape of her neck and her face was hot. She leaned back, feeling his arm still behind her.

"That must have been nice."

"That would be something of an understatement." He cleared his throat. "But, um, I realise that, as *nice* as it was for me, it precipitated a fairly difficult turn of events for you?"

He turned to face her, serious now, the trace of naughtiness gone. "Tess, if I'd had any inkling of what Clara would do, I would have been so much more careful about how and what I told her."

"I know. Don't worry."

"I realised as soon as I got back here that night, I knew I needed to be honest with her, and I knew I couldn't be with her anymore, so I told her that I had feelings for you, and that we'd kissed."

"Uh-huh." Her face was getting hotter and hotter. Having thought that she wanted a deep and meaningful conversation with him, now she wasn't so sure. The Clara aspect of things just made her feel hideously guilty.

"I didn't share any more of the detail," he said. "I mean, there's candid and then there's unnecessarily cruel. I didn't want to do that to her; she's not a bad person."

"No. I know she's not."

"She told me I was a fool, and accused you of various things. She knew about me taking Morris to the vet's and she asked me directly how much it had cost."

"You should have told me, you know. I knew it would be expensive but—"

"I know. And I'm so sorry. I was trying to be, I don't know, chivalrous?"

"Well, I guess it was, in a way. Certainly, the whole 'pet rescue' was pretty heroic."

"I told her you were paying me back, but she didn't want to hear it. She was angry. I guess I underestimated quite how angry... I should have been clearer with her."

"It's easy in hindsight though, isn't it?" Tess smiled at him. "Don't worry."

His expression was earnest. "You must believe me, I would never do anything to undermine you or cause difficulties for you at work."

"Really?"

"Yes, really. What's so funny?"

"You'd do nothing to undermine me?"

"No. Of course not. Honestly, I'd never want to—"

"So, bringing in private specialists, for example, and making it clear that you value their opinion far more than mine, or shouting at me in front of patients and other staff, questioning my professional integrity, or requesting that I no longer be involved in your mother's care... you wouldn't consider that to be in any way undermining?" She was laughing at his expression as her words registered.

"Oh Christ!" He put a hand over his mouth.

"Yes. I mean that was all before your girlfriend nearly got me struck off."

"Okay, so basically I've done nothing *but* undermine you and cause difficulties... with no insight whatsoever. That's really quite spectacular arrogance, isn't it?"

"It's certainly impressive."

"It is an *absolute wonder* that you continue to have anything to do with my family – well, with me specifically." He shook his head in disbelief. "I am just a thorn in your professional side."

"Don't be too hard on yourself. You've certainly made life interesting."

Her heart sank as she said it. He really had made everything *so* much more interesting. Life was going to be boring as hell without him.

Chapter Thirty-Five

A while later they returned to the house. The vast majority of guests had already left but a few stragglers remained. Amongst them, a vaguely familiar figure was walking towards them as they crossed the lawn.

"Dan!" Edward threw his arms around his friend. "When did you get here? Thanks for coming, mate. Really good of you."

"Oh, no problem. I was hoping to come to the funeral, but I didn't finish my theatre list until four. We had a bleeder... Anyway. It's good to see you. Are you managing okay? I imagine it's been a bit of a rollercoaster?"

Edward shrugged. "Yeah, it's not been the greatest few weeks. But I guess we were better prepared for it this time. Better than with Dad anyway."

Dan exhaled sharply. "God yes, I'd forgotten about your dad. Blimey. Not easy." He turned his attention to Tess. "Hi, I'm Da— Oh my God! I know you. Wait... it's Tess, isn't it?

You were on my firm a few years back. Although something's different… weren't you blonde then?"

Tess almost laughed at his evident excitement at having recognised her. "Yes, yes that's right. I was one of your students. Well, one of the students on the firm anyway. It's nice to see you."

"Oh, so you must be qualified now? Which hospital are you at? Local? Oh, it's so nice to…" Dan was looking between the two of them, a light dawning in his eyes. "Wait… so you two *did* get together in the end? Wow! That's great. I always wondered—"

Edward cut in, "Oh, no, mate, we're not together, Tess and I. We're… She was looking after Mum, at the hospice."

Tess had flushed to the roots of her hair. "Yes. I'm, um, doing my GP rotation. I'm in the hospice – at least I was. I'm, well, due to start in practice next week, and Mary was my patient and…"

Dan's mouth was a perfect circle. "Oh… God, sorry, right." He looked at Edward and back to Tess again. "I just thought, you know, after that party…"

Nobody knew what to say and there was a silence for a few seconds. Dan blundered on. "That party. You know, in my flat. When you both… Hang on, have I got this wrong? It was you, wasn't it, Tess? You came with that mate of yours, Donna, yes? And Ed, you were staying at mine for the weekend…" He looked at both of them, confusion spreading across his face. "Are you seriously trying to make out that you don't remember what I'm talking about?"

"Um…" Edward's face was impassive. "The party. Yep. When you had that lovely flat with the—"

"The garden," said Dan. "Yes, that flat. And yes, that party. In the summer. You were, what? About to start with that legal investment team and you stayed... You both stayed in the sitting room, you were, like, chatting all night?" He shrugged his shoulders. "Maybe I got it wrong. Just seems a massive coincidence, that's all, both of you being here and you having met already and... I guess it's not that surprising, really. Bristol's not that big a place and..."

Tess recognised the rambling sentences as the type that she used to fill awkward gaps in conversation and she stepped in to help him out, for all their sakes. "I know. Especially for people who were students here. Doesn't it have one of the highest retention rates for students choosing to stay and work?"

Dan grasped onto the conversational life-raft. "Yes! Yes, you're right, it does. And you're obviously still working here. Me too. I'll keep an eye out for your referrals when you hit general practice. Don't send me too many adenoids, for God's sake. They do my head in. In fact, maybe... if you two aren't..." He gave Edward a quizzical look. "Maybe we should go out for a drink sometime, Tess? Catch up? Ed'll give you my number."

She nodded slowly. This was just too crazy. "Yeah, great, okay." She turned to Edward. "I'll, um, I'd better make a move..."

He looked panicked for the briefest of seconds and then his face settled. "No, I'll tell you what. You go and find Madeleine. I'll have a quick catch-up with Dan and then I'll be with you, help you find your coat and whatever." He slung his arm around his friend's shoulders and steered him away, turning to mouth over Dan's shoulder, "Don't go anywhere. We need to talk."

———————

Tess found Madeleine in the kitchen, dishing out sausages and peas to the children. Pauline had evidently finished all the washing-up before she left, and Tess set to work drying glasses and putting them back in the cupboards.

"They are absolutely shattered," Madeleine whispered as Harvey wobbled drowsily in his chair, trying and failing to spear a pea with his fork so that it rolled off the table to the waiting dogs beneath. "And I feel wrecked too."

She raised her voice slightly to include Edward, who had just walked in through the back door, having seen Dan off. "I'm going to take them up for bath and bed in a moment. And I'll probably do the same myself – early night, get some rest. You okay to sort things out down here, Eddie, lock up and everything?"

"Yes, of course. You go up."

Madeleine turned to put the grill pan in the sink.

"So, you'll be the last ones up then," she said meaningfully. "Pauline's gone back home. The kids and I, we'll be out for the count. It'll just be the two of you."

She dabbed at the pan with a scouring pad in the soapy water.

"Yes, thank you Madeleine. We get the message."

Edward shared an uncertain smile with Tess across the

room and then sat to help Harvey scoop up his peas. Tess placed a hand on his shoulder.

"I think I'll just go through to the other room," she said, wanting to give them a bit of space. She got the impression that Madeleine had things she wanted to say to her brother.

"Goodnight, kids. Night, Madeleine. I'll probably be heading home in an hour, so I won't see you. I hope the rest of your stay goes well, and enjoy the zoo tomorrow!"

Madeleine smiled as she turned from the sink. "Thank you," she said with genuine warmth.

———————

Another hour had passed and the sun had set far behind the wooded copse at the end of the south garden, leaving only a pinkish tinge to the gathering twilight. The dogs were settled in the kitchen, and after a short period of noise from upstairs, the splashing, giggling, tearful protestations and nursery rhymes had finished and all was quiet. Tess and Edward had moved from the large drawing room to a smaller snug which faced onto the same south terrace. The rest of the house was locked and shuttered, but the French doors in this room remained open, allowing a view of the remaining sunset and a welcome breeze. The carriage clock on the mantlepiece struck nine and Tess stood, crossing to the open doors to look out across the darkening lawn.

"I had better be going," she said. "Kath will wonder where I am."

This was a lie. Kath was working tonight and would be

none the wiser as to Tess's whereabouts, but she wanted Edward to understand that she existed for other people outside the bubble that had somehow been created today. He stood and crossed the room to join her by the doors, both looking out over the lawn.

"Yes. I expect she will."

They stood for a few moments in silence, and it was as if a static charge was building between them; the longer they remained motionless, apparently ignoring each other, the fiercer the current between them grew, until it felt like a physical force, pulling them in. They were a few inches apart, but every tiny movement was amplified and seemed to disrupt the air around them. She felt she could almost hear his heart beating, but wasn't sure if the rush of noise was her own pulse or his.

Still looking directly forward, Edward began to speak.

"We need to talk…"

She nodded.

"No, I mean really. talk. About what Dan said." He turned to her. "We *did* meet before. At his party. Like he said. You don't remember it but—"

"I *do* remember it. You were the one who—"

They both started talking over each other and Tess paused. "Go on," she said. "You first."

Edward took a deep breath. "When I saw you, that day in the hospice, when Mum first arrived, you remember?"

She nodded.

"I knew it was you. I'd have recognised you anywhere, even with the different haircut. But I was so… I don't know. So angry about everything, so bloody furious to be there.

And then I see you and all I can think about is you turning me down and it was like, 'Oh, great, here's that girl who rejected me and she's going to be looking after my mother...' And you were ignoring me. It was clear you had no idea who I was, no recollection of that night, and you were just concentrating on your job, doing the right thing. And you were so good with Mum and I just had to get out of there. It was all too much."

"Why didn't you just say?"

"Say what? 'Hi, I'm the bloke you didn't want to go out with five years ago? Here I am again, ta-dah! Except now I've brought a whole lot of extra emotional baggage with me?' And anyway, why didn't *you* say anything? I assumed you'd just forgotten, like I hadn't made as much of an impression as I'd thought."

"But that was what I thought!"

"Well, you were the one who gave me the brush-off all those years ago. If anyone was likely to forget the other, it would have been you; so unimpressed by me that you ran off as soon as I kissed you! What was I supposed to think? I called Dan a week later, but you'd left his firm and he didn't know where you'd gone. I tried to search up your details, but I was typing in things like, 'Tess, Bristol Medical School', which resulted in about fourteen hundred hits. None of which were you. It was hopeless."

"Oh, God! I did that too!"

"The thing was, even if I had been able to contact you, it wouldn't have made any difference. You were with Pete or whatever his name was. You'd already made it clear that—"

"I was scared," she said. "Scared of taking the risk. I'm not very brave really."

"Oh, I don't know about that," he said and looked at her pointedly. "You've done some pretty risky things recently; downright reckless, some might say…"

She blushed. "I know. And look where that got me."

He smiled and brushed her cheek with the back of his hand.

"Jesus. What a mess." Tess shook her head. "I remembered you. Of course I did. But you looked straight through me and I sort of doubted myself, doubted everything, and it just wouldn't have been appropriate to say anything anyway. Your mum was my patient. And then, as the weeks went on…"

"It became harder to mention," he finished for her. "It was like the elephant in the room, wasn't it? Well, along with all the other elephants in the room, like my raging animosity towards the hospice establishment, and your ill-concealed *Socialist Worker* agenda."

She snorted a laugh. "*Socialist Worker*, nice one. God, for a pair of intelligent adults, we've been a bit bloody ridiculous, haven't we?"

They both looked out into the garden, lost in their thoughts until Edward spoke again. "That night at Dan's. It was great. I felt like I'd met someone really special. But then in the morning, when you just ran off…" He turned to her. "This Pete. Are you still with him? Was he the guy in the bar?"

"No. That was Simon."

"Oh, yes. He introduced himself. Seemed nice."

"He is nice."

"Good-looking."

"Yes."

"And is it, you know, serious?"

She pursed her lips together. "He really helped me for a time. He's a lovely, kind man, but we're not... We're not together anymore," she said honestly. "Since the, um, incident a few weeks back."

"You told him?"

"No, it's like you said with Clara, there was no need to be cruel. But it was fairly obvious after what happened that I couldn't continue going out with him."

"I see," he said.

"We're still in touch," she said. "But just as friends."

"Right." He seemed to have come to a decision. He turned towards her again. "So, with that in mind..."

"Yeees."

"I know my family have caused you endless problems..."

Tess remained silent, still staring out into the garden.

"...And I know that I'm not necessarily the most appealing prospect at the moment, being a bit of an emotional wreck and all. I'm clearly still in a mess. Much as I was a few weeks ago, but I am getting there, realising what's important..."

She caught a glimpse of him chewing his lower lip out of the corner of her eye.

"What I really mean," he said, "is that I think there

could be something between us. There's definitely the potential, isn't there?"

She turned to look at him then, and the intensity of his gaze almost threw her off balance. She gave a tiny nod.

"But I also completely understand if you want nothing more to do with me," he said, searching her face for clues. "If I'm just one giant headache you can't wait to get rid of?"

She felt a knot forming in her stomach at the thought.

"But I guess," he said, "in either scenario, if you wanted to stay here tonight? I mean, I'll be leaving in a couple of days. It wouldn't have to be... I don't know. It wouldn't have to mean anything." He exhaled quickly. "I'm getting myself tangled up here. All I know is that I really want you to stay. If you want to. We could just see what transpires..."

There was now a smile twitching at the corner of Tess's mouth. "*See what transpires...?*" she said, and he laughed, putting a hand to her cheek and tracing his finger softly down her neck. She remained motionless but took a sharp intake of breath.

"Yes," he said, now moving his hand to stroke her shoulder, "Besides, I think it would only be fair to let me get my own back for being seduced so mercilessly last time? Perhaps now I'll have a turn at being in charge?"

He leaned in to kiss her, his lips soft against hers, his mouth warm. There was none of the ferocity of the previous encounter; it was almost unbearably gentle, and Tess felt her legs weaken as he bent to kiss the dip beneath her collar bone, running his tongue along it to the tip of her shoulder. He turned her round slowly so that he was behind her, lifting her hair up and kissing the nape of her neck as he slid the zip of her dress down. Tess felt as if her brain had stalled, as if all higher functions had ceased and the rational, sensible part of her had abdicated all responsibility for the rest of her body. Edward spread the fabric of her dress across her shoulders, his mouth hot against her skin. He slid his hand inside the dress and round to her front, cupping one of her breasts through the sheer fabric of her underwear. He then undid the catch of her bra with his other hand and slid the straps over her shoulders, pushing down on the dress so that her top half was exposed to her navel. Tess could feel the light breeze coming in from the garden rippling across her skin as she turned back round to face him and he kissed her softly again on her mouth. Her arms were restricted by her dress as he continued to trail kisses across her throat, down her sternum to her abdomen, kneeling to press his face into the warmth of her body above the folds of fabric bunched at her waist.

Tess didn't know how she was still upright. Her legs were shaking, but he brought his hands back round to unzip her dress completely, letting it fall to the floor in a pool round her ankles. Still kneeling, he leant back and gazed up at her. Her eyes were closed but she could feel him looking, heard him gasp in pleasure at the sight of her.

"Oh, Tess," he whispered. "You are so beautiful."

He pulled her down to the floor beside him, kissing her mouth again, holding her shoulders as he started to move once more down her body. She felt as if she were melting into the carpet, a boiling liquid pool, as his mouth reached the soft curve of her tummy and his hand slid up the inside of her thighs. And then he was kissing the tops of her legs and she was moaning softly, making noises that she could hear from a distance, unaware that they were coming from her own mouth. By the time his tongue was on her and his fingers inside her, she could hold it back no longer. She arched her body up towards him and called out his name, rolling on the wave of molten liquid she had become.

Chapter Thirty-Six

They made it as far as Edward's bedroom, but did not sleep until the sun rose, spending the hours instead exploring each other minutely, both making up for lost time and also aware that this might be their only night together. In the early hours of the morning, when they were lying tangled in each other's arms, exhausted, Tess told him about the recent revelations regarding her father. Over the past few months she'd been dipping in and out of the drawer where she kept Marco's letters, reading them through, but limiting herself to one or two at a time, like treats. She hadn't been sure that she could handle condensing twenty years of life, love, and regret into a single sitting, but she had now read them all, and had been considering getting in contact with him. "I've written him a letter," she said. "I wrote it whilst I was in France with Kath. But I haven't sent it yet. I need to check with Mam, make sure I've got the right address. And make sure she's okay with me doing this," she added.

Edward regarded her seriously. "It is up to you," he said. "Completely up to you. There may be downsides. Neither of you are likely to be the people you have built up in your heads. But from what you're saying, he was keen, *is* keen, to know you, and to have some kind of relationship. It would be your decision how close that relationship became, but I think perhaps you should let him know that you've found his letters, and maybe explain why it has taken so long to respond?"

Tess propped herself up on her elbow. "That's kind of what I thought. The more I think about it, the more I consider how hurt he must have felt by my silence..."

Edward touched her cheek tenderly. "You haven't done anything wrong," he said. "You didn't know. And you're being really sensible, thinking it through rather than leaping on a plane and jetting over to Italy for some big gesture. There's no hurry. He's waited this long, and I suspect many fathers wait a lifetime for a child's forgiveness."

"Yes, you're right."

"And whilst you're understandably hurt and confused about why your mother, sorry, your *mam*," he smiled, "I love the way you say it. Anyway, whilst you're confused about why she acted the way she did, you don't want to pile on the distress. You obviously don't need her permission to contact him, but I get that it needs to be done in a sensitive way."

"Yes, it's tricky."

"But, you're *really* good at that stuff," he said. "Believe me, if anyone can handle that sort of conversation in a kind and empathic way, it's you. I've seen you do it."

"That's a very nice thing to say." She snuggled back down against him. "And whilst you're being so thoroughly understanding…" She sighed. "And while we're on the subject of me and my emotional baggage, there's probably something else you should know."

She told him about Scott, the whole saga, and exactly how wretched she'd felt when she found him with Luke.

"It just made me feel really stupid," she said. "And I was so hurt and so upset, but because of the circumstances it was hard to share it, to tell anyone. If I'd have caught him in bed with another woman then fine, well, not fine, but at least you get a bit of solidarity from the sisterhood. As it was, I felt so ashamed, such a fool for not knowing. I ended up making it really easy for him. I didn't shout or scream at him because I was so confused; I thought it must have been my fault somehow. And he wasn't remotely worried about me or how I felt. The thing about him being gay was that it somehow made the infidelity secondary as far as he was concerned. It was as if the most important thing was that he had been true to himself and finally come out; the fact that he had cheated was less significant. I felt as though, somehow, I had lost my right to be angry. And the trouble was, I was bloody furious."

Edward had been silent throughout but now he smiled. "I can imagine. I've seen you bloody furious before." He pulled her close to him. "You really haven't had the easiest time recently, have you? Scott, your dad, the situation with Clara and the complaint, all the distress that caused. And yet you seem to handle it? To take it in your stride." He shook his head. "I'd be all over the place."

Tess decided not to share the information about her issues with food at this point. There were probably only so many revelations a man could cope with in a single night and besides, she seemed to have a proper handle on it again. "I *was* all over the place," she admitted, "when I first found out about Scott, and for a long while after. I don't think my way of dealing with things is necessarily any better than yours. But I guess you just have to get on with things." She shrugged into the pillow. "Anyway, I couldn't really hate him. I don't think he set out to deceive me; he just fell in love, and the person he fell for happened to be a man."

Edward now had his arm around her shoulders and she was cuddled into him, speaking into his chest, but he lifted her chin to look into her eyes.

"Still," he said, "I imagine that the whole thing must have been quite a shock."

She lay there feeling his chest rise and fall and nodded a little sadly to herself, then he moved his arm from behind her head and brought his face next to hers.

"Mind you," he said, stroking her cheek and gazing deep into her eyes, "I would have to seriously question the sexual orientation of any man who wouldn't want to spend the rest of his life going down on you." He punctuated this with little kisses to her cheeks and neck and she could feel the firm pressure of him building against her thigh. "Speaking of which…" His kisses became slower as he moved down her throat to her breasts and she rolled slightly onto her back.

"You do say the loveliest things, Mr Russell."

"I may speak nicely, Dr Carter"—his voice became muffled as he disappeared under the duvet—"but I'm planning on doing some very bad things to you."

Later that morning, Tess woke to find the bed empty beside her. She lay there for a while just enjoying the heaviness in her limbs and the feathery weight of the duvet on her skin. Whenever she was with Edward her senses seemed to be more highly attuned, as if she were experiencing everyday sensations afresh. She stretched the full length of the bed, feeling the muscles and tendons of her toes and fingers extend. Her cheeks were warm and she realised that she had a ridiculous grin on her face. The hours were passing so quickly and the sun was high in the sky outside their window, throwing bright light into the room. She got up, found a T-shirt of Edward's draped on a chair and slipped it over her head, pressing it to her face to inhale the scent of him that clung to the fabric. She tiptoed to the bathroom, checking for certain that there were no small children in the vicinity first.

Returning to the bedroom, she discovered that Edward had brought her a cup of tea and was sitting propped against the pillows waiting for her with a mischievous look on his face. He told her that Madeleine had already taken the kids to the zoo. "So we don't need to worry about traumatising them when we're swinging from the chandeliers in feats of erotic adventure."

"What you do in your own time, Edward, is up to you,

chandeliers or otherwise." She climbed into the bed beside him and reached over for her cup of tea. "But I am a very busy person. And I have places to be." She took a sip from her tea and raised her eyebrows at him.

He took the mug from her hand and placed it back on the bedside table. "Yes," he said. "I too have places to be. Places I really need to be. But most of those places are somewhere in this glorious body of yours."

She laughed as he slipped his arm around her.

"Do you have to go?" he asked.

"At some point, yes, I really do, much as I'd rather stay." The thought of leaving was awful, but she strove to keep her voice neutral, to enjoy these last stolen moments with him. There was a pause and she closed her eyes, feeling the warmth of the sun on her face.

"I don't suppose there's any way you could come to America with me?" She recognised the same studied neutrality in his voice. He too was struggling to keep his feelings in check. She turned to look at him.

"What? As your private physician?"

"No! Stop being ridiculous. As my, I don't know, girlfriend?"

"Your 'I don't know' girlfriend? Hmmm, let me think…" She stroked his hand and felt the tears prickling at her eyes once more. "Edward," she said. "I have a life here. I have a career, one that I worked very hard to build, and one that I very nearly lost. I can't go running off to America just because some rich, sexy man has clicked his fingers."

"My wealth really bothers you, doesn't it?" He pulled her down further into the bed.

"Yes, but not as much as it used to."

"The sexiness doesn't appear to be a significant problem?"

"I can live with it."

He kissed her lightly on the nose.

"Well, your complete refusal to drop everything and accompany me is frankly outrageous," he said.

"Do you always get what you want?" Tess was genuinely curious.

"Usually," he shrugged, "but not always. And perhaps not this time." He ran his hand up her thigh past her hip to her waist, looking deep into her eyes. "I want to remember you like this, just like this, as you are. You're so beautiful and… I'm sorry I don't really have the words for it…"

"They seem like perfectly adequate words to me. Perhaps you're more eloquent than you think."

He smiled. "You're good for me. That's the thing, I'm not so sure I'm good for you, but you're definitely good for me."

"You sure you're not just a bit overexcited about getting laid?" Tess knew she sounded flippant, but it seemed to be her only protection mechanism against the effect his words were having.

"No." He rolled slightly away from her, a little saddened by her response. "It's not just that, although, Christ, it's obviously been amazing. I mean *you*. You're good for me. You make me a better person."

"Edward…" She didn't trust herself to say any more at this point. There was a part of her that wanted him to pour out his heart, to tell her he loved her as desperately as she loved him. But if that happened, those declarations needed to be accompanied by a promise not to leave her, a promise not to abandon her with these feelings and head off to America, never to return. She knew she could not ask that of him, and as a result she couldn't allow herself to get drawn too far along a path from which there may be no return.

"I know I'm not exactly the most conversant with my feelings," he said, "but I've spent more time considering my emotions in the past few weeks than I have my entire life, so I'm doing my best, and there's something about being with you that just makes sense. I don't know if it's because you challenge me, or because you have higher expectations, or because you understand me more than you realise…"

"That might have something to do with it."

"Well, look," he said, "I don't really know what it is, but I'm better with you. I can sort of imagine myself being better with you for a very long time."

Tess drew circles on his chest, not daring to look up at his face. She felt exactly the same. She'd already imagined their future together. She knew that she had fallen hopelessly in love with him, but despite his candour, she wasn't quite prepared to admit it, not when she stood to lose him. What good would it do to share that information now?

"Edward," she said. "You don't need me in order to be a better person. You are that man already. I saw it that very first time we met. I felt it. And that's not because of my influence. It's nothing to do with me. It's who you are."

Edward sighed. There was a little voice in his ear, the

one he sometimes heard when he was unsure of himself. *She's blown you out again, mate. Take it like a man. You've been here before.* He shook his head. That voice of doubt; it had been particularly vocal when his dad died and when his mother had first been diagnosed, but he hadn't heard it much recently, and knew better than to pay it too much attention, even if it did have a point. He sought to hide his disappointment.

"All this talking isn't solving the immediate problem, I'm afraid, Dr Carter." He rolled on top of her, nudging between her thighs and she gave him a stern look.

"The more times we do this, the harder it's going to be to say goodbye. You do realise that, don't you?" she said.

"Yes. No. I don't know. It doesn't seem to be a compelling reason to stop. I guess it's all a bit of a conundrum…"

She tilted her pelvis to press against him. "A conundrum? Is that what you call it?"

He laughed and pinned her hands down as he slowly edged inside her, watching her facial expression change. "What would you call it?"

Their bodies pressed together and they held each other tightly, both knowing that this was the last time – and when she finally came, she cried a little, just softly enough for him not to hear it. How, she wondered to herself, was she going to give up a man who could make her feel like this, and how long could she maintain the lie that she wasn't hopelessly in love with him?

Chapter Thirty-Seven

They stayed wrapped in each other for a few more moments, their skin warm and sticky against each other. But she knew it was time to leave, and she had to be the one to instigate the separation, if only to give herself some semblance of control. She kissed his shoulder and moved decisively off the bed to pick up her dress, pulling it on and sitting back down next to him, gesturing for him to help her with the zip.

"Oh!" he said. "Don't make me do that. It's like wrapping a favourite Christmas present back up and giving it away."

"Cease your whining, boy, and help a lady recover her modesty."

She laughed as he grumbled to himself, slowly piecing the zip together link by link, and then stood up and hunted around the room for her shoes, slipping her foot into one and hopping to pull on the other when she found it.

"Are you absolutely sure you don't want to run away

with a rich, sexy man?" He swung his legs to the edge of the bed and pulled his shorts back on, trying to sound casual despite the pain in his chest and the tightening of his throat.

"And where on earth would I find one of those?" She leaned back against the window ledge, the outline of the large oak trees in bright relief behind her. He was still sitting on the bed looking at her. "Edward," she said, "Don't look all wounded. I have had the most wonderful, wonderful evening, and night, and morning. And I am not going to deny that there is a part of me that just wants to stay here with you in bed until we get bored of each other, which may be some considerable time, given the things you do to me."

"Well, indeed. It's certainly tempting."

"But you said yourself that you're still in a bit of a mess. You only buried your mother yesterday. You want to rebuild the connections with your family. You wouldn't be able to do that with me in tow."

She continued to speak as she piled her hair up in a loose bun and crossed the room to retrieve her handbag, hiding her face from him as she composed her expression. "The last thing you need at the moment is a girlfriend. You've only just split up with the last one and rushing headfirst into a new relationship would be a disaster. I'm sure as hell nothing like Clara. A bit of a break might give you some perspective on what you really want."

"Okay, point taken. But—"

"And of course, the way this all began… it's not a conventional start to a relationship, is it? We've sort of launched straight into all the high drama and intensity without doing the day-to-day stuff? Who knows how much of this," she gestured between the two of them, "is just both of us clinging to each other in an attempt to escape the turbulence of the past few months? The only way we work this out, decide whether there is something real and solid to link us, is with a bit of space."

She dug her nails into the palm of her hand for distraction, knowing that she had to be pragmatic for both of their sakes. So much of the past month had been governed by emotional responses, and his feelings would still be fluctuating wildly, given the fact that he was actively grieving. She had to be the sensible one today, in spite of wanting to crumple into a heap and beg him not to leave her.

"So, you go. Have a great time in America. You might decide to stay. I can imagine the lifestyle would suit you."

"Tess, don't! Are you crying? Come here."

She crossed the room and sat down beside him. He drew her in, wrapping his strong arms around her as her tears soaked his T-shirt. Her voice was muffled and shaky when she spoke. "I am not actually crying. My face often looks this pink and scrunched up. And watery." She laughed shakily and dabbed her eyes with the edge of his top. "Sorry. Look, if you really do care about my feelings, please don't contact me again unless you're coming back. You might just break my heart if you string me along."

"What? So, that's it?" He looked aghast.

She nodded. "I mean it. No Facebook friending, no Instagram following, no messaging, no calls, nothing. You understand?"

"I do," he said slowly. "But I just don't know how you can be so clinical about it. Have you gone all professional and detached on me? You're not usually so guarded."

"Sorry. I would have thought it was fairly evident from my copious weeping that I am feeling anything but emotionally detached." She rested her head back on his shoulder. "I'm just trying to protect myself. Historically it's not been something I'm great at. And as for being professional, I'm not exactly breaking records on that front either. I mean, it's hardly good practice to have sex with a patient's relative."

"Well," he said, "yes, you've got a point there."

"At least you've got enough self-awareness to know when you're in a mess, Edward. I've been blundering about, making the same mistakes for years, as far as relationships go. I'm riddled with self-doubt most of the time and I need to learn when to leave things alone. Anyway, I can't be that cool and collected if I keep falling in love with unsuitable men, can I?"

She had moved slightly out of the embrace and they held each other's look for a moment – had she said she was in love with him, or that he was unsuitable? Neither of them was sure.

Finally, she picked up her bag and pulled it onto her shoulder. "You will be fine without me, you know you will."

"Well, if that's really what you want… I guess I don't have much choice."

She kissed him gently on the mouth, holding her lips to his for what felt like an eternity, until the salt from both their tears started to seep between their cheeks and she pulled away. "No need to escort me off the premises." She stood to leave. "In spite of what Clara thinks, I have no intention of making off with the family silver!" She turned at the doorway. "You take care of yourself, Edward. You're a really amazing, lovely bloke and I'm going to miss you."

And then she was gone.

—————

As Tess left the house, she felt oddly calm. She strode through the kitchen, patted the dogs, and crunched across the gravel which was bathed in sunlight, before rounding the corner to the stable yard. She was starting to become accustomed to fraught car journeys, and the process of detaching herself from the drama in order to focus on the practicalities of getting home in one piece had already begun. She was determined not to look in her rear-view mirror as her little car pulled out of a driveway better suited to a horse-drawn carriage, an observation only reinforced by Jane Austen's voice in her ear.

"*Parting is such sweet sorrow, dear girl – not one of my lines, you understand, but I consider it entirely appropriate to plagiarise, given the circumstances.*" She sniffed delicately. "*Another you could try is, 'Absence makes the heart grow fonder', although I am unsure as to the veracity of that particular statement. It seems a phrase designed to sustain those of a more fragile and delicate disposition than ladies of our calibre and moral fortitude.*"

Tess was delighted that Miss Austen regarded her so

highly, although she wondered whether her opinion regarding moral fortitude might be somewhat compromised by last night's activities. Her heart was full, but she was in that pleasant state of being physically satisfied before the brain starts to process circumstances and consequences. She knew that over the coming days, perhaps months, she would analyse and review the events of the preceding twenty-four hours in minute detail, considering, reinterpreting, wondering whether particular words held unique significance, whether a certain look or gesture had meant that Edward worshipped the ground she walked on or was utterly indifferent to her – but for now her body was singing, her skin tingling from his touch, and her senses overwhelmed with the smell and taste of him. She wasn't thinking straight, but she didn't want to. She didn't want to analyse her feelings yet; she wanted them to remain pure and unadulterated for a while longer.

Her euphoric state lasted until she got home, by which time the fatigue was starting to kick in. She hadn't eaten or slept for hours, existing on a high-octane combination of desire and adrenaline. As a result, she was now ravenous, and plundered the kitchen in a similar way to her housemate after an on-call shift. She was not seeking food for consolation, purely as sustenance, which, she acknowledged, was as it should be. Edward had made her feel that, somehow, she should be a bit kinder to herself. Their connection had been something magical. To have tainted it with another bout of binging would have been somehow insulting to the memory of what they had shared.

She was in the sitting room, still wearing her dress from

the night before and vacantly spooning cereal into her mouth, when Kath came back from town mid-afternoon.

"Weh-hey there! Love's young dream." She noted the combination of Tess's glowing cheeks and air of general dishevelment. "I take it you've been up all night shagging the repressed orphan? Did you manage a more appropriate venue than a shed this time?"

Tess laughed, almost choking on her cereal, but suddenly the emotional turmoil of the past few hours caught up with her and her laughter turned into untidy sobs, tears trickling down her nose. Kath looked genuinely alarmed.

"Oh, my girl!" She rushed to embrace her housemate. "I'm so sorry. I didn't mean to poke fun at you, or him, or whatever. I can't ever seem to stop myself."

She fussed around Tess, taking the cereal bowl off her and letting her succumb to a full messy wailing, punctuated by hiccups and cries of: "Think I might love him…"; "Probably never see him again…"; and, "What a bloody mess…"

Kath held onto her until the sobs had subsided to an intermittent drizzle and then pulled out her phone, back in practical mode. "Did you use protection?" she asked, and then in response to Tess's sheepish nod, "Every single time?"

"Maybe not every time."

Kath was already dialling the genitourinary medicine clinic; she had their number saved in her phone, as half the patient referrals came through the casualty department.

"You might be thinking a little less fondly about him if

he's left you with a dose of chlamydia or a bun in the oven, babe. I'm surprised at you. I'd have thought your mother would've virtually not let you leave the house without a full-body condom," she said, waiting for the phone to connect.

Tess fell back onto the couch with a groan. "There's just no romance with you, is there."

"When you've seen the kind of things I've seen, my love, the scales fall from your eyes on that score," Kath said. "Did I tell you about the chap who came in a few nights ago with a courgette up his arse? Told me he'd fallen onto it whilst cooking ratatouille in the nude. Had to ask if I was likely to find a red onion and a couple of pointed peppers up there and all! Obviously, wife not best pleased..."

Tess rolled around on the sofa laughing, "You didn't! Oh my God, Kath, poor man. Poor wife! Jesus." She wiped her eyes and looked over at her friend, "What would I do without you?"

Kath brushed the air with her hand. "Pah! Don't be ridiculous. Now get yer arse upstairs and into that shower. Frankly, girl, you reek of sex and it's starting to make me feel a bit flustered."

Chapter Thirty-Eight

Tess spent the rest of the day in bed, drifting in and out of daydreams of a life with Edward that she was never likely to experience. The next morning, Kath said she was allowed one full day to wallow in sentimental indulgence, telling stories and trawling the internet for any trace of him. After about twenty minutes of drooling together over a particular shot taken at a City ball for the diary section of *Tatler*'s website, Kath closed the browser with a flourish.

"Had your fill now?" she asked Tess. "Feasted your eyes sufficiently? Right. We need to be realistic. I'll allow you one visit to that particular website per week, but no more."

"Okay! Okay!"

"I will know. I warn you! Shame I don't have parental controls for our Wi-Fi, but the levels of protection may not extend as far as the *Financial Times*." She looked back at the blank screen. "I feel your pain, believe me. I think I might

358

have to wean myself off him and all, but mate, sure it's got to be done."

"I know. I can't help but feel you're enjoying the cruel prison-warden act a bit much though."

"You could be right. Maybe I've missed my calling… Anyway!" She clapped her hands peremptorily. "You need to start thinking about work. General Practice tomorrow. Yay!"

Tess smiled. She was actually really looking forward to starting in practice and she knew she needed to take her mind off the fact that Edward was leaving for America within the next few hours. As it turned out, his flight took off from Bristol airport about halfway through Tess's first morning clinic, and she was too preoccupied by Dr Sharma's explanation regarding antihypertensive medication to think of him, sitting next to Harvey, pointing out the diminishing bridge and the river from the plane window. That night, when she returned from the surgery, she allowed herself to imagine him just coming in to land and helping his sister steer the children through the arrivals lounge to greet their father. Harvey and Annabelle would likely be fractious and irritable after their journey, but she knew that Madeleine's husband planned to keep them entertained over the following days to allow his wife and brother-in-law the chance to recover from their combination of jet-lag and grief.

She thought of Edward contemplating the prospect of extended rest and relaxation combined with the day-to-day aspects of family life that he had so missed. She could see how easy it would have been for him to simply return to work and plough himself back into the familiar coping mechanisms, blindly following his career trajectory until he woke one day, old and lonely. Instead, he had used the crisis of the past few months to examine his life and, finding it wanting, had taken active steps to rectify the mistakes he'd already made. He had more insight than he gave himself credit for, and she wished she'd told him so when she'd had the chance.

There were many things she now wished she had said, knowing that she probably would not have the opportunity again. She wanted him to know how highly she regarded him, how impressed she was by how he was using his grief to forge closer links with his sister. She wanted him to know how special and treasured he had made her feel, and how that warmth remained with her like a comforting blanket despite his absence. He had encouraged her to think for herself, had admired her strengths, and allowed her to accept her weaknesses. Whatever else happened, she sensed that meeting him again would prove to have been one of the most pivotal moments in her life.

Whilst she silently congratulated Edward on his decision to remove himself from a blinkered working existence, she also knew how therapeutic new career challenges could be. She chose to immerse herself in work for the next few weeks, hoping for distraction, although in reality she thought of him all the time; what he might have said about this, what the expression on his face would have been in response to that, how it would have felt to have cuddled up to his warm body in bed at night, to have been held by him, touched by him again. It was similar to those months after their first meeting; better, because she knew that she hadn't misjudged things, but worse because she now had a much clearer idea of what she was missing out on. Occasionally she broke Kath's rule, searching under both his name and Madeleine's married name for any mention of what he was now up to. His privacy filters, as Tess would have expected, were watertight, but now and then a picture would pop up on Madeleine's Instagram profile of Edward with one of the children, and Tess's heart would leap into her mouth as she saw his tanned, handsome face, smiling and relaxed. But generally, she kept those searches to a minimum, knowing that there might come a time when she would stumble across a picture of him with a woman other than his sister, and that she might just crumble into a billion pieces.

She also ensured that her trips to the other side of the bridge were infrequent, although whenever she took Morris for his check-ups with the vet, she drove past the Russell estate and, in spite of herself, tried to glimpse the window of the bedroom where they had spent the night together. Once or twice she visited the memorial garden in the crematorium, where a plaque bearing Mary Russell's name was regularly adorned with floral tributes. On one occasion she bumped into Pauline, who was, she realised, the source of the majority of fresh flowers. She was thrilled to see Tess and insisted on filling her in on what the family were up to in America, and how much happier Edward sounded when he called to enquire after the dogs and the house, and also to ask how Pauline herself was bearing up.

"He's always been such a thoughtful boy, that one," she

said. "He knows I'm just rattling round that house on my own now, so he calls and pretends it's about something practical." She gestured to the flowers in Tess's hands. "I see you've brought some stocks – Mary's favourite they were. What a kind thought."

Tess looked down at them. "Well, I guessed as much. She always had them in St Martin's; the smell reminds me of her somehow."

"I know. Me too. And how are you doing, Dr Carter? How's that cat of yours? Harvey always asks me."

"Morris? He's fighting fit. Well, other than being a massive chubster. I'm hoping he's now just too fat to get through the window, but I think he's learnt his lesson; he's not tried any Houdini numbers since."

"I'll be sure to let Harvey know. He's been sharing the heroic rescue story with all of his new schoolfriends."

"And how are you doing, Pauline?"

"Oh, I manage okay. Looking after that house is a full-time job – keeps me busy."

"And it's not too hard? Being surrounded by all those reminders of your friend? I know you were closer to her than almost anyone else. Oh, I'm sorry," she put a hand out towards Pauline, "I didn't mean to upset you."

"Oh, Dr Carter. Mary always said that you were a one for winkling the truth out of people. It's nice to know you care, dearie, but I'm fine, honestly. You needn't bother about me."

"Okay, if you're sure. It's been lovely to see you. Anyway, do say hello to the family from me."

"I certainly will. And, you know, she would have been so touched that you brought her flowers."

Pauline squeezed her hand and Tess walked away from the memorial garden with a lighter heart than when she'd arrived, feeling that some of her own sense of loss was easing with the passage of time.

As Morris became stronger and more mobile, the need for any further visits to the vet's diminished, and she began to accept that there was no longer a real excuse to head out in that direction at all. She had taken out the bank loan as planned, and paid off the bill for Morris's treatment in its entirety, requesting that they refund Edward via his credit card. A few weeks later Tess took delivery of an enormous bouquet of flowers addressed to "Dr Carter" and sent to her at home by an anonymous benefactor. She guessed that Edward must have sought her details from Henry, and smiled when she considered the conversation that may have taken place, knowing Henry had a matchmaker's twinkle in his eye at each follow-up appointment. Still, she knew it didn't really signify anything; it was likely just an overblown gesture of gratitude for paying him back.

Similarly, she tried to remain level-headed about a hand-drawn crayon picture of an orange cat that arrived on her doormat one blustery October morning with a Chicago postmark. It was accompanied by another picture of a stick man with large hands and feet standing next to either a green horse or a dinosaur. The figure had a large red smile on his round face, and a caption beneath read "Unkel Ed". Also inside the envelope was a plain notecard, and on it, in an elaborate cursive script, Madeleine had written:

Eddie said you didn't want to be contacted, but Harvey
wanted to send you these. Since he's started at school
he's been churning out pictures like you wouldn't
believe! Thank you for whatever you did for my brother
(I really don't want to know). He is a much happier man
now. Madeleine x

It took a few moments to regain her composure after
receiving this, and Tess struggled to stop herself from
reading a tone of finality into Madeleine's words, as if
whatever transformative effect Tess had once had on her
brother was now complete. However, the pictures took
pride of place in her clinic room at the practice, and patients
often commented on them.

She tried to keep herself occupied with her work, her
family, and her social life, much as she had before meeting
Edward, but it was a challenge not to think of him during
those quiet times, late in the evening, and often she woke
from a restless night having dreamt of him. She thought of
Mary too, returning to the memorial garden now and then,
just to spend a peaceful afternoon in its tranquil
surroundings.

Once she was confident that Clara's complaint was fully
resolved and that there were no further significant shocks in
store for her, she plucked up the courage to contact her dad.
She hadn't forgotten Edward's advice and knew that he
regretted not being able to spend more time with his own
parents. Her mum confirmed that the most recent postal
address on his last letter was the one she had used
previously, and although the conversation was strained, she

understood Tess's need to set the record straight and seek him out, if only to apologise. A few weeks after she sent her letter, she had a reply with a tentative suggestion that they could meet. They spoke on the phone – Marco's English was perfect but had a rolling and extravagant Italian accent – and Tess found herself responding in kind, lifting the ends of her sentences into a question when she was merely stating facts. Kath, overhearing her, creased up in hysterics on the sofa, and told her she sounded like she was in *The Sopranos*, but she couldn't disguise her excitement when she and Tess arranged a trip to Rimini for early in the New Year.

Tess saw Farida intermittently; they went out for coffee or to the cinema, sometimes just the two of them, sometimes with Rob, who had still not quite built up the confidence to ask her out on her own. She also continued to see Simon as a friend, knowing that she had made the right decision about not forcing a romance that did not exist. She wasn't going to make the same mistake and choose the safe option like she had with Pete all those years ago, abandoning passion and excitement for a stable relationship with a man who wouldn't leave her. She knew that getting back together with Simon would have been unsatisfying and would have led to resentment on both sides.

Simon's acceptance of the platonic nature of their relationship impressed her – he never pressurised her into turning it back into anything more. She once mentioned his gallantry to Kath, who responded that maybe he wasn't being a gentleman at all, and perhaps he'd just never really fancied her, which Tess had to concede was possible, although she flicked her housemate the V-sign when she did so.

She sought Simon's advice when she came to look for a flat of her own; Ravi had asked Kath to move in with him, and despite her reservations, she had said yes. "I think he just wants to keep me on the straight and narrow," she had whispered to Tess, but her beaming smile belied the offhand delivery; she was thrilled. The girls' tenancy agreement was due to expire at the end of January, and Tess had saved enough to secure a deposit on a single-bedroom flat in one of the nicer areas of Bristol. It meant that for the first time in her life, she had a real sense of financial security; something that she had worked for; a tiny piece of her own property. When the bank agreed her mortgage application she was almost as excited as the day she'd qualified as a doctor, and her mum was the same. Jake had completed his training and started work, and suddenly it looked as though her entire family were finally starting to free themselves from the financial worries and insecurities that had plagued them for so long.

It was whilst she was with Simon, recently returned from a second viewing of the flat she would ultimately go on to buy, that she first heard about the Russell estate. They were in the agency office, Tess updating Simon as to how her tenancy agreement was proceeding whilst he made her a cup of tea in the tiny shared staff kitchen, when he mentioned a new property that was likely to be coming onto their books. His excitement was palpable, not least because apparently the vendor had specifically asked for him to do the valuation and lead the potential sale.

"It's an absolute stunner, Tess!" he said with obvious relish. "Basically an estate agent's wet dream!"

She rolled her eyes and continued filling in a form about agency fees, but he was itching to show her the photos he had taken earlier that week, and she put down her pen with amusement, turning to the screen where Simon was now opening the sales particulars.

"I owe you one for this," he said as he clicked on the JPEG. "It was that fella we bumped into in the bar that first time we went out. The one you said was an absolute bastard? He kept my business card!"

Tess didn't hear his words. As soon as she saw that first image – the gently rolling lawn, the Georgian façade, greyer in the winter light than the golden summer glow of her memory – she felt a dull pain below her chest. Simon scrolled through the remaining pictures, and she saw the walled garden where she had sat with Edward on the day of the funeral, the kitchen where he had made her breakfast that day when she had arrived from the vet's, awkward with gratitude and embarrassed to have caught him unawares. She saw the drawing room where they had greeted Mary's many friends and well-wishers together and finally, almost so agonising that she had to turn her head from the screen, Edward's room. All those memories, and now, all of it for sale. So, he wasn't coming back. The family were selling up and moving on. She could hardly bear it.

Tess drew a sharp intake of breath, the twisting

sensation in her stomach spreading to her chest, tightening her throat and draining the blood from her head. She put a hand out to steady herself on the desk and Simon looked up.

"You all right, Tess?"

"Oh, yes thank you. I'm fine."

"I know, it's gorgeous, isn't it?" He nodded back towards the screen. "But your little flat is going to be smashing and all. We'll get it fixed up proper job, hey?"

He pushed the cup of tea towards her, shutting down the photos on the screen, reluctant to tear himself aware from such a vision of loveliness.

"It'll be millions," he said wistfully. "Gorgeous manor house and prime land like that. Although they have put in some stipulations. I think they're going to sell a lot of the acreage to the local vet's. Bit bonkers if you ask me; it'd fetch a fortune if it went to developers, but, I guess if you're sitting on that sort of pile, you can afford to be a bit eccentric."

"Yes, I guess so."

"You sure you're all right? You're a bit pale. Anyway, you sorted that form out yet?"

Jane Austen's attempts to soothe her were somewhat undermined by her own distress.

"It is a great shock, my dear. Yes, indeed. A difficult time for us all. But we must endure. We must face the very real prospect that the gentleman to whom you have lost your heart is… never to be seen again…" The wail that accompanied the comment was particularly unhelpful.

Tess didn't share her discovery with Kath until her

housemate noticed her downcast expression and pulled her up on it.

"You'd seemed a bit more sorted, babe?" She patted Tess's shoulder gently. "I thought maybe you were getting over him, but I guess not?"

Tess had not even admitted to herself that her attempts to get over Edward were not going as well as she had hoped. Looking back, the separation from Scott had somehow been easier to manage, his actions having terminated the relationship so definitively that there was at least an element of closure – and some righteous anger – to see her through the tough times. But there was no anger left in her; she had exorcised those demons with the help of Edward, and now there remained only a sadness, a yearning for what could have been. She supposed that with the sale of the house perhaps she would finally be able to shut those feelings down. If she knew there was no chance of rekindling whatever it was that they'd once had, then maybe she could move on herself. She had to try; there was no other option. Edward had made his feelings clear: he was literally moving on, by moving out.

Chapter Thirty-Nine

I t was late December, a few days before Christmas, and the streets were cold and damp, much as they had been the morning that Tess first met Edward almost a year before. Tess was now five months into her GP registrar training, and since her discovery about the proposed sale of the Russell estate a few weeks earlier, she was occupying her time, forcing herself to enjoy the variety of clinical cases she saw. She had missed seeing children and babies during her hospice attachment, and their presence in surgery now caused her much entertainment, although this was sometimes balanced with anxiety about how quickly they could become unwell. She had also missed seeing people who were healthy: pregnant mums excited about their impending arrivals; people with lumps and bumps that turned out to be benign. It was nice to bring good news into people's lives as well as helping them deal with the bad. She was working through the coursework elements for her membership of the Royal College of

General Practitioners and had started to think about the exams she was due to sit in the spring. Although the trip to Rimini would interfere with her revision schedule, she was starting to look forward to meeting Marco. She wasn't sure that she would ever be able to think of him as her father, but by now they had spoken several times, each telephone conversation slightly easier than the previous one, and as Kath said, a trip to Italy was a trip to Italy. She was also spending a lot of her time planning how to decorate her new flat, what furniture to buy, and which colour schemes would best complement the original features Simon had so painstakingly pointed out to her when she viewed it.

It was Saturday afternoon and Tess had returned from a trip to town where she had bought a couple of last-minute presents for her mum and a large table lamp for herself, despite not yet having a table to put it on. She was up in her room, the gifts spread out on her bed and the lamp in a large box next to her chest of drawers, with Morris sitting proprietorially on top of it. Kath was in the sitting room with Ravi, spooning cold spaghetti hoops out of a tin and loudly deriding a medical drama on the television, when the doorbell rang. Kath backed out of the sitting room, keeping her beady eye on the unravelling saga on the screen, and was shouting to Ravi to pause it when she opened the door, her head still turned towards the hall, her hair tied up with an old sock. Turning back to the doorway she was greeted by the sight of a tall, handsome stranger carrying a large suitcase.

He thrust a hand out towards her. "You must be Kath?"

he said in an amused voice, registering her look of open-mouthed astonishment. "I'm—"

"Oh, I know *exactly* who you are, sunshine." Kath ushered him into the hallway and gave him a thorough appraising stare up and down, "And you probably would be worth getting struck off for."

She showed him into the kitchen, plonking the half-empty tin of hoops down onto the counter and muttering, "You wait right there," as she crossed back through the hall to the sitting room. He could hear her whispering urgently, "Rav, *RAV!!* Get yer arse in gear, darling. We are out of here. Now!"

A few moments later, Kath was back in the hallway, dragging a bemused Ravi behind her. "We'll just be popping out for the evening," she said loudly, in the general direction of the kitchen. And then more quietly, "I know. We'll watch it at your place. I'll explain, just get a feckin' move on."

She went to the bottom of the stairs, "Tess, there's a gorgeous man down here. I wouldn't leave him unattended too long or I might jump on him," and then headed past the kitchen door, throwing a large beaming smile in his direction and pacifying her grumbling boyfriend with, "I know, you're gorgeous too, you feckin' eejit, and of course I wouldn't really..." as they left, slamming the door behind them.

Tess had heard the doorbell and immediately her skin had prickled with an anticipatory excitement. She had to stop assuming every unexpected interruption to her daily life was a sign of Edward Russell; it was probably just a delivery driver dropping off the fabric samples she'd ordered, but the sounds of Kath's evident agitation downstairs caused the prickling across her arms and face to intensify and she found that her heart was beating more rapidly, her breath catching in her throat. When Kath finally shouted up to her, she was already at the top of the stairs and caught her housemate's eye just before she left with a disgruntled-looking Ravi. Kath's excitement was palpable in that single glimpse and Tess knew then for certain exactly who was waiting in the kitchen.

"When a young lady is absolutely determined to be a heroine there is little that can be done to prevent it." Jane Austen's voice was bordering on smug. *"Something must and will happen to throw a hero in her way."*

As she took the first few tentative steps downstairs, she felt a growing apprehension. What if he was simply here to tell her that he was selling the house, just dropping by on his way to see the estate agent or his solicitor? What if he was here to clarify something practical regarding his mum or the finances, or tying up the loose ends regarding the complaint from Clara? What if he had met someone else and wanted to let her know in person rather than find out on social media when his status changed, because, let's face it, he would know she'd been checking. All these thoughts raced through her head but then she saw him emerge through the kitchen doorway, stooping to avoid hitting his head on the cupboard door Kath had left open, and she knew immediately from the way he looked at her that it was none of these things. The longing in his eyes exactly mirrored her own expression, their smiles widening as each realised, after such a long wait, that their feelings were reciprocated.

All thoughts of decorum or studied nonchalance vanished. She galloped down the remaining steps and flung her arms round his damp coat, breathing in the scent of him, the warm cashmere, the clean linen, the thrilling aroma of her handsome man. He laughed but hugged her back fiercely, and then they were kissing as if their lives depended on it, tears mixing with the rainwater still damp on his face, hungry for each other as they had always been. She pulled away from him at last.

"You're back! You are actually back." She squeezed him again. "I mean, obviously I'm pretty ambivalent about that."

He laughed.

"I *am* back," he said. "I'm sorted. I've had an amazing time. But I couldn't stop thinking about you."

"Is that so?"

"I mean, frankly it was ridiculous. I *couldn't* stop thinking about you. When I got the message from Henry about the bill, and when Harvey wanted to keep sending you pictures, and when Pauline said she'd bumped into you... Every time I had to keep reminding myself, *she doesn't want me to contact her; she made me promise*. But then we decided to get the house valued and I remembered that boyfriend of yours, and in some sort of ridiculous masochistic way I asked for him to lead the sale..."

"I know! I know. He showed me the pictures. Jesus, I nearly had a heart attack."

"And then when I spoke to him, all I wanted to do was

ask about you, and if he knew where you were and what you were doing, and if he was still seeing you... I was tying myself up in knots and eventually Madeleine said, 'Go home.' She said, 'We'll make a decision about the house later, just go home and everything else will fall into place. Go back to her and tell her you love her, before she hooks up with the estate agent, or runs off with some kindly doctor who is in touch with his feelings and isn't some sort of emotional car crash.' So, I did."

"You did!"

"And here I am. And I love you, Tess. I love you so much. I can't bear the thought of another day without you." He kissed her forehead. "I'm sorry, I was hoping to be just marginally cooler than this. It's not very me, is it?"

"You're not wrong. Quite an uncharacteristic display."

"I don't even care. Although, I guess I am going to feel a bit wretched if... I mean, you haven't, have you?"

"Haven't what?"

"Haven't found a kindly bloke who is in touch with his feelings and isn't going to cause you a moment's stress or anxiety?"

She laughed, shaking her head, and reached to take his hand, leading him upstairs.

"And what on earth would I do with one of those?" she said. "That would be no fun at all."

Epilogue

She wakes slowly, the heat from the July sun seeping through the curtains of the large sash windows, causing her to stir and press up against the warm body lying next to her. He is already awake, propped up on an elbow, gazing down as she emerges from slumber, marvelling at the happiness this woman has brought into his life. She snakes an arm around his broad chest, smiling, knowing even with her eyes closed that he is staring at her, remembering last night. There is a suggestion of noise from the far reaches of the house, a small child's footsteps, light on the staircase, a giggle, a bark.

Madeleine's voice is stern: "Leave them alone! They'll be up in a minute. Poor Tess is going to wish she'd stayed the night in her flat after all if you rotters keep bothering her!" The giggling ceases and the footsteps descend; all is quiet again. Tess looks over to the wardrobe door where her dress is hanging next to Edward's suit. She reaches up to stroke his face.

"How are you feeling?" she asks.

He grins and rubs a hand across her body from thigh to hip, across her tummy and the side of her breast. "Pretty good actually."

She smiles sleepily and prods him with her finger. "No, I mean how are you feeling about today?"

There is a memorial service planned for the morning, a chance to commemorate Mary's life, scatter her ashes, and look back on the past year, a time during which so much has changed. She is still concerned about him, a year on, despite knowing that his emotional scars have healed. She wonders if she will always feel this protective towards him – if, having seen his vulnerabilities and failings so early in their relationship, there is nothing he can now hide from her. He, of course, now knows all about her own weaknesses. She has told him about her previous low self-esteem and even admitted to the binging, something she has never shared with anyone.

She is, again, amazed by how strongly attached she is to this man, someone who entered her life in the most unusual of circumstances and has become the focus of everything she does, every part of her consumed by him, every moment spent thinking of him. She wonders if it is unhealthy to be so obsessed, for one's own happiness to become so intrinsically linked to that of another, but it doesn't feel unhealthy. It feels right.

He is reaching down to his side of the bed and she glances at his back, curious, watching the muscles of his shoulder stretching taut as he leans and returns holding a small box. Her eyebrows lift and her heart starts to beat a little faster. She is now definitely awake.

"I was going to wait until later today. I wanted to do it properly, somewhere nice, but then, this is my favourite place," he smiles at her, "and I can't think of anything nicer than you wearing nothing else but this."

He hands her the box, his eyebrows knitted together for a second – a moment of anxiety. She sees and smooths it away with a smile.

She sits up, opens the box, and inside is a ring. Between two large diamonds sits a square-cut, sparkling sapphire, the colour of his eyes – the colour of his mother's eyes, she realises.

"It was Mum's," he says. "I've had it resized, but obviously, if… you know, if you wanted something else, if it's a bit weird having her ring? Or if… you didn't want a ring at all? If maybe you didn't want to…"

She stares down at the box and the jewels contained within it, and then looks at him, her smile as radiant as the sun catching the diamonds. She's giggling now. Giddy with the excitement of it.

"What are you asking me, Edward? Come on, out with it! What did I tell you about repressing your emotions and hiding your feelings!"

She prises the ring out of its setting and slides it onto her finger, holding her arm out at full length to admire it.

"I want to marry you," he says, not looking at the ring, but at her, gazing intently at her face, earnest and serious despite her attempts at levity. She knows that this will be the pattern of their lives, the ebb and flow, the brooding, the laughing, the sad times, the moments of gentle teasing. This gorgeous, fierce, passionate man is hers. Both challenging each other, supporting each other, there for each other. Always.

"Yes," she says.

———

In the corner of the room the television host claps his hands in glee.

"Janie, old girl!" His voice is tight with excitement. *"Just picture it: A Wedding Special Episode! Fabulous! I'll probably get my own cable channel on the back of this!"*

Jane Austen gives him a side-eye glance and purses her lips to disguise her pleasure.

"It seems likely that I shall be in need of a new bonnet," she says.

Acknowledgments

Firstly, thanks must go to my lovely agent, Tanera Simons, and my wonderful editor, Charlotte Ledger, for both taking a punt on a debut author, writing a rom-com set in a hospice, and publishing in the middle of a pandemic. It's not a classic formula for success but I like to think it was worth the gamble.

Another huge thank you to the amazing people behind Comedy Women In Print and the Romantic Novelists' Association, both organisations who have been stalwart champions of all things Rom and indeed Com, and have been endlessly generous and supportive of the writers within their respective folds. In fact, the online writing community generally has been nothing but a force for good; a sounding board during the bleak times and a chorus of trumpets for even the tiniest of celebrations. Thank you to everyone who has shared the literary love online and in real life.

When I started writing *Love Life* as a romantic comedy, I

knew immediately that I wanted to set it in a hospice – a cathedral of powerful human emotions and the perfect place to observe a whole range of relationships. Over the years I've worked closely with palliative care teams looking after terminally ill patients and I know that there will be hospice staff out there averting their eyes from some of the more ridiculous components of *Love Life*'s plot. Clearly what happened in the shed would be in contravention of many aspects of the GMC's code of conduct for a start, but in writing *Love Life* I wanted to celebrate the work that hospices do and bring the conversation about dying out into the open. I would also like anyone who has enjoyed the book to donate to their local hospice if they are able. These remarkable institutions receive minimal state funding and are almost entirely reliant on charitable donations. As a result, a proportion of profits from every copy of *Love Life* sold this year will go to hospice charities.

But anyway, back to me.

Friends – I would love to name you all but because I want to stay under the radar, I'm afraid you all have to stay under it with me. You know who you are – old friends (yes, you girls from school), local friends (for local people), medical friends and just generally anyone who has ever been nice or kind or even tolerably polite to me. It all counts. It all matters.

My parents and my amazing sister are responsible for shaping me into the kind of person who felt she could do anything, and be anything she wanted. They are the reason behind the absurdly inflated sense of my own abilities that led me to write a book, so you can blame them.

And finally, to my husband, Mr Peach. I always assume that you know how much I love you, but it doesn't hurt to be reminded. You are everything to me; my port in the storm, my number one cheerleader, my favourite and my best. So, to you and the three little peaches who fill me with joy – all my love for all my life.

ONE MORE CHAPTER

One More Chapter is an
award-winning global
division of HarperCollins.

Sign up to our newsletter to get our
latest eBook deals and stay up to date
with our weekly Book Club!
<u>Subscribe here.</u>

Meet the team at
<u>www.onemorechapter.com</u>

Follow us!
 @OneMoreChapter_
 @OneMoreChapter
 @onemorechapterhc

Do you write unputdownable fiction?
We love to hear from new voices.
Find out how to submit your novel at
<u>www.onemorechapter.com/submissions</u>